UNTIL
I LOVE
AGAIN

JERRY S. EICHER

HARVEST HOUSE PUBLISHERS
EUGENE, OREGON

Scripture quotations taken from the King James Version of the Bible.

Cover by Garborg Design Works

Cover photos © Chris Garborg; Bigstock

This is a work of fiction. Names, characters, places, and incidents are products of the author's imagination or are used fictitiously. Any resemblance to actual persons, living or dead, is entirely coincidental.

UNTIL I LOVE AGAIN
Copyright © 2016 by Jerry S. Eicher
Published by Harvest House Publishers
Eugene, Oregon 97402
www.harvesthousepublishers.com

ISBN 978-0-7369-6589-7 (pbk.)
ISBN 978-0-7369-6590-3 (eBook)

Library of Congress Cataloging-in-Publication Data

Names: Eicher, Jerry S., author.
Title: Until I love again / Jerry S. Eicher.
Description: Eugene Oregon : Harvest House Publishers, [2016]
Identifiers: LCCN 2016000193 (print) | LCCN 2016004506 (ebook) | ISBN
    9780736965897 (softcover) | ISBN 9780736965903 ()
Subjects: LCSH: Amish—Fiction. | Mate selection—Fiction. | GSAFD: Love
    stories. | Christian fiction.
Classification: LCC PS3605.I34 U58 2016 (print) | LCC PS3605.I34 (ebook) |
    DDC 813/.6—dc23
LC record available at http://lccn.loc.gov/2016000193

Printed in the United States of America

16 17 18 19 20 21 22 23 24 / LB-GL / 10 9 8 7 6 5 4 3 2 1

Chapter One

Susanna Miller pulled back on the buggy reins, and her horse Charlie came to a halt as the traffic light turned red. Susanna casually looked to her left and suddenly let out a gasp, not believing her eyes. When the light changed to green moments later, Susanna's gaze was still on the illuminated sign in the parking lot of DeKalb Seed and Feed. It took the honking of the car horn behind her to break Susanna's trance. She let the reins fly as Charlie lunged forward.

As she drove by, she glanced over her shoulder at the sign one final time. *Yah*, it said what she thought it said: Happy Birthday, Susanna Miller. Susanna groaned. If *Daett* or anyone else from the community saw this, there would be questions she didn't want to answer.

Susanna hung on to Charlie's reins as he trotted out of town and made the sharp turn off of Highway 17 onto Maple Ridge Road. Perhaps the fact that she was on the final days of her *rumspringa* would make any explanation more acceptable. She had been given free rein by *Daett*, but that was about over now. And this sign might be the straw that would break the proverbial camel's back. *Daett* had allowed her freedom in the hope that her *rumspringa* time would accomplish its intended purpose. *Yah*, she was supposed to taste what lay out there in the *Englisha* world, and in so doing, come to realize why those things were not allowed among her people.

But *Daett* hadn't intended things to go as they had. Things like her friendship with Joey Macalister. She had kept that hidden from everyone, because, really, Joey was only a friend—nothing more. She need not alarm her family. Her *rumspringa* was almost over and she was ready to settle down—or was she? That was the question. She had told herself she was done with the *Englisha* world… but when she was with Joey, she wasn't so sure. When she was out with him, the world outside the Amish fence beckoned, tossing her emotions back and forth each weekend.

The birthday sign she had passed—if she was honest—warmed her heart as much as it alarmed her. Joey had placed the words there himself, or more likely, he had asked his cousin Marisa, who worked at the seed and feed, to set up the birthday greeting. Joey meant no harm, but an Amish girl's name should never be seen on an *Englisha* sign whether she was on her *rumspringa* or not. Such a thing would obviously mean she was a close friend and perhaps more than a friend with some *Englisha* person. *Daett* would wish to know who that was, and all the details.

Her friend, Emma Troyer, claimed that one's *rumspringa* in her aunt's community in Ohio allowed for friendships with *Englisha* people, but Susanna couldn't imagine that here. Amish life in New York's North Country was a controlled affair. *Daett* had already given her more freedom than anyone in the community thought was appropriate.

Susanna sighed and pulled back on the reins as Charlie approached the Millers' driveway. She turned in with a quick look around the barnyard. *Daett's* buggy wasn't there. It was just as well. She didn't want to see him at the moment. Not with the memory of the illuminated sign still haunting her. *Daett* would understand neither the sign nor her friendship with Joey. No, *Daett* would want to end her *rumspringa* time if and when he learned of this. He would no doubt put pressure on her to attend the community's upcoming spring baptismal classes.

"It's about time you thought about settling down," *Daett* had said only last week with a grin, but underneath his beard the lines had deepened on his face. She knew *Daett* well enough to know that he was worried, and so was *Mamm*. *Mamm* didn't tease like *Daett*, but of late *Mamm's* steps had grown slower as each weekend approached and Susanna spent time away from the homeplace.

Susanna climbed out of the buggy to unhitch Charlie from the shafts. She led him toward the barn while her thoughts whirled. Neither *Mamm* nor *Daett* knew where she was spending her time on Saturday nights, and that was how she intended things to stay. She had let *Mamm* think she was at the usual parties the other young people attended in Heuvelton.

The result was that neither *Mamm* nor *Daett* knew of the quiet hours she had spent at Joey's house over the past few months—nor of her newfound love for music. She had even learned to play the piano at Joey's, much to her own surprise. She had picked it up more easily than even Joey's mom, Beatrice, had imagined she would. And by now, Susanna had grown to love the feel of her fingers moving across the keys. *Yah*, she had taken to music like a duck to water. She was better now than even Joey, who had been taking lessons from his *mamm* for years.

Daett would never understand how such a fancy thing had gained a hold on her. The community sang songs at the Sunday services, but it wasn't the same as music from a piano. She could never explain the difference to *Mamm* or *Daett*, which was why she hadn't tried.

Susanna pushed open the barn door, and her younger brother Henry hollered from the back of the barn, "Home from a hard day's work, I see. Oh, and happy birthday."

"Thanks." Susanna forced a cheerful note into her voice.

"Did you pass *Daett* on your way home?" Henry asked as he tossed a bale of straw into the stall beside Charlie's. A cloud of dust drifted upward.

Susanna drew a long breath before she answered. "*Daett* went to town?"

"Yep!" Henry's voice no longer had its tease. "James is still in the field, but the axle broke on the wagon I was driving. I think it's been cracked for a while. Anyway, *Daett* hoped to reach the hardware store before they closed."

"I didn't see him." Susanna turned Charlie into his stall. "I guess *Daett* must have passed through before I started home."

"Must have," Henry allowed. "Or were you daydreaming?"

"I was minding my own business," she said, and hurried past him to exit the barn.

Henry's chuckle followed her. Susanna closed the barn door and continued her rush across the lawn. If *Daett* was going to the hardware store, he would surely pass the sign at the seed and feed. No doubt he would have words to say upon his return, but the matter was out of her hands now. She couldn't do anything but pray and hope.

Susanna entered the house by the washroom door and tried to smile as she opened the door to the kitchen.

"*Goot* evening," she sang out, mustering up as much cheerfulness as she could.

"*Goot* evening," *Mamm* replied. She was bent over the stove, and at once, Susanna started to set the table for supper. She counted the pieces under her breath, hoping to settle her nerves. A knife and fork each for *Daett* and *Mamm*, and then there were her brothers. She laid out the place settings for Henry, James, Noah, and little Tobias. *Yah*, all brothers. She was the only girl in the family, but she didn't mind. A sister would be great, but her brothers didn't bother her much. And she was allowed the freedom to drive her own buggy on Saturday nights, a tradition she had begun before Henry turned sixteen. She liked all of her brothers, from Henry down to three-year-old Tobias, who was now peering at Susanna around the kitchen doorway.

Susanna gave him a smile. "You want to sit down? Wait for supper?"

Tobias shook his head as *Mamm* said, "Better wait. He'll just be poking his finger into the food before it's dished out."

"Will you?" Susanna asked with another smile.

Tobias solemnly shook his head again, his tousled hair covering his ears. Tobias needed a haircut, but *Mamm* had been too busy this week. Perhaps Susanna should try her hand at haircuts. Her fingers could skim over the piano keys, so why couldn't they handle the scissors? *Mamm*, though, had always kept the task for herself, and none of Susanna's brothers would let her experiment on them.

"Don't tempt him," *Mamm* said. "You know he's hungry."

"*Yah*," Susanna agreed. "He's always hungry."

Mamm ignored the remark and said, "Ernest Helmuth came by today. I saw him speaking with *Daett* out in the barnyard. He sure was looking toward the house often enough."

Susanna pressed her lips together, but *Mamm* continued as if she hadn't made the point. "I'm sure he was hoping for a glimpse of you."

"Doesn't the man know I work each day at the DeKalb Building

Supply?" Susanna snapped. "I would think that would be the first thing to learn if you're interested in a woman."

"Come now," *Mamm* chided. "Ernest has plenty of things on his mind. He cares for his two small girls all by himself, with no *frau* and all of his farmwork. You ought to pay more attention to the man at the church services. That and…" *Mamm* focused on the pan in front of her, with the point temporarily forgotten.

But Susanna knew what *Mamm* meant. Both *Daett* and *Mamm* had taken a liking to the widower Ernest Helmuth, and unless she missed her guess, they planned to push her into a marriage with the man.

"Ernest is such a good *daett* to his little girls since their *mamm* passed," *Mamm* continued. "Any man with such a tender touch would make a woman happy."

Susanna kept her voice low. "What if I'm not interested?" There was no way Tobias could understand this conversation, but he studied their faces with interest.

"Of course you wouldn't be." *Mamm's* statement was tinged with frustration. "You've not given the man a fair chance. You're getting older, Susanna, and it's high time to think of settling down."

"And if I do that, how will you handle the house by yourself?" Susanna asked in a desperate attempt at distraction.

Mamm wasted no time in batting down the excuse. "Look how we're living now, Susanna. You work at the building supply part-time and some weekends, and we're making out okay. There's no reason for you to turn down an eligible man's interest. A suitable marriage partner for you is more important than how I'll run a household of boys by myself. A woman's place is in the home, Susanna, and not out there in the *Englisha* world." *Mamm* waved her hand in the general direction of the town of DeKalb. "I should never have agreed to let you work in that place, but what's done is done, and we can only go forward from here."

Susanna pressed her lips together again. This discussion was familiar territory. She wasn't attached to her job because it was part of the *Englisha* world, but it was useless to tell *Mamm* so. That was the only reason *Mamm* could imagine for Susanna's hesitation in joining the spring instruction classes. So far she had not told *Mamm* the real reason, but perhaps she would have no choice once *Daett* came home from the trip into town—if he noticed the sign.

If Joey had only known the trouble it was going to cause, he wouldn't have asked Marisa to put it up. But Joey didn't understand her world like she did his. And Joey had no intention to learn about her Amish world. That much he had made clear more than once. Not that it mattered. Susanna had no plans for their relationship to move beyond friendship. She planned to settle down in the community eventually, and Joey was headed for law school.

Mamm put a smile on her face. "Are you daydreaming about being Ernest's *frau*? That's sometimes the first step, you know. Even before you know if the relationship will work out. *Yah*, Ernest is a fine man, Susanna. *Daett* thinks highly of him, and so do I."

"No, I'm not thinking about him," Susanna retorted.

The smile stayed on *Mamm*'s face. "Then think about those two cute little girls of his. Don't you just love them? You'd have a right decent start at a family from the get-go, Susanna. And you would be spared the pains of bearing them."

Susanna felt the heat rise to her face. She glanced at Tobias. He still regarded her with that intense look of his, as if he understood every word, which wasn't possible. This conversation wasn't decent for adult ears, and hopefully it was unintelligible to three-year-olds.

"I almost invited Ernest and his girls for supper tonight," *Mamm* continued, "but I thought that might be a little too much and too soon. You should give him a few smiles at the services and encourage his heart, though. He's lonely, Susanna. And it's a great honor for our family that Ernest is thinking of you as his future *frau*. You should get down on your knees and thank the Lord instead of hesitating. You might lose him."

Susanna gave *Mamm* a sharp glance and opened her mouth to speak, but closed it again. She had heard enough about Ernest for one evening. The boys would soon be in for supper. And there was *Daett*'s buggy just now, coming down the lane.

A chill crept up Susanna's back as she hurried to move the hot food over to the table. *Mamm* gave her frequent sideway glances but said nothing more about Ernest Helmuth.

Chapter Two

An hour later, Susanna reached over to tug Tobias's hand as he attempted to smear an extra layer of butter onto his bread. "Don't do that," she chided. "Enough is enough."

"But I like butter," Tobias protested.

"Susanna's right," *Daett* chimed in. "We must be moderate in all we do." *Daett* gave his young son a smile. "Life offers many choices and we must choose what is right, which means restraining ourselves on things that might not be wrong in themselves."

Tobias appeared puzzled at this deep lecture over such a small offense, but he settled back on his bench without further protest. Susanna glanced again at her *daett's* face. He had given no indication of having seen the sign at the seed and feed. Was it possible he had overlooked it?

"Pass the potatoes again," *Mamm* said to Susanna. When she didn't respond, still gazing at her *daett*, *Mamm* repeated the request.

"She's thinking about Ernest Helmuth," James teased. "I saw him here today, speaking with *Daett* for much longer than necessary. The poor man must have greatly desired a glimpse of Susanna on the porch."

"Oh, stop it," Susanna ordered. "Must the whole community know about this?"

James chuckled.

"I think we should speak of something more decent," Henry said.

"Thank you." Susanna gave him a grateful smile. "Glad someone has *goot* sense among the males of this household. I—"

Daett cleared his throat, and Susanna stopped in midsentence. "The love between a man and a woman is not a matter of shame," *Daett* lectured. "That goes for you, James, as well as Susanna. We can tease each other, but let's not forget that the Lord made Adam and Eve and placed them on this earth to multiply and replenish the land. This is a sacred task, and we must take our duty with soberness and prayerfulness before the Lord."

"Amen," *Mamm* added.

There was heat rising up Susanna's neck again. Odd, how this subject never came up at the Macalister home. Such plain talk had little place among the sounds of beautiful piano music and regular family chitchat.

"See, she's all red-faced," James teased. "We have a wedding coming up this fall if I don't miss my guess."

"Mind your own business," Susanna retorted, as all four boys chuckled at her embarrassment.

Daett's grin faded and he appeared ready to continue his lecture, but instead he said, "Let's have dessert, please."

Mamm bounced up before Susanna could move, and brought over cherry pies and a pitcher of milk. *Mamm* stopped with a flourish. "Something a little special for Susanna's birthday today. It's not much, but we all know how Susanna likes cherry pie."

"So do I," Tobias said as he eyed the lightly browned pies. "But we could use some ice cream on top."

James cut himself a large piece and glanced at his brother. "You do have fancy tastes tonight, but this is *goot* enough for me. Nothing matches *Mamm*'s cherry pies, even without ice cream."

"Thank you, James," *Mamm* said, smiling. "But remember not to praise your mother's pies once you're married."

Daett appeared amused. "You can say that again."

"Now, I wasn't talking about you." *Mamm* reached over to pat his arm. "Boys, your *daett* has been more than kind when it comes to comparisons with his mother."

"That's because you're so *goot* at cooking," *Daett* said. "Cherry pies especially."

Mamm beamed with happiness. "See, that's how it's done, boys. Look and learn from your *daett*."

"I'm looking," Henry said. "I just haven't seen the young girl that's right for me."

Laughter spread around the table, and Susanna joined in. "She'll come in due time," Susanna comforted Henry. "You're still pretty young, you know."

"*Yah*, but old enough to look around," Henry shot back. "And I do have cause to worry. Look at how Sarah Beth swoons every time James comes around. I can't even get a smile from a girl with James right there to grab all the attention. And he's younger than me!"

Daett spoke up. "That's enough, boys. We accept what the Lord gives, Henry. Keep your hopes up, son, and the right girl will be along. That's the way it works when we walk in the will of the Lord."

"You're such a dear, Ralph," *Mamm* cooed. "You have such sound advice to give all of our children."

Susanna smiled as James and Henry hid behind their spoonfuls of cherry pie. She appreciated *Mamm* and *Daett*'s affection for each other, even if it embarrassed her brothers. She wanted to be like them when she married.

An image of Ernest Helmuth's bearded face appeared in Susanna's mind, and she lowered her head. Ernest wasn't exactly what she envisioned as husband material.

Thankfully *Daett* soon called for the closing prayer of thanks, and Susanna followed the boys into the living room where *Daett* had his Bible open. She found a seat on the couch, and he began to read.

"'The Lord is my shepherd; I shall not want.'" *Daett*'s deep voice filled the living room.

Why had *Daett* chosen this familiar Scripture tonight? Susanna wondered. Did he seek comfort for himself, or was this to encourage her to face the truth no matter where the road led?

"'I will dwell in the house of the Lord forever.'" *Daett* concluded the psalm and closed the Bible. He looked around the room and took them all in one by one until even James squirmed on his chair. Finally *Daett* spoke. "*Mamm* and I would like to have time alone with our daughter this evening, so Tobias and Noah, would you boys please go upstairs to your rooms? James and Henry can start the work in the kitchen."

After the boys all left silently, casting a mournful glance at Susanna, *Daett* started right in by asking, "Do you have something you'd like to tell us, Susanna?"

Mamm had obviously not been let in on what was going on, as she looked at *Daett* and asked, "What do you mean, Ralph? What's this all about?"

"I think we should let Susanna tell us," *Daett* said. "It would be best that way."

Susanna took a deep breath. "Do you mean the happy birthday sign?"

"*Yah*, of course." *Daett* leaned forward.

"A happy birthday sign?" *Mamm* interrupted.

Daett held his hand up and *Mamm* fell silent.

"It's…" Susanna began. "It's some friends that I know. They didn't tell me they would do this, or I would have objected…"

"In the middle of town where anyone can see it." *Daett's* voice was more statement than question. "Those must be some friends."

"She's…" *Mamm* tried again.

Daett turned to her. "Susanna's name is on a well-lit sign at the seed and feed store in DeKalb. The sign says, in big letters: Happy Birthday, Susanna Miller. The whole community will know by morning, and we will have much explaining to do. I'd at least like some answers before Deacon Herman calls."

"Susanna!" *Mamm* exclaimed. "How did this happen?"

Susanna swallowed but found no words.

Daett's voice cut through her fogged brain. "You can begin anytime."

"I…" Susanna began. "I didn't know this would happen, I really didn't, but Joey must have told his cousin Marisa about my birthday, and her parents own the seed and feed store."

"You know this Joey well enough that he would put up your name without asking you?" *Daett* had leaned forward again.

Susanna looked at the floor. "I suppose so," she allowed.

"We had best stop beating around the bush, Susanna." *Daett's* voice was stern. "Did you meet this Joey at the parties in Heuvelton?"

Susanna nodded, but this wouldn't satisfy, so she added, "I met him there, but then I also went to his house."

"Each weekend after the parties?" *Mamm* asked in horror.

"I don't go to the parties anymore." Susanna lifted her head to meet their gazes. "There. Now you know. Joey's my friend—and that's all."

Moments later *Daett* reached over to touch the cover on the Bible, but he said nothing. *Mamm* was likewise silent.

"And they taught me to play the piano," Susanna blurted out.

Daett's face paled. She had expected this result, but the sight still shocked her. *Daett* and *Mamm* had no idea what beautiful piano music sounded like, and she wasn't about to explain. She had already said too much.

"Do you love this man?" *Daett* finally asked.

Mamm gasped at the question, obviously fearing the answer.

"He's my friend," Susanna answered. "That's all."

"Is this why you've been hesitating about the baptismal classes this spring?" *Daett* asked.

"*Yah*, I guess," Susanna acknowledged.

"You surely know the depth of my shock and sorrow," *Daett* said. "This is not what *rumspringa* is for. I told you this when the Troyer sisters jumped the fence a year ago. You are not to form attachments with *Englisha* people. This will trouble you when it's time to come back. I trusted you, Susanna, enough to give you the freedom I thought you needed. Perhaps I was wrong."

"I didn't intend things to turn out this way," Susanna said. "It just happened. I wish you could understand."

Daett's hands trembled. "We had best speak no more about this matter tonight. I'll talk with Deacon Herman if he inquires about this, and ask for patience as we pray for the Lord to help us through this difficult time. But you must seek the Lord's will on your feelings for this boy, Susanna. None of our people marry outside the faith. Surely you know this."

"I do," Susanna told him. "And I'm sorry. But, as I said, Joey's just a friend."

"Friend or not, he's *Englisha* and he's a young man. That can only mean trouble eventually."

Susanna hung her head as *Mamm* remained silent.

Daett began again. "We will consider this matter settled for now. From now on, you will drive into town with Henry on Saturday nights." *Daett* tried to smile. "I should have insisted on this for some time, but we thought to make an exception in your case."

Now what did that mean? Likely *Daett* had been his usual considerate and decent self—and was disappointed to find out that Susanna's *rumspringa* had gone off course. The time had come for rules and restrictions, and she had no one to blame but herself. She ought to promise she would return Ernest Helmuth's attentions at the next Sunday services, but her stomach turned at the thought. Instead, Joey's face floated in her mind, and the tears stung. What a mess she had gotten herself into. Susanna rose to her feet and beat a hasty retreat up the stairs.

Chapter Three

As Susanna fidgeted with the pins on her dress, the late Saturday evening sunlight streamed through the bedroom window and spilled on the hardwood floor at her feet. She studied the beam and moved her bare foot into the light. Should she obey *Daett's* orders tonight? She drew her foot back and sighed. James had already left, and Henry was waiting in his buggy. She really didn't have much choice, but perhaps later in the evening she could slip away or find some other way to meet Joey. Maybe Henry could be talked into cooperating. They could drive past Joey's house on their way to Heuvelton, and then she could run inside for a moment and explain to him why she couldn't see him. And if no one was home, she could at least leave a note on the door.

But of course Henry wouldn't stop so she could see Joey. Henry was solid as a rock and would not let her out of his sight all evening. That was why *Daett* had assigned her to Henry's care, but she just *had* to see Joey tonight. She had to explain her absence.

"Susanna!" *Mamm's* voice called up the stairs. "Henry's waiting."

Susanna plunged in the last pin and stifled a shriek when the end pricked her finger. How clumsy she had become. Only ten-year-old girls stuck their fingers when they dressed themselves. This only added to the shame she had felt all week as *Mamm* hovered over her.

"Did Joey stop by your work today?" *Mamm* asked each evening after Susanna came home from the DeKalb Building Supply.

In a way, she was glad Joey hadn't stopped by. *Mamm's* anxiety would only have increased. But the downside was that she missed Joey. At least *Mamm* and *Daett* didn't know that. She had half-expected *Daett* to demand that she quit her job this week, but he hadn't.

"Susanna!" *Mamm* called again. "You can't keep Henry waiting."

"Coming," Susanna called out, grabbing her shoes. She dashed out the bedroom door barefoot taking the stairs two at a time.

"Do be careful!" *Mamm* chided at the bottom of the stairwell.

"*Yah, Mamm.*" Susanna stopped so *Mamm* could inspect her dress.

"Go." *Mamm* motioned toward the front door. "You look decent enough. And be sure to stay with Henry. *Daett* has told him to watch over you."

Susanna suppressed a protest and ran for the door. The screen door slammed behind her. The sound was rebellious, like how she felt inside. All week she had acted humble and submissive in front of *Mamm*. What a bundle of contradictions she had become, so unlike her former self. What was wrong with her? Why couldn't she be stable like her brothers? She had taken chances in her *rumspringa* time that none of them had.

As she approached, Henry leaned out of the buggy and grumbled, "I'm not like a boyfriend that you can keep waiting."

"Sorry," Susanna muttered. She climbed in and shoved her shoes under the buggy seat.

Henry shook the reins and called out, "Getup, Ranger." When the horse had settled into a steady trot, he gave Susanna a sharp sideways glance. "You can put those shoes on now. I'm not arriving at the gathering with a sister in her bare feet."

"In a moment," Susanna said. "I have a question first. What's different about me, Henry? Sometimes I feel so rebellious, and none of you boys are like that."

Henry smiled. "Don't worry. It's just a rough spot, I suppose. You'll settle down now that Ernest is making eyes at you. I saw you give him at least one smile at the service last Sunday. That's *goot*. I hope you gave him lots more that I didn't see."

"You just imagined that," Susanna protested. "If I remember right, I didn't look at him all day."

"Oh? There's not another widower you're making eyes at, is there?" Henry said with a grin.

Susanna made a face at him.

Henry laughed. "Ernest is a *goot* catch, you know. And those little girls of his, they are cuter than buttons."

"You've noticed his girls?" Susanna asked.

Henry snorted. "*Yah*, of course! They sit on Ernest's lap each Sunday. Naturally I'm interested in the man my sister will marry and the daughters that will become my nieces."

"You're such a dear, brother," Susanna teased, reaching over to slap Henry's arm.

"Hey," he protested.

"Sorry." Susanna gave him a sweet smile. "Like I said, I'm still feeling a little rebellious."

Henry sighed. "You'll come to love Ernest soon enough." He jerked his head with all confidence and pulled Ranger to stop for the turn onto Highway 17.

"I'm not so sure about that," Susanna muttered under her breath. She reached under the buggy seat for her shoes and put them on while Henry drove toward Heuvelton.

"That's better," Henry said once she was finished. "Now we're ready to face the big wide world this evening."

"What if Joey looks for me tonight?" Susanna asked. "I mean, he could. He knows where the Amish youth hang out."

Henry's face clouded over. "You'll tell him you're spoken for, and that's that."

"But I'm not spoken for. And I like Joey...as a friend," Susanna said.

Henry gave Susanna a stern look. "That's not the way to talk, and you know that."

"Sorry, I can't help it," Susanna said. "It's my rebel nature. I have all these desires inside me for forbidden things. How come you don't? How come you were able to leave your *rumspringa* time behind so quickly?"

Henry's voice was steady. "It was easy. There's nothing out there in the *Englisha* world for us, Susanna." He waved his empty hand toward the approaching city lights. "That's what *rumspringa* is for. We're to settle the matter in our hearts."

"Then why is it not settled in mine?" Susanna glared toward the town. "You know I've tried."

"*Yah*, I do," Henry assured her. "And *Mamm* and *Daett* also understand. This is only a storm that will soon pass."

Susanna kept silent.

Henry finally cleared his throat. "Maybe we should both think about joining the baptismal class in two weeks. I'd be willing to attend if you will."

Susanna sat up straight. "You would? For my sake?"

"Of course." Henry's grin was lopsided. "I was ready anyway. I've seen plenty of what's out there."

"You're such a dear, Henry, and so kind." Susanna sighed. "Why can't I be like you?"

"You're close enough," Henry said. "You're just a little different, but that's okay. Ernest will get a decent *frau* when he weds you this fall, and you'll be happy with the man for all the days the Lord gives you together. You'll raise those little girls up to melt some man's heart someday."

Susanna gave him a sharp glance. "Did *Daett* tell you to say all this? You're not usually this talkative."

Henry elbowed her playfully. "That's because you've never driven with me before on a Saturday night. Look what you've been missing out on."

"How do you know I'm the one who's been missing out on Saturday nights?" Susanna teased.

Henry gave her a wry look. "I don't think I like the direction of this conversation. Promise me that you'll join the baptismal class with me."

"I'll think about it," she said. "And don't worry. I'll behave tonight…wherever we're going. And where *are* we going?"

"Just the usual," he chuckled. "But I guess you've forgotten what the usual is?"

"Like *boring*," Susanna said. "Let's see, you'll drive around town for a while and then stop and eat hamburgers with other Amish young people."

Henry grunted. "And what's wrong with that? Don't you like hamburgers?"

Susanna rolled her eyes. Henry had obviously experienced little of what she had in the *Englisha* world, but that was because he was one of the decent Amish young people.

"You'll enjoy yourself tonight," Henry encouraged her. "Think of the evening as the last look before the door closes on the glitter of the *Englisha* world."

Susanna winced, but said nothing as Henry tightened Ranger's

reins once they approached the edge of Heuvelton. Several other
buggies appeared from the side roads and fell in line behind them.
Susanna waved over her shoulder, and the girls inside returned the
greeting with smiles on their faces.

How happy they all were. Why couldn't she be happy with them?
Deep down she knew the answer. She wanted to see Joey, not the
other Amish young folks…but tonight she couldn't do anything
about that. She would have to make the best of things. Susanna
waved toward several more of the buggies and forced herself to smile.
Surely Joey would understand. He was familiar enough with Amish
ways to figure it out.

"We're stopping for hamburgers at the Heuvelton Deli," Henry
announced. "Then we'll drive down to the river and eat them along
the water's edge."

"That's okay with me," Susanna agreed. But the word *boring* was
on the tip of her lips.

"Here we are," he announced minutes later. "Heuvelton's finest
fast food at your service."

Ranger pulled to a stop, and Susanna gasped. Surely this couldn't
be… Was that Joey's car she saw? *Yah!* And there he stood with his
arms crossed, wearing the biggest smile she had seen in a long time.

Somehow he had found out their plans and had come to look for
her. She couldn't stop her heart from pounding like Ranger's hooves
on the open road.

Chapter Four

Susanna hesitated at the restaurant door. Joey hadn't approached her even after her smile of welcome. Henry had tied Ranger securely and had followed her toward the entrance. "Is something wrong?" he asked.

"No," she told him. "I'm okay."

Henry didn't appear convinced. "If you want to, we can stay here instead of going down to the water with the others. Whatever makes you happy."

Susanna nodded, but she didn't move. Why hadn't Joey come over to greet her? Maybe Joey knew she was uncomfortable with Henry along. Maybe he even thought Henry wasn't her brother. Susanna took a deep breath.

"I need to speak with someone. I'll be right back," she said, and scurried off.

"Who?" Henry hollered after her.

Susanna didn't pause to answer amid her dash across the parking lot.

Joey turned toward her as she approached. "So I'm not going to be ignored," he teased. "I thought for a moment you had gone into hiding."

"I'm sorry, Joey," Susanna said. "Things have come up, but I can explain."

"Dating someone?" he asked with a glance toward Henry, who was still standing by the restaurant door with a frown on his face.

"That's my brother," Susanna whispered. She forced a smile. "Would you like to meet him?"

Joey glanced around at several of the Amish young people who had paused in the parking lot and were now beginning to stare at them. "Things feel a little tense around here all of a sudden," he said. "Maybe we could get away somewhere."

Susanna tried to laugh. "Oh, they won't bite. Come, I want you to meet my brother Henry and some of the others."

Joey shrugged and followed her across the parking lot. Henry was still frowning, but Susanna ignored him and said, "This is Joey, Henry. And Joey, my brother Henry. He was kind enough to bring me into town tonight."

Questions danced in Joey's eyes, but he only nodded and greeted Henry. "Good evening. How are you?"

Henry hesitated. "Fine," he finally said, "and a *goot* evening to you."

Henry led the way inside while Joey held the door for Susanna.

"We're going down to the water's edge after we've purchased food to eat," Susanna said. "You want to come along?"

"Sure!" Joey's face brightened. "Sounds like a great plan, and I'll get to partake in a little Amish life." Joey looked over his shoulder at several of the Amish young people who had entered behind them. They chattered to each other in Pennsylvania Dutch, and Joey grinned. "But then there's Amish talk. You'll have to speak my language when I'm in earshot—none of this German stuff when you address me."

Henry kept his back turned and acted as though he didn't hear

Joey's prattle. Susanna smiled but kept quiet. She didn't know what to say. Henry's response to Joey had been understandable, but the others were showing their disapproval even more distinctly. What was wrong with everyone? She was still on her *rumspringa* and had done nothing excessive. She hadn't sought Joey out in the past week, nor had she tonight. Besides, they were only friends, so there was no reason for everyone to act this way. Maybe she should just leave with Joey. *Daett* would be upset, but Henry wouldn't be blamed. But she'd better not. She was rebellious, but not that rebellious.

Susanna kept her gaze away from the others as she stood behind Joey and waited to order.

Henry had already placed his order and was still frowning. Maybe Joey was right. They should go find a place they could talk. She couldn't leave Henry to drive home alone though. How would she get home? If Joey took her home, that would spell disaster. *Daett* might confront Joey. She didn't want that, so she would have to settle for something less. Maybe Joey could go down to the river with them, if the others—

"Hey, your turn!" Joey whispered.

Susanna jumped. "Sorry. I was daydreaming."

"What would you like, miss?" The young man behind the counter appeared amused.

"The same as him," Susanna said, not caring. She couldn't even remember what Joey had ordered, but his choices were always delicious.

She glanced over at Henry, his face now dark as a thundercloud. The implications of her ease and comfort with Joey had not been lost to him. This was exactly why Henry had been entrusted with her care, to prevent contact with Joey, and he obviously felt like a failure.

Susanna met Joey's gaze and smiled, but she looked away at once. She shouldn't display her real emotions here. In the meantime she wouldn't think about the disapproval of those around them. She'd think about Joey and the *goot* times they'd shared. It was likely this would be their last night together, which was an awful thought. When their orders were ready, Henry tugged on her arm. "Susanna! Here's your order. Come with me. Now!"

When Susanna hesitated, Henry tugged again.

"But he's coming too." Susanna sent a quick glance toward Joey.

"That I am," Joey responded.

"Not in the buggy," Henry snapped, his voice a bit too loud. "Now come." He pulled hard on Susanna's arm this time, and she gave in. Joey could follow them in his car. That was best anyway.

"You're making a scene," Susanna muttered on their way out. Her sandwich bag caught on the door frame, but Henry didn't stop. The bag ripped, and a piece of brown paper stayed behind. At least her sandwich was still in her hand.

"I'm not making a scene. You are," Henry grumbled. "I'm not the one who made plans to meet their *Englisha* loved one in the middle of Heuvelton."

"I didn't plan this, Henry. And besides, I'm on my *rumspringa*," Susanna retorted.

Henry untied Ranger and climbed in the buggy before he answered. "Your *rumspringa* needs to end. You're marrying Ernest. Let's keep that truth in front of our eyes."

"Why are you making such a big deal about this? It's not as if I want to marry Joey. We're just friends," Susanna protested. Henry didn't answer but drove Ranger out onto the street at breakneck speed.

"Slow down," she ordered.

"We're going home," he said, his face set.

"No, we're not," Susanna shot back.

Henry said nothing as the waters from the town's river appeared in front of them and the road toward home became visible across the bridge.

"Joey will follow us home," Susanna said. "Is that what you want?"

Henry pulled back on the reins and looked at her. "Are you telling the truth, Susanna? Would he follow us?"

"I don't know for sure," Susanna admitted. "But he might. He will want to know what's going on. I told him we were headed to the water."

Henry pondered the point for a moment. At the last second he pulled left on the reins. The open buggy tilted to the side as they made the turn. Two blocks later Henry pulled off the street and onto the riverbank. Ranger came to a halt, and Henry let the reins hang loose. There was no place to tie up, but Ranger had been here before. The routine was established.

"You behave yourself now," Henry said out of the corner of his mouth. "And *Mamm* and *Daett* need not know about this."

"Thank you," Susanna told him. "I appreciate what you're doing for me."

Henry didn't answer, but he climbed down from the buggy with his bagged sandwich in one hand. Susanna tried to breathe evenly. That Henry should offer to keep this evening a secret warmed her heart, but his offer would only go so far. The word would get around the community from the others that she had asked Joey to join their gathering. She would deal with that later.

With trembling hands Susanna climbed down from the buggy. She almost tripped when her foot hit the ground, but she caught herself with one hand on the wheel. Thankfully Joey hadn't pulled in yet. He didn't need to see this display of clumsiness. The rest of the evening must be perfect, since it could be her last with Joey. She forced a smile as Joey parked across the street and with quick steps crossed over and came to a stop beside her.

"Is everything okay?" he asked.

"*Yah*, I've got things straightened out with my brother…for now. Thanks for following us down here," Susanna said.

Joey smiled and took her hand. "Come," he said. "Let's walk by the river and find a nice spot to sit and eat away from the others."

"I couldn't agree more," Susanna said with a quick glance over her shoulder. Henry had backed off and joined the others. It was right that she should spend what could be the last evening of her *rumspringa* with Joey, Susanna told herself. She already knew the others disapproved, so what greater damage could she do?

The tinkle of the flowing water filled Susanna's ears as they walked along the bank. Her hand grew warm in Joey's tender grasp. She smiled up into his face and leaned against his shoulder. Was he more than a friend? Maybe he could be someday, if only their relationship would be allowed to continue and grow. But that could never be.

"How about here?" Joey asked. He didn't wait for an answer before he lowered himself onto the grass.

Susanna smoothed her dress before she followed Joey's example. A desire to pull off her shoes and run her feet through the spring grass came over her. But did she dare? *Yah*, she would. With a quick motion, Susanna set her sandwich on the bank and slipped off her shoes. The socks came next. Susanna didn't look up at Joey as she moved her feet through the grass. When she dared glance at his face, his smile was all the answer she needed.

"We used to do that in the summertime when we were kids," Joey said. "But we got away from the practice. Looks like you hung on."

"It's not something to let go of," Susanna said. "That's what our people believe."

"For once I like an Amish custom." Joey grinned. "Nice feet."

Susanna reddened and tucked both of them under her dress. "You shouldn't say things like that."

"What? Complimenting your feet? Come on, Susanna. Is that so wrong?"

"I guess not," Susanna managed. "Thanks for caring enough to find me tonight. I was hoping you would."

"Well, we missed you at the house last weekend, so we were beginning to wonder. Is something going on I should know about?"

"I…" Susanna began but then stopped. "Let's not talk about it, please. Let's enjoy the evening and this moment."

"Then there is something going on." Joey studied her face. "Please tell me, Susanna. I would hate to think you won't come by the house as often…or any more at all. Is it something we've said or done? Do your parents object? Would it help if I spoke to them?"

Susanna shook her head. That was the exact wrong approach. But how could she explain? Susanna began again. "I…really can't tell you. Not now. Not at this moment."

"Well then, will you promise me you won't disappear without a trace?"

"You know where I live." Susanna forced a laugh. "You can always stop by." There, she had said the words despite her misgivings, but she simply couldn't help herself. She didn't want this to end. Not tonight. Not ever.

Chapter Five

Ernest Helmuth paused near his barn door for a moment, having just finished his chores. His sister Katherine would have breakfast ready by now, but he wanted to savor this quiet moment alone. Sunday morning had dawned with clear skies, and the warmth of a south wind was blowing up from the valley below. The trees were ready to bud, and the ground was bursting with new life. Tomorrow he would be in the fields for the last of the spring plowing.

The Lord had blessed even as He had taken away. Naomi was gone, and he had mourned her death for months. The sorrow still lingered along with a deep discontentment. Naomi would never come back, but there should be a *frau* in the house with breakfast prepared for him. His seventeen-year-old sister, Katherine, had taken over since Naomi's passing, and she had handled the household duties with grace and joy in her heart. He was not ungrateful, but even *goot* things must come to an end. He could not impose on Katherine forever, nor on the good graces of his parents. At their age, they could use Katherine's help on the homeplace. Instead he had Katherine tied up with the care of his two young girls, Lizzie and Martha. He compensated his parents for Katherine's time, but that didn't get the work done at home.

"We are glad to help out where we can," *Mamm* often told him.

Daett always nodded, and sometimes said, "When your heart is healed, son, then we will think of what comes next."

He knew what that meant. He was eventually expected to find and marry a proper woman who could care for Lizzie and Martha. His parents continued to wait, but action would also be expected from him. In fact, he should already have a Sunday evening date lined up with an available unmarried woman from the community. There were plenty of decent choices from which to pick. Two young widows lived in the district, but he had settled his mind on Susanna Miller—and more than just settled. The truth was, he was completely taken by the girl. He couldn't keep his eyes off of Susanna at the Sunday services, and he had made several unnecessary trips over to the Millers' place on needless errands in the hopes he would get a chance to speak with the girl. But Susanna hadn't appeared, and he had been reduced to incoherent mumbles in his conversations with Susanna's *Daett*, Ralph.

"Nice weather we're having, isn't it?" he had asked. "The Lord has been gracious again this year."

"*Yah*," Ralph had allowed. "That it is. We receive both the rain and the sunshine as from the Lord's hand."

"I used to enjoy the rain as a boy," Ernest had said. "I used to take my shoes off to clomp through the barnyard puddles. I appreciated the heritage the Lord gave us from a young age. Seems like my heart has always been with the community and the life we live here. May the Lord's name be uplifted and praised among His people."

Ralph had looked strangely at him. "We all have our memories, I suppose. And I, too, love our way of life."

"Well, tell Susanna hello for me," Ernest had managed before driving quickly out of the lane.

He was sure Ralph understood and even approved of his intentions, but he knew that Ralph would likely approve of any man from the community who called on his daughter. He had learned of Susanna's past from his parents after he mentioned Susanna's name a few weeks ago in their presence.

"All the older people know this," his *Mamm* had informed him. "Ralph made his wishes known years ago when he took Susanna into his home after his marriage to Linda. No one is to speak to Susanna about her past. I doubt she even knows the truth herself. Of course, people can tell the tale when their sons show an interest in her, so I'm sure the story has been told often. The girl is quite *goot*-looking, and doubtless has generated plenty of interest. You should consider what we told you, Ernest. Considering her background, Susanna could be unstable. Look at the reports we've been getting on her wild *rumspringa* time. She's not the *frau* to replace Naomi, Ernest."

"No one can replace Naomi," Ernest had told them. "And this interest I have in Susanna is of the Lord." So they had fallen silent and let the matter lie.

The story of Susanna's past had not changed his mind. There was no reason that the sins of the parents should be held to the child's account. The Lord had said so Himself in the Old Testament. Susanna was not to blame. The blessing of the Lord was on the girl, and there should be no obstacles in his path to marrying her. He would approach Susanna directly. It just wasn't the time yet.

But *Mamm* was right on one point. By now many of the unmarried men in the community knew the true story of Susanna's birth. Yet none of them had the courage to continue their pursuit of Susanna's hand in marriage. They did not have his faith. The Lord had given him great grace in this matter. Perhaps this came because of the pain he had suffered after Naomi's death. Did not the Lord give back what He took? He could think of no other reason to explain the confidence that stirred inside of him. Susanna would be his *frau* by this fall, and he would be the man to comfort Ralph's heart.

What a great honor had been bestowed upon him. Ralph and Linda had doubtless spent many a sleepless night in prayer for their daughter. How else had Susanna matured into the beautiful girl that she was? Maybe what *Mamm* said about Ralph not having done everything right was true, but he had made up for his mistakes by raising Susanna correctly. Susanna's *rumspringa* time would be over soon, at which point he would speak with Ralph. That might even happen the next time he saw the man. There was no reason not to. Susanna would make any man a decent *frau*, if that man could overlook her past.

Look at the *goot* character the woman had. Susanna knew how to cook and keep house as well as the other women in the community. Maybe someday he would tell her about the deep pit the Lord had rescued her from, but on the other hand, some things were best left in the Lord's hands. He would use wisdom in the matter. The urgent thing was to proceed with his plans.

"Ernest!" The call from his sister brought Ernest out of his reverie. "What are you daydreaming about now? I've had breakfast ready for twenty minutes."

"I'm sorry," Ernest muttered, hurrying toward the house. "I was just thinking of the fine Sunday morning the Lord has given us."

Katherine eyed him with skepticism. "Well, breakfast is cold by now," she said, retreating with a frown on her face.

Ernest hung his coat near the living room stove and followed Katherine into the kitchen. Both Lizzie and Martha were sitting in their normal places with smiles on their faces.

"*Goot* morning, *Daett*," four-year-old Lizzie called out.

Ernest paused to kiss the top of Lizzie's head. A small white *kapp* would soon cover her lively curls for the church services, but Katherine hadn't gotten to the task. Three-year-old Martha peered up at him, and he leaned down to kiss her chubby cheek. Martha glowed, but said nothing. The girl needed a *mamm*, Ernest reminded himself. Katherine was doing a *goot* job, but there was nothing like a girl's own *mamm*.

"You're dawdling again," Katherine said. "Sit." She pointed to his chair.

"*Yah*, I know," Ernest grumbled. "You don't have to be so bossy."

"You need bossing," Katherine said. "*Mamm* told me so this past week. She said to make life miserable for you, and then perhaps you'd hurry and do the right thing and…" Katherine looked away. "But I suppose it's not decent to speak of such things, even with my own brother."

Ernest chuckled. "It's decent if plainspokenness is called for. And you'll be thinking of such things yourself before long. I saw Joe Schrock give you smiles last Sunday after the service. You didn't seem to object. Are you speaking with each other at the young people's gatherings?"

"That's none of your business," Katherine snapped. She sat down on the kitchen chair and glared at Ernest. "Stop teasing me and pray, please. I'm hungry."

Ernest stifled his laugh to bow his head in silent prayer. At home, his *daett* led out in a spoken prayer, but he had never developed the practice with Naomi. Perhaps he would once he wed Susanna. That would be a worthy moment to move on with his spiritual development. For now, he declared only the "Amen" with gusto.

Katherine passed him the plate of eggs and scolded, "You're mighty cheerful this morning after all that daydreaming."

Ernest only smiled as he helped Lizzie and Martha with their food.

"You are taking *Mamm*'s advice to heart, aren't you?" Katherine continued.

Ernest shrugged. "It depends which advice you are referring to. If it's about marrying again, then *yah*, I'm taking it to heart. I know you're doing a great job here, but I also know I shouldn't be keeping you much longer. I'm hoping I can soon ask a woman home on a formal date. In fact, I have already spoken with her *daett*—sort of."

"*Goot*!" Katherine said. "So is it Laura or Hannah? You know that's who *Mamm* thinks you should consider. And she's right. You could be married to either of them this spring yet."

Ernest paused with his fork lifted. "I know that's what *Mamm* thinks, but what makes you believe I'd ask either of those women home for a Sunday evening date?"

Katherine waved her hand about. "Well, all three of you have children and you've all been married before. It only makes sense. So is it one of them? You can tell me. I won't say anything until you say it's okay."

Ernest didn't answer as the image of Susanna's face appeared in front of him. Her beauty took his breath away and he stopped chewing for a moment.

Katherine waved her hand in front of his face. "You're spacing out again, Ernest. So which one is it?"

Ernest didn't answer. He could imagine Susanna sitting right where Katherine was sitting now. She looked so at home and at peace. Susanna was the woman for him.

"So which one is it?" Katherine leaned forward. "It's got to be Hannah or Laura. I know Laura's a little on the heavy side, but

Hannah goes the other way and could use a few pounds. I, of course, understand that. Hannah has suffered a lot since her David passed last year. She would be my pick. The pounds would come back if you wed her and brought happiness into her life."

Ernest kept his face passive. Let Katherine think she was correct. That was better than guessing games. The girl didn't need to know of his interest in Susanna Miller, and *Mamm* obviously hadn't told her. The matter could remain secret until he took Susanna home from the hymn singing, which would be soon, he hoped.

"Ernest!" Katherine's voice rose again. "I give up on you. But just for the record, I'm sure I'm right. You wouldn't fall for Laura. She's not your type."

"What is my type?" Ernest asked.

Katherine's face lit up. "The man speaks. I think Hannah's your type."

Ernest grinned and remained silent. He was through with this conversation, but he couldn't shut Katherine up without offense. The girl would have to speak her fill.

"I know I'm right," Katherine continued. "Hannah would make a decent sister-in-law. She's a little on the moody side, but I can't blame her. You'll cheer her up, and with the extra work around the house, Hannah would regain her health fully. And your two little girls…" Katherine glanced at Lizzie and Martha. "They are the sweetest things. You'd be *goot* for each other, and Hannah's son Isaac would fit right in with this family. I'd say the Lord has opened the door wide, Ernest, if only you have the sense to walk through it."

Ernest laughed. "Okay, enough of that. On my part I feel sorry for the extra work we've been for you since Naomi passed. But you have done well. In fact, you've gone way above anything I could have expected."

"Thank you," Katherine said. "That's nice of you to say, but you're changing the subject. I still think you should ask Hannah home soon—perhaps this evening."

"*Yah*, I know you favor Hannah," Ernest said. "But I'm not of a mind to ask Hannah home from the hymn singing—not this evening or perhaps ever."

Katherine gave him a sharp look. "Well, just remember what *Mamm* said. You must do more than think about things."

Lizzie looked up at him to chirp, "What must you do, *Daett*?"

Ernest smiled down at her. "You're too young for this conversation, Lizzie. Just eat your eggs before they get cold."

Katherine gave him a glare. "Lizzie's eggs got cold a long time ago while their *Daett* dawdled at the barn door."

"You'll never capture young Joe's heart with that scowl," Ernest teased.

Katherine made a face at him. "Maybe that's already happened, brother of mine. Sorry to disappoint you."

Ernest shrugged and dished out the oatmeal for both girls. He didn't much care for young Joe, but Katherine wasn't about to ask for his opinion or listen to any feelings he might express. He stirred the milk into the oatmeal as his mind drifted back to Susanna Miller. He'd see her today, and his heart would beat faster. She'd sit in her usual place among the unmarried girls. Behind Susanna would be Laura and Hannah, seated in the married women's section as widows did, but neither woman stirred his emotions like Susanna.

Katherine's voice cut through his thoughts. "You have that same look on your face that Susanna Miller did last night down by the river in Heuvelton. That girl's in love with that *Englisha* boy, Joey Macalister. She's headed for lots of trouble, if you ask me. Falling in love with *Englisha* people while on your *rumspringa* is about the worst thing that can happen."

Ernest stared at his sister. "What did you say?"

"If you'd listen instead of daydreaming," Katherine told him, "you would have heard the first time. I said that Susanna Miller is playing with fire. Hopefully she'll come to her senses. We can't have more of our young people jumping the fence like the Troyer sisters did last year, or we'll soon not be allowed out of the house on Saturday nights."

"*Yah*," Ernest agreed, even as his mind raced. Susanna was in love? At least Katherine seemed to think so, and with an *Englisha* man? Katherine must be wrong, just as she was wrong about him and Hannah.

"Can we give thanks now?" Katherine said. "I have to clean the kitchen and change both girls before it's time to leave for the service."

Ernest nodded and bowed his head for a silent prayer. All he could see, though, was Susanna's face.

Chapter Six

Joey slowed for the turn onto Maple Ridge Road. Ahead of him lay the Millers' place. His foot hesitated a moment on the accelerator before he pressed down again. Susanna had said he could stop by whenever he wished, so he would. Something smelled of trouble—and with the Amish being so strict, the trouble could be just about anything. He knew this trip was risky. If he wished to win Susanna's affection, a little discretion might be in order. There was no sense in offending her family or the Amish community.

On the other hand, was there any hope that he could capture Susanna's heart and earn the community's approval of their relationship? None, if he knew the Amish. The way the Amish young folks had acted in Heuvelton the other night had convinced him of that. He had forgotten that people still existed who didn't marry outside of their faith. His only access to Susanna was because of her traditional *rumspringa* time, when their young people sampled the outside ways to decide if they really wanted to stay Amish.

One thing was certain. His plans did not fit the Amish way of life. And yet his interest in Susanna now went beyond friendship even though Susanna seemed oblivious to the fact. She always referred to him as a friend. Why, he wasn't sure, because if he had to guess, he felt certain Susanna shared his feelings. At any rate, it was time he at least faced the truth. He loved Susanna and he wanted to pursue a deeper relationship with her. The Amish community would have to deal with that. If she left the community, she wouldn't be the first one to do so. He had heard from Susanna herself that sometimes young folks in the community "jumped the fence," as she had called it.

Joey slowed for the Millers' driveway and eased his Toyota up to the barn. Two buggies were parked nearby with their shafts turned toward the road. Apparently someone planned to use them later in the day, but on a Sunday afternoon, surely everyone would be home.

Joey stepped out of the car, the gravel crunching under his feet. He hesitated for a moment. Did he dare approach the front door? That was what a normal suitor did when he called on his girl, but this was no normal situation. The contrast between his vehicle and the two black buggies could not be starker. As if in answer to his question, the front door opened and a tall, bearded Amish man walked out. The man, likely Susanna's father, pulled down the brim of his hat and headed toward Joey with a purposeful step. Joey waited. Apparently a confrontation lay ahead. But where was Susanna? She must have seen him drive in. From the look on the man's face, he had certainly surmised who he was. Should he leave? Avoid trouble? But how would he explain his retreat to Susanna later? He couldn't expect her to bear all the burden of their obviously unwelcomed relationship.

Joey planted on a smile and greeted the approaching man. "Good afternoon, Mr. Miller. You have a nice place here."

Susanna's father stopped a few feet away. His face was somber and his eyes were blazing. "And you are Joey, I presume." He didn't wait for a response. "You are not welcome here, Joey. Please leave before there is further damage done to my daughter's heart. And you are not to see her again. I want to make that clear. Her *rumspringa* days are at a close, and she will be staying home on the weekends from now on. Susanna belongs to the community, not the outside world." The man waved his hand toward the distant town. "Do you understand that?"

Joey cleared his throat. "I came to call on your daughter, Mr. Miller."

"Ralph is *goot* enough," he interrupted. "We do not call each other fancy titles around here."

"Okay, Ralph then." Joey shrugged. "I don't wish to offend you."

"In that case you should leave at once." Ralph's voice was clipped.

Stubbornness rose inside of Joey. People didn't normally give him orders. "I'm not planning to do your daughter any harm. You have nothing to worry about from me."

"You have already done harm," Ralph said. "I should have put my foot down a long time ago, but I didn't. Now it's time. Susanna belongs with us and the community."

"I didn't know you could own people these days." A hint of a smile played on Joey's face. "I think the days of slavery are past."

Ralph didn't seem flustered. "We all belong somewhere, Joey, and Susanna's world is here, at our house. Someday it will be with her husband when the Lord unites them in holy marriage."

Joey pulled himself up straighter. "Mr. Miller...I mean, Ralph, am I not also a man?"

"Out there, I suppose you are." Ralph smiled for the first time. "But in here you are not a man of the community. That is what matters. You will have to answer before the Lord for how you live your life, but we also have to answer for how we live ours. A man violates his conscience at the risk of his own soul."

"But what of Susanna?" Joey asked. "After all, she invited me to visit."

"She did not know what was in her best interest," Ralph replied. "You will leave now and not come back. Do you understand?"

Joey didn't move. "I would like to speak with Susanna first. Not to insult you, Ralph, as you are her father, but…"

The man's eyes blazed again. "*Yah*, that I am. And I am charged with determining what is best for her. I tell you again that Susanna's happiness does not lie out there. Now go. You have done enough damage. Much prayer will be needed to repair the wrong you have done. We may even have to speak of things with Susanna that only the Lord should speak to her heart. Now leave."

Joey turned, but hesitated. What could he do? This was the man's property. He couldn't force entry to see Susanna. He'd just have to find Susanna the following weekend in Heuvelton. But hadn't Mr. Miller said she wouldn't be going out anymore? He turned back to face Ralph again. "You will keep your daughter home now on the weekends?" he asked. "Did I hear right?"

Ralph nodded. "You heard right. Susanna will be here where she belongs."

"She knows our house is always open to her," Joey protested. "Susanna enjoys the time she spends with us. Have you heard her play the piano? She's still learning, but Mom claims that with the proper training, Susanna could go far. Would you keep that from your daughter? Hasn't the Lord given us music to enjoy?"

Ralph opened his mouth but closed it when the front door burst open and Susanna hurried out. She ran off the front porch and slowed only for the last few steps to halt in front of them. She glanced between her father and Joey. "*Daett*, I want to speak with Joey," she said.

Ralph held out both hands as if to shoo her back inside. "You should not even be out here with this man."

Susanna's voice was firm. "Joey is my friend."

Ralph stepped closer with his hands still raised. "Go in the house at once, Susanna. We have much to speak of, but now is not the time."

Susanna didn't move. "If you won't let us speak here, then I'll leave with him so we can speak somewhere else. *Daett*, I'm sorry, but there is nothing you can do about that."

"You must not do this," *Daett* said, not moving.

Susanna reached over to touch his hand. "Please don't make this more difficult than it is. You know that I love you and *Mamm*, but I must know for sure before I settle down. Isn't that what *rumspringa* is about? Have you not told me so many times yourself?"

Ralph still didn't move. "You must love the Lord above all else, Susanna. I cannot give my word or blessing to this thing. You must not leave."

Tears filled Susanna's eyes. "Then I must leave without your blessing, *Daett*. It grieves me deeply, but it cannot be otherwise. My heart would never know itself again if I don't."

Joey held his breath. Slowly her father yielded and stepped back. Joey reached for the passenger's door handle and held it open. Without a word Susanna climbed in, her face set. Joey hurried over to the other side, slid in, and started the engine. As he drove away, he checked the mirror to see Ralph still in the yard with his hat off and his head bowed. It was as if he was praying. This he had not expected. His family was religious, but this was…well, way out there. In his world there were no confrontations in the front yard followed by prayers toward heaven.

Joey accelerated and eased the car back onto Maple Ridge Road. Susanna still hadn't spoken. Joey glanced back to the Miller home for a final look. Ralph was still standing in the yard with his head down, his hat on the grass by his feet.

"Just take me to your house," Susanna whispered, tears on her cheek.

Joey reached over to touch her hand. "You don't have to do this," he said. "I mean, I'm not trying to break anyone's heart or tear your family apart."

"Just drive," she said. "You're breaking no one's heart that wasn't already broken."

Joey took her hand again and didn't let go until he pulled into the Macalisters' driveway. He parked beside the garage and sat still for a moment.

"Shall we go in?" he finally asked.

Susanna didn't move. "Give me a moment, please." Her voice choked. "I don't want your *mamm* to see me like this."

"My mother's not home," Joey said. "We have the house to ourselves."

Susanna's face lightened. "Then let's go in."

Joey opened his door and hurried around to the other side of the car, but Susanna had already climbed out. He took her hand and led the way toward the house. "Where were you when I drove in at your parents' place?" he asked.

Susanna gave him a small smile. "I was in my everyday dress. I had to change."

Joey chuckled. "I'm sure you looked fine. You left me to face your father's wrath alone."

Susanna dropped her gaze. "I knew you could handle *Daett*. He's only upset because he cares so much for me. I don't know why he has to clamp down so suddenly on my behavior. I guess I have no one to blame but myself, but maybe I wouldn't be so rebellious if he'd be slower to act. Sometimes it's almost as if…"

"What?" Joey asked. "Almost as if what?"

"I don't really know," Susanna said. "The way he is so protective. It's as if…as if he knows the temptations…himself. But that can't be. *Daett* has always been Amish through and through."

"He certainly was today," Joey said.

"Joey, thanks for coming to the house. This was painful, but it was bound to happen sooner or later."

"I'm glad I came too," he said, leading the way inside.

Susanna made her way straight to the piano and sat down on the bench. Her fingers seemed to drift for a moment, until she found the right keys. Slowly the music rose, one note at a time until the melody formed itself. Joey walked closer to look over Susanna's shoulder. The tune was unfamiliar to him and complicated. The sounds rose and fell, angry at first, followed by strident tones that grated the soul. Then high notes descended toward subtle sounds of beauty and agony mixed together.

"That was beautiful," Joey whispered when she paused.

Susanna didn't answer as the tempo picked up again. Joey listened. Susanna was playing from her heart. Joey closed his eyes. What would it be like to have such a woman as his wife, to cherish her with all of his heart—a woman so beautiful, more beautiful than he had dared imagine a woman could be? Joey kept his eyes closed and willed the music to continue.

Chapter Seven

When Joey took Susanna home late that afternoon, both *Daett* and *Mamm* were waiting for her.

"Come, we must talk," *Daett* said as soon as she walked through the door. She took a seat on the couch, and *Daett* continued, "This cannot go on, Susanna."

Susanna lowered her head and offered, "If it will make you feel better, I'll stay home from the hymn singing tonight as my punishment."

"You will do no such thing," *Mamm* said. "The very thought of making this disobedience public is simply unthinkable. People know too much already."

"I could say I was ill." Susanna wrinkled up her face. "I kind of am."

"You're not ill," *Mamm* said. "And neither are you sorry for what you did."

"Instead, we will go with you to the hymn singing!" *Daett* decreed.

"That won't do any good," Susanna said. "Do you really think I'd see Joey on the way there and leave with him again? Besides, I'll be with Henry and James."

"There is no other way. All of our nerves are on edge."

Susanna forced a laugh. "What do you expect? That I'll see Joey on the road and elope? Besides, Henry, James, and Matthew will…" Susanna stopped.

"We're going with you, and that's final," *Mamm* said. "And then afterward, we're going to have to have a talk. You need to know—"

"Please, not now," *Daett* interrupted.

Mamm faced *Daett*. "She must be told, Ralph. She should have been told long ago. Maybe that's why the Lord is punishing us for our deception."

Daett paled but said nothing more.

Susanna focused first on one face and then the other. What was *Mamm* talking about? What must she be told? Was there some punishment in store for her? Had a marriage with Ernest Helmuth already been arranged?

"We will speak with her after the hymn singing!" *Mamm* said. "I have put up with this secret for long enough."

Daett reached over to touch *Mamm's* arm. Distress was written deep across his face. "We can still turn this around, Linda. We don't have to speak of the past. Susanna will listen to reason."

"Look how she's acting now," *Mamm* snapped. "No, she must be told!"

Susanna cringed and sat lower on the couch, thoroughly confused. Maybe time spent at the hymn singing—where they sang praises to the Lord—would clear everyone's mind. In the meantime she wouldn't worry about this secret *Mamm* spoke of. Everyone had secrets, and they eventually spilled. Look at her and Joey.

"Are we having supper tonight?" young Noah called from the kitchen doorway. "I'm starving."

"*Yah*, of course." *Mamm* attempted a smile. She glanced back at Susanna before she dashed off.

"I should join *Mamm*," Susanna said to *Daett*, who stood in front of her. Tears were running down his cheeks and into his beard. Susanna rose to her feet and wrapped her arms around him.

"I am still your father," *Daett* whispered.

"*Yah*, I know." Susanna gazed up at him, holding back her own tears. "And I do love you, you know that?"

Daett turned his eyes toward the window. "You will always be my daughter," he said. "My only daughter."

A lump gathered in Susanna's throat.

Daett's hand reached down to lift her chin. "You are so beautiful, Susanna, so like your…" *Daett* stopped with a distant look in his eyes.

"Like *Mamm*, *yah*?" Susanna pulled on his hand. "I know."

"You are my daughter," *Daett* repeated. "This I will never forget."

"*Yah*," Susanna agreed. "But what do you mean?"

She waited but *Daett* didn't answer. She was ready to speak again when *Mamm* called from the kitchen doorway. "Susanna, I need your help."

Daett's hand lingered on hers before he let go. There was sorrow in *Mamm's* eyes when Susanna turned to face her, but *Mamm* hid the look at once with a grim smile. "I really do need your help."

"*Yah*, I'm coming," Susanna said, hurrying into the kitchen.

"What did you do when you left with that guy this afternoon?" Noah glared up at her from the bench.

Susanna didn't answer, but gave him a smile. What was there to say about all this that a ten-year-old boy could understand?

Mamm stood at the stove and turned to give Susanna an accusing look. *Mamm* said no words, but Susanna heard them plainly enough: "*Look at the kind of example you're setting for the younger ones.*"

She already knew she was a bad example. But what she wanted

to know was why. Weren't brothers supposed to be the wild ones? Yet neither of the two oldest, Henry and James, had exhibited any of the rebellion she manifested on weekends—or during the week, for that matter. Wasn't she part of this family? *Yah, Daett* had made the point only moments ago.

Susanna pulled the plates from the upper cupboard and avoided Noah's steady gaze. He followed her with his eyes as she set the table. A quick retort wanted to escape her lips, but Susanna suppressed the words.

"What were you doing with that *Englisha* boy today?" Noah finally asked again.

Mamm spoke up for her. "Susanna is sorry for her actions, so don't worry about it."

Noah's gaze still followed her.

Now shame filled Susanna at the memory of those moments in the Macalister home this afternoon. The music had seemed to pour from her fingers without any thought on her part. Noah knew nothing about *Englisha* music or what happened on *rumspringa*. No, she was the one with secrets, and terrible ones at that.

A plate slipped from Susanna's fingers and crashed to the floor. She gasped and waited for *Mamm*'s sharp rebuke, but only silence filled the kitchen. *This is an omen if ever there was one*, she thought to herself. An omen of what lay ahead of her if she continued in her rebellion. Then she gazed to her feet to see the plate in one piece.

"It didn't break," Noah said with amazement on his face.

"That was awful clumsy of you, Susanna!" *Mamm* still chided. "Thank the Lord no harm was done, but next time…"

Mamm cut off her words to pick up the plate. But her meaning was plain enough. There was a limited time of grace left in her life in which to reform.

"It twirled twice in the air," Noah said, his face glowing with admiration. He was obviously impressed for all the wrong reasons.

Susanna's cheeks burned. She forced herself to slow down and set each plate with care. With her head down, she set the utensils on the table.

She glanced over to Noah and said, "You could help set these."

Noah shrugged and reached for the spoons without objection.

As Susanna placed the last of the forks, she gave Noah a smile. "Thank you for your help."

He glowed again but said nothing. *Mamm* placed the bowl of soup on the table and gave Susanna a quick glance before she called out, "Supper's ready, Ralph. Call the boys. We'll be late already."

Daett's footsteps moved toward the front door, and his voice filled the house as he called toward the barn, "Supper, boys. Come at once."

Moments later the utility room's screen door slammed, and the sound of chatter from Henry and James could be heard. Small Tobias had come in behind them, after having watched his big brothers at work. They all fell silent once in the kitchen. Each one pulled out a chair and sat down at his customary place. *Daett* was already in his seat.

"We're all going to the hymn singing tonight," Noah announced before *Daett* could say anything.

"Hush," *Mamm* said. "We're ready to pray."

Noah appeared sheepish and ducked his head. Susanna pressed her eyes shut and focused on *Daett*'s prayer. Somehow she must gain control of herself.

"Now unto the most high God," *Daett* was saying, "we give thanks tonight for the meal prepared before us. We are unworthy of even this, the most humble of gifts that You, O Lord, have bestowed upon us. Forgive us of our ungratefulness and the murmuring that stirs often in our hearts. Make us truly grateful for what You have given by Your gracious hand. Amen."

"Amen," the others echoed.

Henry piped up immediately. "Someone please pass the soup. I'm starved. I thought supper would never come."

"Susanna was being rebuked," Noah offered. "That's why supper is late."

Silence fell around the table.

"We will speak of something else now," *Daett* finally said. "Susanna will seek repentance in her heart."

The tinkling of soupspoons resumed, but Susanna kept her head down. Her older brothers all knew of her transgressions, and they would respect *Daett's* instructions not to discuss them at the dinner table. But the events of the day still left a heavy silence at the table. The seconds ticked past, and thankfully James soon asked, "What's this about the hymn singing, Noah?"

"We're all going!" Noah proclaimed, the glow back on his face.

"But why?" James asked. "Not that I'm complaining."

"Then just be thankful," *Daett* said. "We're not discussing this, remember."

James shrugged and turned his attention back to his soup bowl.

"Can I ride with you?" Noah piped up.

Susanna kept her head down as her brothers sparred and made the arrangements for who would ride with whom. She would go with Henry—that was already a fixed point. Now if only the rest of her life could be that simple.

Chapter Eight

Later that evening, Susanna followed *Mamm* out of the hymn singing to the washroom, where they had left their shawls. *Daett* had gone out the front door with Henry and James ten minutes earlier to ready their buggies, but why *Daett* was in such a hurry to leave wasn't her concern. What she wanted to know was why *Daett* had engaged Ernest Helmuth in a long conversation before the hymn singing. They had spoken so long that *Daett* and Ernest had entered the house only moments before the first song began. To make matters worse, the two had their heads together before *Daett* had left with Henry and James.

What kind of plans had *Daett* made with Ernest? Had they discussed some sort of arrangement for her to be married to him? It didn't seem likely. Amish parents didn't force their daughters into unwanted marriages.

"Why didn't you return Ernest's smiles tonight?" *Mamm* chided as the washroom door closed behind them. "Surely you noticed them."

"How do you know I didn't return them?" Susanna asked.

"*Did* you?" *Mamm* said, searching for her shawl in the pile.

They both knew the answer. Susanna remained silent as they

slipped their shawls on and left. *Yah*, she had glanced once in Ernest's direction, but the memory of Joey and the *wunderbah* afternoon she had spent with him rushed into her mind, pushing thoughts of Ernest away. How could forbidden things bring such joy into her heart? She would think no more about Ernest Helmuth tonight. Instead, she would focus on the conversation *Daett* had promised would occur once they arrived back at the house. Likely *Daett* had another lecture ready for her, or some hint at what he had said to Ernest. What else could it be?

"Henry's buggy is over there. I'm going that way," Susanna muttered before slipping away from *Mamm* into the darkness.

"See you at home," *Mamm* called after her. "Wait up for us. Remember!"

Susanna kept her head down and didn't answer. *Mamm* knew she would obey. That much she could do.

Henry greeted her. "Hi, there. Your chariot is ready."

Susanna chuckled in spite of herself. Henry's humor was always appreciated, especially in tense situations. She should keep him around for the rest of the evening, but that likely wasn't possible.

"I'm surprised Ernest doesn't have you in his buggy already," Henry cracked. "I do declare, the man was sending longing looks your way all evening. I thought for sure he had a date up his sleeve."

"Stop it," Susanna scolded. "I'm going home with my handsome brother as I'm supposed to."

"Woohoo!" Henry said with a low whistle. "I like that."

He fastened the last tug and motioned for Susanna to climb into the buggy. She did, and Henry tossed her the lines. With a flourish Henry pulled himself up while Susanna held the reins tight.

Susanna sighed and settled into the buggy seat. She handed the reins over to Henry, and they took off down Bishop Enos's lane. Susanna caught sight of Ernest Helmuth's face in the yard as they passed. The man had his head down and was headed for the barn. His two little girls hadn't been with him tonight. Maybe Henry had been right. Perhaps the man did have hopes that she would allow him to drive her home after the hymn singing.

"I just saw Ernest," Henry said. "He'll be following us home, no doubt."

"Stop teasing," Susanna said.

"He's like a coonhound with his nose to the scent," Henry added with a laugh.

Susanna stared out into the darkness and didn't respond. She pressed her hands together and listened to the steady beat of Ranger's hooves on the pavement. The turn onto Maple Ridge Road was a mile down, but she wished the ride would go for hours. Even with Henry's teasing, there was a measure of peace inside the buggy that likely wouldn't last once they arrived at the house.

"I think you deserve better," Henry finally offered. "You should think about that."

Susanna looked at him. "Really! So you're coming to your senses?"

Henry didn't laugh. "I don't mean Ernest. It's that Joey fellow who's beneath you. And there are other options beside Ernest," he added. "I saw Emory Yoder making eyes at you a few months ago."

"Stop it," Susanna ordered.

"Would you accept a date if Emory asked to take you home?" Henry asked.

"I'm not responding to that," Susanna told him.

"It's just as well," Henry went on. "I don't think Emory is interested anyway once it comes right down to it."

"Would you stop talking about me?" Susanna got in edgewise.

Henry ignored her. "In fact, Emory isn't the only one to lose interest. I seem to remember not long ago Mark Troyer was smiling your way quite a bit. But not lately."

Susanna pressed her lips together. Was this true? Both Emory and Mark had considered her, but changed their minds? Henry would have this straight, but she had been too wrapped up in Joey to notice. So why didn't an Amish man other than Ernest Helmuth follow through on his interest in her? Not that she was interested in them, but still…what was wrong with her?

Susanna pushed the dark thought away as Henry pulled back on the reins. They bounced into the Millers' driveway and came to a stop near the barn door. Susanna climbed down to wait while *Daett* drove his buggy in behind them with James, Noah, and Tobias in the backseat. *Mamm* stepped down and walked with Susanna toward the house while the men unhitched the buggies.

"Can't we just go to bed and forget about all this tonight?" Susanna begged at the front door. "It's already late."

"You would be up till midnight if you were on a date," *Mamm* said. "We are going to talk tonight, Susanna. *Daett* has it all planned. Besides, it's way past time to get this out in the open."

Susanna wanted to protest further, but resistance was futile. She took her seat on the couch and waited. The minutes seemed to drag into hours before the voices of her brothers and *Daett* came from the washroom. The kitchen door slammed next. Henry paused for a moment at the sight of her on the couch, but he hurried on when *Daett* made a quick motion with his hand toward the stairs. Noah wasn't so easily persuaded. He walked past *Daett* and came to a stop in front of Susanna. "What have you done wrong now?" he demanded.

Susanna tried to smile. "Don't worry about me, Noah. Just go to bed."

"But I want to know," Noah protested. "Why doesn't anyone tell me anything?"

Mamm hurried over and hustled Noah up the stairs and closed the door behind him. Susanna sat up straight as the sound of another set of buggy wheels could be heard in the driveway. *Mamm* and *Daett* exchanged looks, and *Daett* rushed outside again.

"Who is that?" Susanna asked. Visions of a visit from Deacon Herman flashed through her mind. Had *Daett* gone to such extremes? Surely her transgressions didn't merit a visit from the deacon on a Sunday evening?

"It's Ernest Helmuth," *Mamm* said, her lips set firmly.

Susanna drew a long breath. "You have set up a date with the man—for me, without asking me?"

"No, but behave yourself," *Mamm* said. "This is the end of the line, Susanna. That's all I can say. At least your *Daett* has the sense to finally tell you the truth."

Susanna tried to breathe as the room tilted on its axis. Something serious was afoot, and she had no idea what. One couldn't be married without consent, even if her parents wanted her to. Susanna quieted the wild thoughts and clasped her hands tightly. No matter what caused her parents to act this strangely, she would survive. She always had before. Besides, *Mamm* and *Daett* loved her and wanted the best for her. She would take comfort in the thought.

The front door opened, and Ernest followed *Daett* inside. Ernest held his hat in his hand and didn't appear too happy, but that was understandable. What man would if he were in a woman's home uninvited at such hours and under such circumstances?

"Have a seat," *Mamm* told Ernest, offering him a chair. Ernest sat down and squirmed, his hat still in his hand.

"I'll take that," *Mamm* said, and Ernest handed over the hat. *Mamm* laid it gently behind the stove.

Daett waited until *Mamm* returned to her rocker. "This is a most serious moment in our lives," *Daett* began. "I had always hoped this time would never come, but I see I was quite wrong, and I beg forgiveness from all of you. First from Susanna, but also from *Mamm* and now from you, Ernest. I have wronged each of you greatly, even though I have tried these many years to make things right. It seems my sins have followed me, and now others must suffer for what I have done."

Daett paused and *Mamm* reached over to hold his hand. Susanna kept her eyes on Ernest's shiny, black Sunday shoes. Nothing seemed real or appropriate at the moment. Was *Daett* going to say something that would change her life forever? *Yah*, somehow she knew he would, as if the words had already been spoken. But what? She couldn't imagine, though the cloud hung heavy and dreadful over the whole house.

Daett cleared his throat. "I would have wished to never tell you this, Susanna, but now I must so that you will understand why Ernest is here. He has offered to marry you this fall after you have been through your baptismal classes."

Susanna gasped. "But *Daett*, this cannot be. I—"

Mamm hushed Susanna with a wave of her hand. "Listen to what your father has to say."

Daett's face was white, and *Mamm* touched his arm as he continued. "Once I tell you what I have to say, you will understand, and I think you will agree to Ernest's offer." *Daett* hung his head for a moment. "The truth is, you are my daughter, Susanna, but *Mamm* is not your mother. That is what we have never told you. You were born of an *Englisha* woman before *Mamm* and I were married. Your real *mamm* was a girl named Mindy Whithus who died shortly after your birth. You were taken care of by other people until Linda agreed to marry me. After our wedding, you came to live with us, and *Mamm* has always done her best to treat you as if she had birthed you."

Susanna let out a gasp as *Daett* continued. "I know this is a shock to you, but I did what I thought was the best. I always will be grateful to Linda for her love and her willingness to accept me as a husband after such a sin. You should also be grateful for how Linda has taken you in as her own daughter, all without complaining or interfering with how I have raised you. I can only say how really sorry I am. I know that you have not sinned, Susanna, and that some of your troubles are a result of my own sin. Even so, Ernest has agreed to do for you what Linda did for me. Ernest will take you as his *frau* if you are willing. He will love you, and together you will bury the past. If you think anything else can be done, Susanna, you are wrong. None of the other young men from the community will take you as their *frau*. If you haven't already noticed, then I can assure you this is true. Their parents will not allow them to marry a girl who has wild *Englisha* blood in her. And please don't protest, Susanna. You have not helped in this matter. Even this afternoon when you left with this Joey fellow, you have shown us beyond a doubt that this is true. Something must be done or you will jump the fence into the world and be lost from us forever. Ernest is a kind man to consider taking you as his *frau* under these circumstances. And a brave man, I must say. We will all be forever in his debt."

Daett paused and dropped his gaze while *Mamm* glanced toward Susanna. Only now, this wasn't her *mamm*. The thought tore through Susanna and left a fiery trail in its wake. How could this be? How could it be that her real *mamm* was an *Englisha* girl?

Ernest spoke for the first time. "I believe we can make it together, Susanna. I know this is a shock to you, and I had my doubts whether this was the best way to approach things. I most desperately had wished to begin our relationship under different circumstances, but your *daett* has assured me that there isn't much time. He thinks this is the best way to handle things. He wants you to know that I am willing to stand by you. I hope you understand."

Susanna tried to focus. Had Ernest spoken to her? The living room spun in slow circles around her. She tried to speak, but no sound came out of her mouth. *Mamm*'s hand reached for hers, but the gas lantern on the ceiling slowly dimmed and Susanna felt herself sliding sideways on the couch. *Daett*'s concerned cry was the last thing Susanna heard.

Chapter Nine

The next few days seemed to drag by as Susanna wrestled with the news that would change her life forever. What else in her world was not what she thought it was? The very question brought her to the edge of fresh tears.

The following Sunday morning dawned with a clear sky, and a slight breeze blew in from the Adirondacks. The smell of cedar and spring was heavy in the air. Susanna closed the window of her upstairs bedroom and then climbed back into bed and pulled the heavy quilt over her head. She had left the kitchen after the breakfast dishes were finished. If she didn't go back down soon, *Mamm* would be up to check on her, but Susanna would not go to the church services today. *Mamm* had to know that. The shame was too great. Plus, she still couldn't think straight. Since she had passed out that evening on the living room couch, the horror of who she really was gripped her—and to think that most of the community knew all along. The ones from *Mamm* and *Daett*'s generation had kept the origin of her birth a secret, divulging the information only to their sons if they showed an interest in her. This was why no community man had asked her home from the hymn singing.

Surely by now everyone knew that she had wild *Englisha* blood. Those had been *Daett's* own words last Sunday night. Nothing could change that. If she had behaved herself in her *rumspringa* time, the past might have been overlooked—but she had stretched the limits of what was permissible. Even if she hadn't, she might have never received a decent marriage proposal from an Amish man. The truth was, she was an outcast.

Susanna buried her face in the quilt, but this time no tears came. Tears were a thing of the past. She had cried for three days straight last week. At least she had thought to send Henry to tell Mr. Kenny that she would not be in for work this week at DeKalb Building Supply.

"She's not feeling well," Henry had told Mr. Kenny.

Mr. Kenny had sent word back. "Tell Susanna we hope she gets better."

But she wouldn't get better. Not from this. There was only a cold numbness that filled her body. Her family had shown her nothing but tenderness, but that only made matters worse. Wasn't kindness part of the reason she was in trouble? If *Daett* hadn't given her so much leeway in her *rumspringa* time, maybe she wouldn't have met Joey and his family. And then she wouldn't have...

A soft knock on the bedroom door made Susanna pull the quilt higher over her head.

"Susanna," *Mamm* called.

Susanna buried her face deeper.

The doorknob turned and *Mamm's* footsteps approached. "Susanna, you must get dressed. We will leave for the service when the men finish the chores." *Mamm* paused. "You are going along. You have to face the people sometime."

Susanna didn't answer.

Mamm tugged on the quilt. "This is no way to behave, Susanna.

We've given you plenty of room to adjust all week, but things are what they are, and it's time you faced them."

Susanna jerked the quilt off her head to answer. "That I am an *Englisha* girl?"

"No!" *Mamm* was horrified. "You are not an *Englisha* girl, so stop acting like one."

"You heard what *Daett* said." Susanna's eyes blazed. "I have wild *Englisha* blood in me."

Mamm's face clouded. "Your *Daett* is not always wise in his choice of words, as he once wasn't in his choice of girlfriends. But he is still your *daett*, and you are still his daughter."

"I'm not facing anyone today, other than Joey if he stops by."

"Susanna, please!" *Mamm* grabbed her arm. "You are doing no such thing."

Susanna almost pulled back, but *Mamm* meant this for her own *goot*. Truth was, she had acted all week like a *bobbli*, but she couldn't help it. Her entire life had been a lie. How did one deal with that?

"You are still my daughter," *Mamm* said. "*Yah*, you should have been told about your *Englisha mamm* when you were young. I'm sorry now that I didn't insist, but maybe it's not too late for us to start over. I love you, Susanna, as if you were my own. That has not changed." *Mamm* took Susanna's hand. "I raised you and loved you as only I could."

Susanna managed to nod. There was no sense in hurting *Mamm* unnecessarily. What *Mamm* said was true. She couldn't imagine how her own *mamm* could have mothered her better. "Did you know my real *mamm*?" Susanna asked.

Mamm looked away. "We had best not speak of her. Some things are best left with the Lord."

Susanna leaned closer. "So you *did* know her, yet you married *Daett*."

Mamm meet her gaze. "I have forgiven your *daett*, as you must forgive him. There is no *goot* in speaking of the past."

"But there is *goot* in speaking of one's *mamm*," Susanna insisted. "I have a right to know. In fact, I must know."

Mamm's face softened, but she still hesitated.

"I must know," Susanna continued. "I will only learn it from other people if you don't tell me."

Mamm's voice caught. "Your *mamm* looked much like you, Susanna. I didn't know her well, but we saw each other while I was on my *rumspringa* time. Things were different back then. Few of our young people jumped the fence, so we mingled freely with the *Englisha* people. Which was all to our own shame, of course."

Susanna ignored the comment. "How old was I when you married *Daett*?"

Mamm thought for a moment. "Six months or so. Your *daett* saw his mistake early, and he was glad that I didn't reject him once I knew. We had dated a few times, but our relationship was nothing serious. He offered Mindy the chance to join the community and marry him, but she wasn't interested. Mindy told him she would raise the child by herself." *Mamm* looked away. "Your *daett* promised his financial support, and he would have kept his word. Did he not take you in when the time came?"

"And so did you." Susanna softened and reached out toward *Mamm*.

Mamm pulled her close for a hug. "I loved your *daett*, more than I can say. And a child is not to blame for her parents' mistakes. Don't you see that's why *Daett* has been so concerned for you and this Joey fellow? You must not follow in your *daett*'s sins, Susanna. Be thankful that Ernest has given you a marriage offer. I know you might not love him yet, but love comes slowly sometimes. Once you say the marriage vows this past trouble can be forgotten forever, and love will come even quicker then. No one need speak any more about this matter."

Susanna caught her breath, but the words of denial stuck in her mouth. She had not agreed to marry Ernest, so why was everyone assuming she would? Was her silence the same as assent? Ernest wasn't a bad choice for a husband, and he must be a *goot* man. How else could his two girls have turned out so cute? But she didn't love him. She had always planned to love a man before she dated him, much less marry him. Yet *Daett* and *Mamm* were correct. If she wished to marry in the community, she had no choice other than Ernest. She could remain single, but the shame would be great, perhaps too great to bear.

"Come now," *Mamm* said. "The men are in, and we need to leave soon. I'll help you dress."

"I'm not a *bobbli*," Susanna protested.

Mamm's smile was thin. "Sometimes we need extra loving care. Now get out from under the quilt."

Susanna got out of bed slowly. All the strength seemed to have left her body. She couldn't resist anything at the moment. "Is Ernest planning on courting me today?" The words came out as a croak.

Mamm's smile vanished. "Not yet. Your *daett* had the sense to tell him to wait until you have had a few baptismal classes behind you before he makes any official move. Bishop Enos will look more favorably on the matter after that."

"Baptismal classes!" The room spun in circles.

Mamm nodded. "Starting today, *yah*. That's all the more reason you must attend the services. You can't miss the first class."

"But I'm not ready to join," Susanna whispered. "Nor can I be Ernest's *frau*. I don't love the man."

"You will love the man in time." *Mamm* leaned closer to hold up a dress she had selected for Susanna. "We'll help you just as we're doing now. There is no other answer. We cannot have you bear the shame of a single life—not for this reason."

Bitterness against *Daett* rose inside of Susanna, but she couldn't go there. She hadn't said a word to *Daett* all week, other than a mumbled "*goot* morning."

Daett had stayed out of her way, no doubt realizing she needed the space. *Daett* always seemed to understand her needs, but this morning she must face him.

"It's time you spoke with your *daett*," *Mamm* said, as if reading Susanna's thoughts. "You can't attend the baptismal classes while there is silence between *Daett* and you. The Lord only blesses the heart that is open."

Susanna waited while *Mamm* placed the straight pins in the sleeves of her dress. She could have done those herself, but it felt *goot* to hold still at the moment. Perhaps someday she could move again, but right now there was only numbness inside of her. The coldness began deep down and didn't stop until it reached every part of her body.

Mamm took Susanna's hand, and they walked out of the bedroom and down the stairs together. *Daett* looked up from his chair, alarm filling his face, as they entered the living room. He must have sensed that Susanna was ready to speak to him about the matter.

Susanna squeezed her eyes shut, and her words began in fits and starts. "How could you have not told me before, *Daett*? Couldn't you just have...even a hint? Would that have been so wrong? Would I have died? It feels like I have now. You had all this time! All these years! How did you think I would never find out?"

Tears formed in *Daett*'s eyes. "I am guilty of all you say, Susanna, and of even more. My sins follow me to this day, and their sorrow has come on you. I dare not ask your forgiveness. I wish only to make right what I have done wrong, so far as it is in my power to do so."

Weakness swept over Susanna, and the anger left. *Daett's* words had that effect on her. They always had. She loved the man, and yet...

Daett stood up to stand beside Susanna. His arm slipped around her shoulder and he pulled her close. "You will always be mine," *Daett* said. "*Mamm* feels the same way. We can't change the past, but we can help shape the future with our choices. The way has been opened for you, Susanna. I know it will not be easy, but we are here to stand with you and to walk the road beside you. Ernest will be a *goot* husband for you, and you will love his girls. And someday, if the Lord wills that other *kinner* be given to you, we will have our first grandchildren to love and to hold. They will never know that sin once cast its grave shadow upon your life. The Lord will see to this, as we walk in His ways."

Susanna leaned against *Daett's* shoulder. What else could she do? She had no strength to hold up her head, let alone protest.

"*Mamm* must have told you about the baptismal classes by now," *Daett* continued. "Take courage, Susanna. I told Bishop Enos about our situation this week, and he will make things easy for you. All you must do is get up on your own two feet and walk upstairs. Nothing more is required of you."

Mamm spoke up. "Susanna will do this. I know she will."

Chapter Ten

Some twenty minutes later, Henry pulled on the reins to turn Ranger toward Deacon Herman's place on Bush Road. This section of the pavement didn't go far, and Susanna waited for the moment when the deacon's driveway came into sight. When she saw his place, the line of buggies beside the barn was still short, so *Mamm* had been correct—early was better this morning. Fewer people would be around to see her shame. She ought to wear a sign around her neck that read, "*Yah,* I have an *Englisha mamm.*" Maybe the shame would end sooner that way.

But on the other hand, she must not allow this bitterness a voice. Most of the community would know what had transpired last week. They would still be kind to her. She could be thankful for that. She shouldn't blame the community for how they saw things. The world on the other side of the fence was a dangerous thing. There were reasons why no young unmarried Amish man would take her home from the hymn singing—or ever would. *Englisha* girls were known to leave their husbands after the wedding vows were said. Not even baptism would cleanse that fear from their minds. Only an experienced widower like Ernest figured he could take a chance on her

Englisha wildness. And the next widower who showed an interest might be a worse option than Ernest—if such a man ever dared.

"Easy there, boy," Henry muttered to Ranger as he slowed for the turn into Deacon Herman's driveway.

There was no danger that Ranger would overturn the buggy, but Henry must have felt the need to say something. They had driven in silence all the way from home.

"Hold it there, boy," Henry muttered again, bringing Ranger to a stop at the end of the sidewalk.

Susanna climbed carefully down the buggy step. The path to the house was empty of women at the moment, but the last thing she needed was a clumsy spill.

Susanna took a deep breath and forced her feet forward. She paused before she opened the washroom door, hearing the low murmur of women's voices coming from inside. Maybe she should flee right now and leave the community permanently. Joey would help her leave, but did she really want to? That was the question. She was too confused to know right now. Better to go with the flow. That road had been mapped out for her. What did it matter if she married Ernest and didn't feel anything for the man before the wedding? That was better than thoughts of jumping the fence. Susanna pressed her lips together and opened the door.

Benny Yoder's *frau*, Beth, and John Chupp's *frau*, Esther, had been whispering together. They looked up when she walked in with startled looks on their faces. Both managed to smile. After a quick "*goot* morning," the two women grabbed their young daughters and scurried out of the washroom.

Susanna dropped her shawl on the table. At least she hadn't been treated with outright rejection. There would, of course, be lingering questions in many minds until she said the wedding vows with Ernest. Even then there would be a few who would wait to see if she would still jump the fence into the *Englisha* world and leave Ernest without a *frau*—for his lifetime. That was the horror an *Englisha* *frau* could inflict on an Amish man.

Susanna hesitated, but pressed on into the kitchen. The sooner she faced this, the better. Acting guilty would only make matters worse. The small group of women turned to face her when she entered.

Thankfully Bishop Enos's *frau*, Lydia, hurried out of the small group and held out her hand. "*Goot* morning, Susanna. I'm so glad you came. I hear you plan to attend your first baptismal class this morning."

"*Yah*, I guess." Susanna kept her head down, but the relieved looks on Beth's and Esther's faces were plain to see. This they had not expected. But what could anyone say if the bishop's *frau* approved of her? One by one the women came forward to shake Susanna's hand and wish her a *goot* morning.

Even Beth and Esther joined in the conversation afterward. Nothing more would be said about her problems, but doubts would remain. Her whole life hung by a thread. Not much pressure would be needed for it to break.

Susanna stood against the farthest wall to await the start of the service. More women came in from the washroom and the kitchen soon filled up. Susanna moved into the living room to escape the crush. Several of the smaller children were clinging to their *mamms'* hands, and Susanna noticed Ernest's two little girls ahead of her. They were with Ernest's sister, and both of them looked up to smile at Susanna.

Had Ernest described her to them as their future *mamm*? That wasn't possible. Or was it?

Susanna chided herself as thoughts whirled through her mind. This was no attitude to have on the morning of her first baptismal class. Somehow she must walk through this experience with her heart turned toward the Lord, no matter how unjust her circumstances were. *Daett* was the one who had borne a child with his *Englisha* girlfriend. Now she, Susanna, had wild *Englisha* blood in her. Was that why she felt so comfortable around Joey and his family? Because he was one of her people? The community must be right in their judgment of her. Did not a longing to see Joey sweep over her even now?

Ernest appeared in front of her, and Susanna let out a little gasp.

"*Goot* morning," Ernest greeted her as he collected his two girls from his sister. He had an amused smile on his face.

Susanna looked the other way and didn't answer. She wasn't his girlfriend or *frau* yet, and she didn't have to respond to him. He could write her attitude off as haughtiness if he wished. Ernest had been present when she passed out last Sunday evening, but apparently he still didn't understand that her heart was torn to bits. But she shouldn't complain. A perceptive man was a high expectation for a girl in her situation to have. She was clearly *Englisha* at heart and should be happy with what the Lord had given her.

Ernest smiled at her as he led his girls to the men's side of the room. He appeared quite satisfied with himself, but why shouldn't he be? She planned to attend the baptismal class this morning. That was almost the same as a promise to be Ernest's *frau* in the fall. She had been such an easy catch for Ernest—all things considered. On the negative side, her reputation didn't seem to faze the man in the least. No doubt forbidden fruit had its own allure.

The first of the older women began to file into the living room and take their seats. Susanna kept her head down until the line of single girls formed. She stepped into place behind Emma Yutzy, who gave her a faint smile. Susanna smiled back. Emma had always been nice to her, and that was unlikely to change. The line of girls took their seats and Susanna made sure to keep her gaze away from the married men's section. She had enough on her mind without dealing with Ernest's glances in her direction.

Moments later the first song was given out, and the appointed singer for the morning's service led out in the haunting tune. The song's German words had been written in prison cells by their persecuted forefathers over five hundred years earlier. Shame filled Susanna as the singing filled Deacon Herman's home. Here she was, upset over her troubles brought on by sin, while her forefathers had suffered for the sake of righteousness. She ought to mourn and thank the Lord for His mercy. Instead she was wallowing in self-pity.

On the second line of the song, Susanna lifted her chin while Bishop Enos rose to his feet and led the line of ministers up the stairs. They moved in slow motion, and no one else stood to follow them until the last minister had reached the top of the landing. Susanna watched out of the corner of her eye as several unmarried men rose to their feet. Susanna waited. Should she stand, or were there more men to follow? Surely she wouldn't be the only girl to attend the baptismal class. If she didn't stand soon, it would be too late. Susanna tried to move her feet, but they wouldn't respond.

Then she saw Emma Yutzy slowly rise. Susanna reached out to grasp the corner of Emma's dress. She didn't dare pull, but the touch was all she needed. Strength flooded her body, knowing she was not alone this morning. Emma would also attend the baptismal class. Truly the Lord must care about her situation, for He had provided for her need.

Susanna stayed close to Emma on their climb up the stairs, and Emma turned around to offer another smile at the top.

"Thank you for being with me today," Susanna whispered.

"I'd say you're the one who is with me," Emma whispered back. "I thought I would be the only girl in the class."

Susanna gave Emma a quick hug before they entered the bedroom where the men waited. Bishop Enos smiled up at them when they walked in and motioned toward chairs set up beside the boys.

The bishop greeted the class once Emma and Susanna had seated themselves. "*Goot* morning, everyone. You can all relax now. No one is going to eat you."

Chuckles passed around the room, and Emma's face glowed with happiness. Susanna tried to smile, but her expression froze in place. The joy from moments ago flew far away. Baptism was a momentous decision in the life of an Amish young person, and she was attending the class on less than honorable grounds. She had been forced in. Yet she was here, and with Bishop Enos's approval. The thought kept her from a hasty retreat back down the stairs to the living room.

Bishop Enos cleared his throat and his face sobered. "As you all know, this is not a light choice you have made to walk up the stairs this morning. In the Lord's eyes you have made your first steps toward an openly expressed godly life. By this summer you will state your desire publicly to live a life pleasing to the Lord and His church. For this, I commend all of you. We will do what we can to support and admonish each of you in the upcoming months, but in the end the decision to continue your walk is up to you. The Lord presses no one into His service, and neither does His church. We are all laborers together in the Lord's vineyard."

Bishop Enos's voice continued, but Susanna closed her eyes and thought of Joey and the piano in the Macalisters' living room. She could feel her fingers moving over the keys and the music pouring out into the room. Her heart rose and fell with the sound until Bishop Enos's words could no longer be heard.

Chapter Eleven

The following week, Ernest Helmuth left his two small girls in Katherine's care and drove early in the morning toward the Millers' place. Ernest clucked to his horse, Gambit, and headed off past his fields. As the buggy passed the pasture the cows lifted their heads to watch. Most of them were heavy with calves, others had been milked on time, and all of them appeared contented. Ernest believed in performing his duty toward man and beast alike. He supplied plenty of grain for his animals at each milking, and there was hay in the barn and spring grass growing high in the fields.

Ernest's thoughts turned to his lost Naomi. Why did the Lord take such a *wunderbah frau* from him when she was so desperately needed? Obviously the Lord did what He wished, and that was enough of an answer. Ernest was not a complicated man who ran around looking for things that weren't there. It was enough that the rain fell from the skies on his fields, and that he had a roof over his head and plenty of wholesome food on the table. It was also enough that the Lord seemed to bless his desire for another *frau*. The hope was strong in his heart that he could win Susanna's love. Had not the road been opened in front of him? Of course, Susanna still wasn't paying him any attention at the church gatherings, but that would come. He could wait.

"Give the woman some time," Susanna's *daett* had said on Sunday.

There hadn't been time for a lengthy or private conversation with Ralph, but maybe today there would be. Ralph might have suggestions for how he could move Susanna's affection toward himself while he waited. If he needed an excuse for the visit, there was always a reason to talk about farming. Most of his cows were due to bear their spring calves soon. Ralph might be willing to help out if Ernest ran into a crisis situation. The veterinarian out of Ogdensburg was always on call, but Ralph's help would incur a much lower bill. They could talk in the barnyard, and perhaps Ernest could catch a glimpse of Susanna.

"She's quitting her job in town this week," Ralph had assured him on Sunday. "Susanna will agree to this now that she has taken her first baptismal class." This was all for the best—to quit her job and stay closer to home under the circumstances.

Ernest jiggled the reins and turned onto Maple Ridge Road. Gambit sped up, but moments later Ernest pulled back on the reins. Speed wouldn't look decent upon his arrival, much as he wanted to swing into the Millers' driveway with a flourish. His heart beat faster at the very thought of Susanna. At this moment she might be at the kitchen window busy with the dishes. If he hurried, he might have a look at her face before she drew back.

Ernest sighed and slowed down even more. He must be patient with the girl. The days would pass, followed by the months, and by this fall Susanna would be at his home every morning. They would be man and wife. Susanna would fix his breakfast and sit at his kitchen table while they ate. He wouldn't have to steal glances at her face. He could touch her hand and perhaps even give her a kiss before he left for the day's fieldwork. He was in love with the woman. There was no question about that. Not since the day when he first saw Naomi, when she had arrived in the community from Ohio to visit her relatives in the North Country, had his affections been so captured by a woman.

"Whoa there," Ernest called out to Gambit. He turned into the driveway and pulled to a stop by the hitching post. The kitchen window was in plain sight, but no form was visible behind the pane of glass. If he'd had enough nerve, he would have climbed down from the buggy and walked right up the Millers' front door to greet Susanna with a "*goot* morning." But he had expressed enough bold-ness already. This was the time for winning the woman's heart, not forcing her hand.

The barn door cracked open and Henry, the oldest of the Miller boys, peered out. Henry grinned and ducked inside again. Obvi-ously Henry knew of Ernest's intense interest in Susanna and was steering clear until the dust had settled.

Ernest jumped down from the buggy and tied Gambit to the hitching post. Before he reached the barn door, Ralph pushed it open and stepped outside.

"*Goot* morning," Ralph greeted him.

"*Yah*, and *goot* morning to you," Ernest replied. He stole another quick glance toward the house.

Ralph followed Ernest's look and smiled. "You'd be thinking of Susanna, no doubt?"

Of course, Ernest wanted to say, but he lowered his head instead. "The Lord has blessed me with hope, *yah*. And my thoughts are never far from her."

"Do you wish to speak with her this morning?" A smile filled Ralph's bearded face.

Ernest shook his head. "Only with you."

Ralph nodded. "You're a wise man, Ernest, and one of great faith.

Susanna still mourns the loss of her *rumspringa* time even though she has taken the first step in the right direction. I hope you know that."

"I do." Ernest drew himself up. "And I hope to win the woman's love, Ralph. Naomi's heart was mine for a few precious years. Surely that is a gift the Lord can give again."

Ralph nodded. "As I said, you are a man of faith and courage, for which I'm very grateful. I may never be able to properly tell you how much." Ralph's face sobered. "The shame of my daughter jumping the fence into the world would overshadow me for the rest of my days."

"That would be a shame not easily covered," Ernest agreed. "But we must not doubt Susanna's future. We can believe the Lord is on our side and is greater than the temptations out there in the world. Susanna is an excellent woman at heart, even with—" His words stopped when a face appeared in the kitchen window.

Ralph caught Ernest's look and turned in that direction. "I do love that girl," he said. "And you're the man who can win her heart, Ernest, if anyone can. I will help where I'm able. Of that, I want to assure you."

"*Yah*, I will win her heart," Ernest said. His gaze was still fixed on the kitchen window, but the glass was empty now. He cleared his throat. "I'm the one who is grateful, Ralph. Your daughter is a beautiful woman."

"*Yah*." Ralph turned back to face Ernest. "But beauty has its downside. I hope you know that."

Ernest smiled. "The Lord will be with me. Of this I am confident."

"Pride can be an awful trap," Ralph muttered.

Ernest swallowed twice before he answered. "Surely you're not having doubts?"

"Not about you," Ralph said. "It's Susanna. Will she stay on the right path until her baptism? That's the question I've been asking myself the past few days."

Ernest didn't answer at once. He wouldn't lose Susanna. He couldn't. He needed a *frau* his heart could love. "We must trust the Lord," he finally said.

Ralph continued as if Ernest hadn't spoken. "Linda thinks the *Englisha* man won't leave Susanna alone. Already we've seen his vehicle driving past the place a few times. Thankfully Susanna was upstairs and didn't notice. We will do what we can, Ernest, but the girl has a mind of her own. Be warned of that and ready for a rough road to your wedding day. Susanna is humbled at the moment, but emotions come and go. Surely you know this?"

"Susanna will not jump the fence," Ernest said. "We must see to that with the Lord's help."

"*Yah*, but I can't keep her in the house morning, noon, and night." Ralph forced a chuckle. "She's already defied me by leaving with Joey for an afternoon a while back."

"No, you can't lock her up," Ernest agreed. "Our people do not resort to such measures, but we must pray and believe for the best."

Ralph sighed. "We will take courage then and not think dark thoughts." He stared down at his shoes for a moment. "My past sins cloud my counsel, Ernest. You must grant me patience and understanding, although I expect that is difficult for a man of your character. You never committed great sins in your youth."

"We all have our faults," Ernest assured him. "And you have cleansed your ways since then, and still seek to cleanse them." Ernest forced a laugh. "How else would you let such a man as myself near your beautiful daughter?"

Ralph laughed too. "We will say no more on that, but there also lies your danger, Ernest. You must pray for us, that we know how to handle this *Englisha* man." Ralph paused for a second. "If this Joey does come around again, do you have words of wisdom for me? I didn't do too well the last time he was here."

"I will pray for you, but I'm no man of great wisdom. I'm a simple man," Ernest said, with another glance toward the house. "You know, perhaps I *should* speak with Susanna this morning after all. I mean, how can I compete with this Joey fellow if the man has personal contact with Susanna and I don't?"

"You'd best wait," Ralph warned. "I know patience is difficult, but Susanna's heart is tender at the moment. Give the girl some time. We have already pushed the matter fast enough."

Ernest's face fell. "So tell me. Is this Joey handsome?"

Ralph looked away. "I'm afraid so, and he's from the world, Ernest. Everything about him is from out there."

Ernest straightened his shoulders. "We must not despair, Ralph. The Lord is on our side. There is too much at stake for us to lose your daughter. You have suffered enough, and as for me, I need a *frau*."

Ralph glanced toward the ground, but there were tears in the man's eyes. He wiped them away and looked up at Ernest. "You came for something else, perhaps?"

Ernest chuckled. "*Yah*, most of my cows are bearing soon. I thought perhaps you could give me help in an emergency or offer some advice. I've never had this many cows ready to birth calves at the same time."

Ralph grinned. "Stay up all night with your cows. You have no *frau* who would complain of your absence. But I'm here if you need me. Come fetch me, night or day."

Ernest smiled. "Thanks. I was hoping I could call on you…if need be."

Ralph sobered again. "As for Susanna, we must stay in prayer about all this. The Lord cares for even the smallest matters in our lives, but that doesn't mean we won't have to check on our cattle in the middle of the night. Much as we may have to spend sleepless nights in watch for my daughter."

"*Yah*, I'm willing to do whatever it takes," Ernest said. "We will pray for the wedding to be soon, and that the Lord will be with us until then. In the meantime, I had best be going."

Ralph nodded. "We will let you know if there is trouble with Susanna, and you do the same for us with your cows."

"May the Lord guide and keep us." Ernest turned to walk back to his horse. Ralph stood in the same spot even after Ernest had climbed in the buggy.

"Getup there," Ernest called to Gambit, and the horse took off up the lane. Ernest couldn't resist one last glance toward the kitchen window, but the glass was empty. The danger from this *Englisha* man bothered him more than he wished to admit. Ralph was not a man to exaggerate danger, and he knew more about the worldly ways of men than Ernest did. Hadn't Ralph sired a child with an *Englisha* woman? Thankfully the Lord turned such sins into *goot* things. Susanna plainly showed that grace in her life, but still…

Ernest jiggled the reins and urged Gambit onward. His farm had been neglected long enough while he chased after a woman. Yet this chase was necessary, and from the looks of things, he would be spending a lot more of his time trying to secure Susanna as his *frau*. He would not back down, though, he told himself. The wedding would be this fall. Ralph and Linda would help him make that happen.

Ernest drove on and listened to the beat of Gambit's hooves on the pavement, and by the time he pulled into his own driveway, a smile was back on his face.

"Whoa there," Ernest called out as he brought Gambit to a halt by the barn. Katherine opened the front door, and both girls came running out to meet him. Ernest let the reins fall as he leaped down from the buggy and gathered Lizzie and Martha into his arms. They both burst into giggles and kissed his bearded face.

"I was first!" Lizzie declared to her sister.

"No you were not," Martha insisted. "I kissed *Daett* first."

"I did!" Lizzie retorted.

Ernest silenced both of them with a touch to their lips. "Shush now, both of you. *Daett* has given you a hug and you've kissed him. Now he has to work in the fields."

"Okay," Martha said. Lizzie turned to run back to the house, and Martha followed without hesitation.

Ernest smiled as he watched the two girls reach the house and vanish indoors. How could Susanna not love the two little ones? Maybe that was his answer. He would take Lizzie and Martha along for his next visit to Susanna. Perhaps he could even send the girls over to say hello to Susanna some Sunday at the meeting. *Yah*, that might work, but how would he explain things to Lizzie and Martha? The girls needed a reason they could understand. He couldn't just say, "I'm going to marry Susanna this fall, and she will soon be your new *mamm*." Both Lizzie and Martha were too young to hear such grown-up news. But he would take the girls along to the Millers' place. That much he could do. Both girls would enjoy a visit, and so would Susanna.

Ernest smiled and unhitched Gambit from the buggy.

Chapter Twelve

It was a cool, moonless night, and Joey shivered as he waited in his car. He was parked under the large oak tree south of the Millers' place. Any closer to the house and someone would see him. Susanna would have to travel the distance on foot—*if* she came to meet him. That remained the big question.

After all, Susanna might not have received the letter he sent, and even if she did, Susanna might have a family engagement for the evening that would prevent her from meeting him. He should have been man enough to stop by and ask to speak with Susanna in person, but her father had been outside the barn the last time he drove past. One look from the road at the man's stern face had been all Joey needed. Contact with Susanna by that route was doomed.

So he had begged for an official DeKalb Building Supply envelope from the manager for his missive. Mr. Kenny hadn't agreed until Joey had provided further details—enough to enlist Mr. Kenny's grudging support.

"Only once," Mr. Kenny had warned him. "And if the Miller family finds the letter or Susanna hands it over to them, and if Mr. Miller comes in here to ask why I was involved, I'm telling him the truth."

"Fair enough," Joey had allowed.

Mr. Kenny had grinned. "I don't want to lose any Amish business over this fuss."

"You won't," Joey said, hoping he was telling the truth.

"Okay, then," Mr. Kenny said. "I hope this all turns out well. I do like the idea of giving the woman a choice. Susanna's a nice girl. I want to see her happy, whatever she decides."

Joey had smiled and left with the empty envelope in his coat pocket. At home he had composed the letter with care. Just the right words were needed, but his normally ready tongue had seemed to fail him. What if Susanna was really happy with her Amish life? But that couldn't be. He had only to think of the way she caressed the piano keys. Besides, Susanna had hinted at problems with her family. Surely she would find a way to sneak out of the house and meet with him. If not, he would check again tomorrow night. His instructions had been plain enough.

> *Dear Susanna,*
>
> *I hope this finds you well. Sorry for the subterfuge in contacting you, but I don't know any other way that doesn't cause worse problems for you. Be assured that Mr. Kenny gave me the envelope and knows why I want to contact you. He thinks very highly of you and wants to see you happy. I'm sure he'd give you your job back if you decide you want it.*
>
> *But that's not why I'm writing. I would like to meet with you, Susanna. I miss your friendship, and something doesn't seem right about your current situation. You wouldn't tell me why when I dropped you off at your house that Sunday afternoon. Maybe you will now. I hope you trust me enough to confide in me.*

But if you are really happy with the present situation, I
want to hear that too. If you tell me you don't want to
see me again, I guess I can accept that—eventually.

Please meet me under the large oak tree south of
your place. It's where the lane goes into Mr. Williams's
farm. No one should disturb us there, or I'll take you
into town if you wish. Anywhere you are most com-
fortable to talk. I'll be under the tree in the dark of the
moon on Wednesday and Thursday evenings at ten.
Your music still haunts me, Susanna. Don't silence
such beauty or banish from your life the joy God has
given you.

Hope to see you,
Joey

Joey peered into the darkness. How long should he wait? He had
said ten o'clock, but Susanna might have been delayed. The clock
on his dashboard said twenty after. He would wait a few more minutes. There was still tomorrow night, but he was sure Susanna would
come tonight if she'd come at all.

Joey opened the car door and stepped outside to stretch his legs.
There were tight knots in both of them and in his shoulders. He
swung his arms to loosen the muscles. How must Susanna feel if he
felt this tense as he waited? Susanna would have to sneak out of the
house and find her way through the fields. She wouldn't come by
the road. That would be too obvious. He should have chosen a closer
spot, Joey chided himself, but he hadn't dared. As usual Susanna
bore the heaviest end of this deal, but it couldn't be helped.

"Joey." Her soft whisper made him whirl about.

"Susanna?" he called back.

Her form slowly became visible. Her breath came in short gasps. He reached for her hand.

"You did come!" Joey opened the car door. "Sit inside until you catch your breath."

She shook her head and then leaned against his car. "This is fine. I'm just…well, I had to hurry."

Joey glanced toward the Miller home, where a low light burned in a window. He couldn't remember whether it had been there before.

"I'm so sorry about this," he said. "Were you seen?"

Her fingers clung to his. "No. Oh, Joey, it was such a relief to hear from you. I…" Her voice trailed off.

Joey stepped closer. "I care about you, Susanna. I hope you know that, and that I'm worried. What is going on?"

Susanna dropped her gaze. "I can't tell you, Joey. Or rather, I'm ashamed to tell. There are things…" She stopped again. "Oh, I wish that everything could go on the way it did before. I lie awake at night in bed and hear the music in my head. I can hardly stand it, but what else can I do?"

He hesitated. "Has something else happened?"

She bit her lip. "I can't say what's wrong, Joey. *Daett* committed a horrible sin…and I never knew."

He regarded her for a moment. "This sounds like riddles to me. Can you tell me what he did?"

A tear trickled down her face. "No, Joey. My people are still my people, and I will bear their shame with them."

"What shame? I still don't understand."

She looked away. "Can't we speak of something else? Just hold me. Whisper to me that everything will be all right."

He opened his arms and pulled her close. "Whatever troubles you, I'm here," he said. "Shall I take you home with me? You can stay there for a few days, and we'll find you an apartment after that. Mr. Kenny will give you your old job back. You don't have to live like this, Susanna."

She looked up at him. "If only, Joey. If only I could, but there is…" She buried her face in his chest. "Oh, I can't say it. I'd lose even you, Joey…"

He reached up to hold her hand. "You're talking in riddles again. Please tell me what happened, Susanna."

She wiggled out of his arms and glanced toward the house. The light was burning brighter now. Or was there another lamp in the window? Joey couldn't tell.

"They'll be looking for me soon," she said. "I thought I heard *Mamm* stirring in the bedroom when I went out the washroom door, but I couldn't wait and look. I can't climb the roof the way my brothers can." Susanna gave a little laugh. "Breaking a leg would have been a real disaster, on top of sneaking out to see you."

"The only disaster will be if I don't see you again," he said.

She shook her head. "I don't think I can. Don't you see how my life is?"

"No, I don't see," Joey said. "I wish you would tell me, but since you won't…or can't…just know that I'm here, and that I'll always be your friend."

"I have to go now." She turned her gaze toward the house and then back to Joey. "I can't thank you enough for what you brought into my life. I wish it could have gone on forever."

Joey reached for his belt and unclipped his cell phone. "Here!" A plan raced through his mind. "Take this. Keep it turned off until you want to call me. The battery should last a while. You can call me at home." He reached in the glove box of his car, pulled out a pen and a pad of paper, and scribbled down the phone number.

Susanna stared at the phone in her palm. "No. I cannot take this.

Mamm is up, I'm sure, and she will be able to tell by my face that something's wrong. She'll know!"

Joey looked away. Desperation gripped him. Somehow he must stay in touch with Susanna.

He reached back into his car and pulled out a bag that had held his fast-food dinner. "Here. Better yet. I'll get a spare, and we'll put the cell in this bag and leave it under this oak tree. You can come out tomorrow to retrieve it."

Susanna nodded and then said, "But please don't ever call me. I'd never be able to explain the sound of a cell phone ringing."

He nodded. "I promise, but don't forget to call me if you need to."

A smile played on her face. "I promise."

"Oh, Susanna." Joey reached for her hands and she clung to them. "Get in the car with me," he begged. "We can leave and never come back to whatever problem you have here."

"I can't leave. These are my people." She pulled herself away, her face solemn. She glanced across the darkened field. "And you don't know everything about me, Joey. I really must go now."

Joey took a step after her, but Susanna had already disappeared into the darkness. He heard the soft twang of barbed wire in the field along the ditch line, followed by silence. She had left as quietly as she had come. Like a night owl on the wind currents, Susanna could probably see in the dark.

Joey smiled after her, more convinced than ever that whatever Susanna's trouble was, he would see her through it…somehow. He took another glance toward the Millers' house before he climbed in his car and turned the key, the headlights cutting a broad swath across the fields in the dark night.

Chapter Thirteen

Susanna paused near the barn and looked back over her shoulder. She gasped at the sound of the car engine, and the stream of light that flooded the fields south of the Miller home. Whoever was up in the house would surely see the sudden appearance of Joey's headlights. The chance to slip into the house unnoticed was past. Nor could she claim that she had been out on a midnight stroll.

Susanna watched as the headlights bounced past the house and faded into the distance. She could have gone with Joey but had chosen not to. Now the results of her decision must be faced. Susanna set her shoulders and approached the front porch. The dim light in the house had moved into the living room, so someone was waiting for her. Her heart pounding, Susanna went up the steps and pushed open the front door to see *Mamm*'s worried face framed in the light of the kerosene lamp.

"Susanna!" *Mamm* grabbed her arm.

Before she could respond, *Daett* entered from the bedroom and his stern face joined *Mamm*'s worried one. "How long have you been out, Susanna?" he demanded.

"Not long." She dropped her gaze to the floor, but it was a little late for a display of humility.

Daett's words were clipped. "An *Englisha* vehicle just cut on its lights moments ago south of the house. Does that have anything to do with you?"

Why couldn't you have had some sense, Joey? Susanna didn't say the words aloud, but she groaned quietly.

"Does it?" *Daett* demanded. "Tell me the truth. Why were you out at this hour of the night?"

"I went to meet Joey," Susanna whispered.

Mamm gave a little shriek, and *Daett* reached over to slip his arm around *Mamm's* shoulder.

Mamm held the kerosene lamp off to the side with one hand and clung to *Daett* with the other. "Oh, Ralph, how could this happen?"

Daett held *Mamm* close and whispered, "My sins continue to haunt us. I'm shamed beyond words, and I pray this will end soon. If not, I will have to go out of the house dressed in sackcloth and ashes."

"A lot of *goot* that would do us." *Mamm* let go of *Daett* and pulled out a handkerchief to dab her eyes. "It's time you dealt with this daughter of yours. I've tried to stay hopeful and think the best, but this is too much." *Mamm* let out a loud cry and handed the lamp to *Daett*. Without a backward glance she fled toward the bedroom.

Daett and Susanna stood motionless, as if frozen in place. Was this all her fault? How could it be? She had not chosen an *Englisha* woman for her mother. That had been *Daett's* choice, and he was the one who had kept the truth hidden for so long.

Susanna gave *Daett* a quick glance. What horrible thoughts these were. *Daett* wanted nothing but the best for his family, yet only moments ago she had clung to Joey with desperation. Susanna stared at the darkened hardwood floor. Oh, the horribleness of it all! She was being torn asunder by these conflicting emotions, and there was nothing anyone could do about it—she least of all.

Daett finally broke the silence. "We should sit and talk." He lowered the lamp onto the desk. "Come." *Daett* took Susanna's hand, and together they sat on the couch.

Her whole body stiffened. *Daett*'s lecture would be long, and her heart would be torn into smaller pieces. Why did all of this have to happen to her? Had the Lord no mercy on her situation?

Daett's voice caught. "I loved your *mamm*, Susanna—that is, your *Englisha mamm*—as I love you. The Lord forgive me, but I did."

Susanna drew a long breath and looked up into *Daett*'s face. Had she heard right? The words finally came. "Then why did this happen to me and you? Why did she die? Why are we not together?"

Daett winced. "You should know the answer to that question, Susanna. You have been brought up among the people. The Lord does what He does, and He does not ask us for permission."

"So my real *mamm* had to die so things could be made right for us?" The words were bitter, and Susanna looked away from *Daett*'s face.

Daett hung his head. "I don't know the answer to such things, Susanna. I am a simple man. I wish that Mindy could have lived and married me here in the community. But she chose not to."

Susanna looked again at her *daett*. "So it was the Lord's will that I be raised in the community. That's why *Mamm* had to die?"

Daett shook his head. "If you had been raised by Mindy, the Lord would have watched over you. But you were not. So this is His will, and you should not fight it, Susanna."

"And is this the Lord's will, that I lock myself away in marriage to a man I do not love?"

Daett met Susanna's intense gaze. "So this is what troubles you— marriage to Ernest? But it must not. Any woman can learn to love, and Ernest will be kind to you. He will hold you close to his heart and cherish you. His two small children will fill your days with fruit- ful labor. You are not being locked away. You are being given a new life. Your heart should be filled with gratitude for the patience the community has with you and with me."

How could she forget that point? The whole community held itself together somehow. What affected one affected them all. She had always relished the closeness, but now the weight of the community bore down on her until she couldn't breathe. *Daett's* voice broke into her thoughts. "Susanna?"

"*Yah?*" Susanna didn't look at him.

Daett placed his hand back on hers. "I know I speak difficult words to hear, but the truth will set us free, bitter though they sound."

Susanna was tired. What could she possibly say that would make any difference? What could she say that didn't sound defensive or accusative? Finally, she said, "I had best go to bed." Susanna stood, but *Daett* pulled her back down.

"We haven't solved anything tonight, have we?"

"Did you expect us to?"

Daett paused for a moment. "I'm sorry that my faults continue to follow me. In this I must again admit my error. I have been too easy on you these past years. I know that now, and yet my heart still struggles. What am I supposed to do?"

"You're asking me?" Susanna stared at him. "Am I supposed to agree to anything while I'm torn apart on the inside? I need some time. This is all too sudden for me."

Daett shook his head. "On that you are wrong, Susanna. We should baptize you next week and have your wedding the week afterward, but that's not possible. More time will not help you. Still, I understand your desire for what cannot be. I, too, once dreamed of things that lie out there, or rather of bringing those things into the community. What a fool I was. I thought I could take an *Englisha* woman as my *frau*. I asked Mindy if she would marry me, but she told me no, that she was not part of my world. How will things be different with this Joey of yours? He cannot bring our two worlds together in marriage."

"But he does not mean to," Susanna protested. "We have said nothing of marriage. We are only friends."

A brief smile played on *Daett's* face. "In this you are not wise, daughter. The man loves you. Trust me. That you do not love him gives me what little hope I have. The Lord has left your heart open for a proper man. We must take advantage of the situation before it's too late."

Susanna sighed. "Too late for what? I have no plans to jump the fence."

Daett smiled. "Mindy was a *goot* woman, Susanna, just as this Joey is probably a *goot* man. The problem is that Mindy wasn't meant for me, and Joey isn't meant for you."

"Just one more thing then. How did *Mamm* die?" Susanna asked.

"Toxemia," *Daett* answered without hesitation. "Why she didn't go to the hospital sooner, I don't know. Or why her…" *Daett* stood and paced the living room floor in front of Susanna. "No," *Daett* muttered. "I've been there a thousand times before and I will not go there again. I did what I thought was right. Mindy did what she believed was right, and so did everyone else. I will go mad if I continue to question the past." *Daett* pressed his fingers into his forehead and sat down again on the couch.

Susanna reached over for his hand, but *Daett* pulled away.

"I'm sorry," he said. "I should not have said what I did just now. These regrets are understandable, but they are not from the Lord."

"I do not blame you for wishing you were married to Mindy," Susanna whispered.

Horror filled *Daett's* face. "Susanna, no! I did not mean that! I'm torn, that's all. I was speaking out of my worry over your situation and my blame for it."

But *Daett* did mean it, Susanna told herself. Tears filled her eyes at the thought. How different life would have turned out if *Daett* had married her real *mamm*, Mindy. Had her *mamm* been so heartbroken that she had ignored her own health needs? Had Mindy loved *Daett* more than she dared admit? Why else had all this happened? But if Mindy and *Daett* had stayed together, Susanna wouldn't have brothers—Henry, James, Noah, or Tobias. Oh, it was all a horrible, confused mess.

"Come!" *Daett*'s voice broke into Susanna's thoughts. "Enough has been said tonight. Too much, I'm thinking, but I am tired of these secrets. Perhaps it's best if the heart finally speaks and the Lord sorts all these things out."

"What will you tell *Mamm*?" Susanna motioned toward the bedroom with her hand.

"I will tell her we must all pray about this," *Daett* said. "Only the Lord can help us. But in the meantime, we will work on getting your heart ready to love, Susanna. You must marry Ernest. There is no other way." *Daett*'s face glistened with intensity.

Susanna looked away, numbness filling her whole body.

"We must get to bed," *Daett* repeated. "The work doesn't stop tomorrow just because our hearts are troubled."

The tears stung again as Susanna clung to *Daett*'s arm on the short walk to the bottom of the stairs.

"Try to get some sleep," *Daett* whispered in her ear.

"*Yah*, you too," Susanna whispered back.

They parted at the bottom of the stairs with a quick hug. The bedroom door squeaked behind them, and *Daett* shooed her on with a quick wave of his hand. Susanna took the steps in the darkness, each board familiar and dear. How many times had she climbed these stairs since her childhood? This had always been home; she had never thought otherwise. To leave home for what was not home, even with Joey at her side…could she make that choice? The question tore at her heart, and Susanna pushed it away. She couldn't think anymore tonight. Once she reached her bedroom, the door across the hallway opened a small crack. Susanna stopped short. No face was visible, but she could see starlight through the window on the other side. Had Henry stayed up to question her?

Susanna waited, but it was Noah who whispered, "Where were you, Susanna?"

"Don't burden your mind about it," Susanna whispered back. She approached the door, and it opened wider. She reached inside to find Noah's tousled head, and she pulled him close.

"But I worry about you," he said.

Susanna pressed back the tears. "*Yah*, I know. Just pray for me, Noah. And now, go back to bed."

Noah obeyed, and Susanna closed the bedroom door behind him. She choked back a sob and hurried into her own room to bury her face in the pillow under the heavy bed quilt.

Chapter Fourteen

On Thursday morning, Susanna came downstairs in the early morning hours. The men had already left for the barn. She had waited until she heard the washroom door slam before venturing out of her bedroom. Susanna set the kerosene lamp on the table and watched the flicker of its flames play on the kitchen wall. Her mind wouldn't focus from lack of sleep, but that was her own fault. She could have gone to bed early like the rest of the family, but bedtime was a dreaded event of late. Sleep wouldn't come, and when it finally did come, it was filled with troubling dreams of what might lie ahead of her.

But that was also her fault. She had retrieved the cell phone Joey left from under the oak tree the very next morning after they had met. The knowledge that she could now call him anytime she wanted only increased the pressure. Already she had been tempted to call just for a chat, in hopes that hearing Joey's voice would lift her spirits.

Mamm's soft steps behind her jerked Susanna out of the daze.

"*Goot* morning," *Mamm* greeted her. "You're still not sleeping well, I see."

"*Goot* morning," Susanna muttered back. She busied herself with the breakfast preparations.

Feelings between her and *Mamm* hadn't been *goot* since the night she had gone out to meet Joey. What *Daett* had told *Mamm* of their conversation she didn't know. Whatever it was, *Mamm* had become more guarded around her. The tension was high. She found herself longing for her old job at the DeKalb Building Supply, where people talked to each other without issues between themselves. She even missed the ride to and from work. The silence had been peaceful then.

Maybe she even missed her daily exchange with the *Englisha* people. Maybe because she was herself half-*Englisha*? That thought had never occurred to her before *Daett*'s startling revelation. That stain seemed permanent now, even if she said the marriage vows this fall with Ernest. She would always be half-*Englisha* in an Amish world, and if she jumped the fence, she would be half-Amish in an *Englisha* world.

"You should try to accept your lot in life, Susanna," *Mamm* said softly, as if reading her thoughts. "Rebellion against the Lord's will only causes more trouble."

"Sorry," Susanna whispered. "I'm just trying to sort through some things right now. Believe me, I'm not after more trouble."

"You only have two choices," *Mamm* said. "To follow the Lord's will, or to go your own way. The only right choice is to submit to the Lord's will."

"*Yah*, I know," Susanna said. "I'm trying, but it's hard when you aren't really sure—"

"Well, to help you be sure," *Mamm* said, "Ernest is dropping off his girls for the day so you can spend some time with them. Get to know them and let them get to know you too."

Susanna turned to stare at *Mamm*.

"Don't you think that's a *goot* idea?" *Mamm* asked. "You have to come out of your confused world, Susanna, and begin to walk on the road the Lord has shown you. This will help."

"Ernest is dropping off his girls? Without asking me?"

"*Yah*," Mamm said. "This will do both of you a lot of *goot*, but especially you. I liked the idea right away when Ernest asked me after the Sunday service if he could bring his girls over for the day. Think about it for a moment, Susanna. Isn't it time you see more of the man and his *kinner*? You will be his *frau* by this fall, and you need to act more like a woman about to be a wife and an instant *mamm*. Besides, the way you've been acting isn't right. The Lord can't be pleased with your actions. You have so much you could be thankful for even with the trouble you're in, but instead you choose to pout and ignore everyone around you."

Susanna looked away. "I'm not trying to be difficult, and I want to do what is right. It's just that I don't know. Marrying a man I don't love seems like getting in even more trouble than I'm in now."

"I've told you a hundred times, you *will* love him," Mamm declared.

Susanna sighed. It was no use. "Well, if I'm going to have the girls for the day, let me at least take them somewhere for a while. I need to get out of the house for a few hours. Anywhere."

Mamm looked up. "Okay, I'll give you this much. You can take the girls for a buggy ride before lunchtime. That should be safe."

"Oh, *Mamm*," Susanna groaned. "Why must you be so hard on me? It's beginning to seem like a prison here in my own home."

Mamm turned around to face Susanna. "You lost my trust when you went out the other night to meet that *Englisha* man. When you begin to show us that you plan to make the right choices and serve the Lord, then maybe we can let up a little."

Susanna winced. "Do you have to be so sharp with me, *Mamm*? I'm hurting, you know."

Mamm's face softened a little. "I know I can be harsh, but your *daett* has treated you like a *bobbli* all your life, and it's time it ended. If you had been made to face things earlier in life, maybe we wouldn't be in this mess. Instead, *Daett* let you run around all over the county like a loose hen, and of course you ended up consorting with *Englisha* people. What did Ralph expect, considering..." *Mamm* gave Susanna a meaningful look. "You did have an *Englisha mamm*, Susanna. The truth is the truth. I told the man this often, but *Daett* has a stubborn mind. Just like you. Now look where his leniency has gotten us. I say it's time for someone with some sense to be in charge, which is why I'm thankful for Ernest. I told the man on Sunday that he needs to handle you with a firm hand. He wasn't sure about that since he's so taken with you, but I'm saying it. It's time you changed your attitude toward Ernest. You need to start giving him some encouragement before he changes his mind. I know for a fact there are two widows in the district who would take the man's marriage offer in a snap. And here you are, with the man's heart in your hand, moping around like there's a funeral ahead of you."

Susanna started to speak but then stopped. A protest was useless, but she could speak up for her real *mamm*. "Why are you so hard on Mindy? *Daett* speaks nothing but *goot* about her."

Mamm's eyes blazed. "Your *daett* would be wiser if he forgot that girl instead of dawdling around in his mind about how things might have turned out. He knows this was all for the best. We cannot coddle the world in our hearts, Susanna. *Daett* thinks he understands that, but he doesn't. I have come to regret the sympathy I gave Ralph for his past, and I say the same thing to you. Now is not the time to wallow in maybes, but to make the right choices for the future. You must go through with your baptismal classes and marry Ernest by this fall. That decision starts today with his little girls. Be a *mamm* to them. Hold them. Cherish them. Give them the motherly love Ernest can't give them."

Susanna looked away. "I could try, I guess."

"*Goot*! You would do well to listen to me, Susanna. You may not be my daughter in the flesh, but I raised you as my own."

Susanna couldn't keep the catch out of her voice. "Do you wish you hadn't married *Daett*?"

Mamm didn't flinch. "No, I would do it all over again for the love I feel toward your *daett*. And I have come to love you too, Susanna. Don't doubt me on that. It's just that love isn't enough. We must also live right. This is not the time for fuzzy feelings. It's a time for careful walking in fear of the Lord, because the eyes of the community are on us."

"I know, and I wish they weren't," Susanna muttered.

Mamm ignored her, and moved the oatmeal bowl to the kitchen table. Susanna found the sugar canister in the cupboard and filled the jar to the brim. The clatter of the men in the washroom filled the house moments later, and *Mamm* added another piece of firewood to help her finish frying the last of the bacon. Susanna pressed out a small crease in the tablecloth and took over at the stove while *Mamm* went to call Noah and Tobias.

Her brothers came in one by one and took their places at the table. Henry regarded Susanna with a long look, but he said nothing. It was Noah who offered the first smile of the morning. Susanna stepped away from the stove to give him a tight hug, and Noah grunted in protest.

When they were all seated, they bowed their heads in prayer and then ate in silence. The clock on the kitchen wall ticked loudly. *This can't continue*, Susanna told herself. They had once been a happy family around the breakfast table. Now there was only a glum stillness.

As if in protest, three-year-old Tobias threw his spoon toward the floor, where it landed with a bang against the side of the stove.

"Don't do that," *Mamm* chided. She returned the spoon, and pressed the boy's hand on the handle for a few seconds. "Behave yourself now, Tobias."

Finally Henry spoke up with a quick glance in Susanna's direction. "When is Susanna getting baptized?"

"Hush," *Daett* chided. "We will not speak of the matter at the breakfast table."

"Ernest's children are coming this morning," *Mamm* announced with forced cheerfulness. "Susanna is taking care of them for the day."

"They are cute girls," James muttered. "At least there's that to be thankful for. But when is the wedding? That's what I want to know."

"All children are cute," *Mamm* said, ignoring the question.

Henry guffawed. "Cousin Elisabeth's aren't. I don't care what anyone says."

Daett gave his eldest son a warning look. "Be careful what you say, Henry. Those things have a way of coming around later and biting you."

James chuckled. "Hear that, Henry? You and Charlotte Yoder—"

James ducked as Henry swatted at him. "Stop it. Charlotte couldn't have anything but cute children."

Noah perked up and waved his spoon about. "What I want to know is when will Charlotte marry Henry?"

Henry turned red as a beet and said nothing. James laughed and answered for him. "We don't know yet, and neither does Henry. He hasn't dared ask the girl home, but you'd better think about something else, Noah. You're too little for such thoughts."

"No I'm not," Noah protested. "I'm going to marry Beth when

I grow up. I gave her my pencil to use at school yesterday, and she kept it all day."

There was a ripple of laughter around the table, and Susanna joined in. Maybe the tide had begun to turn.

"She sounds like a *goot frau* to me," James told Noah with a straight face. "You keep that little girl in your sights. Don't let her get away from you."

Noah nodded solemnly. "I won't!"

Chuckles were followed by silence again when *Daett* bowed his head for a silent prayer of thanks. They all kept their heads down until *Daett* said "amen." No one moved afterward until *Mamm* had brought the family Bible in from the living room and *Daett* opened the pages.

In a solemn voice, *Daett* read, "'O Lord, our Lord, how excellent is thy name in all the earth! Who hast set thy…'"

Susanna tried to listen, but her mind drifted away. In an hour or so Ernest would be here with his two girls. Would he want to speak to her? *Yah*, they would have to talk with each other. She would have to force words out of her mouth and place a smile on her face. She had to—if she wanted to stay in the community. And she did. She wanted to make the same *goot* choices *Daett* had. She wanted to leave behind the *Englisha* world she had tasted briefly and grown to love. But then there was Joey. And the piano. And her job at DeKalb Building Supply.

Susanna shut down her thoughts and listened to the last words *Daett* was reading. "O Lord, our Lord, how excellent is thy name in all the earth!" *Daett* closed the Bible. "Let us pray," he said. There was a shuffle of feet as they knelt, and *Daett's* voice rose and fell with the morning's prayer.

Please be with me and help me, Lord, Susanna prayed silently. She squeezed her eyes tightly shut. *I don't know myself anymore. I'm lost in my sorrow. Can You help me?*

There was no answer, but she didn't expect one. Some comfort was all she could hope for, and a sense of peace did seem to drift over her heart.

"Amen," *Daett* said seconds later, and they all stood to their feet. Her older brothers made a beeline for the washroom. *Daett* paused to smile at *Mamm* before he followed his sons.

Once the washroom door had closed again, *Mamm* said, "Noah, you get ready for school now." Noah shuffled toward the stairway.

"Tobias, you go up with Noah. I'll be up in a minute," *Mamm* said. "Susanna, you clean the kitchen while I tend to Tobias. And be sure and change your dress before Ernest comes. You're talking with him if I have to drag the two of you together by your ears."

Chapter Fifteen

An hour later, with the drapes on her bedroom window drawn, Susanna slipped into a clean everyday dress and placed each pin with care. Then, on second thought, she considered that *Mamm* would probably prefer she wear a Sunday meeting dress.

But surely not her best dress. Ernest would get the wrong impression if she showed up in such attire. He'd think he'd won her heart already, when the truth was completely otherwise. The truth was, Ernest had a lot of work ahead of him if he wished to win her love before the wedding. Was he up to it? Or did he even care? Did she hope he cared? Did she want this to happen? The questions raced through her mind, but Susanna pushed them away.

She must try and make the relationship with Ernest work. She didn't want to jump the fence into the *Englisha* world, and she didn't want to leave *Daett*. He had chosen the life of the community. Could *Daett* be wrong to have made the choice he did? She had only to envision his kind eyes and feel his tender touch on her hand to know the answer to that. If she chose to jump the fence, the sorrow that would descend upon *Daett* would tear at her heart. *Daett* was right, and she would follow his footsteps. Only that road led to success. Look what had happened to her real *mamm*, Mindy, when she refused to follow *Daett* into the life of the community. *Daett* had offered to marry Mindy. What guarantee did Susanna have that a greater disaster did not lie ahead for her if she rejected Ernest's offer? A life lived in sorrow and regret could be worse than death.

Susanna pushed the last pin into her dress. With that done, she turned to open the drapes wide. The bright sunlight burned her eyes as she peered out and saw Ernest's buggy parked beside the barn. *Mamm* fluttered about near the door of the buggy, where both of Ernest's small girls sat up on the seat. How had Ernest driven in without a sound? She must have been deep in her own thoughts not to hear. She stepped away from the window and made her way slowly downstairs. At the bottom of the steps, Susanna forced her feet onward—past the front door, off the porch, and into the yard.

Ernest looked up with a grin on his face as she approached. *Mamm* stopped her fluttering about and froze in place.

Susanna greeted Ernest with a smile. "*Goot* morning."

"*Goot* morning." His grin grew wider. "You're awful perky this morning."

"We're so glad for this chance, Ernest," *Mamm* gushed before Susanna could speak. "I'll take the girls into the house, and you can speak with Susanna for a few moments. I'm sure you have some catching up to do. But I just want to say again how much we appreciate you coming by this morning and giving us a chance to watch your girls for the day."

Mamm reached into the buggy and lifted Lizzie down to the ground with a twirl. "Hey, big girl. Now you're on the ground."

Lizzie giggled. "That was fun. Do Martha now!"

"Coming right up," *Mamm* said, glowing with happiness. *Mamm* glanced toward Ernest before she reached back into the buggy and brought Martha down with a flourish.

Martha smiled but didn't say anything.

"They'll be just fine here, I see." Ernest's grin was still in place. He gave both girls a quick hug. "Be *goot* for Linda now, and give Susanna a chance to get to know you."

Susanna forced herself to smile. "I'm sure they will."

That Ernest was taken with her was plain to see. She should be thankful for his attentions. He was her only hope if she wished to stay in the community with a *goot* reputation. She glanced at his bearded face and tried to smile again.

"You two chat now," *Mamm* said.

"*Mamm*," Susanna protested. "I…"

Mamm ignored her and waved over her shoulder as she led the girls toward the house. Lizzie also waved as if she were going on a road trip and wouldn't see either of them for a long time.

"My daughters are the apple of my eye," Ernest muttered. "So like their *mamm* it breaks my heart sometimes."

Susanna dropped her gaze to the ground. She should say something in sympathy, but the words stuck in her throat.

Ernest grasped his horse's bridle as if he needed a lifeline. "I…I just want to say you're doing the right thing, Susanna, in caring for my girls today. I know your *Mamm* agreed to this, not you, but the gesture must also be in your own heart or you would have objected."

Susanna opened her mouth to correct him, but Ernest continued. "This must be difficult, pulling yourself away from the world out there and getting to know me better. I know that I'm finding my way along the pathway myself, and yet I often cheer my heart by telling myself that the Lord has promised to bless the sacred marriage vows no matter how we arrive at them. I wish, like you do, Susanna, that this awkwardness between us wouldn't be necessary, but things are the way they are. I hope you continue to open your heart to me and give me a chance."

Ernest stared off into the distance and Susanna waited.

"I miss my dear Naomi," he said, "more than I can say. I had hoped we could grow old together, but the Lord had other plans. And now my heart is drawn to you, Susanna. I would give you the place that Naomi once had, even though you were not my first choice. I know you understand that, and I know that I may not be your first choice either. So forgive my boldness this morning, but I have waited a long time to speak with you. There are many things heavy on my heart. The love between a man and a woman is a strange thing. As Solomon said, it's mysterious like the ways of a serpent upon a rock. Whatever the road holds ahead of us, the Lord will be with us and help us. Of this I am most confident."

"I am sorry for your loss of Naomi," Susanna whispered.

Ernest nodded. "Thank you, and let me say something else. I imagine you have lately wondered why your *daett* committed the sins he did in his youth. I want to tell you that I don't hold these things against your *daett* or against you, Susanna. Some in the community might not be so understanding, but the Lord has given me grace in my heart to see that these things can be overcome."

Susanna's voice broke. "I love *Daett* regardless of what he did."

Ernest didn't seem to notice as he continued. "What a shock it must have been for you to learn that your *mamm* was *Englisha*. I can imagine your horror. No doubt you thought there was no choice left for you but to leave the protection of the community and jump the fence. This *Englisha* man who befriended you was no doubt right there, ready to lead you into this temptation." Ernest gave Susanna a smile. "But take comfort. The Lord has supplied a way out of temptation. The Lord has again done what He promised. As Moses stood before the mighty Red Sea and parted the waters with his uplifted rod, so I can imagine your *daett* has stood before the waters of his great sorrow and lifted his hand toward heaven. And now a way has been opened for you, Susanna. I would not have wanted Naomi taken from me—for any reason. But now that the Lord has chosen, I'm glad I can be part of His plan to save you from the world. Our faith and the community believe in redemption. Bishop Enos and Deacon Herman both understand my feelings for you and my faith in the Lord's hand. I have been open with both ministers about my plans. I know the way is dark for you right now, and perhaps I'm not much of a catch or the one you dreamed of. But the Lord knows Naomi loved me, and it looks like I'm all you've been given, Susanna." Ernest gave her a quick glance. "There are, of course, my two daughters. The Lord has blessed me with them. I encourage myself daily with such thoughts, and I'm sure you will too once you know the girls better." Ernest fell silent and gazed off into the distance again.

Susanna's head spun as she hung on to the buggy wheel.

"Your *daett* has a nice farm here," Ernest finally said. "I can see you're used to a decent place, and I hope mine matches your upbringing. If you have any doubts, you're welcome to visit my farm soon, and I'll show you around the place. There is still a little debt on the property, but we're doing—"

"Your place is just fine," Susanna interrupted. "But there's more to life than a nice farm."

Delight filled Ernest's face. "Those are wise words. You come highly recommended by your *daett*, Susanna, and I can see why. That is what a true woman of the Lord would say. Truly my life will be graced with abundance whether I prosper financially or not. I have felt this in my heart for some time about you, but to hear the words from your own lips cheers my heart more than I can say."

"I…" Susanna hesitated. "Ernest, I don't know how to say this, but there's still…"

Ernest silenced her with a wave of his hand. "Don't say it,

Susanna. I can see the modesty on your face. Praise for you is in order. You are a beautiful woman who has graced her heart with the Lord's glory. I'm sure you still have your doubts at times, but take courage. If the Lord wills that we will spend our lives together, we will live blessed lives. We will grow in grace as our spirits are daily prepared to live in a better country beyond this world. This is what I believe, and I wish to raise all of my *kinner* in faith and in fear of the Lord. I care not what the world offers out there." Ernest gave Susanna a quick glance. "In a way I'm glad these next few months will not be easy for us. Suffering cleanses the heart of what doesn't belong there. Even in me this suffering can produce *goot.*"

"I...I know I have much to improve too, I'm sure," Susanna stammered.

Ernest regarded her with a steady gaze. Then, as if he knew enough had been said, he replied, "Well, I had best be going. This has been a *goot* conversation, and I have perhaps said too much, but they were things that needed saying. I look forward to many more of these moments in the weeks ahead. Maybe soon we should plan on a more formal time together—perhaps on each Sunday evening after your baptism, but not before then. It's not that I don't trust you, but we must be careful with how things appear. Until then, I will stop by to speak with you from time to time."

Susanna hung her head. No words would come out of her mouth at the moment.

Ernest appeared pleased. "Then I'll be seeing you today at suppertime. Your *Mamm* was kind enough to invite me to eat when I return to pick up the girls. The Lord knows Katherine feeds us well enough at home to satisfy any man, but I do need to meet your family and become better acquainted. Katherine will also appreciate the evening off. She might sneak a drive past Joe Schrock's place." Ernest grinned. "I'm just kidding. Katherine is a woman of the Lord as you are, and she wouldn't do anything inappropriate. She does have her eye on the young Schrock boy, though. They might even be married by the wedding season after this one, which is all the more reason…" Ernest grinned again. "Well, you can see how all this has been guided by the Lord's hand. But like I said, I had best be going."

Susanna stepped back and Ernest climbed in his buggy. "Lizzie and Martha will love you," he assured Susanna.

Susanna swallowed and nodded.

Ernest waved and clucked to his horse. The buggy whirled out of the driveway with a flourish. Susanna had been unable to raise a single protest to his plans the whole time he spoke, but so be it. Perhaps this was all for the best. From the looks of things, Ernest wouldn't have listened anyway. Susanna lowered her head and made her way slowly toward the house.

Chapter Sixteen

That afternoon Susanna sat on the front porch watching as Ernest's two girls raced in the yard. Lizzie would first lead Martha to the old oak tree and then point toward a distant point before hollering, "Off we go!"

Lizzie always led, but Martha did her best until she collapsed in the yard from sheer exhaustion.

"Let's try again," Lizzie would say. "I'm older, but you can run fast."

She ought to get up and show Lizzie what a fast run looked like, Susanna thought, but her whole body ached with weariness. She was tired after the day's work and with the constant care the girls needed, but deeper down the tiredness didn't come from physical labor. Ernest's promised return at suppertime hung like a dark cloud over her head.

"Cheer up," *Mamm* had ordered several times that day. "I could see Ernest's happy face this morning all the way from the kitchen window. You have nothing to worry about, Susanna. You've charmed the man completely. You ought to give the Lord thanks each waking moment of the day."

Susanna had winced but refrained from comment. *Mamm* meant no harm, but how could Susanna be thankful for Ernest's long-winded, bombastic words? The man could see nothing but himself and her beauty. That point was plain to see. The real reason for Ernest's interest and his willingness to overlook her past lay in the Lord's gift to her of *goot* looks, which came from her *Englisha* mother. Ernest had settled his mind on her from far less lofty motives than he professed. His faith moved him, *yah*, but she knew there was more, much more. But if she brought up the matter, *Mamm* would refuse to ascribe such lowly thoughts to Ernest, so what was the use?

Susanna stood to her feet and walked up to the porch railing. "Come, girls," she called across the lawn. "Time to get the two of you cleaned up for supper. Your *daett* will be here soon."

The two girls stopped their play at once and ran toward her. They were obedient children, no question about that. Ernest had raised them well, which wasn't a surprise. He didn't look like a man who would spoil his children—or a *frau* for that matter—with a lack of discipline. *Yah*, Ernest would run a tight ship. She would have an adjustment in front of her if she married the man, since *Daett* had always ruled her with a light hand. The change would not be easy.

Lizzie came to a sudden halt in front of Susanna and peered up into her face. "Would you run with us, just once please?"

Susanna smiled. She couldn't resist that plea, and from somewhere the energy came. "Okay." Susanna took Martha's hand in hers.

Lizzie jumped up and down with excitement, and Martha had a gleam in her eyes. Susanna grabbed Lizzie's hand, and with a little girl on either side of her she marched back to the oak tree.

"That way, that way!" Lizzie hollered and pointed toward the barn. "All the way to the door."

Susanna hesitated. "I don't know about that. That's a little far."

"Please!" Lizzie begged.

Susanna hitched up her dress a few inches in preparation for the run, and Lizzie did the same.

"Get ready…go!" Lizzie yelled.

Martha made no attempt at the run as they took off, but flopped down on the grass to giggle in sheer delight. They must make quite a sight, Susanna told herself—a full-grown woman and a little girl in a race for the barn door. She held back so Lizzie could stay a few inches ahead of her. Lizzie still strained and gave it her best. Slowly Susanna crept ahead. She was tempted to hold back and let Lizzie win, but such trickery wouldn't work with Lizzie.

They raced along, and Susanna threw her head back as Lizzie panted beside her. This was like the excitement she used to experience in her school days when games were played at lunchtime. Those days were long gone, but perhaps she was still a little girl at heart.

"I'm going to win!" Lizzie yelled out, as if to encourage herself.

With an exaggerated gasp Susanna threw herself at the barn door and pretended to collapse on the ground. Lizzie did the same, but for more valid reasons.

"Oh, that was such a *goot* run," Lizzie said, nestling up against Susanna. "And *Daett* was here to watch me run almost faster than you did." Lizzie pointed down toward the end of the driveway.

Susanna sat up straight and stared in horror. There was Ernest in his buggy with the horse pulled off to the side of the lane. He had a good view of the lawn, and a grin nearly split his face in half. Obviously the man had seen the whole thing, and she had failed to notice his approach. Susanna groaned.

Ernest clucked, and the buggy started moving down the lane and toward the barn.

Lizzie leaped to her feet and ran down the lane in a wild dash.

This couldn't be allowed, Susanna knew. Horses spooked easily, and little children ended up in unexpected places as a result. Lizzie must be stopped. There was no choice but to run the girl down. All the strength had left her body, but Susanna forced her feet to move. Her dress caught on her shoes in the run, but she didn't dare pull up the hemline. She had already been humiliated, and she wouldn't allow it to happen again. Susanna's breath came in short gasps by the time she caught Lizzie and pulled her to the side of the lane. Ernest's buggy hadn't moved in the meantime. He awaited the outcome of his daughter's foolishness from the safest spot.

"I wanted to tell *Daett* hello." Lizzie tried to wiggle out of Susanna's grasp.

"You don't run toward buggies that are still moving," Susanna's voice squeaked. "Don't ever do that again!"

Susanna could hear Ernest cluck to his horse, and the buggy pulled closer to stop in front of them.

"*Daett, Daett,*" Lizzie hollered, dancing on both feet.

Ernest leaned out of the buggy, and Susanna dared to peek at him. "I see you have my daughters in firm control," he said.

Susanna lowered her head and didn't respond. The answer was obvious. Lizzie had gotten away from her.

"That was some run you took earlier," Ernest said. "I'll have to come back more often if I get to see such *wunderbah* things as my daughters at play with you. I see the day must have gone very well indeed."

Susanna kept her gaze on the gravel in the driveway. Ernest didn't seem to need any response. "I was telling myself on the way over that it wouldn't surprise me if the Lord gave me another sign of His *goot* blessing on my hopes, Susanna. And lo and behold, I pull in the driveway and see all the signs I need. My daughters love the woman I love, and my heart is filled to overflowing with joy and happiness."

Lizzie interrupted her *daett*. "Will you come run with us?"

"Ah, now that's a funny joke," Ernest chuckled. "I'm afraid I'm a little old for such wild exertions. Now, step back from the buggy so I can drive to the barn."

When Susanna and Lizzie arrived at the parked buggy, Ernest climbed down and wrapped Lizzie in a tight hug. He stood up to wave toward Martha, who still stood by the oak tree. Martha waved back but didn't move. Susanna motioned with her hand for Martha to come, and obediently the three-year-old broke into a run. Ernest met Martha halfway, picked her up, and carried her back nestled in his arms. Ernest's smile said it all. Since his arrival they had functioned as a little family, and she had fallen into the role of *mamm* without a hitch.

Heat flamed into her face, and Susanna leaned down to take Lizzie's hand. "Come, let's go inside."

"Aren't you going to wait until I unhitch?" Ernest protested.

Susanna ignored the question and held out her hand for Martha. "Supper will be ready when you come in," she told him.

Ernest set Martha down. He didn't appear pleased, but he said nothing. Rather, he patted Martha on her head. "You run along with Susanna, and I'll be in presently."

Mamm met Susanna and the girls at the front door with a frown on her face. "Why are you coming in, Susanna? You should have waited until Ernest came with you. Surely you two aren't…" *Mamm* glanced toward the barn. "Things were going so well from the looks of it."

"I have to go upstairs," Susanna answered.

"Why?" Surprise showed on *Mamm*'s face. "Ernest will be in any moment, and I need help with the table."

"I won't be long." Susanna didn't wait for an answer but made a dash for the stairs. What possessed her she had no idea, but she had to get away for a few seconds. *Mamm* and Ernest wouldn't understand, but she didn't care. The *Englisha* blood in her hadn't died out yet. Ernest thought he had everything under control, and she had done nothing to dissuade him. Well, the time had come for a little resistance—the kind of resistance she could manage. She would call Joey. *Mamm* and Ernest would never know, but she would know in her heart what had been done. She would go to the other end of the house. A phone call would be safe there. No one would hear.

Susanna drew in a long breath and slipped into her room, certain she was losing her mind. For one thing, she didn't feel one bit guilty about what she was going to do. And she knew she should feel very guilty.

Susanna found the cell phone at the bottom of her dresser drawer. She had wrapped it well enough to hide its form. The moments ticked by as she undid the folds of clothing. With care she placed the phone in her dress pocket and reentered the hallway. Her younger brothers' voices rose and fell in the room across the hall, and Susanna tiptoed toward the far end of the house, where the spare bedroom lay. She stepped inside and closed the door behind her. She perched herself on the narrow ledge and pulled the phone out to stare at it. What if Joey didn't answer? But she had to try. Susanna focused and dialed the number Joey had taped on the underside of the phone.

Susanna pressed Send and waited. The phone rang once and then twice. Her whole body tensed when Joey's voice answered, "Susanna. You called!"

"Oh, Joey," she whispered, and the tears came. She couldn't help it.

"How are things?" His voice was very concerned. "You sound like you're crying."

"Okay, I guess." Susanna quickly wiped her eyes. "We have visitors for supper, but I grabbed a few moments. I just had to speak with you. It's been so hectic around here, and I needed to hear your voice."

"Hectic?" he said. "In an Amish home?"

Susanna laughed in spite of herself. "*Yah*, you could say so, though stressful is more like it. We are—" She stopped. There was no way she was going to tell Joey about Ernest Helmuth, nor about how she was supposed to fall in love with an Amish man.

"It's good to hear from you," Joey said. "When can I see you again?"

Her voice caught. "You know it's not possible under the present circumstances. I'm trying to make peace with my heritage, Joey. Please try to understand."

"But you're calling me on a cell phone." The illogic hadn't escaped him. "I'm glad you did. I've been hoping you'd call so I could hear the sound of your sweet voice."

"Oh Joey, don't say that." The tears came again. "If you only knew." Coming from him, the words sounded perfectly sincere and honorable. Why couldn't Joey be an Amish man?

Noises came from the hallway outside the spare room. "Joey!" Her voice was urgent. "I have to go. Please don't be offended. Can I call you again sometime? I don't know when, but please say yes."

"I gave you the phone for that very reason." His voice was puzzled. "Of course you can."

"Thank you, Joey. You'll never know what this means to me."

"Ah—" he began.

"I have to go," she repeated. "I really do."

"Okay. Call again when you can," he said.

Susanna pushed the End button and slipped the phone back into her dress pocket. The tears came in a gush, but she didn't care. Her face would be red from crying when she went downstairs, but let *Mamm* think what she wished.

Susanna opened the bedroom door to find an empty hallway. The noise she'd heard must have been made by her brothers headed downstairs for supper. She walked slowly down the stairs, trying to regain her composure.

Ernest was seated in the living room with Lizzie and Martha on his lap. He looked at her with a question on his face.

"I have to help *Mamm*," she told him, and hurried on.

Susanna entered the kitchen. "Where were you?" *Mamm* asked. "I needed you."

Susanna just said, "Well, I'm here now," and then began to set the table. She called her brothers in from the front porch, where they had gone to play while they waited for supper. She managed a smile toward Ernest when she walked through the living room, and he beamed from ear to ear.

The whole family was relaxed by the time *Daett*, Henry, and James came in from the barn. They appeared pleased at the sight of Ernest seated at the table with his two girls. Thankfully Susanna didn't have to say much as *Daett* said the prayer of thanks and the food was passed around.

Ernest gave her a smile from time to time, but he didn't embarrass her with overt attention. After supper and a prayer of thanks, Ernest followed *Daett* into the living room while Susanna helped *Mamm* with the dishes.

"You did well at supper," *Mamm* said. "Ernest was relaxed with the family and everyone enjoyed his company. Your feelings for Ernest will be falling in line soon. You wait and see."

Susanna kept her head down and didn't answer. Thankfully *Mamm* let the subject drop. Ernest stuck his head in the kitchen doorway a few moments later to say, "I'll be seeing you, Susanna. We have to run. I have chores. Thanks for the *goot* supper. I really enjoyed my time here tonight."

"You're welcome," Susanna said, but she didn't move away from the kitchen sink.

Ernest nodded and left.

"You should walk him out to his buggy," *Mamm* said. "And help him with his girls."

"No, I shouldn't," Susanna whispered back.

Mamm sighed. "I suppose I should be satisfied with the progress we've made today."

Susanna kept quiet—her head down, her hands busy with the dishes.

Chapter Seventeen

A few days later, dusk had fallen outside the Helmuth home. Ernest looked up from his rocking chair to face Katherine, who stood in front of him with a determined look on her face.

"The girls are in bed now, and we can talk," she said.

Ernest ignored Katherine for a moment.

"Woohoo?" Katherine waved her hand in front of Ernest's face. "I'm still here, and I'm going nowhere until we talk."

Ernest motioned toward the couch. "Sit down then. I can't talk to you while you're standing there."

Katherine complied.

"You have something on your mind?" Ernest teased, leaning forward.

Katherine tried to glare at him but failed. "You don't have to tease," she said. "Lately, you've been so cheerful and dreamy. I know it's serious between Susanna and you, but I still want to know—is the wedding planned yet?"

"Are you asking so you can plan your own wedding with young Joe Schrock?" Ernest teased again.

Katherine blushed. "You know he hasn't asked me home from

the singing yet, but he might if I can drop a word to his *mamm* that your wedding is planned for this fall."

Ernest reached over to pat Katherine's arm. "You needn't have worries about Joe waiting on news of my plans before he asks you home. He'll get around to that soon enough. The Schrocks are known to take their time in everything they do, but all of them are solid people. You're the woman for him, Katherine, and I can assure you that Joe knows this. I can tell by the gleam in his eyes when he looks at you at the Sunday meetings. If he should ask me about you—which I doubt he'll need to—I'll give him the most glowing report I can. You have run my household since Naomi passed with excellence and with a devotion to duty. Joe couldn't ask for anything better in a *frau*. Not if he looked for years through all of our districts."

Katherine's blush deepened. "Hush," she scolded. "I don't need to hear all that. I know that Joe's heart is turned toward me, and I know that the Schrocks take their *goot* time about these things. That's why I want to know if your wedding will be this fall. If it's not, Joe might think I'll be tied down here for years to come. I need to let him know I'm available whenever he's ready."

Ernest nodded. "That's fair enough, and the truth is, we haven't set a date yet. But I do plan to marry Susanna this fall."

"That's not much of an answer," Katherine said.

Ernest nodded, and the room faded from before his eyes. He imagined Susanna's form as she ran with Lizzie toward the Millers' barn. The girl was light of foot and graceful as the deer that grazed on the meadows below his freshly mown hay field. He was sure Susanna would never have allowed him to see her in such a state if she had known he was sitting in his buggy watching her. How gracious of the Lord to allow him such an endearing glimpse of the woman he loved.

"You're a totally hopeless cause tonight," Katherine muttered, and got up to leave.

Ernest smiled up at her. "I'm in love."

"I hope the deacon can talk some sense into you tonight," Katherine said. "What's he coming over for anyway?"

Ernest sat up straight. He had forgotten about Deacon Herman's request after the service on Sunday. "Have you got a moment some night this week?" the deacon had asked him.

"For you, I'll make time," Ernest had answered.

Deacon Herman had chuckled. "I thought I'd stop by and catch up on things, but it's nothing that can't wait, of course."

Ernest had nodded, not wanting to ask questions. Deacon Herman wouldn't divulge the reason for his visit anyway, but he couldn't imagine he was in trouble with the church *ordnung*. That was usually the reason the deacon stopped by. He was one of the most upstanding members the community could wish to display to the world.

Katherine waved her hand in front of his face again. "Do I have to dig for that too?" She didn't wait for an answer, but disappeared into the kitchen.

"Thanks for reminding me," Ernest hollered after her.

Katherine wouldn't eavesdrop once Deacon Herman arrived. The Helmuth children had all been brought up to respect each other's privacy, but Katherine would ask him afterward for details.

As he heard the sound of a buggy pulling in the driveway, Ernest got up from his rocker and hurried out the front door and across the lawn. Deacon Herman had tied his horse to the hitching post when Ernest arrived at the buggy. The deacon turned and greeted him with a cheery, "*Goot* evening there, Ernest. I see your sister's got the place still in one piece."

Ernest laughed. "*Goot* evening, and *yah*, Katherine has been a great blessing to me. I don't know what my girls or I would have done without her."

Deacon Herman smiled. "The Lord provides grace as it's needed. I hear you expect some further grace supplied, perhaps with a *frau* this wedding season."

Ernest grinned from ear to ear. "Susanna Miller has been given to me straight from the Lord's hands. She is a woman full of grace and glory, and Susanna is all that a man who wishes to follow the Lord's will could desire. I could speak all night on that subject, but I'm sure you are aware already of what a blessing Susanna will be to me."

Deacon Herman gave Ernest a quick glance. "I see you're in love, and that is *goot*. The Lord intends for us to marry and bear *kinner* for the next generation. I was a little afraid you had forgotten that command, but I see you were just a little slow getting around to it."

Ernest leaned against the buggy wheel. "All in its own *goot* time, deacon. You can't hurry the Lord, you know. He grinds His grain fine. Isn't that what you preachers say on Sunday? It seems one's faith gets tested in real life at times." Ernest paused to glance in Deacon Herman's direction. The man had a slight smile on his face, so he took the teasing well. Ernest cleared his throat. "I have always appreciated your efforts on the community's behalf, deacon, so don't get me wrong. Preaching and teaching the Lord's Word cannot be a small or easy task. I know I wouldn't be nearly as *goot* about it as all of you are, so I guess that's why no one ever voted for me. They must have read the Lord's mind—"

"Ah," Deacon Herman interrupted. "I understand how you feel, Ernest. None of us choses to walk in the church's holy calling, but all of us are brethren together, as you well know. We must keep our hearts equally holy before the Lord."

Ernest brought his head up with a jerk. "You're not saying that

I...please don't tell me this is about some *ordnung* transgression that caused this visit. I have been most diligent, deacon, I can assure you. Although with my sorrow at Naomi's passing, and perhaps with my girls I have missed something in their dress or comportment? Katherine tries, but she is still young. You know that, surely?" Ernest stopped. Deacon Herman must have shaken his head some time ago, but Ernest hadn't noticed.

Deacon Herman smiled again as he said, "If you'll let me get a word in edgewise, I'll explain the reason for my visit."

Ernest looked toward the ground and ran his shoe in circles through the gravel. "We can go inside to talk, if you wish. It would be more comfortable. There's an extra rocker open." Ernest forced a laugh. "Not for too long, I hope, but it's empty now."

Deacon Herman coughed and Ernest fell silent again. There was no reason for nervousness. He had done nothing wrong.

"It would be best if we spoke out here," Deacon Herman said. "I know you trust your sister fully, but I wish to speak plainly on a matter."

"What is it, then?" Ernest asked.

"This concerns Susanna," Deacon Herman said, "and your plans to wed the woman. This is what you intend, is it not?"

"Of course." The words leaped out of Ernest's mouth. "All my hopes are in that direction. Susanna's in the baptismal class, and Ralph has given me his full approval. I mean, who else would marry the woman after how she has conducted herself? I know the ministry had hoped that no signs of Susanna's *Englisha* mother would surface in her character, but now that they have, what else could—"

Deacon Herman silenced him with an uplifted hand. "I know you are taken with the woman's charm, Ernest. And Susanna is a beautiful girl."

"Beautiful as the Lord intended," Ernest leaped in again. "But

Susanna's intentions are plain enough. She plans to deal with the
effects of her *Englisha* mother's influence with submission and obedience to the Lord and to the church. What more—"

"And to you?" Deacon Herman interrupted again.

"*Yah*, once I wed her." Ernest allowed his puzzlement to show.

Deacon Herman attempted a smile. "In the meantime, there are
some concerns that the ministry has about Susanna."

Ernest opened his mouth, but Deacon Herman lifted his hand
to say, "*Yah*, you are right. Susanna is attending the baptismal classes,
and she says all the right words and has all the right actions."

"So what…?" Ernest tried again.

Deacon Herman continued, "The woman doesn't appear happy,
Ernest. Not as she was before she began the baptismal classes or you
began your relationship with her. We haven't spoken with Ralph on
the matter. The man has enough on his mind. But you are the one
who hopes to win Susanna's affections, so we thought this should be
taken up with you. Perhaps you two have spoken of her happiness?
Do you know any reason that might account for Susanna's sorrow?
Does she mourn her life among her *Englisha* friends? Does she still
speak with that *Englisha* man who had the birthday greeting placed
on the store sign in DeKalb for her?"

"You could ask her," Ernest interrupted. "Why—"

Deacon Herman shook his head. "These questions involve you.
We don't wish to place Susanna in an uncomfortable situation, since
we think the answer to all of these questions is probably a *yah*. Her
feelings cannot really be held against her, other than maybe her contact with the *Englisha* man, but even that can easily be repented of.
Perhaps she has already taken care of that. We do have some confidence in her *daett*, that he can lead his family right. Our question is,
why has your relationship with Susanna not drawn her away from
all these things and brought her happiness? I don't mean to meddle,

but are you promised to each other? If you are, she must love you, and…" Deacon Herman let the sentence hang.

"Of course she loves me, as any godly woman would," Ernest protested. "Susanna fears the Lord and wishes to walk in His ways. I am a blessing that she is thankful for."

"I wouldn't argue with that, but…" Deacon Herman searched for words. "Surely you know that trouble could wait down the road if Susanna's heart is not truly yours. Forgive me for even saying this, but we do have to look at how things appear, and you should see the woman's face during the baptismal classes. Susanna is very unhappy. Even if she weds you, if she is not at peace, things could…" Deacon Herman looked away and sighed. "Not having a *frau* now is difficult for you, Ernest, but having a *frau* who might be tempted to jump the fence is worse than difficult. Surely you have thought of that possibility?"

Ernest shook his head. "I have not. I am a man who trusts the Lord, and so far all the signs point toward His blessing on our eventual union."

Deacon Herman shifted on his feet. "Be patient with my boldness, Ernest, but can you tell me how Susanna reacted when you asked her to be your *frau*?"

Ernest snorted. "I didn't know the ministry had descended to asking after the sweet words lovers speak to each other. I thought you had plenty of other things to occupy you—such as people who break the *ordnung*." Ernest waved his hand about. "I will not speak of private things we told each other. It would not be fair to Susanna."

"This is serious, Ernest," Deacon Herman probed. "I mean no offense, but some questions must be asked. I thought this one might shed light on the situation and ease our minds."

"I will see to Susanna's unhappiness," Ernest said. "I love the woman, and Susanna is my responsibility."

Silence settled between the two men for several moments. "I guess I should be going," Deacon Herman finally said. "I hope there are no hard feelings."

"None at all," Ernest assured the deacon with his best smile. "I'm sorry you had to trouble yourself in the first place. If this continues, I beg for your patience, but I can assure you that Susanna's heart is in the right place. She will do what is right."

"I'm glad to hear that," Deacon Herman said as he turned to climb back into his buggy. Ernest hurried forward to untie the deacon's horse and toss in the tie strap. With a nod of his head, Deacon Herman drove out of the lane.

He would have to visit the Millers again soon, Ernest told himself. Susanna needed instructions on how to comport herself in public. That was plain to see. He had tried to woo the woman with his young daughters, but it seemed that strong words were also needed. As Susanna's future husband, it was his duty to speak them.

Chapter Eighteen

Joey paused in the aisle of the DeKalb Building Supply. The face of the Amish girl ahead of him seemed familiar. He had seen her before, but where? She glanced in his direction, and Joey smiled. The girl dropped her gaze and hurried around a corner. So much for his attempt at communication with an Amish female. He wanted to ask her if she knew Susanna, and if so, how was she doing? Was she happy in her isolation? Was Susanna on some kind of probation?

But who exactly to talk to about Susanna—that was the question. An Amish girl seemed his best bet. The faces of the bearded men forebode nothing but trouble, and the younger men might have a romantic interest in Susanna. They might be even more hostile to his questions than the older men.

He would have to take a chance. That's all there was to it. He was convinced Susanna didn't belong in the Amish community. The impression he had was of a cloistered nun locked up in some medieval convent, all without the young woman's consent. The whole affair was wrong. Susanna must be under some duress. Her voice on the cell phone had convinced him of that. He must make contact with her, but he couldn't bring himself to drive to the Millers' place without Susanna's permission. That could be a minefield, and Susanna's father might broadcast Joey's attempt to the others. Then he would lose what little hope he presently had of making contact with someone from the community.

Joey paused for a moment. Why was the Amish girl in the store familiar to him? He thought harder, and the memory of his last evening in Heuvelton with Susanna drifted through his mind. That was where he had seen the girl. She had been in the group of Amish young folks before they broke off to eat down by the river. Maybe the girl would remember him, which would make the introduction easier. He must try, whether his attempt was successful or not.

Joey hurried down the other side of the aisle and nearly ran into the girl at the corner. "I'm so sorry," he said, while his feet found solid footing. "But may I speak to you for a minute?"

"Speak to me here?" she squeaked. The girl looked up and down the aisle as if she might flee.

"I'm Susanna Miller's friend," Joey blurted out. It was sink or swim.

"Susanna's friend! Oh, *yah*, I know." The girl stared at him. "You are Joey then."

"Yes," he admitted. "And I need your help."

She hesitated. "Someone might see us, and that would not be *goot* now that Susanna—" She stopped.

"What's your name?" He attempted a disarming smile.

The effort seemed to bear fruit, but her words were still terse. "I'm Luella Mast, but why do you want to speak with me about Susanna? She's not supposed to have contact with you."

He hesitated and searched for words. "I know that," he began. "But I don't know why. Can you tell me?"

Luella's words were clipped. "She's through with her *rumspringa* time."

Joey wrinkled his brow. "I don't understand exactly what that means, but can you explain why she's not working here any longer?"

Alarm showed on Luella's face. "Susanna's taking baptismal classes with several others. More than that, I'd best not say."

Joey looked around. He felt like a dancer who didn't know his next move. One mishap and there would be a terrible tangle of feet. Luella would bolt before he could blink.

"I had best be going," Luella said. She began to move away.

Joey made one last desperate stab. "Maybe you could tell me how to find someone who can help me find out what I want to know. Some friend perhaps?" He didn't dare add anything further.

Luella shrugged. "I doubt it. We take care of our own problems, you know."

He put on his best smile. "I'm not trying to…" He searched for words again. "Please, just tell me where can I find someone."

Luella hesitated and then said, "I shouldn't be telling you this, but you could ask Emma Yutzy. I feel sorry for Susanna, and so do several of us. Emma's in the baptismal class with Susanna. Emma hasn't told me anything, and she may not tell you, but it's not right what's happening between Susanna and—" Luella clamped her lips shut. "I've said too much already. Go speak with Emma and see what she tells you. But leave my name out of it."

"How can I find Emma?"

A slight smile played on Luella's face. "I suppose you wouldn't know. The family lives on Maple Ridge Road, a few miles past Susanna's place. They have a roadside stand, and Emma works there each day except Wednesdays and Sundays, of course." Luella gave him a sharp look and closed her mouth. She hurried off without a backward glance.

Joey waited until Luella was out of sight before he retreated in the other direction. He had come into the building supply after something, but he couldn't remember what. Whatever it was could wait. A visit to this Emma's roadside stand likely would bear no more fruit than this conversation, but he must try—and the sooner the better. He didn't understand Susanna's situation, and the conversation with Luella had done nothing to assuage his fears. The whole community apparently knew something he didn't.

Joey hurried out to his car and headed north toward Maple Ridge Road. He risked a drive past the Millers' place, but surely no one would recognize his vehicle in the middle of the day. He didn't slow down, so hopefully they would think nothing of it even if he was spotted. He turned left onto Maple Ridge Road, and soon the Millers' homeplace came into view ahead of him. Joey kept an even pace. A wagon with a team of horses bounced out of the barnyard as Joey zipped past, and the young man on the flatbed looked his way to wave. Joey kept his face turned, but lifted his hand in a return wave. A woman's form appeared in the front window for a moment, but the profile was too heavyset for Susanna. He would go home by a longer route. He had best stay away from the Millers' place in the daylight hours. The risk was simply too great.

A mile farther down the road, Joey slowed and began to watch for signs of a roadside stand. The first one came into view, and the sign stated simply Yutzy's Fresh Fruit and Vegetables. The words were hand drawn onto a piece of plywood, which was nailed to a tree. The stand appeared around the next bend, and Joey came to a stop a few car lengths away. No house could be seen, but a lane ran past the stand and into the trees nearby. A girl around Susanna's age was standing behind the wooden counter, where the vegetables appeared fresh and plentiful. *The Yutzys must have a greenhouse,* Joey decided. He couldn't imagine a regular garden producing so much bounty this early in the season.

Joey opened his car door and stepped out.

The girl greeted him with a bright smile. "Hi, can I help you?" Her quick glance took in the rows of vegetables set up along the counter.

Joey smiled back. "Your produce appears excellent, ma'am, but that's not why I'm here. Are you Emma?"

She hesitated. "*Yah*. And you are…?" Recognition filled her face. "You must be Joey."

Joey winced. "That I am. I hope that's not a problem."

Emma lowered her head. "It's not with me, but with some it would be."

"That's what I need to speak to you about." He leaned on the counter. "Someone who wished to remain anonymous told me to ask you. I need information about what's going on with Susanna."

She tilted her head. "I don't know about this. It doesn't seem right."

"Please," he begged. "I need to know."

"Then why don't you speak directly with Susanna?" she asked.

"You know why," he said. "I don't need to explain the ways of your people to you, do I?"

A smile flitted on her face. "*Yah*, I know. We are strange sometimes. But you really don't know about Susanna?" Emma regarded him with a steady gaze.

Joey kept his response simple. "No, I don't. Can you tell me?"

"But if Susanna hasn't told you…" Her gaze was still on him.

"I've asked," Joey protested. "But she won't say, and now I don't have any contact with her, unless—" Joey stopped. He had best not mention the cell phone.

"I'm in the baptismal class with Susanna," Emma said. "Doesn't that mean anything to you?"

Joey threw up his hands. "Not really. I don't understand the rules of your community."

A smile played on Emma's face. "But you've found me. You're persistent, if nothing else."

"Can you help me?" Joey tried again.

Emma didn't answer as the beat of a horse's hooves arose faintly from beyond the bend. Alarm filled her face.

Joey bent over to examine the vegetables as the buggy came into view. He turned his head enough to catch sight of the man's long, bearded face and hands firmly on the reins. Emma recovered sufficiently to smile and wave toward the man, who was obviously her father. Joey dug in his pocket for his billfold and lifted a sack of freshly dug potatoes to the countertop. He placed a twenty on the counter, and Emma reached for it as the man in the buggy drove past. Emma looked up to smile again as the man's gaze swept over them, but he didn't stop.

"Are you sure you want these potatoes?" Emma asked once the buggy had disappeared beyond the tree line.

"I'm not going to back out of this so easily," Joey muttered. "We'll eat potatoes all week, I guess."

To his surprise Emma giggled and gave him his change.

His hand hesitated on the potato bag. "Do I have to beg, Emma? I need help, and I'm thinking Susanna does too."

She looked away for a moment. "I cannot tell you about…" She shook her head. "Susanna should tell you, and I will tell her she should."

"But I—"

She interrupted, saying, "If you come back next Wednesday on my day off, I will pick up Susanna for a buggy ride. You can meet us beyond the stand about a mile down the road. There's a grove of trees there, and we won't be seen. I don't dare take her toward town, but out here no one seems to think we can get in trouble."

"Thank you," Joey whispered. "I cannot tell—"

She cut him off again. "Susanna is very unhappy, and my heart hurts for her. It's not right what's happening, and Susanna needs to…" She stopped again. "You just come, okay? You can speak with her then." She hesitated and then added, "Don't think this is just for Susanna's sake. I have my own reasons too."

The form of the buggy appeared in the trees again, the beat of the horse's hooves muffled.

"I'll be there," Joey told her. He grabbed the bag of potatoes and beat a hasty retreat. The buggy with the stern-faced man in it stopped by the stand as Joey climbed in his car. The man jumped out to unload several boxes of vegetables, green stems hanging over the sides. Joey waved and drove off quickly.

Chapter Nineteen

Susanna looked up from the supper table as the sound of buggy wheels floated in from the driveway. *Mamm* leaped to her feet to peer out the kitchen window. A big smile spread over *Mamm*'s face. "It's Ernest!" she exclaimed. "He must have come to pay Susanna a special visit tonight. Now isn't that a great honor?"

"Why can't they act like normal couples and date on Sunday evenings?" Henry grumbled. "Isn't it about time for that? Now they'll be out on the porch all evening, and we'll have to tiptoe out the washroom door."

"Now, Henry," *Mamm* chided. "Remember whose side you're on."

Henry faked a smile and went back to eating his pecan pie.

"Susanna," *Mamm* continued, "you should go up and change. Ernest must see you at your best."

Truth be told, *Mamm* had probably arranged this meeting. But *Mamm* always did what she thought best.

"Go!" *Mamm* waved her hand toward the stair door. "You can finish your pie later."

"We should pray first," *Daett* spoke up.

"Without finishing the meal, Ralph?" *Mamm* exclaimed.

"We can give thanks for all that is on the table," *Daett* said, attempting a smile.

Mamm gave in, and the rest of the family lay down their forks to bow their heads.

"Our Father who art in heaven," *Daett* prayed. "We give You thanks for the supper we have eaten and for the strength given to our bodies. Bless now the rest of the evening, and especially Susanna and Ernest as they continue to seek Your will for their lives. Amen."

Susanna made a quick dash for the stairway, but she slowed down once she was out of sight and took the steps one at a time. As she entered her bedroom, Susanna wiped her eyes and sat on her bed. For a minute she thought about what would happen if she refused to change into her Sunday dress and put on a torn apron instead. That would be an appropriate gesture. Then Ernest could see her as she really was. Only he wouldn't. He'd think no one had warned her of his arrival. No, she would prepare properly. Susanna plucked her best Sunday dress from the closet and quickly slipped into it. Ten minutes later the last pin was in place, and Susanna made her way back down the stairs.

"That was fast," *Mamm* said, obviously pleased. "Just keep up your courage, dear. You will soon be in love with the man." *Mamm* patted Susanna on the shoulder. "Go meet him on the front porch. *Daett* is talking with him out by his buggy. Just sit down and wait. He'll come."

Susanna nodded and made her way out to the porch. The movement caught the attention of Ernest from where he stood, facing the house. His head jerked up, and his words to *Daett* stopped. *Daett* also turned, and Susanna quickly sat down with her back to them. Moments later, she heard Ernest's footsteps on the walk. She clutched the arms of the porch chair and waited. She would think of Ernest's two cute little girls, Lizzie and Martha. They were so adorable—she couldn't help but love them. Maybe in the days and weeks ahead some of that natural affection would spill over into feelings toward Ernest. She had to keep up her courage.

"*Goot* evening." Ernest appeared in front of her, his bearded face grim. "Can I sit down?"

Susanna didn't move and Ernest sat down anyway. He took in her Sunday dress with a quick glance. "I see your *mamm* told you of my coming."

Susanna didn't respond.

Ernest cleared his throat and began. "Your *daett* has assured me of your continued obedience and willing heart. That encourages me, but that's not why I have come tonight." He cast a sideways glance at Susanna and went on. "I think it's time you and I had a more detailed talk about what lies ahead of us."

Susanna just nodded. She didn't want to have a conversation about an engagement. She wasn't even close to ready yet, but perhaps Ernest had something else in mind.

"I would have brought the girls along," Ernest continued, "but we really should talk, just the two of us…I hope you understand that, Susanna."

Susanna nodded again and waited.

"I intend to love you in the same way I once loved Naomi," Ernest went on. "I hope you understand that too." He hesitated. "There's something I should ask, although I didn't want to move ahead too quickly…" Ernest paused again.

Susanna glanced at him, but said nothing.

"You will be my *frau* this wedding season, won't you?" Ernest's voice was tense.

Susanna took a deep breath. "Ernest, please don't push me into that. I understood your offer from the beginning, but I need more time before I commit myself."

"But I thought this was all decided," Ernest said.

"I know you thought that," Susanna allowed. "So do *Mamm* and *Daett*."

Ernest seemed to relax. "*Yah*. But we—you and I—we've never made it official that you would wed me. That…" Ernest's voice drifted off. "I'm sorry, this is most awkward and I wouldn't have brought it up, but…well, I think we should make it official and soon. For your sake too. It will end your waffling back and forth all the time. Making up one's mind does wonders sometimes. The road straightens out, so to speak." Ernest fiddled with his hands, his gaze on the porch floor.

Susanna stared at him. She had never seen the man this nervous. "It's best, Ernest, if we do this right. Do you really want a *frau* who doesn't love you? But on the other hand, if I wish to stay in the community and have a decent reputation, I have to marry you. The only other option would be to jump the fence into the *Englisha* world."

"Which you won't take!" Ernest's tone was sharp. "And I do understand how things are, Susanna. Of course no one wants to force you into a marriage with me, even if that would be the wisest choice. I hesitate to say this since I'm on the receiving end, but…" Ernest paused to take another tack. "Susanna, what is out there in the *Englisha* world besides grief and sorrow and heartache and broken homes? Or children who run wild in the ways of sin, and all the emptiness that comes from a life lived for one's self?" The smile was back on Ernest's face. "Surely you can see the right choice. There really is no other one to make. And many a woman in a second marriage enters into it with her confidence set in the Lord, believing that love will come in its own time."

Susanna allowed her confusion to show. "So you think I shouldn't hesitate, or ask questions, or make sure my heart is in this?"

"I think you know the answer to that," Ernest said. "Of course, the enemy of your soul casts doubts upon a decision like this. But you should side with the Lord and put an end to the tactics of the enemy. You should say the words, '*Yah*, I will marry, Ernest.'" He smiled crookedly.

Susanna looked away and didn't answer.

"So is the silence your way of saying *yah*?" Ernest asked.

"No," she finally said. "I know you and everyone in the community wants me to decide about my life your way…but it's my life and my future. I have to do this my way."

Ernest frowned. "It seems to me you've been doing this your way long enough. Why can't you commit yourself? That's the first step in the long journey back to an Amish life."

"Because…" Susanna searched for words. "I just *can't*. Marriage is a lifetime decision, and it's being forced on me out of the blue. Not that long ago I was in my *rumspringa*, and suddenly I'm in a totally different world. I just can't say *yah*, Ernest. I'm sorry. You'll have to wait on me."

Ernest nodded. "I will try, Susanna. The Lord knows you are worth the wait. But can you give me some comfort that in the end you will decide to wed me? That my time is not wasted? But here I go, doing the same thing your *daett* did. He has been easy on you, and look where that has led you. No *goot* fruit comes out of tolerating wrong. It would be best if you'd agree at once to marry me, and we can work out the details after that. The longer we wait, the more difficult this will become. That's what I fear."

Susanna pressed her lips together. She should say *yah*, but she just couldn't. The wild *Englisha* blood of her *mamm* must be the cause of this rebellion, but that couldn't be helped either.

"Please, Susanna," Ernest begged. "These are not difficult words to say. You know that in the end you must—and *will*—say *yah* when

Bishop Enos asks if you will take me as your husband on our wedding day."

"Please do not push me." Susanna bit off the words. "I need more time, and nothing will change that."

Ernest's smile changed to a glare. "I see why no one else will take you as his *frau*. You have rebellious *Englisha* blood in you. There is no question about that, but a *goot* husband can handle such rebellion. I have the promise of the Lord on my side. The faith of the others may falter, but I have my hope fixed on the rock that does not move, Susanna—the Word of the Lord." Ernest paused to gaze across the open fields, apparently lost in his own thoughts for a moment. "Marriage is honorable in all," he finally continued. "And if I may add my own words to the Scriptures, this is true even when the woman has an *Englisha* mother. The Lord will be with us."

"*Yah*, He will," Susanna agreed. "We just don't know *how* He will be with us. We don't know if it will be in marriage."

Ernest's face was set. "Let me set one thing straight, Susanna. You will no longer go to the Sunday meetings, or anywhere else in the community, with that long, sorrowful look on your face. You will be my *frau* someday, and my cheerful *frau* when we've said the vows. It's time for your attitude to change. I'm offering you decency, a *goot* life in the community, and respect from everyone. On top of that I bring two *kinner* to the union that you can love and adore. What more could you want? So smile in public and show your gratitude for the blessings the Lord has showered upon you. Things could have gone much differently if I had not been around to offer you a chance at marriage."

Susanna didn't move on the swing. He spoke the truth. She had much she could be thankful for. It was time she gave the man some respect, so she attempted a smile in his direction and added, "You will make a *goot* husband for your next *frau*, I am sure."

Ernest didn't seem to notice the implication of her words as he glowed from ear to ear. "I must be going now," he said, getting to his feet. "This has been a profitable evening, all things considered. We need to have more of these talks as our wedding day approaches."

"As you wish." Susanna said, keeping her head down.

Ernest still seemed pleased. "*Goot* night then. I'll see you later."

"*Goot* night," she whispered, listening as his footsteps went down the porch steps and out toward the barn. Moments later the beat of his horse's hooves crunched on the gravel in the driveway. Susanna forced her breathing to even out, and whispered a quick prayer toward the heavens. "Thank You, dear Lord, that I didn't say impossible words tonight that I must take back later. Thank You for helping me as I try to do Your will."

Chapter Twenty

The following Sunday service ended exactly at twelve o'clock, and the tables were set up for the noon meal. Susanna helped with the first rush of service. Once things had calmed down, she stood along the living room wall with several other girls to catch her breath.

"How are you doing this morning?" Katherine Helmuth asked Susanna.

Two of the other girls turned their heads to listen.

Must Katherine be this obvious? Susanna pasted on a smile. "Okay, I guess," she chirped. "Maybe we'll get to eat at the next table and replenish our strength."

They all laughed, and thankfully Katherine leaned back against the wall and asked no more questions.

Ernest's gaze was fixed on her from across the room. She was sure of this. Ernest had followed her every movement all day. Her nerves were worn thin by this whole mess. She tried her best and had assumed a cheerful attitude all day. She had even offered Bishop Enos a smile before the morning baptismal class began upstairs. Bishop Enos, for his part, had appeared pleased with her efforts, as had Ernest when she caught his first glance during the sermons.

Surely Ernest could leave her alone for a few moments. The stress was wearing on her. But what else could be done? She had to submit to the man. Somehow her *Englisha mamm*'s wildness must be overcome. Clearly Ernest was the answer, but what bitter medicine the Lord had chosen for her.

A touch on Susanna's arm caused her to jump. "Skittish, are we?" Emma whispered in her ear as the other girls moved back toward the kitchen. "You've been acting strange all morning. Is something wrong?"

"I'm fine," Susanna whispered back. What was Emma up to? Why was she so curious?

"Ernest has been looking at you all day as usual." Emma smiled wryly. "I'd say he's quite smitten."

Susanna tried to chuckle, but the sound came out like fingernails on a chalkboard.

"And you were smiling at Bishop Enos this morning," Emma added. "That was unusual."

"I'm trying...to show I'm happy," Susanna tried again, but from the look on Emma's face, she had only made things worse.

"Can I come home with you this afternoon?" Emma asked. "I think you need cheering up."

"Of course," Susanna agreed at once. "There's nothing going on until the hymn singing."

"Then it's settled," Emma said. "Can I ride along with you and Henry?"

"I don't think Henry would object." Susanna opened her eyes wide. "Is this what I think it is?"

Emma smiled. "I think Henry is quite capable of his own advances, if he's interested—which he isn't."

"But you..." Susanna persisted.

Emma shook her head. "No, I just want to talk with you. I've had you on my heart all week. Well, since early this week to be exact."

"Then let's see if we can get on the next table," Susanna suggested.

Emma stuck close to her as they waited in the kitchen, beyond Ernest's gaze. Ten minutes later they helped clear the first round of tables.

There were plenty of places at the end of the living room table, and both girls took seats alongside Katherine and several others. Bishop Enos led out in a prayer of thanks, and the younger girls served the table. Susanna tried to join the light chatter, and she sent plenty of smiles all around since Ernest had a clear view of her from where he stood against the wall with several of the men.

The meal ended with another prayer of thanks from Bishop Enos, and Susanna motioned with her head. "There go Henry and James leaving for the barn now. We'd best go tell them so James can ride home with *Mamm* and *Daett*."

Emma squeezed Susanna's hand, and they hurried through the living room and the tight kitchen quarters. Once in the washroom, they found their shawls and draped them over their shoulders. With Susanna in the lead, they crossed the lawn and arrived at Henry's buggy as he came up with his horse. There was no sign of James.

"What's this all about?" Henry teased. "Did I invite someone home while I was asleep?"

"Oh, stop it," Susanna chided him, but Emma seemed to enjoy the tease.

"Am I not a worthy catch?" Emma teased back. "You'd have a difficult time doing better, I'm thinking."

Henry roared with laughter. "Truly this is a woman bold and brash. I wouldn't have thought it of you, Emma. You appear so meek and mild in the service."

Emma chuckled and held up the buggy shafts for Henry. "Let

that be a lesson in appearances, young man. Not all things are as they seem."

Henry's laughter was lower. "You sound like Susanna."

Susanna climbed in the buggy and let the sound of their happy chatter wash over her. The tears threatened to flow, but she held them back. This afternoon was not a time for sorrow. Emma had reached out to her in compassion, and she was thankful. Susanna lifted her heart toward the heavens for a quick prayer. *Thank You, Lord, for Your grace. You must have known the load had become too heavy for me to bear.*

James's holler came from behind them. "Hey, what's going on here?"

"Just an extra rider," Henry told him. "You'll be walking home."

"No I won't," James retorted.

"Sorry about this," Emma cooed. "I fell in love with Henry this morning, and I had to ride home with him this afternoon already."

Henry's hoot caused several men in the yard to look their way.

James grinned from ear to ear and said loudly, "Well, Henry could have done worse, I guess."

"If you both don't stop this…" Emma's face grew red. "I didn't mean for you to broadcast my teasing to the world."

James glanced at his brother. "Now she sounds like Susanna."

"That's what I just said," Henry agreed. "Maybe we should bring her home more often, and they could straighten each other out."

"Sounds *goot* to me." James chuckled and hurried off.

"What brothers you have," Emma told Susanna as she settled into the buggy.

"*Yah*, they are decent men," Susanna said, scooting over to one side of the seat. Emma did the same, and Henry tossed in the lines to climb up and sit between them.

Henry took a moment to look around and proclaim, "My, what

a day. I have two *goot*-looking girls in my buggy. How privileged indeed."

"Just go," Susanna said. "You'll make a scene."

Henry grinned and jiggled the reins to steer Ranger out of the driveway. Susanna tried to stifle herself, but giggles overcame both girls by the time Henry pulled out on the blacktop road. She had never known Emma to act this way, but then again, Emma had never come home with her before. Maybe the Lord had allowed their friendship to develop so she would have another firm support once she married Ernest.

Susanna's face darkened at the thought, and she turned to gaze across the passing landscape. Her silence wasn't noticed as Henry and Emma resumed their chatter.

"What's your horse's name?" Emma asked.

"Ranger. Do you like it?"

"Will you change it if I don't?"

Henry chuckled. "I doubt that, since my marriage prospects to you have been so cruelly wrenched out from under my feet."

Emma joined in his chuckle. "Your horse is a plodder, so it probably wouldn't help anyway. That's what his name should be—Plodder!"

"Oh, don't you have such nice, kind things to say?" Henry pretended great bitterness.

"The horse suits you quite well, I'm thinking," Emma shot back.

Their laugher pealed across the open fields. "So what really brings you home with us?" Henry finally asked.

Emma hesitated before she answered. "I thought Susanna needed some cheering up."

"I appreciate that," Henry allowed as he turned onto Maple Ridge Road. Minutes later he pulled back on the reins and turned into the Miller driveway.

"Well, here we are. Thanks for the wedding thoughts," Emma said, and the two laughed again as Henry came to a stop by the barn.

Emma jumped out first to help Henry unhitch. Susanna hung back and watched them. Maybe there was a romance between the two of them that neither wished to admit? They sure seemed to enjoy each other's presence.

But soon Emma's attention turned back to Susanna. Henry left for the barn with Ranger, and Emma didn't gaze after him. Instead she faced Susanna and offered a soft smile. "Sorry about all that. I got to chattering with Henry and forgot why I came home with you."

"Don't worry about that," Susanna said. "I was enjoying the time. The Lord knows I need the diversion, so thanks. Shall we go in the house?"

"That would be great." Emma fell in line behind her. "Maybe we can go somewhere and speak in private?"

"Sure, we can go up to my bedroom. But first…do you and Henry have something going after all?" Susanna attempted a tease.

Emma ignored the comment as they walked through the empty house and up the stairs.

"What a lovely room!" Emma exclaimed when they entered Susanna's bedroom. "I haven't been here in a while."

"Well, I'm glad you're here now," Susanna said. "So was I so terrible this morning with my forced cheerfulness that I need a lecture?"

"Of course not," Emma said. She came over to sit beside Susanna on the bed. "I feel bad about this whole situation, that's all. I can't believe the community is doing this to you. You shouldn't have to marry Ernest if you don't want to."

Susanna stared at Emma. "Well, you're about the only one in the community who thinks that way. Is that what you're here to tell me? Because if it is, I sure need to hear it!"

Emma reached for Susanna's hand. "I don't want to shock you, Susanna, so I don't know where to start with this. But…" Emma looked away. "I don't know how to say the words, or how much I should say—because if you really are in love with Ernest, I don't want to interfere." She gave Susanna a quick glance.

Susanna stared. "What are you saying?"

Emma looked away again. "*Do* you love Ernest, Susanna?"

Susanna shook her head.

Emma let out a long breath. "I didn't think so. But now that I know for sure, I can say this. I met Joey last week. Or rather, he looked me up. And I promised I would speak with you."

Susanna grabbed Emma's arm. "You spoke with Joey? Where? What did he say?"

"Just a minute, slow down." Emma rubbed her arm.

Susanna stood to pace the floor. "Where have you spoken with Joey? And why?"

Emma hung her head for a moment. "Maybe I can explain. Let's just keep it simple and say that I know I should be ashamed of myself for even bringing Joey's message to you—but I'm not. I can't help seeing how unhappy you are, Susanna, and I have my own reasons for being concerned. There's your happiness, of course, but there are also other things. Some of them personal…but let's start with this: How can a marriage between you and Ernest ever work? I mean, really, seeing how you feel… Have you thought of what would happen to Ernest if this marriage doesn't work? If you were to jump the fence after you're married to him, he would have to live with that for the rest of his life. He would be terribly unhappy."

"*Yah*," Susanna agreed. "There's no *goot* answer. But what did Joey want from you?"

"He wants to speak with you, and you must go to him, Susanna. It's all arranged. I'll come by this Wednesday and pick you up. We already have a spot planned, where Joey will meet us. If you don't want to go at all, no one needs to know about this plan. Or if you *do* want to go, to cut your ties with Joey, that will be fine too. He just needs to know. He's very worried about you. And so am I."

"You?" Susanna asked. "Why?"

Emma hesitated. "Of course I care about you...but I also care about Ernest's happiness."

Emma dropped her gaze for a moment. "*Yah*, I'll admit that I couldn't stand to see Ernest marrying you if you won't make him happy. If you're happy with Ernest, I won't complain—but if you're not, then why would you marry the man and ruin both of your lives? What if things become so bad that you jump the fence after the wedding? There is more to a marriage than vows, Susanna. Surely you know that. And if you left Ernest after becoming his *frau*, you'd be condemning him to a single life. The man could never marry again while you're alive. And I'm the one who would have to stay behind and watch Ernest endure his loneliness."

Susanna stared at Emma. "You care for Ernest?"

Emma reddened. "He doesn't notice me, Susanna. So that's not the point."

"But you do!" Susanna clutched Emma's arm again.

"Okay, *yah*, I admit it. Even though I know I don't have a chance," Emma said. "There are plenty of widows in the community who have set their *kapp* for Ernest. You know that."

"But you do care," Susanna insisted.

Emma looked away. "*Yah*. I'd have taken Ernest ever since his Naomi passed, but he won't give me a sideways glance. I don't blame the man for that, but that doesn't mean I don't care for his happiness. Think well before you turn down Joey's offer. Maybe if you speak with him, it will settle things in your heart. After that, if you want to cut off the relationship and be truly happy in the community, I will say no more. I can stand having my silly heart broken. I'm not the first girl to have a crush on a man, so I'll accept the Lord's will. But you need to find where your heart is and follow it, Susanna. Nothing else matters…" Emma's voice trailed off.

Susanna reached over to lay her hand on Emma's arm. "*Yah*, I will speak with Joey. You can pick me up Wednesday."

Emma's smile grew. "You will go?"

"*Yah*," Susanna said and then opened her arms. Emma rushed into them, and the two clung to each other.

Chapter Twenty-One

When Wednesday morning rolled around, Susanna came slowly down the stairs with both of her hands clutching the handrail. Emma had driven in the driveway moments before, and if Susanna appeared nervous as she passed *Mamm* in the kitchen, *Mamm* would know something was up.

"Wednesday's my day off from the roadside stand," Emma had chirped on Sunday afternoon to Susanna's *mamm*. "I could come by and pick Susanna up. I think she would benefit from a morning's drive. I know I like them. We could both enjoy and soak in the beauty that the Lord has written into nature."

Both *Mamm* and *Daett* had regarded Emma with skeptical looks, but *Mamm* had finally nodded. "You have cheered Susanna greatly with your visit today, so maybe getting out of the house later in the week would also be good for her."

Emma had smiled, and that had been the end of the matter. Only it wasn't. The shame of their deception made Susanna's knees weak. Who would have thought that Emma could be up to such a thing? Emma had always been the decent one. Emma was such a credit to the baptismal class, and she would make an upstanding member of the community once she joined.

Susanna clenched her hands and forced herself to move forward. Would she make a decision today that would set the course of her entire life? If she decided to marry Ernest after the visit with Joey today, she would soon become a married woman with two *kinner* in her care. And today might be the last time she'd speak to Joey, even as just a friend. Susanna's heartbeat quickened at the sobering thought, and her face flushed.

Mamm looked up when Susanna walked into the kitchen. "You're ready, I see."

Susanna kept her head about her. "I hope this isn't inconveniencing you too much. I know there is a pile of mending on the sewing room floor, and…"

Mamm silenced Susanna with a quick shake of her head. "I'll manage. It's not as though you'll be home much longer anyway, what with the wedding this fall." *Mamm* broke into a smile at the thought. "I'm so thankful the Lord is supplying help in your hour of need, Susanna. Emma has always been your friend, but now she's becoming a very special friend."

Susanna forced herself to look at *Mamm*. "Well, I'd best be going. Emma's waiting."

"Enjoy yourself." *Mamm* reached up to push a few loose hairs back under Susanna's *kapp*. "If this drive does you *goot*, I'll have to tell Ernest he should take you out next week."

Susanna forced herself to smile. "That's not necessary, *Mamm*. Ernest's a busy man with his farm and his two *kinner*, and I…"

"Just run along now." *Mamm* squeezed Susanna's hand. "We'll talk about Ernest later."

Susanna dashed out the washroom door, still trying to quiet the pangs of her conscience as she hurried across the lawn. She had not lied, and neither had Emma. They simply had not told the whole truth, which wasn't far from lying. But why worry about the matter now? She would soon be with Joey.

Emma leaned out of the buggy to greet her. "*Goot* morning. Are we still on?"

"*Yah*, of course," Susanna said as she climbed into the buggy.

Emma seemed to relax a little. "You took forever to come out."

"So why didn't you come inside?" Susanna asked.

Emma jiggled the reins and guided her horse back onto Maple Ridge Road before she answered. "For the same reason you're red-faced, I suppose. My conscience is giving me deep stabs of panic. I've never told so many half-truths in my life."

"But if this outing settles the matter, then it will be worth it, don't you think?"

"*Yah*," Emma said. "Especially if it will settle the matter between Ernest and me. If you marry him, I can move on."

"Would you really marry Ernest?" Susanna said. "If he asked you?"

Emma shrugged. "I want Ernest's happiness first and foremost, and he can't keep his eyes off of you at the Sunday services. How could I compete with that? Ernest barely knows I'm alive."

"But, Emma!" Susanna exclaimed. "You would make a much worthier *frau* for Ernest than I ever would. Please believe that."

"He doesn't seem to think so," Emma intoned. "Or he would have noticed me by now."

"Then he's just plain wrong…and maybe blind too," Susanna said.

Emma stole a sideways glance at Susanna. "I wish I had what you have—whatever that is."

Susanna sighed. "And I wish I had what you have, but I don't. The Lord knows I've tried, but I can't turn myself into the decent *ordnung*-abiding woman I should be."

Emma jiggled the reins. "Then we must hope you find an answer today, because I don't want to do this again. My conscience will never allow it. It's already going to bother me for an awful long time."

Susanna nodded. "At least something will come out of the morning. You've given *Mamm* an idea. She'll have Ernest's ear at the next Sunday meeting, and he'll be over every week to give me buggy rides."

Emma forced a laugh. "Unintended consequences, it seems. Those always pop up."

Silence hung in the air, and moments passed before Susanna dared speak the words. "And what if Joey convinces me to jump the fence? What happens then?"

Emma shivered. "Please don't say that. I only pray the Lord has mercy on my weakness, and I hope I have judged correctly. I have only Ernest's best interest in mind—and yours, of course."

Susanna drew a long breath as she saw Joey's car in front of them, parked along the road. Emma pulled back on the reins. Whatever lay ahead of them this day, the moment had come. Susanna stilled her conscience with a loud whisper. "There he is."

"*Yah*, the *Englisha* man you love," Emma said, as if the fact couldn't be disputed.

Protests rose to Susanna's lips, but instead she asked, "How long can we stay?"

Emma bit her lower lip. "That's up to you, but you only have this one chance. Remember that. I'm not doing this again."

Susanna focused on Joey's face. He had stepped away from the car and was now moving toward them. Feelings of delight stirred inside of her. How many hours had she spent at his home? Hours in which happiness had filled her heart, and joy had risen in her soul. How could that all have been wrong?

"You should tell him everything," Emma whispered as she brought the buggy to a stop. "He wants to know." Emma leaned out of the buggy to greet Joey. "*Goot* morning. I see you're here."

"That I am," Joey said with a smile.

Susanna forced herself to speak. "Hi, Joey."

Joey came over to Susanna's side of the buggy before he answered. "Good morning. I'm so glad that you came."

"And I'm so glad to see you. You just don't know…" Susanna pressed back the tears. This was not a *goot* start, but she couldn't help it.

"What on earth are they doing to you?" Joey reached inside the buggy to touch her hand. "You have to tell me, Susanna. We don't have much time this morning." He glanced up at Emma. "Do we?"

"We have all the time it takes," Emma said. "I told Susanna I can't bring her here again."

Joey gave Emma another quick glance. "Thanks for bringing Susanna to me. I know there was risk involved."

Emma waved her hand toward Joey's car. "Why don't you two sit in the car, and I'll drive down the road a bit and park—out of sight, of course. You can find me in the first lane into the woods when you're finished."

Joey glanced between the two of them before he asked, "Is that okay, Susanna?"

"*Yah.*" Susanna didn't hesitate, but climbed down the buggy step with Joey's hand still in hers. The touch made her heart throb, but it soothed her at the same time. She wanted to cry and laugh all at once.

"Take your time," Emma hollered to them before she clucked to her horse and drove off.

Joey stared at the buggy for a moment. "That's a nice friend you have there."

"*Yah*, she is," Susanna agreed.

"So tell me. Are you okay?" Joey's hand was still in hers.

"I'm trying to be," Susanna managed.

"Let's go sit," Joey said, leading her toward the car.

Susanna followed him and he opened the car door for her. She slid inside, careful not to look up at his face. She couldn't without breaking into tears. Whether they would be tears of happiness or sadness, she couldn't tell.

"How have you been?" he asked.

"I'm making it so far, but barely." Susanna pasted a smile on her face.

Joey nodded. "I'm really worried about you. I haven't heard a thing since you called that night. I mean, is the cell phone still working?"

"The battery is fine." Susanna made a wry face. "I can't charge it, but I haven't used the phone either."

"That's just the point," Joey said. "Why don't you call? Don't you want to speak with me?"

Susanna looked away. The answer was obvious. The problem was how to tell him about Ernest and his marriage proposal, and the baptismal class, and Ernest's cute *kinner*, and the community life she wasn't even sure she wanted to live.

"You need to tell me what's troubling you, whatever it is," Joey said. "That is…unless you want me out of your life for good. If that's what you need to tell me today, I can leave and never bother you again."

This was her moment, Susanna told herself. She could mumble the words and Joey would stay true to his word. There would be no pressure and no assumptions and no…

Susanna caught her breath. "Joey, I can't talk here. For some reason, I want to be at your house. Can we go pick up Emma and drive to your house?"

Joey smiled. "That would be perfect." He reached for the keys and started the car.

Chapter Twenty-Two

Twenty minutes later, Susanna held her breath as Joey turned into the Macalisters' driveway. The familiar sight of the house swept over her. Here she had spent so many happy hours on the weekends. Those delightful times now seemed as if they were lost in the shadows of yesterday.

"Here we are," Joey said.

"*Yah.*" Susanna didn't look at him, but reached for the door handle. She had made her mind up when they were parked along Maple Ridge Road and hadn't wavered since. She would come here and tell Joey everything.

"So this is where you live, Joey?" Emma asked from the backseat.

Susanna turned to answer. "*Yah,* isn't it nice? Are you coming in?"

"I guess so," Emma said, following Susanna out of the car.

Emma glanced around as if the place held a grave danger for her.

"Let's go inside." Susanna took Emma's arm. Joey caught up with them and ran ahead to unlock the front door.

"Home sweet home," Joey proclaimed after opening the door. "Welcome to our humble abode."

Emma's arm trembled under Susanna's touch. "I can't believe

I'm doing this." Her gaze shifted quickly around the room. "Is this where you used to come?"

"*Yah.*"

Emma didn't say anything as her eyes widened.

"You're not comfortable here," Susanna said. "We'll make this fast and drive you back to the buggy."

"No! Take your time," Emma ordered. "We must get this matter settled once and for all. I certainly am never coming back here again."

"Hey, you two," Joey said. "What are you whispering about? This isn't Dracula's den."

Susanna managed to laugh, but Emma appeared puzzled. Clearly they were worlds apart in their understanding of the *Englisha* life. But Susanna didn't need a reminder of that right now.

"Where can I go while you talk?" Emma asked. "Is there a backyard?"

"No, you're staying," Susanna said. "I want you here. Is that all right, Joey?"

"Whatever you want will work for me."

"I don't think it's right," Emma protested.

But Susanna insisted. "You're going to hear this."

Emma needed to know what had happened between Susanna and Ernest. Stepping inside the Macalisters' house had emboldened her. It was almost as if she had come home, only that wasn't possible. This was not her home.

At Joey's direction, the two girls took seats on the couch, and Joey seated himself on the sprawling rug by the fireplace.

"Okay, if everyone's comfortable, tell me all, Susanna. I want to know," Joey said.

Susanna fixed her gaze on the familiar outline of the Macalisters' stone fireplace. Above the mantel were two stones that intersected to form an angel's face. She needed to see angels right now.

"My parents," she began, "or the people I thought were my parents, are not really my parents." She didn't dare look at Joey. "Well, sort of. My father is my father, but the woman I thought was my mother isn't. I was born to a Mindy Whithus, and she came from what the community calls the *Englisha* world. That would be your world, Joey. I was conceived before my *daett's* Amish marriage, and I was taken into my *daett's* home after Mindy died. She died soon after I was born, and I was raised without this knowledge even though the older people of the community knew. *Daett* had requested their silence. I guess they thought *Daett* would tell me when the time came. If I had turned out like the rest of the Amish young folks, the matter would have faded from sight. But I didn't turn out the way they had hoped. My *daett* was slow to face the facts, but the rest of the community wasn't. I clearly displayed the tendencies of my *Englisha* mother, and the truth is, they don't know half of what I did over here on the weekends." The angel on the fireplace faded in and out of her focus, and Susanna's voice choked.

"Please continue," Joey said, his voice soft. "I haven't heard anything incriminating so far."

Susanna wiped her eyes. Why did Joey have to say such a nice thing at the wrong time? She tried to smile at him but couldn't.

"I am to be married off," Susanna finally whispered, "to the only Amish man who will take me. He is a widower, and all I have to do is attend the baptismal classes and be baptized soon afterward. After the wedding my past indiscretions will fade away, washed off by the sacred vows of marriage, I suppose."

Joey sat up straighter on the fireplace rug. "Do you love this man?"

Susanna kept her gaze on the stone angel. "Do I have to answer that?"

Emma spoke up. "No, she doesn't love him! That's why we're here."

Joey glanced between the two of them. "If you don't love him, why would you do this, Susanna? I think I know you pretty well that this is not who you are. This would be nothing more than an arranged marriage." Joey allowed the horror to tinge his voice. "What about the life you love out here, Susanna? And your music? I can't imagine a woman who can play the way you do taking a man she doesn't love as her husband."

"Music?" Emma gasped. "Susanna plays music?"

Susanna ignored Emma. "I want to do what is right, Joey. I know that makes no sense to you, but this is what the people I trust say is right."

"But what about *you*?" Joey insisted. "What do *you* think is right?"

"*Yah*," Emma interjected. "What you feel toward the man you marry is very important. It would be wrong for you and wrong for him if you were to marry Ernest when you don't love him."

Susanna turned to face Emma. "But you're only saying that because of your feelings for Ernest. You know our community doesn't think that way."

"But if you left Ernest heartbroken after the wedding, how would you live with yourself?" Emma countered. "And think of the pain you'll leave me in too."

Joey's head swiveled back and forth between the two of them.

"Sorry, Joey," Susanna muttered. "We talk a different language, so bear with us."

"Yeah, some translation would be nice," Joey said.

Susanna gave Emma a quick glance. She shouldn't betray Emma's trust, even to explain things to Joey. "Maybe we'd best leave that topic alone," Susanna said.

Joey shrugged. "As you wish, but you have done nothing to be ashamed of, Susanna. I can understand, I guess, why you might give in to the pressure the community has brought to bear on you. But you really shouldn't. You're a wonderful woman, Susanna. You're bigger than this. You're loyal, and decent, and beautiful on top of all that."

"Stop it," Susanna ordered, lowering her head. "Don't say such things."

"Maybe I should explain the problem to Joey," Emma said.

"Go ahead and give it a try," Susanna allowed. "But—"

Emma hurried on. "See, Joey, the man who has offered to marry Susanna is well-thought-of in the community and is not without other options. His name is Ernest Helmuth, and there are at least two widows who would gladly accept a marriage proposal from him. Neither woman would trouble herself with questions the way Susanna does. To the community's way of thinking, Susanna has led a wild life. The question then is, how can Susanna predict what will happen after she says the marriage vows with Ernest? What if she wishes she hadn't married him? She doesn't love the man by her own admission. What if she doesn't learn to love Ernest after the wedding, as everyone claims she will? If Susanna should decide to leave Ernest after the wedding, that would be absolutely awful. And even if she didn't leave him, what if she stayed with him out of a sense of duty? I don't think Susanna could keep that up for the rest of her life. It would only mean trouble."

Joey grunted. "You people sure do look at things differently. But from what I'm hearing, I agree that Susanna shouldn't marry someone she doesn't love."

"I wish you could persuade her of this," Emma said, exasperation in her voice.

Joey laughed. "And how would I do that? By giving her an executive order not to marry this Ernest guy?"

"I am being ordered around enough already," Susanna got in edgewise. A smile flitted on her face in spite of herself.

"Susanna is stubborn," Emma muttered. "You can't talk sense into her easily."

"Why should that surprise anyone?" Susanna asked. "Remember, I have an *Englisha mamm*."

"The bottom line is that no one can make this decision for you, Susanna. You have to decide for yourself. But I have confidence in you," said Joey. "I believe you'll make the right decision when all is said and done. And now, at least—I think I understand what's going on."

Emma was grim-faced. "*Goot*! At least we haven't wasted our time. I didn't take this risk just to make more trouble."

"If there's trouble over this, don't worry. They'll blame it all on me," Susanna said.

"Come," Joey said. "I want to hear you play the piano before we go back."

"Play?" Emma exclaimed. "I didn't come over here for that."

Susanna ignored Emma and walked over to the piano bench. Joey followed and leaned against the piano with expectation. Susanna closed her eyes, and her fingers found the keys. She pressed down gently, and a melody soon overflowed into the whole house. The dark weeks that had passed rose in her mind, and the music washed them away. She saw Ernest, and Lizzie, and Martha, and their smiles. Her fingers moved faster, searching for the right sounds.

Her memory returned her to a time when she thought she was purely an Amish girl and she thought her *mamm* really was her mother. The carefreeness swept over her as the music rose higher. Susanna didn't hold back—the longing, the love for her people, the friendship with Joey, and the loss, the desire to have back what no longer was, the impossible sorrow of knowing that this never could be. She swept her fingers across the keys one last time and then stilled the piano with both hands.

Joey's face came into focus in front of her. Susanna stood to her feet and raced for the front door with Joey close behind her. Emma was already there, her eyes round like saucers. Life would never be the same for any of them. She had met a fork in the road—and having chosen a path, she could no longer turn back.

Chapter Twenty-Three

Susanna and Emma stepped out of Joey's car and hurried toward the parked buggy. Emma climbed in while Susanna turned to Joey and said, "I'm sorry for the trouble I've been today, and for—"

He silenced her with a touch of his finger on her lips.

Susanna trembled. Would Joey take her in his arms right here in front of Emma? Besides, weren't they only friends? And yet, she wanted very much for him to hold her right now. She wanted to feel his strength. She wanted to forget the world that lay only a few short miles down Maple Ridge Road. She never wanted to see Ernest Helmuth again, or hear him speak, and she certainly did not want to say the marriage vows with him this fall.

Susanna took a deep breath. "I have to go back, Joey."

His eyes searched her face, and he gripped both of her shoulders. "Susanna, I'll always be your friend, but listen to me. Back there at the house, I heard with my own ears what's in your heart. You are not what they say you are. You don't have to marry this man if you don't love him. There's a way out. All you have to do is call me. I'll help you."

Susanna looked away and said nothing. What was there to say?

"You can break out of whatever is holding you back, Susanna. It's in you. I know it is. Don't let them do this to you." His fingers dug in. "Do you want me to talk to this man?"

"No!" Susanna gasped.

"Then at least be honest with everyone about who you are." Joey gestured toward the buggy. "Besides, think of Emma. She loves this Ernest. Wouldn't moving aside and letting her have him be the reasonable thing?"

Susanna struggled to breathe. What Joey said was true. How could she marry Ernest when she knew Emma loved him and she didn't?

"But how can I leave?" Susanna's cry rose into the air. "My family is here. The life I know. It's all I planned for myself."

"You cannot go on like this," Joey told her. "I think you know that."

She reached for him and pulled him close. The sobs came quietly once his arms closed around her. She nestled her head against his shoulder, and the world seemed to float away. How *wunderbah* it would be to never leave Joey's side. She could imagine the two of them as they floated off into the bright sky, high above all of this trouble. Oh, if only they could!

Joey's soft voice broke into her thoughts. "Susanna, you must do something about this. I don't know what, but something. You can stay at our house temporarily if it comes to that—whenever you're ready. Mom and Dad would welcome you, and we'd find a more permanent apartment quickly. I have connections, and Mr. Kenny will give you your old job back."

Susanna cut him off. "Joey, I don't know what I can do—but you're right that something has to be done. I have to face things." Susanna's voice caught. "I guess that's what I haven't been doing. But now I'll try."

He opened his arms with reluctance, and she stepped away.

Susanna looked up at him and tried to smile. The effort failed, and she buried her face in his chest again. "Joey, just hold me tight for a moment longer. I know none of this makes sense. I don't make sense. My life doesn't make sense! What I'm doing doesn't make sense, but I guess I was born without sense."

He rocked her gently. "You will do the right thing. I know you will. And, Susanna—I love you." He cleared his throat. "I love you, and this will turn out right. I know it will."

Susanna didn't dare look at him or she would never leave. How could he say such *wunderbah* words that soothed her heart? And yet she knew they would be awful words for him to say in front of *Daett* or Ernest. How could she think of being strong and accepting the love of an *Englisha* man? That was what she was doing. Ernest had never held her in his arms. And if he had, it wouldn't be like this.

Susanna pushed away and muttered, "Thank you, Joey, for everything."

"Be strong now," Joey called after her.

Susanna still hadn't looked back when she reached the buggy and pulled herself up to settle on the seat beside Emma. "Is he still there?" Susanna whispered.

"*Yah*," Emma told her. "I'm sorry to have overheard some of your conversation. I shouldn't have been here."

"It's okay," Susanna said. "In a way, I'm glad you were here."

Emma turned the buggy around. "Susanna, it seems to me you made your choice today. And for what it's worth, I think it's the right one. Not just for you, but for Ernest. We both know he wouldn't want to marry a woman who could love an *Englisha* man."

"*Yah*," Susanna agreed.

As Emma drove past Joey's car, edging her way back onto the road, Joey waved and Susanna leaned out of the buggy to wave back.

"Don't fall out of the buggy," Emma quipped. "I wouldn't want that on my hands."

Susanna smiled and settled back into her seat with a sigh.

Minutes later, Emma pulled into the Millers' driveway. "You will tell them then?" she asked Susanna.

Susanna pressed her lips together. "I guess I'll have to." She climbed down from the buggy and looked up at Emma with gratitude. "Thank you for being my friend today. I'll never forget this. I pray you won't get in trouble."

"I hope so too," Emma said with a smile. Then she turned the buggy around and drove off.

Susanna walked up the driveway toward the house, her heart like stone as she thought of what was ahead of her. *Daett* and *Mamm* and Ernest must be told that she had sneaked off to meet Joey. If she didn't tell them, she would feel the weight of her guilt until she confessed. Was Joey worth it? She had only to think of his arms wrapped around her to know the answer to that question.

Susanna forced her feet forward as her mind raced. So much of her life had been half-truths. She once thought she had been born and raised in this house the way her brothers had, but she hadn't been. She once thought she was an Amish woman, but she wasn't. She once thought that what *Daett* wanted was what she would always want, but she didn't. She once believed that her heart would always be in the community. Now she saw that was wrong too.

Susanna quickened her steps, and *Mamm* met her at the front door with a nervous smile. "That was a long ride. Did you have a *goot* time?"

Susanna looked away. "There is something I must tell you."

Mamm tried to laugh. "That's an awful serious note after a *wunderbah* time spent with Emma. Did Emma tell you she has her eyes set on Henry and can't get his attention?" *Mamm* teased.

Susanna went into the living room and seated herself on the couch. "We went out to see Joey," Susanna said, not meeting *Mamm*'s gaze. The shame of the whole thing turned her cold, and yet she must tell the truth. Emma would if Susanna didn't.

Mamm's voice was weak. "You did what?"

"Emma arranged for me to meet Joey this morning, and we ended up going over to his house. That's what took so long."

Mamm stared for a long moment. "I'd best get *Daett*." *Mamm* got to her feet and reached for the back of the couch.

Susanna stopped her with a touch of her hand. "Let me tell *Daett*, please. It's best that way."

Mamm didn't protest. Her face was bloodless when she turned to enter the kitchen, no doubt to busy herself and keep the pain at bay.

Susanna stood, moving toward the front door with her outstretched hand. Tears stung her eyes, and once out on the porch, the afternoon breeze blew across her face. Susanna stopped to feel the coolness rush over her. She hadn't noticed the wind on the walk in from Emma's buggy. How much of life was like that right now—buried under a load of sorrow and questions? If she could only move past this point in her life and live the way she had before, carefree and with an open heart. But that couldn't happen. It was too late.

Susanna moved forward again, slowly walking toward the barn. Perhaps *Daett* was in there. She opened the door to peek inside. The dim darkness was broken by the soft clink of horse harnesses and the low murmur of voices in the back of the barn. Susanna stepped forward.

Henry's cheerful voice greeted her first. "Come to help with the manure cleaning, I see. I'd say it's about time after riding around all morning with Emma." Henry laughed and stopped to lean on his pitchfork.

Daett's voice was more serious. "Why don't you boys take this load of manure out while I speak with Susanna?"

"But it's not full yet," James protested.

Henry seemed to understand. "Let's go," he told his brother.

The two climbed on the manure spreader and left, sending sober glances back over their shoulders.

Daett stated the obvious. "You have something to say."

Susanna nodded, unable to speak.

"Perhaps we had best sit down." *Daett* didn't wait for her answer before he took Susanna's arm and led her to a low wooden bench near the haymow. "Sit," he said, and sat beside her.

Susanna gathered her thoughts as *Daett* waited. Finally, she began.

"Emma and I went to see Joey this morning," she said. "He wanted to talk in depth with me, so we met and he took us to his house."

Daett was quiet for a moment and then said, "You will have to tell Ernest. He needs to know."

"Do I have to?" Susanna buried her face in her hands.

"*Yah*, you will do what is right," *Daett* said. He slipped his arms around Susanna's shoulders and pulled her close. "You will always be my daughter. Nothing will change that, and we can hope Ernest will understand. We just have to figure out how to help you leave the past behind, Susanna. But the Lord will help us."

Susanna lifted her face toward the silent barn walls, sobs raking her body. *Daett's* kindness tore at her. If he had yelled and chastised her she would have understood, but not this.

"I don't think I can leave it behind. That's the problem," she managed.

Daett held her tight and whispered, "*Yah*, you can. You must. Go now and help your *Mamm* in the house. I'll let Ernest know so he can come over after supper."

Susanna got to her feet, but she couldn't get a word out. What was there to say?

"We'll make it through this together." *Daett* tried to smile. "That's what our people do."

Susanna tore herself away and rushed out of the barn. She slowed her steps once she was in the yard, pausing near the front porch to let more wind blow across her face. Her whole body ached, but she would not think about that right now. She would help *Mamm*, and work, and work, and work. Maybe that would help ease the pain.

Mamm opened the front door and asked, "Did you speak with *Daett?*"

"*Yah,*" Susanna replied. "He will tell Ernest, and Ernest will be over tonight. Until then, I will work and not think. If I think any more, I'll go mad."

"We never go mad with the Lord on our side," *Mamm* said.

Susanna didn't respond, but hurried past *Mamm* to take the stairs up to her bedroom and change into her work dress.

Chapter Twenty-Four

That evening during supper, Susanna had tried to join in the chatter around the table but hadn't been very successful. Nor had she been able to eat much. Thankfully no one had commented on her obvious distress. Surely her brothers had questions about her talk this morning with *Daett* and about Ernest's announced visit later in the evening. The questions went unasked and unanswered.

Once the table was cleared and the boys sent upstairs, Susanna helped *Mamm* wash the dishes until sounds in the driveway signaled Ernest's arrival. *Daett* got up from his rocker and went outside to greet Ernest.

"Come," *Mamm* told Susanna. "These dishes can wait until later."

Susanna stifled her protest and followed *Mamm* to sit on the couch. They'd wait here until *Daett* came in with Ernest. What would happen beyond that, she had no idea. Maybe she was expected to get down on her knees, beg for forgiveness, and promise to never see Joey again. That she couldn't do.

Susanna cringed when the front door opened. She kept her gaze on the floor as *Daett* and Ernest entered the house.

"*Goot* evening, Ernest," *Mamm* greeted him.

"Please be seated," *Daett* said.

Mamm moved from the couch to her rocker as feet shuffled all around her.

"Susanna." *Daett*'s voice brought her head up. "I have told Ernest the whole story, but it would be best if he also heard the words from your own mouth. Confession is *goot* for the soul."

Susanna opened her mouth, but nothing came out.

Ernest spoke up. "I want to assure you I'm not forsaking you—even though what happened this morning has shocked me to the depths of my soul. I can't begin to think what may have caused such an action on your part, Susanna. Your *daett* assured me there are reasons that we may not understand. Of course, I will expect that the most strict measures be taken with you to keep you accountable, and that a confession be made in front of the ministers when you take your next baptismal instruction class. I'll speak with Deacon Herman and see that this is requested of you if you don't volunteer. But I'm sure you will, as your conscience must be bothering you awfully."

Daett cleared his throat. "You should be very thankful that Ernest is so understanding, Susanna. Not all men would feel this way. Most men would cut off a relationship with you if they heard such news."

"I want to do my part in Susanna's search for repentance," Ernest continued. "The Lord knows that my daughters need a *mamm* badly. It's best, I'm thinking, if we work through these problems instead of ending the relationship." Ernest gave a mirthless laugh. "Our people believe in restoration, so it's proper and right that we put into practice what we preach. I must say, though, that I never thought we'd get into a situation quite like this."

From where within her it came, Susanna had no idea—but she found herself sputtering, "Ernest, I'm not sure you're right. Perhaps we *should* call the whole thing off. You can leave with no hard feelings from me. As for your girls, I know there are plenty of widows in the community who would love a marriage proposal from you. Any of them could give you the wedding you want this fall and be the kind of *frau* you need. They would most certainly not be the kind of *frau* I'd make for you. Surely you can see that."

"Susanna!" *Mamm* exclaimed. Shocked silence settled over the living room.

"Did I just hear what I heard?" Ernest asked. "Susanna is picking my next *frau* for me? Whoever heard of such a thing?"

"She didn't mean it," *Mamm* explained. "The stress of this morning has affected her mind. And Susanna has barely eaten all day. I'm sure she'll be better by tomorrow. Just to be sure, I'll see that she eats right after you leave."

"Maybe she ought to eat now," Ernest said. He turned to Susanna. "You shouldn't say such things. The Lord is in this match, and it wouldn't be decent to switch horses in midstream."

"You're right, Ernest," *Daett* assured him. "You wouldn't do something like that. You are a man of your word, but still…I wouldn't blame you if you wanted to adjust your course. Susanna has given you plenty of cause to do so, and I will say nothing in the least against your character if you change your mind."

"I am committed." Ernest sat down and leaned back in his chair. "As any God-fearing man should be. I stayed by my first *frau*'s side through her illness, and I cannot do less with Susanna."

"But I don't love you, Ernest," Susanna tried again. "I've already told you that. There are other women in the community who can love you."

Ernest stared for a moment. "You seem serious about this. Has someone said something I ought to know about?"

Susanna paused. It was not her place to reveal Emma's crush. "I speak only for myself," she finished. "But I am sure there are other women in the community who can give you what I cannot give."

"Your *daett* says it was Emma Yutzy who took part in this deception with you. Has she been planting these ideas in your head, Susanna? Is she why you went to meet your *Englisha* friend this morning? All this begins to make sense now. The nerve of the woman. To think that…" Ernest snorted at the thought. "Emma will be dealt with. This surely disqualifies her from continuing in the baptismal class, to say the least."

"No! That's not what I meant." Susanna tried to stand, but collapsed back onto the couch.

"That's a little harsh, don't you think?" *Daett* said.

"Not with an important issue like this," Ernest retorted. "I have taken a great risk with Susanna. What will the community think if my judgment is called into question? Emma is to blame for this escapade—that's what I say. The matter could not be clearer in my mind. She has gotten things into her head no woman should dare think." Ernest waved his hand about. "Emma would have me take her home from the hymn singing by her own choosing. She's almost making her own marriage proposal like the *Englisha* people do. That's the message Emma is sending—as if I would pick her over Susanna!"

"*Yah*, we understand," *Mamm* said, reaching over to touch his arm. "But do calm down. You'll have our boys coming down to see what the matter is, and I don't want this broadcast further than necessary. We are shamed enough already."

"Emma meant this only for your best interest and for mine," Susanna tried again. "She really does care for you, and I don't. And you can't blame Emma if she does have a crush on you. At least she's looking out for you. And besides, Emma has said nothing about a marriage proposal from you."

Ernest glared. "The best love comes after the vows are said. I've been a married man, Susanna, and I know. Before the vows, men and women only dream of love—that's what both you and Emma are doing. I don't dream because I know where the Lord causes true love to grow. Am I not demonstrating this love to you right now? What would you do if I turned my back on you? Would you jump the fence into the world? Would you, Susanna?"

"I hadn't planned to," Susanna managed, "but…"

"See there!" Ernest proclaimed with a triumphant look. "That proves my point."

"But I was with Joey this afternoon, and I was greatly comforted," Susanna whispered. "That may not be love yet, but it's better than what I have with you."

"What did you say?" Ernest stared at her.

"You don't want to know." *Mamm* tugged on Susanna's arm. "I have to get her something to eat. This discussion has gone on long enough for someone in Susanna's condition."

Ernest opened his mouth to protest, but *Mamm* already held Susanna by the arm and propelled her toward the kitchen as if she were still a small girl.

"I wanted him to hear that," Susanna whispered.

Mamm ignored her and pulled out a kitchen chair. "Sit!"

"Why won't you listen to me?" Susanna continued. "I'll just tell him all this later."

"You just go right ahead," *Mamm* retorted. "If you do, then my part in your recovery ends. I'm doing this for your *daett*'s sake and not for yours. I always thought I could call you my own daughter when the Lord chose not to give me any, but I don't know anymore. You should get down on your knees and thank the Lord that Ernest still wants to marry you after this morning's capers. What were you thinking, Susanna? Or did Emma plan all this last Sunday afternoon when she was over here? Is that what happened?"

Susanna opened her mouth, but *Mamm* cut her off. "You don't have to say a word. I see the truth, but it's still your decision—

regardless of what Emma told you. Responsibility is the first order of business, and I know Emma is your friend, but friends don't help their friends jump the fence. From now on you're staying away from her. That's all I can say. And keep your mouth shut about the details of your time with Joey this morning. Enough has been said already."

"Emma is as honest as the day is long," Susanna tried again. "She has Ernest's best interest at heart. What if I were to leave Ernest after I've said the vows with him?"

Mamm stopped, a slab of ham in her hand. "You would do such a thing?"

"Maybe?"

Mamm shook her head. "You wouldn't. That much I know about you."

Susanna buried her head in her hands on the tabletop. What was the use? All her life she had imagined a long courtship, filled with drives home from the hymn singings on Sunday evenings. Some handsome young man drove the buggy, though the man's face had never been clear in her mind. But the young man she had hoped for had never appeared—and now she understood why. She had only been dreaming, the way all of her life had been a dream. A false dream!

"Eat!" *Mamm* pushed the sandwich into Susanna's hand.

Susanna tried to take a bite, but her hand trembled too much to lift the sandwich.

Mamm sighed and sat down beside her to cut a piece. "There. Maybe that will help."

Susanna picked up the bite of sandwich and put it in her mouth. She chewed but couldn't swallow for the longest time. *Mamm* cut off another piece and waited. She'd be here all night until she ate, Susanna was sure. With a great effort the first mouthful went down.

"That's better," *Mamm* said. "You'll get through this, but I do declare I've not seen so much patience expended on one girl in my lifetime."

Susanna pressed back the tears as *Daett* peeked into the kitchen. "How are we doing?" he asked.

"She's eating," *Mamm* said, as if that solved everything.

"Ernest would like to speak with Susanna before he goes." *Daett* motioned over his shoulder. "He's waiting. Can she come now?"

"I suppose so." *Mamm* got to her feet and helped Susanna stand. "Can you walk without my help? It would look better if you did."

Susanna didn't respond. She needed all her strength to face Ernest again. Slowly she moved forward and into the living room. Ernest had a warm smile on his face and motioned for her to sit. Susanna looked over her shoulder, but *Daett* had stayed in the kitchen with *Mamm*. She was on her own. Her legs weakened under her, but Susanna managed to lower herself gracefully to the couch.

Ernest took her hand in his. "I'm really sorry that Emma has led you into temptation, Susanna. She will be dealt with kindly, but I will see to it that something is done. This cannot go unpunished."

"She meant this for good, and for your sake. Can't you see that?" Susanna forced herself to meet Ernest's gaze.

Ernest's smile was still kind. "You're a true friend to say such things, but Emma doesn't know what's in my best interest. The fact that she tells you she does is wrong of her. She will be stopped, and our wedding this fall will still happen. Surely you will consent now that this awful thing is behind us. Think on that for a few days and see if I am not right. I wanted to tell you that my offer still stands in case you sorrowed overmuch or blamed yourself for this weakness. This isn't your fault. The Lord will help us through this valley. We will make it together."

"But Emma—" Susanna tried again.

Ernest shook his head. "Good night now. Try to get some rest, and just don't give in to temptation again."

Susanna dropped her gaze and said nothing, but Ernest didn't seem to need an answer. He let go of her hand, and seconds later the front door closed behind him.

Chapter Twenty-Five

Saturday morning found Ernest sitting at his breakfast table, idly staring at the wall. Thoughts churned through his mind, and a great weariness filled him. He had left the Millers' place full of confidence that Susanna's escapade with the *Englisha* man could be handled easily, but doubts had come afterward. Now he had experienced another sleepless night, and the day was beginning whether or not he was ready. Little Lizzie, seated beside him, tapped his arm. He looked down at her, but she had her mouth stuffed full of bread and jam at the moment and couldn't speak.

"Don't eat so fast," he chided, and then went back to his thoughts.

"What's wrong with you this morning?" Katherine asked for the second time since they had sat down to eat.

Ernest tried to smile. Katherine was still ignorant of all that had transpired this week with Susanna, and she could stay that way for a while—at least until further measures had been taken to contain the damage.

"It's not something I'm doing wrong with the housework, is it?" Katherine asked.

"Of course not." Ernest reached across the table to squeeze

Katherine's hand. "You couldn't do a better job keeping this house. For that I will always be grateful."

"It's your wedding this fall, then." Enlightenment dawned on Katherine's face. "You must really be in love if you're so taken up with the plans. Was that what your trip to see Susanna was about earlier this week? Has the wedding been moved back a bit perhaps?"

Ernest looked away before he answered. "Everything will be okay, I think. But I have to call on Deacon Herman before he leaves the house this morning."

"About the wedding?"

"It's not about—" Ernest began, but caught himself. "Don't worry," he tried to tease. "Joe Schrock still likes you, and he hasn't done anything bad."

Katherine gave him a skeptical look. "I already know that. It's you I'm worried about."

"Everything's fine," he proclaimed, jumping up from the table without the usual prayer of thanksgiving.

He felt Katherine's gaze following him out the door, but Ernest didn't look back. He had already told her where he planned to go, and that was all the information Katherine needed. Her concern touched him deeply, but she couldn't do anything about his problem with Susanna.

Ernest entered the barn and threw the harness on Gambit. Five minutes later he was in the buggy and driving out of the lane. He urged the horse on and within minutes pulled to a stop beside Deacon Herman's barn. Several cattle in the barnyard lifted their heads to stare at him, but Ernest ignored them as he glanced around. Deacon Herman should still be in the barn at this early hour unless he'd had a late breakfast. Ernest had hoped to arrive before there was any chance the deacon had left on his Saturday church rounds.

Once Deacon Herman learned of Susanna and Emma's escapade

this week, there might be other stops for the deacon to make. The least of which was a long conversation with Bishop Enos. The next baptismal class was tomorrow, and Emma Yutzy must be dealt with. On this he was more convinced than ever. Susanna had given in to weakness, but Emma had been the tempter. No other answer made sense. Emma's bold ways could not go unchecked. If she was left alone, everyone in the close-knit community could be affected eventually.

Ernest climbed out of the buggy to tie Gambit to the hitching ring, which was nailed on the side of the barn. Herman still hadn't appeared, but he must be in the barn. If not, Ernest would walk up to the house and check.

The barn door creaked as Ernest pushed it open. "*Goot* morning," he called out. "Anyone around?"

A muffled voice called from the direction of the haymow. "Over here."

Ernest walked toward the voice, and Deacon Herman appeared with a bale of straw in his hands. The deacon chuckled. "I thought you'd find your way in. I'm just tossing the horses their bedding for the day before I hit the road on church business."

"Long list, huh?" Ernest muttered. "I'm afraid I have another one to add, and a big one at that."

"You could arrive with a little more cheerful news, you know." Deacon Herman smiled in spite of his words. "But it's the way things go, I guess." He spread the straw liberally in one stall before he moved on. "So what's been happening that you have to pay me this early morning visit?"

"Susanna Miller and Emma Yutzy," Ernest said as he followed the deacon's steps. "The two got themselves into a heap of trouble this week, and Emma's to blame, if you ask me. That's what needs looking into. The girl should be thrown out of the baptismal class tomorrow. What she's done cannot go unpunished. How can we exist as a community if such things are tolerated in our women, let alone from our unmarried women? The nerve of the girl!" Ernest ended his exclamation with a kick into the newly spread straw. "I have never seen anything quite like this."

Deacon Herman laughed. "That does sound serious, but perhaps you should begin at the beginning. Give me all the details as you know them. And don't leave anything out. Maybe it won't be as serious once you tell the story in the light of day. Sometimes things turn out that way, you know."

Ernest snorted. "I doubt it in this case. Susanna's *daett* had me over, and we discussed it thoroughly with Susanna, so I'm thinking the light of day test is already behind us. Things aren't looking upward much. Even Ralph says—"

Deacon Herman silenced him with an upraised hand. "Just give me the story. You can fill in Ralph's part when you get there. I do have to get on the road, you know, and from the sound of it this will make my day even longer."

"Sorry." Ernest hung his head. "But this is trying my patience too. Please understand that." When Deacon Herman didn't respond, Ernest hurried on with the story. He talked for nearly twenty minutes with no pause but to take his breath.

"I see," Deacon Herman commented when Ernest finished. "So Emma is in love with you?"

"I did not say that," Ernest sputtered. "She thinks she is, and what a woman thinks can be a very dangerous thing. Emma must be dealt with. We cannot have wild imaginations floating around in the community like this, causing damage to our people. Look at what has happened already between Susanna and me."

Deacon Herman gave Ernest a sharp look. "Tell me about that. Did you ever get things straightened out with Susanna?"

Ernest glared. "After our initial talk, Susanna was much happier at services the next Sunday. You have to admit that. I still plan to marry the woman this fall, and that's that. Susanna is seriously considering my proposal, especially since she has been unsettled by her own weakness this past week. Surely you have no objections to the match? I mean, after all, I am a widower who should have been married a long time ago, what with my two small *kinner*. Already I'm tasking my sister Katherine's endurance way above what is normal. Katherine should be at home helping our *mamm* instead of housekeeping for me. That way—"

"I know that," Deacon Herman interrupted. "And Susanna did seem a little happier after my talk with you, but my *frau* thinks there is still a sadness underneath. Not that I would know such things about women, but that's what Rebecca told me on our drive home from the Sunday services."

Ernest stared in horror. "You speak with your *frau* about church matters?"

Deacon Herman smiled. "No, I mentioned nothing about you and Susanna. Rebecca offered me the information on her own. See, Rebecca's not the only woman who's concerned about Susanna and you. There are others, including Bishop Enos's *frau*, Lydia. They like to see young brides in love and glowing with happiness. That is the way of our people, you know."

"But Susanna is," Ernest objected. "And this is all beside the point. Can we get down to business and deal with Emma? The woman must have some punishment. Surely you don't think otherwise."

Deacon Herman nodded. "I will stop in and speak with her before I see Bishop Enos this afternoon. I'm sure a confession in private might be what is needed. I can't imagine that Emma would be tempted to jump the fence the way Susanna is. And the woman does have affections for you, it seems, so we can't—"

"This is outrageous!" Ernest exclaimed. "How can you speak so? I have Susanna to worry about, and our wedding this fall. And you talk of confessions for the woman who led Susanna astray. Why, Emma should be banned if it were possible. But since she isn't a member, dropping her from the baptismal class is the least you could do."

"Are you now in the ministry, Ernest?" Deacon Herman didn't smile. "Be careful of what you say and the orders you give."

Ernest tried to simmer himself down. It wouldn't do any good to rile up Deacon Herman at this point. Still, something had to be done.

Deacon Herman regarded Ernest for a moment before he spoke again. "I can see what you're thinking, Ernest. 'Wait until the rest of the community finds out about this.' Well, I'd advise you to keep quiet until the ministry can get to the bottom of it. What Susanna and Emma did is very serious. Let me be clear about that. You are correct in saying that we can't tolerate such things, but the truth is, Susanna may be the root of this problem. I'm thinking you may be too blind to see straight on the matter. You're too taken with Susanna's beauty, but the rest of us aren't. Susanna has been a problem for many years—in fact, ever since Ralph took her into his home as a child. Many questioned the wisdom of such a move, but we don't have hearts of stone. Jesus reached out to sinners while He walked on this earth. We wished to follow Christ's example, but in the meantime there was, and is, a real danger that Susanna will never be one of us. You can't force these things, Ernest. Susanna had an *Englisha mamm*. That can never be changed. We wanted to give Ralph a chance to raise his daughter in the faith, but things can only be taken so far. You have spoken correctly that this is not a light matter, and neither is taking a *frau* like Susanna. On that point, you should take into account your own preaching, I think."

Ernest caught his breath and turned away. "I can't believe this," he muttered. "Surely Bishop Enos doesn't think this way."

Deacon Herman shrugged. "The bishop is as concerned about this situation as I am. We cannot have someone in our midst who is not one of us."

"But Susanna is—" Ernest stopped. The deacon would not be convinced. He might as well save his words and reputation. A rebellious attitude was not wise, even if he thought he was right. "I just hope the ministry makes the right choice on this matter," Ernest said instead.

"That's better." Deacon Herman smiled.

Ernest stared at the ground. "I'd best be going, then, but I still plan to wed Susanna this fall. Whatever happens, that won't change. She will be agreeing to it soon."

"I would think you should have Susanna's consent to be your *frau* by now. Doesn't that trouble you?" Deacon Herman had his gaze fixed on Ernest.

Ernest searched for words. He could not lie. "I have had my doubts, *yah*, especially this past week, but I also trust in the Lord. I have the faith that Susanna can be the *frau* I desire to have. The wedding vows would make our union sacred, and that's *goot* enough for me."

"I see." Deacon Herman moved away from the stall door. "And yet I don't see. This whole situation with Susanna has been murky ever since I've heard of it. That's not *goot*, and I'm gravely concerned. I'm sure you agree, Ernest. We must see clearly on this."

Ernest didn't hesitate. "I *do* see clearly. Susanna will not leave me once she has said the vows. Of that I am sure."

Deacon Herman shrugged. "The vows are not meant to keep a person inside the fence, Ernest, but rather to keep trouble out. Think about that. It seems to me you're using the sacred words for all the wrong reasons. You would cage a woman's heart when she longs for the freedom that we do not believe in. She may desire the freedom the *Englisha* world gives."

"But Susanna cannot marry another man from the community! You know no one else would take her. Her only hope is to marry me!"

Deacon Herman nodded. "This is true, but maybe they are wiser than you are. Maybe Susanna does not belong with us. Maybe Emma has more sense than you do. That's what I'm saying."

Ernest sputtered but could find no words. This was indeed an outrage, and one he had not expected. He turned on his heels and stomped out. Gambit looked up when Ernest slammed the barn door behind him. This display of temper wouldn't help, but the deacon already thought the worst of him. A little temper tantrum could do no more harm. The deacon needed to know Ernest took this affront seriously. If things kept moving in this direction, Bishop Enos might forbid his marriage to Susanna. That must never happen.

Ernest untied Gambit from the hitching ring, climbed back in the buggy, and sped out of the deacon's driveway at a fast trot.

Chapter Twenty-Six

Later that afternoon, Joey pulled into the Millers' driveway. The barn door was swinging back and forth on the gentle afternoon breeze. Several buggies sat in front of the barn with their shafts turned toward the road. No doubt the buggies would be in use tomorrow for the Sunday service. How he dared to stop in today was the question. And yet he felt he must speak with someone from the Miller family. After meeting with Susanna and hearing about her plight, he must respond. Maybe Susanna's father was the man to once more approach. Were not the Amish men in charge of their households?

A young man peered out of the barn door and stared at him. The face vanished, and Joey climbed out of his car. This made things easier, now that someone had shown himself.

Joey strolled toward the barn door but stopped when Susanna's father stepped out.

"Good afternoon, Mr. Miller," Joey greeted him. "I wonder if I could speak with you for a moment."

"I thought I told you that my daughter must be left alone," Ralph replied. "Why can't you *Englisha* people listen?"

Joey met his gaze. "I think Susanna has decided that question for us, Mr. Miller. She came to see me this week, in case she hasn't told you."

The man winced. "Susanna told me everything that happened. But Susanna was lured into something that wasn't in her best interest. That's being taken care of now by the man who will marry her this fall. Did Susanna tell you that? About her upcoming marriage?"

"But not to a man she loves," Joey shot back.

Ralph stepped closer. "We are a people of community, young man. Susanna may not feel all that she should at the moment for Ernest Helmuth, but love comes softly at times. It does not come in a rush, despite what you *Englisha* seem to think. We are here to help Susanna, not to harm her. Let us be clear about that. Susanna is my daughter, and I will keep her in the life that is best for her. Your world has nothing to offer her but heartbreak and sorrow and regrets."

Joey regarded the man for a moment. "You sound as though you speak from experience. Would this concern Susanna's mother? Are you sure that your feelings aren't colored by your own history in my world?"

Ralph's gaze shifted. "We will not speak of what I did wrong," he said. "*Yah*, I sinned, but I have done what I could to make things right again…and the Lord gave me the opportunity to do so when Susanna was brought to our home. I will not allow you to undo the work of the Lord just because—"

The front door of the house swung open behind them, and Ralph turned to see Susanna approaching.

"There's your answer," Joey said as Susanna came closer. "What you're doing to Susanna isn't right. I will do everything in my power to show her that she doesn't have to go through with this."

"You have the world and its temptations on your side," Ralph shot back. "I have only the Lord and love in my heart for my daughter."

"Then you should give Susanna her freedom," Joey said.

Ralph didn't answer, but turned to face Susanna. He held out both hands to her. "My daughter, do not give in to this temptation. Not again. We love you, and so does Ernest. Tell this young man to leave."

Susanna stopped in front of her father and took his hands in hers. "*Daett*, I know you want what is right, and so do I. I've wanted to stay in the community, but I also want what is out there. Don't blame my real *mamm* or Joey for that. It's the fault of my own heart, and there's no use pretending otherwise. Ernest may think he knows what is best for himself, but he doesn't deserve a *frau* who pines for the world. How do I know if my marriage vows would hold me faithful? I'm glad Joey came by. It gives me a chance to get away, to maybe clear my mind. I have to follow my heart, *Daett*, instead of fighting it all the time. I'm sorry that I'm doing this again, but I have to go."

Susanna leaned forward and kissed her *daett*'s bearded cheek. "Joey will take me to his place to spend the afternoon with his family. Then he will bring me home."

Ralph dropped his gaze and said nothing. His shoulders sagged.

"I'm sorry, *Daett*. I don't mean to hurt you." Susanna gave him another quick kiss and wiped the tears from her eyes before she turned to Joey. "It seems like we keep coming full circle. Will you take me?"

"Of course." Joey reached for her hand.

Ralph's mournful gaze followed them on their walk toward the car. Joey opened and closed the car door for Susanna before he climbed in himself. Ralph stood at the same spot when Joey glanced over his shoulder. Susanna didn't look back as Joey started the car and drove out of the lane.

"You did the right thing," Joey assured her. "I'm once again glad

I stopped by. I struggled with the decision and wondered if it was the right thing to do, but when you came out on the porch all the fog cleared away."

Susanna tried to smile. "I sort of feel like I'm sliding down a long chute to who knows where. I can't stop, and soon there won't be any going back. In fact, I may already have passed that point. This can't go on, you know. I've shattered *Daett's* confidence in me and the confidence I had in myself. Oh, Joey." Susanna reached for his hand. "What am I going to do?"

"You're going home with me right now," Joey said. "That always seems to help."

"You are a godsend," Susanna whispered, and a wisp of a smile formed on her face. "You seem to know what needs to be said at all the right times."

Joey smiled. "I'm glad to help, although I don't think your father thinks I'm much of a help."

Susanna's face clouded. "No, but you are to me."

"And that's all that matters to me," Joey said with a grin.

"Joey, can I change my mind?" Susanna asked. "Instead of going to your house, can we go down to the river in Heuvelton for a while and sit along the water's edge?"

"Your wish is my command," Joey said.

Susanna's slight smile turned into a beam of light. "That would be perfect. What better music than the Lord's very own water falling over the rocks? If there's time, maybe we can go by your house afterward."

"That sounds like a plan," Joey said, and silence fell in the car as they approached the outskirts of the Heuvelton.

Minutes later, Joey pulled into the parking lot by the riverbank. Susanna took in the view through the car window. "You first brought me here all those months ago when this whole affair began.

Neither of us knew how tangled the web would become. To you, I looked Amish—but I wasn't really. How could you be my friend? Back then and even now?"

"Do you really need to ask?" Joey answered as he climbed out of the car to open her door. "Here's your answer." He took her hand in his and led her to the river's edge, where they sat on a log. The murmur of water filled the air, and the smell of spring blossoms drifted over them. They had come to the right place from the look on Susanna's face. She seemed lost in her thoughts, but peace was finally written on her face.

Moments later she spoke. "Thanks for bringing me here. It's so peaceful and so right somehow. I don't know how to say it. I wish our lives were like this, perfectly in harmony with how the Lord made things. But I don't think my life will ever be right again. I don't see how it can, regardless of what choice I make."

"I don't agree," Joey protested. "I've told you before, I have confidence in you. You will make the right choice."

Susanna shook her head. "You don't really know who I am, Joey. I'm half this and half that. I don't think you can really understand how I'm torn between two worlds."

Joey didn't protest this time. She was right. He couldn't know her pain. He didn't understand what it was like to have his affections torn in two directions. But he could see how Susanna was attracted to the life of the community and how she loved her father.

"Do you think I could make a go of it in your world?" Susanna glanced at him. "If I jumped the fence, as we call it?"

Joey didn't hesitate. "Yes. I have no doubts you could make it. You have a brain, you have plenty of talent, and you're beautiful."

Susanna blushed and looked away.

Joey wanted to continue. He wanted to tell her how gorgeous she would be in a proper dress, with her hair done by his mother's stylist—but that might confuse her more. She might be ready some-day, but not yet.

"Despite my *rumspringa*, I really don't understand your world," Susanna said. "I understand the Amish world."

"You could learn," he offered. "It would come naturally with time."

Susanna winced. "Do you mean it would come naturally because of my birth mother?"

Joey shook his head. "No, but you really mustn't be angry with your mother, Susanna. She gave you life, and she must have loved your father. Things might have been different if she hadn't passed. No doubt she would have raised you in her world, and—"

"So do you think I'd be better off if I had never been Amish?"

Joey hurried on. "I don't deal in might-have-beens. Things are what they are. What I'm saying is that your mother loved you, and she still would love you—the way your father does. That would be true whatever your choice is."

"Whatever my choice is?" Susanna looked away.

"Yes, whatever your choice is," Joey said, slowly wrapping his arm around her shoulder to pull her close. She winced at first but then settled back.

They clung to each other as the moments ticked past, with only the sounds of the river before them and the town behind them.

"That was the best answer I was given in a long time," Susanna finally said.

Joey smiled and stood to his feet. "Shall we stop in at my parents for a few minutes to say hi and then get you back home?"

Susanna nodded and followed him back to the car.

Chapter Twenty-Seven

On Sunday morning, Susanna kept her head down as she entered Deacon Herman's home before the start of the service. Several of the women stared at her as she walked past. They all knew of her escapade this past week, but what would happen with her was the question. *Daett* had been tight-lipped last night after she defied him again and spent the afternoon with Joey. Clearly this had to end soon. *Daett* had gone somewhere for at least two hours after she came back. When *Daett* returned, his face showed his sorrow, written in long lines on his weather-beaten brow. That she had caused the agony in *Daett's* heart tore at her own. Yet her time with Joey had been important. She needed to be with him yesterday. Where their relationship would go from there she didn't know. Joey hadn't pressured her about the future, nor would he.

When he had dropped her off after the stop at his parents' place, he had just given her a brief hug and said, "Thanks for a great afternoon. I'm so glad you agreed to come with me."

The tears had slipped down her cheeks, and she had stood frozen to the ground until Joey had said, "You'd better go in now. Just remember to let me know if you need anything."

Joey understood her in a way that baffled her mind and ripped at her heart all at the same time. Only *Daett's* love had ever gotten this close to her, but Joey was only a friend. She had kept that refrain firmly fixed in her mind all last night. *He's a friend…he's a friend… he's a friend.*

Joey couldn't become more to her. How could he? Beyond that question was how to handle her *daett* without hurting him more. If he had yelled at her last night or brought Ernest Helmuth back with him to lecture her, perhaps she'd have felt better this morning. But *Daett* hadn't. His distress had only grown deeper.

"*Daett* still loves me," Susanna whispered to herself. She chose a spot in the back corner of the kitchen to hide, but she forced herself to look up when the unmarried women began to form a line and enter the living room. Someone touched her on the elbow, and Emma's sober face was bent close to hers.

"I'm sorry about all this," Emma whispered. "Maybe I didn't do the right thing after all."

"It's okay," Susanna whispered back.

Deacon Herman's *frau*, Rebecca, glanced at them, and Emma fell silent. Susanna tried to give Rebecca a smile, but the effort was weak. At least Rebecca had a friendly look in her eyes, so perhaps Deacon Herman had not turned against her. How that was possible, she didn't know. The deacon had to enforce the church *ordnung*, and she had violated plenty of those rules since her last baptismal class. *Daett* must have gone to Deacon Herman's place last night, if for no other reason than to clear his own name. What she had done could not be hidden even if *Daett* had wanted it to be.

The line of unmarried girls moved toward the living room doorway, and Emma squeezed Susanna's hand before they entered and the men could see them. Susanna squeezed back but kept her gaze fixed on the hardwood floor. Moments later she had to look up to maneuver around the benches, and the blaze of Ernest's anger from across the room pierced her. Susanna winced and hurried on. Emma had turned bright red, so she must have noticed Ernest's look as well. Apparently Emma also considered herself the object of Ernest's outrage.

Susanna didn't look up when the first song number was given out. She would have to stand soon, and she needed all the strength she could muster. The song began, and on the second line, Bishop Enos rose to his feet. He slowly led the line of ministers upstairs. Out of the corner of her eye, Susanna saw the men from the baptismal class get to their feet one by one. She waited until Emma moved and then followed her. With downcast eyes, they both made their way across the room. Susanna caught another glimpse of Ernest. His eyes were still blazing, but a touch of sadness was now written on his face. Ernest must know he was losing her. The man thought he was in love with her, but when Susanna compared Joey's tender looks from yesterday with Ernest's this morning, Ernest stood no chance—even if Joey was only her friend. But what unholy thoughts to have on her way to the baptismal class! This must stop! Maybe she should confess everything to Bishop Enos once they reached the room upstairs. The problem was that she wasn't sorry. Not sorry at all.

A sigh escaped Susanna's lips. Emma didn't seem to notice as she led the way into the bedroom. The men were already seated across from the ministers on one side of the room, leaving two chairs open for them. Emma tucked her dress in and sat down. Susanna did the same, her gaze glued on the floor. That was the proper reaction for an Amish girl. Now if she could only repent.

Bishop Enos spoke first. "*Goot* morning to all of you on this Lord's day. We are thankful for another night's sleep in which we could rest our weary bones." Bishop Enos paused to chuckle and rub his knees. "There's not much left but bones in these legs, but let me keep on the subject." Several of the ministers joined in the bishop's laughter. Emma didn't smile, and Susanna couldn't crack a smile if she tried.

Susanna forced herself to look up when Bishop Enos continued. "Anyway, we are here, and another day is upon us. I pray we can live it in a manner that pleases the Lord. I also hope that we can worship Him in the beauty of holiness."

A chorus of "amens" came from the ministers.

Bishop Enos nodded and waited a moment. "Apparently we have some issues which must be resolved along those lines. Deacon Herman informs me that two of our baptismal applicants have strayed from the straight and narrow road and must be called back to the Lord's will." A deep silence filled the room as Bishop Enos paused. No one moved a muscle. Bishop Enos cleared his throat before he began again. "I am, of course, deeply sorrowed by this report. What a tangled web we do weave, as the *Englisha* poet once said. I had hoped all of you would take this time to learn more deeply of the Lord's ways and the community's ways, but this apparently is not the case." Bishop Enos's gaze drifted down the line of baptismal candidates and came to rest on Susanna's face.

Hot streaks of fire ran up her neck. Shame filled her heart, but no words would come. The bishop didn't expect any—at least not yet.

"It seems Susanna Miller is the most grievous transgressor," Bishop Enos said. "I had hoped better things from Ralph's daughter, but I guess one never knows what lies in the heart until it is tested."

"I am mostly to blame for this," Emma gasped.

Bishop Enos turned toward Emma. "And how is this, young sister? Are you also tempted with the things of the *Englisha* world? Do you also have an *Englisha* boyfriend?"

The words of protest sprang to Susanna's lips, but she clamped her mouth shut. She had spent time with Joey, so Bishop Enos spoke the truth in part. Susanna trembled and held the sides of the chair so her hands wouldn't shake.

Emma remained silent too.

"I thought so," Bishop Enos said to Emma, and turned back to Susanna. "What have you to say for yourself, young woman? It seems you've had quite the experiences since we last met."

"I…I don't know what I can say that will be helpful," Susanna said truthfully.

Bishop Enos glanced at Deacon Herman. "The deacon here tells me that you've made several contacts with your *Englisha* boyfriend from your *rumspringa* days. Surely you know that as a baptismal candidate you are to take seriously the vows you plan to make this fall. At least, I assume you still plan to make them." Bishop Enos paused and waited.

"I…" Susanna began again, but she got no further.

"I see," Bishop Enos said. "It's that bad. Would you mind telling us what your plans are? I was led to believe you are considering Ernest Helmuth as your future husband. Is this not true? Normally I wouldn't speak of wedding plans in public like this, but the situation calls for frank speaking, Susanna. I hope you understand."

"I do," Susanna managed.

Bishop Enos waited again, but he continued when she didn't speak. "We have always had concerns about you, Susanna, ever since your *Englisha mamm* passed away and you came to live with your *daett*. Yet we are a caring people. The community did not wish to rush into judgment about you, since you could not help who your parents are. Those things lie in the will of the Lord, and He thought best to bring a child out of your *daett's* sin. This we did not wish to hold to your account. For his part in this, your *daett* made his peace with the Lord and offered his confessions in a baptismal class very similar to this one. That same opportunity is in your power, Susanna. You can make your apologies for your own past choices—first to the Lord and then to all of us. We must speak plainly, of course, in front of these witnesses, so nothing can be hidden. You must speak even if you have sinned greatly with this *Englisha* boyfriend of yours. Perhaps that is what lies at the root of your drawing back into the *Englisha* world."

"Joey is just my friend," Susanna whispered. "He is an honorable man."

"I see," Bishop Enos said. "But you understand we are to forsake our friends who are in the world. Are you willing to do this and to make your confession?"

Susanna choked and said nothing.

Bishop Enos sighed. "So it is as we always feared. I had hoped for your *daett*'s sake things would never come to this. He has invested years in your godly development. He no doubt has wept many tears of regret for his own past, and prayed fervently that his sin would not be passed on to you. And yet, here we are with your heart drawn into the *Englisha* world. No amount of love will change that—only your choice to fully forsake what lies out there will bring you back." The bishop gestured toward the bedroom window. "Even then the road from out there is often long and difficult, but we are willing to walk it with you. Please believe that. But you must choose the road. The miles may be rocky, but I believe for your *daett*'s sake that the Lord will give us grace for the journey. Can we begin that walk this morning with a full confession from you and a vow to leave the *Englisha* world behind forever?"

Susanna's mind whirled as tears crept down her cheeks. All she could think of was *Daett*'s love and care for her. All that Bishop Enos said was true. How could she be so ungrateful? How could she walk away from *Daett* and his faith? How could she even think of jumping the fence? Many wished they had been raised in a godly community like hers, so why couldn't she appreciate all that had been given to her?

Susanna stifled a sob and tried to speak clearly. "I'm very sorry for the trouble I've caused you and *Daett* and the community, and the shame of it all, and my own ungratefulness. I wish I had never been born at times, but I was brought into this world, and now I am what I am. I can do nothing about that."

Kindness filled the bishop's face. "We can all change, Susanna. The Lord washes clean a sinner's heart if he confesses. And Ernest will love you and take you as his *frau*. There is a way out. You don't have to leave us."

"But you don't understand," Susanna began. "I don't love—" She stopped. Her relationship with Ernest was not an appropriate subject. She could not expect the bishop to see what she meant anyway. He had never looked into Joey's eyes and seen what she had seen. The bishop had never felt his fingers move over the piano keys, nor heard the room filled with sounds like the angels must sing in heaven. It was all useless. "I'm sorry, I just can't," Susanna finished.

"Can't what?" the bishop asked.

"Do what you want me to," Susanna replied.

"Then you know what that means," Bishop Enos said.

"I do," Susanna said. She stood to her feet and silently walked out of the bedroom.

Chapter Twenty-Eight

The buggy ride home after the service was full of silence. Susanna sat in the middle with James on one side of her and Henry, holding the reins, on the other.

"So what was all that about?" James finally asked. "I know you met with that *Englisha* man again last week, but a little confession to Bishop Enos should have taken care of the problem. Instead you came down from the baptismal class before anyone else did."

Susanna bowed her head at the memory. *Mamm* had looked up at her and burst into tears right there in front of everyone. When Bishop Enos had led the ministers downstairs after their meeting, he looked as if he had just presided over a funeral.

"You must have—" James stopped. "Oh well, what does it matter? I just wish you'd act normal for a change. I don't need the whole community to think I have a strange sister."

"Does this have to do with your wedding with Ernest this fall?" Henry asked. "Because if it does, then coming down early from the baptismal class will be pretty bad for your reputation. *Daett* has always gone easy on you, but if you ask me, he ought to chew you out good for this."

Susanna wiped away a tear. How was she to break the news to her brothers? Bishop Enos had finally made things abundantly clear to her. After that painful session in the baptismal class, she must explain things to *Daett* first. The time had come to make her choice. Why she couldn't have seen this before was beyond her, but to speak with her brothers first on the matter...that she couldn't do.

"She's not going to answer us," James said as if Susanna weren't in the buggy.

Was this what she would become to her family? A person who had never existed? Would the years she had lived with them be as if they had never been? If so, how could that be? They couldn't act this way. She was a part of them, and if she left, that wouldn't change—and yet it would. She had to leave. That was what Bishop Enos had finally made clear. The bishop hadn't said so in words, but he had succeeded where others had failed.

"She's still our sister whatever she's done," Henry said.

A sob escaped Susanna's lips, and the tears rolled down her cheeks in a cascade.

James took a stab in the dark. "What did Ernest do to you?"

"Nothing," Susanna choked.

"What about that *Englisha* man?" Henry asked.

"Joey is a *goot* man," Susanna whispered. "He wants only the best for me."

"Sometimes nothing needs to happen to make a woman upset," Henry said. He gave James a superior look. "That's lesson number one in dealing with a *frau*."

"She's not our *frau*," James said softly. "I think sisters should tell their brothers what's wrong with them."

Should she tell them? The question burned. But how could she explain herself kindly, and without telling *Daett* first?

"I guess we'll find out soon enough," Henry muttered. "It's a shame that everyone always knows things before we do. Look at what we learned just a few months ago about Susanna's birth, and here most of the community had already known." Henry gave Susanna a quick glance. "It's still hard for me to believe you had an *Englisha mamm*."

"I'm sorry," Susanna whispered. "I didn't choose my *mamm*, you know. And can you imagine how I felt when I learned it? And then having Ernest, a man I don't love, forced on me as a husband—all because no other man from the community would take a chance on a woman who had an *Englisha* mother?"

Henry didn't appear convinced. "That's not the whole truth, you know. If *Daett* had been stricter with you in your *rumspringa* time, and if you hadn't taken up with that *Englisha* man, maybe things would have turned out differently. And Ernest is a decent match for you. He's got plenty of character, and they say a woman can fall in love after the wedding."

Susanna could no longer keep the anger out of her voice. "Do you plan to marry a woman who doesn't love you?"

James piped up. "Is this what the problem is? You don't love Ernest and don't want to marry him? Well, no one's making you."

Susanna stared out across Ranger's back. The familiar sound of his gait rose and fell in the soft afternoon sunlight. "I know they're not," she said. "But if I want to be part of the community and sit among the married women and have *kinner* and not be an *old maid* who stands on the edges all her life…" Susanna's voice trailed into silence. How could she explain that above all she wanted to please *Daett*? His sorrow over the past would never end if she remained unmarried. *Daett* would always see her single state as the Lord's punishment for his mistakes. No, she had reached for the best the community had offered and had fallen short because of her own weakness—as *Daett* had done years ago himself. In this she truly had been her *Daett*'s daughter. Now they would both have to live with what she had done.

"She's fallen mute again," Henry said as he pulled back on Ranger's reins and turned the buggy into their driveway. "Whoa, there," he called out as they came to a stop by the barn.

Susanna jumped down and fled toward the house. Henry and James would understand, even as they shook their heads at her actions. They had always been kind to her, but now her time with them was past. She would have to leave the house soon, maybe as soon as next week. How and when she didn't know. The questions buzzed until her head hurt.

The beat of a horse's hooves came from the distance, and Susanna turned to flee upstairs but then paused. *Daett* and *Mamm* would arrive any minute, and she might as well face them now. With a fixed face Susanna seated herself on the couch and waited. Long moments passed until footsteps sounded on the porch floor. Noah peeked in first, followed by Tobias. They had apparently been instructed not to ask questions.

"She's on the couch," Noah said.

Susanna looked away as the tears began again.

Mamm's voice came next. "Everyone upstairs now," she ordered, "and change into your everyday clothes. I don't want one more smudge on your pants than what is already there."

Susanna didn't try to smile as her younger brothers trouped past her on their way upstairs. *Mamm*'s soft footsteps came up to her, followed by *Daett*'s heavier ones. Their rockers creaked as they sat down. Only then did Susanna force herself to look up and utter all she could muster.

"I'm sorry," she whispered. "I can't tell you how very sorry I am."

Daett lowered his head and looked away, but *Mamm* reached across the couch to touch Susanna's arm. "We know you are."

"But that doesn't change anything, does it?" Susanna continued. *Mamm* was too kind to speak such words, but they were true. Nothing could change what had happened today.

"Ernest hasn't given up yet," *Daett* said. "He plans to come over in a few minutes. I told him to give us some time alone before he arrived, but I doubt he'll wait long."

Susanna groaned.

"You must speak with him," *Mamm* said, sitting up straight in her rocker.

What was Susanna to say? She sat silently. She didn't want to talk with the man. They would only go in circles again.

Mamm's voice grew urgent. "You *must* speak with him! He obviously still has his offer of marriage open, even after all of this."

Susanna kept her voice to a whisper. "I wish he didn't."

Daett winced and turned to face her. "Susanna, you are my daughter. I have loved you with my whole heart. I have wanted only the best for you. Obviously I've failed you through my own weakness." He cast his eyes toward the ceiling. "Forgive me, dear Lord, for my sin, and my inability to stop it from affecting those I love. Truly You have spoken in Your holy Word that the ways of a transgressor are hard. I bear my shame in great sorrow, and yet what is the use? I have lost the daughter I love."

"You still have four sons," *Mamm* said. "I have given them to you out of my love for you. Do you count them as nothing?"

Daett hung his head for a moment before reaching for *Mamm's* hand. "You are right, Linda. I'm sorry." *Daett* tried to smile.

"You must let go of the past now," *Mamm* chided. "Everything is not your fault. Susanna bears some blame for this. She has made choices."

"*Yah*, it's true. I have made choices," Susanna volunteered at once. Silence again settled over the room.

"Where do we go from here?" *Daett* finally asked. "I spoke with Deacon Herman at the dinner table, and he says the church has done all they can do. If you refuse to repent, it would be best if you leave the community." *Daett's* voice caught. "I understand this. I know that the standards of the community must be maintained, and this is a blight that must be removed. They've tried their best. You were so close to the end, Susanna. Ernest Helmuth would have married you. Why did you have to turn back and destroy the only life you've ever known?"

"Well, it's done now." *Mamm* tried to comfort *Daett*. "And it can't be undone easily if what Rebecca told me is true. Bishop Enos would find it difficult to trust Susanna again after what happened today."

Susanna stood. She couldn't bear this any longer, but *Mamm* grabbed her arm and pulled her back. "We must speak even the difficult words," *Mamm* said.

"So what do you want to say?" Susanna asked. "Why don't you just tell me what a failure I have been as your daughter?"

Mamm's glance was not unkind. "I have tried to love you as my own, Susanna. The Lord knows I've not always succeeded. I confess that to you, and beg your forgiveness. Perhaps if I had been able to forget that you are not my daughter things could have turned out differently. So perhaps we all are to blame. I do not consider myself guiltless."

"This is not necessary," *Daett* protested.

"*Yah*, it is," *Mamm* told him. "I have been silent far too often because I feared my own heart. I was afraid I would spoil your daughter if I interfered, Ralph. Rather than fear, I should have joined in with her training and said the difficult things. I should have protested when you gave Susanna so much leeway in her *rumspringa*. *Yah*, I was wrong to remain silent—and yet I was afraid to speak up. I doubted myself, and look where we are now. May the Lord have mercy on all of us."

Susanna buried her face in her hands and was silent. *Daett's* soft voice murmured beside her as if she wasn't even in the room. "You have been a *goot frau* to me, Linda. I could not have asked for a better one. Yet I know I have failed you often. The memory of Mindy was in the back of my mind in bringing up Susanna. I see that my efforts to bring her up to not be like her real *mamm* only made things worse. I don't dare ask your forgiveness, as I don't deserve it, but I still am sorry for what I have done."

Mamm took *Daett's* hand in hers and stroked his arm. "You are forgiven, Ralph. How could I do otherwise with my own faults so fresh in my mind?"

Daett opened his arms and *Mamm* stood up to hug him. The two clung to each other. Susanna watched as tears streamed down *Mamm's* face. This was the relationship the community offered those who abided by its rules. She had been given the chance to have this, but she had failed. Now all was lost. She would call Joey this afternoon. She must leave this place of her childhood once and for all because she no longer belonged. Susanna stood and slipped upstairs, and no one protested her departure.

Chapter Twenty-Nine

Barely fifteen minutes after she had run up to her room, Susanna heard the sound of buggy wheels pulling in the driveway. She peeked out of the bedroom window, and as she expected, it was Ernest who had arrived.

She turned to take slow steps back to her bedroom dresser, where a small quilted cover hung over each side. Susanna ran her fingers along the soft edges and remembered that *Mamm* had made it for her sixteenth birthday, in honor of the start of her *rumspringa*. It was to be a reminder that her heart should always stay close to home.

Susanna tore her gaze away from the quilted cover. It was just another piece of her life she would be leaving behind. *Yah*, she would leave today. Before nightfall, even. Why, she wasn't sure. Perhaps if she stopped too long to think, doubt would enter her heart. There was no other way. She could not fit into the community. She had tried her best, and now she must move on.

With one hand Susanna opened the top dresser drawer and searched for the cell phone. She'd tell Joey to give her two hours to pack. She couldn't take much with her anyway. Her Amish clothing couldn't be worn in the *Englisha* world—at least not for long. She wouldn't be one of those people who lived with one foot in each place.

Susanna punched in Joey's number and pressed Send. "Pick up…pick up," she whispered as the phone rang. What if Joey didn't answer? It was a Sunday afternoon, and Joey surely wasn't sitting round waiting for her to call.

The phone beeped, and a voice said, "This is the Macalisters'. Please leave a message."

Susanna took a deep breath and spoke rapidly. "Don't call me back, Joey. Can you just come pick me up around six or so? I'm leaving the community for *goot*. Sorry for the short notice, but things have happened rather quickly. If you can't come, I understand. I'll set out on foot and catch a ride into Heuvelton the best I can."

Susanna slipped the phone back into the drawer and closed it. If Joey didn't come, he'd make contact with her tomorrow. She would call him from a hotel and let him know where she had landed. Phone conversations would no longer be a problem once she was out of the community.

A quick knock came on the bedroom door, and *Mamm* called out, "Susanna, Ernest's here. You need to come down."

"*Yah*, I'm coming," Susanna called back.

There was silence in the hallway for a moment. "Why are you dawdling?" *Mamm* asked.

Because I don't want to see him, Susanna almost said, but she bit back the quick retort. Instead, she crossed the room and opened the door. *Mamm*'s worried face appeared in the darkened hallway. "Are you okay?"

"*Yah*, I'll come down," Susanna answered.

Mamm seemed satisfied and led the way downstairs. "There's still time to change your mind," *Mamm* whispered over her shoulder, just before she opened the stairwell door.

Susanna didn't respond. The look on her face said enough. *Mamm* sighed and fell silent.

Daett stood to his feet when they entered the living room. Ernest was already standing and looked toward Susanna with sorrow etched on his face. At least his anger from the church service was no longer there.

"You two can speak outside on the porch," *Daett* said, motioning with his hand toward the front door.

The hopeless expression on *Daett's* face was almost more than Susanna could take. How could she live with herself after this? She wanted to rush over and give *Daett* a hug, to tell him she had changed her mind—that instead she would be the daughter he had always hoped she would be. She wanted to say that she would never disobey him again, and that she would be Ernest's *frau* or anything else he wanted, if only life could be made right again. But that wouldn't change anything. They all needed to face that which could not be changed.

Ernest didn't look at her but led the way outside. There he settled on the porch swing, its chains creaking. Ernest still harbored that same sorrowful look. Susanna sat down beside him and said, "We don't have to do this. I've made up my mind to leave."

Ernest sat up straighter. "But I'm still willing to wed you. That is not going to change. I have my two daughters to think of, and my love for you."

"No, Ernest. I'm not saying the marriage vows with you." Susanna tried to sound forceful. "I could never be the kind of *frau* you want."

His anger flared. "I'll decide that—not you or anyone else. Please, Susanna, reconsider this. I can speak with Bishop Enos and something can be done."

"I am not promised to you," Susanna said. "I never was, and even if I had promised, would you want a *frau* who was always regretting her proposed marriage to you? I don't think so."

Ernest's anger still lingered. "Don't be telling me what I think,

Susanna. I want a *frau* to take care of the house and my two daughters. Your heart will settle down once the marriage vows are said, and you will begin to care for Lizzie and Martha. Maybe I should have brought them along this afternoon so you could be reminded of your duties."

Susanna looked away. "I know my duties, Ernest, and they are to avoid marriage to a man I don't love. Nothing else can be right if I don't stay true to what I know. I'm not—"

"You're speaking like an *Englisha* woman," Ernest interrupted. "This is not what you have been taught. Your *daett* did what he knew was right by raising you to be a faithful member of the community, and that duty includes marriage to me. You cannot do anything else, Susanna. Not if you want to do what is right in the eyes of the Lord."

Susanna met his gaze. "I have struggled long and hard over this, Ernest. So please don't make things worse. You know I love *Daett*, and I would gladly live the life he had planned for me. But I have also told you that I will never agree to marry you without loving you. What is wrong with you that you continue to insist on a marriage without love? Is it because I had an *Englisha mamm* and you think I must accept you?" Susanna stopped. Ernest's mind appeared miles away as he stared off into the distance.

A slight smile played on his face. "I believe none of this," he said. "With your marriage to me, the Lord can meet the needs of my daughters. Our marriage would comfort my heart and turn your situation from something evil into something *goot*. You must not blame the Lord for what was done wrong in the past, but rather give thanks for the blessing He brought out of this horrible situation. That's still possible, Susanna."

"I am leaving tonight," Susanna whispered.

Ernest's head jerked up. "Haven't you been listening to a word I said? How many times do I have to say this? You don't know what you're doing. I'm not going to sit idly by while you ruin your life. With my *goot* word on your behalf, I'm sure the little kerfuffle you caused in church this morning can be smoothed over with Bishop Enos. I'll go talk with Deacon Herman right now. All you have to do is behave yourself in the future, and everything will be all right."

"No, it will not be all right. I'm sorry I led you on this long." Susanna hung her head. "I was only trying to do what was right. Somehow I thought everything would work out and everyone would be happy. I was wrong."

"It *can* work out all right, Susanna!" Ernest persisted. "You are your own worst enemy! Forget this foolishness. Where would you go anyway? Who do you know out there in that evil world?" Ernest waved his hand toward the horizon. "What will happen to you? How will you ever find the love you have experienced here in the community? And what about your affection for your *daett*? Consider the shame you're bringing on him."

Susanna stood to her feet and stepped away from Ernest. "We have said enough!"

"You're not leaving like this," Ernest ordered. "Sit down again at once until you're ready to repent."

Susanna didn't respond, but opened the front door and stepped inside the house. Ernest sputtered something behind her, but she closed the door on him. *Mamm* stared openmouthed at her.

"I'm sorry," Susanna whispered. "I'll be out of here soon, and then you won't have to—" Susanna stopped in midsentence and fled back up the stairs. Of what use were apologies? The longer this was drawn out, the more painful the experience would become. *Daett* already looked like a lost and forlorn little boy. But she would think no more. The time had come for action.

Susanna went into her bedroom and peeked out the curtains.

Ernest was standing beside his buggy, apparently lost in deep thought.

She turned from the window, went out into the hall, and headed to the storage room at the end of the house. Noah and Tobias were looking out of their bedroom door at her. She gave them a quick smile, and they went back to their play.

Susanna opened the storage room door and found a small suitcase. That was all she would need. Most of her clothing would stay. She returned to her bedroom and with quick movements packed the suitcase. The last item was still laid out on the bed quilt when she heard a car in the driveway. Susanna raced to the window to make sure it was Joey and then returned to close the suitcase. With the handle firmly in her grasp, she made her way back downstairs.

When she walked into the living room, *Mamm* had tears on her cheeks. But *Daett* came over to envelop her in his arms.

"Oh, Susanna," he whispered. "How I have loved you, and how greatly I have failed you."

"You have not failed," Susanna said. "But I must do what I think is best." She continued to cling to his strong arms. She never wanted to let go, but she must.

"How did Joey know to come?" *Mamm* asked.

Susanna hesitated, but *Mamm* didn't wait for an answer. She hurried toward the washroom door. "I'll call the boys, so they can say their good-byes."

"Don't!" Susanna stopped *Mamm*. "I don't think I can bear it now. Just tell them I love them."

Susanna untangled herself from *Daett's* arms, grabbed her suitcase, and fled out the front door.

Chapter Thirty

The walk across the lawn toward Joey's car seemed to take forever. Susanna forced herself to look back, but the front porch was empty. A sob escaped her, and she swallowed quickly. Joey didn't need to see her turning into a blubbering mess. She was not the first girl to ever leave home. At least she had a friend to call to support her decision. Susanna caught sight of movement in the barn window, where James's face peered out. She should have let *Mamm* call the boys in to say their good-byes, but the pain would have been too much to bear. Maybe soon she could come back, and…

"Susanna." Joey spoke her name softly. He came closer and held out his hand. She took it, and he helped her into the car.

"Are you okay?" he asked as she settled into her seat.

"*Yah*," she said. "I think so."

"Your message was so unexpected," he said, sliding into the driver's seat. "I'm sorry for how difficult this is, but I had hoped this day would come eventually."

Joey started the car and backed up to turn around near the barn. Henry and James had come out of the barn to watch them leave, but neither of her brothers moved or waved. She couldn't make out the looks on their faces, but she knew happiness was not written there. Her own heart throbbed and tears rolled down her cheeks.

Joey reached over and squeezed her hand. "No one said it would be easy," he offered. "But I'll do all I can to help in the weeks ahead."

"Joey, I already owe you so much," Susanna said. "If you'll just give me a place to stay for a night or two, I'll find something and be out of your hair, and out of your life."

Joey stopped Susanna with a touch of his hand. "Nonsense. I told my mother before I left that you were coming. She said you're welcome to stay for as long as you wish. She understands. She told me she remembers Mindy Whithus and what happened back then. She never realized you were the baby she delivered before she died."

Susanna was silent for the rest of the trip. Silence was exactly what she needed. That and comfort.

"Here we are," Joey said as he pulled in the driveway.

Susanna waited until Joey stopped the car and came around to open the door for her. She could have climbed out herself, but Joey wanted to help in whatever way he could—and she wanted him to. He touched her heart deeply with his actions. She wished she could show him how much, but all she could do was look up into his face and whisper, "Thank you."

"I am honored," he said, with one hand on the car door. With the other he reached for hers. Then he retrieved her small suitcase from the backseat. "Shall we?" Joey motioned toward the front door.

Joey's mother, Beatrice, opened the door with Joey's father, Langford, only a step behind. The two smiled a warm welcome, and Beatrice wrapped Susanna in a hug.

"You poor thing," Beatrice cooed. "Joey told me all about what happened. I can't believe people would act like that in this day and—"

"Mother," Joey cut in. "Susanna feels bad enough already."

"I'm sure you do." Beatrice backtracked at once. "I'm sorry for adding my criticism to your pain, but do come in and make yourself at home. It's not as though you're a stranger."

"Hi, Susanna," Langford said with a smile. He offered a handshake, his grip firm.

"You sure you don't mind my staying here?" Susanna glanced down at her Amish dress. "I guess I should go shopping this evening and get something…more appropriate."

Langford smiled. "I'm around Amish people every day. They are godly, hardworking people, and it's a privilege to have one of their daughters staying in my home."

"Thank you," Susanna said. "That's why leaving is so hard for me."

"That life is not for everyone," Langford added quickly. "You just make yourself at home with us, and don't think too much right now. I'm sure things are very confused in your mind. But at least Joey here will keep you straight."

"He has been more than kind." Susanna managed to smile.

Langford patted Joey on the shoulder. "He's a decent kid, if I can say so myself."

"Father," Joey muttered, "I'm to blame for Susanna's break with her family, if anyone is."

"No, you're not," Susanna protested. "There's no one to blame but myself and my inability to fit in with the community."

Langford regarded her for a moment. "I'm sure you're the least to blame, Susanna, but now's not the time to speak of blame. You're probably hungry and in need of a good night's rest."

Susanna nodded and said, "I think you're right. Thanks for understanding."

"Come." Beatrice took Susanna's arm. "We've already had supper, but let's see what we can find in the kitchen for you."

Susanna allowed herself to be led. She was hungry—there was

no question about that. How that was possible, she didn't know. Hunger and sorrow didn't go together. Susanna's head drooped as she felt another pang of remorse over what had to be.

Beatrice noticed and turned to give Susanna another quick hug. "The first few days will be the hardest," Beatrice said. "After that, things will look up."

"Thanks," Susanna whispered. Beatrice was kind to say the words, even if Susanna felt her life could never be right again. "You're so kind to take me in. I'll try not to be a greater burden than necessary and to move on quickly toward the next step of my journey."

"Hush now," Beatrice told her as she opened the refrigerator door. "What shall it be? We have cold cuts for sandwiches. I think we have some leftover fried chicken."

"Anything will be fine," Susanna said. "A sandwich is all I need, and I can make it myself. I think I know where everything is."

Beatrice hesitated but then sat down at the kitchen table. "Okay, but I'll listen while you work. Tell me a little about what happened, dear. That helps sometimes. Oh, the cheese is in the bottom drawer, and the knives are to your left."

Susanna busied herself with the sandwich and didn't answer at once. Beatrice waited in a comfortable silence. When she was done, Susanna brought the sandwich to the table and sat near Beatrice. Should she offer a prayer of thanks? Beatrice answered the question when she smiled and bowed her head for a silent prayer.

"I suppose you could use plenty of prayers in the days ahead," Beatrice offered when they lifted their heads again.

"*Yah*, I could," Susanna agreed before taking a bite of her sandwich. The food tasted *wunderbah* and then some.

"Is the sandwich okay?" Beatrice asked.

Susanna nodded. Her mouth was full. She surely must appear ill-mannered, but hunger had overtaken her.

"Shall I make another one for you?" Beatrice asked a moment later.

Susanna swallowed before she answered. "No, this will be plenty. Thank you, though."

"So, can you share a little about your leaving home this afternoon, or is it too painful?" Beatrice asked.

Susanna stared at the last of her sandwich for a second. "How much has Joey told you?"

Beatrice grinned. "He's a man. Not much, believe me."

Susanna chuckled and wrinkled her brow, and then she began the story. If Beatrice had been a stranger, Susanna couldn't have said a word, but Beatrice was now a friend, so the whole story poured out quickly.

"I considered marrying Ernest for what I thought were the right reasons," Susanna finished, "but thankfully I came to my senses in time. Emma's insight helped, and Joey's, of course. I couldn't have made it without him."

"Does this happen often in the community?" Beatrice asked.

"Oh, no," Susanna hurried to say. "It's because I have an *Englisha* mother that there was so much trouble. That's why I turned out the way I did. No one could change that."

Doubt was in Beatrice's eyes. "It's seems as if your father would have wanted what was best for you instead of trying to marry you off to this Ernest fellow," she said. "But never mind. You're safe now."

Susanna looked away and didn't answer. She felt anything but safe, but her feelings couldn't be trusted at the moment. Ernest's warning about all the dangers once she jumped the fence into the world rang in her ears.

"Are you sure you don't want another sandwich?" Beatrice offered again. "Or some chicken?"

"No, thank you. I'm finished." Susanna forced herself to smile.

"And thanks for listening to my story. Somehow it does help that someone else knows. I don't think I could have told Joey everything I told you."

"I understand." Beatrice touched Susanna's arm. "Now, what shall we do for the rest of the evening?"

Susanna didn't think too long. "I need to go shopping," she declared.

"On a Sunday?" Beatrice showed her surprise. "You're Amish and also tired, I'm sure."

"Maybe tired," Susanna allowed. "But I'm no longer Amish." Her words were steady, but she couldn't hide the pain on her face.

"You poor thing." Beatrice came close to give Susanna another long hug before she asked, "Do you have money? Things aren't cheap from the stores, and I know you're probably used to making your own clothes."

Susanna's head spun. She had placed all of her savings in the pocket of one of the dresses she had packed, but it wasn't much. Now her two hundred dollars seemed even smaller. She would have to make the money last and spend with care until she could begin her job again at the DeKalb Building Supply. "I guess I don't have much," Susanna allowed. "I'll have to make things by hand as usual—*Englisha* things, of course, if you'll let me use your sewing machine."

Beatrice wrinkled her face. "I'd be glad to help out, but I don't own a sewing machine. Maybe you could rent one from the local dry goods store."

"Then I guess I should rest this evening instead of shopping," Susanna allowed. A great weariness swept over her. "If that doesn't impose too much on you."

"You'll have to stop saying that," Beatrice chided her. "We're here to help until you can stand on your own two feet. But come, the men will wonder if the kitchen has eaten us up."

Susanna nodded and followed Beatrice back to the living room. Joey stood when they walked in, but Beatrice motioned for him to sit. "We're not going anywhere the rest of the evening. Susanna needs her rest."

Yah, she needed to rest. And then she glanced over to the familiar piano. Susanna walked toward it, and Joey quickly joined her. A peace settled over her as they approached the bench and took their places.

Susanna touched her fingers to the keys. Slowly she searched for the music as the pain throbbed in her heart. What she found was quietness where the chords touched the deepest part of her and loosened yet more tears. Susanna ignored everything around her as she continued to play.

When she stopped, silence filled the room.

"That was lovely," Langford said in a hushed tone.

Susanna's fingers moved on the keys again. She played with more confidence this time, her thoughts on the future that lay ahead of her. She might never love again, but she could live. Was this not the beginning of a new life? It was, Susanna decided, and her fingers moved even more swiftly on the piano keys.

Chapter Thirty-One

Ernest sat at his supper table and tried to hide his irritated feelings. A short temper had followed him in from the barn. He had almost attacked a hay bale with his foot but decided not to lest he stub his toe.

"How was your day, *Daett*?" Lizzie chirped as she ate her soup.

Ernest managed a smile. "*Goot*. Eat plenty of food now, so you can sleep well. Katherine's soup is the best as always, you know."

His sister gave him a wry look from across the table. She knew the soup was average, tossed together hurriedly amid her other household work. Katherine was not happy with him, and he couldn't blame her. He wasn't happy either, but what could be done about it now? Deacon Herman had let Emma off lightly for her recent escapade. And now, according to what Bishop Enos's son Paul had told him this morning in town, Susanna had left with her *Englisha* boyfriend on Sunday evening right after he left the Millers' house.

The embarrassment of it all stung him deeply. Why hadn't Ralph found the time to drive over and tell him that Susanna was gone? But of course, Ralph hadn't wanted to face things. The man had handled Susanna with soft gloves all her life, though strong discipline

had been needed. But regrets weren't going to help. There must be
something he could do to bring Susanna back. He needed her, as
did his two daughters. And since this morning an idea had started
to form in his mind that might work. He could speak with one of
the neighboring bishops and ask for their intervention. He could
point out how the situation had been handled incorrectly, and how
a harsher punishment could have kept Susanna at home with her
daett. Maybe Susanna could still be brought back if she saw discipline applied to Emma, the way it should have been done. It was
worth a try, and the sooner the better.

"Have you told them?" Katherine interrupted his thoughts to
motion toward the two girls.

Ernest shook his head.

"But you must, and tonight," Katherine said in a loud whisper.
"Pretty soon someone else will."

She had a point, but he didn't want to tell his girls that Susanna
would not be their *mamm* after all. That would close the book on
the subject, and he wasn't ready to give up yet.

When he remained silent, Katherine threatened, "I will tell them
myself if you don't."

"Okay!" He let his exasperation show. "I'll tell them."

"Tell us what, *Daett*?" Lizzie asked.

You don't want to know, Ernest almost said. Katherine gave him a
sharp look as if she had read his mind, but he finally got the words
out. "Girls, Susanna may not become your *mamm* after all."

Lizzie pondered the information for a moment before she
objected. "But Susanna used to smile at me at the Sunday service
when I ran up to her. Of course she's going to be our *mamm*."

"She held me once," Martha piped in.

"Just don't think about it right now," Ernest said, more harshly
than he meant.

"You call that telling them?" Katherine glared at him. "It's time you faced the truth, Ernest, and began looking for another *frau*. I can't stay around here forever, you know."

"You're right," Ernest admitted. "I have to do something."

Katherine didn't appear convinced of his intentions and seconds later began again. "Emma spoke with me at the Sunday service, she—"

"What's that woman saying now?" Ernest's voice rose to a roar.

Katherine gave him another glare. "Calm yourself, Ernest. She was just talking with me. You know she's in love with you, don't you? You ought to consider her. That wouldn't be much different from considering Susanna—since you seem to prefer young women over widows."

Ernest forced a laugh. "Not that long ago you were trying to push the Widow Laura on me, or was it the Widow Hannah?"

"Don't mock me." Katherine's words were clipped. "I could leave and go home, you know. What would you do then? Send the girls with me?"

Ernest flinched and didn't answer.

Katherine didn't back down. "You are going to do something, aren't you?"

"I'm going right now," Ernest said, springing to his feet. "But it's not what you think," he said over his shoulder as he closed the wash-room door behind him.

Outside an early dusk had fallen, and Ernest grabbed a light coat before he exited the house. He shouldn't be out late on a Wednesday evening if he planned to work tomorrow. The summer chore load was heavy right now. On top of that, his field of hay was cut and still lay behind the barn. Tomorrow it should be raked and baled. Still, the matters of the soul must be attended to. He needed a *frau*, and he wanted Susanna to fill that place. Badly! She would be a perfect *mamm* for little Lizzie and Martha. And Susanna must not waste her life among the *Englisha* people when the Lord had such a *goot* work prepared for her in the community. She must not!

With his face set, Ernest harnessed Gambit and hitched him to the buggy. He jiggled the reins and drove rapidly out of the lane. Bishop Mark was from the district to the north and lived on Old Canton Road. Ernest could be there in twenty minutes if he hurried. The conversation shouldn't take too long, and he'd be back in time to give Lizzie and Martha a quick hug before their bedtime.

Katherine insisted on the gesture each evening. Katherine said the girls needed extra attention from their *daett* with their *mamm* gone. He imagined Katherine was right on that point, but she was not right about Emma. He could not reward Emma with a proposal after her disloyal actions. What kind of example would that set if Emma was given a place in his home after playing such a prominent role in Susanna's departure? And as for the two widows who would gladly take up his wedding proposal, he didn't want either of them as his *frau*.

"No!" Ernest shouted out the side of his open buggy door. "Susanna is to be my *frau!*"

The sound echoed in the woods as if to mock him, but he set his face again as the miles rolled under his buggy wheels. The man who gave up easily was not worth much. This battle was his to fight, and the prize was having Susanna back where she belonged as his promised one. In a few months she would say the marriage vows with him, and he would not have to worry about her departure again.

Bishop Mark's place appeared ahead, and Ernest slowed down to turn into the driveway. A mad dash up to the bishop's barn would be the wrong way to begin a conversation. He was already on thin ice with this visit, so he had to walk carefully.

With slow motions Ernest pulled back on the reins and climbed down from the buggy. He tied Gambit to the ring on the barn wall, and approached the front door. The bishop's *frau*, Esther, answered the door.

"*Goot* evening," she greeted him.

Ernest nodded. "*Goot* evening. Is the bishop at home?"

"*Yah*." Esther held open the door. "He's sitting right in here. Come on in."

"I won't be long," Ernest assured her. "And I'm sorry for the intrusion."

"We have heard of your situation," Esther said. "That's terrible how things have been going over in Bishop Enos's district."

"They *are* terrible," Ernest agreed, taking off his hat. He turned his attention to the bishop seated in his rocker. Obviously he didn't have to give a detailed description to the bishop of why he had come. "*Goot* evening, bishop," Ernest began. "I thought a little counsel from another source would be wise."

Bishop Mark stroked his beard for a second before he answered. "*Yah*, we've been hearing about things from your district. Lots of trouble in the Lord's vineyard, it seems. The enemy lets loose little foxes all the time."

"But there is safety in the multitude of counsel, is there not?" Ernest hastened to say.

Bishop Mark stroked his beard again. "From what we've been hearing, one of the little foxes has left the Lord's vineyard. That's much to be thankful for, I would say. Do you not agree?"

"I don't know," Ernest sputtered. "It's not all what it seems. Or maybe you haven't heard the whole story or don't know Susanna Miller that well. The fact is, after her…well, her wild *rumspringa*, Susanna was settling down, and we were moving toward our plans for our wedding day this fall. But Emma Yutzy stepped in and convinced Susanna to meet her old *Englisha* boyfriend. Susanna never

would have done so on her own, so you can see why I'm upset. I
think the situation can still be saved if the proper measures are taken.
As it is, Emma got by with nary an admonition…and as you say,
Susanna has left." Ernest hurried on. "At least that's what I wanted
to ask you about. Surely there is no harm in asking after wisdom
from the Lord's assigned leaders in the community."

Bishop Mark's hand stopped halfway down his beard, and he
regarded Ernest with a steady gaze. "You would question the wisdom of your own bishop then?"

"Of course not, but—"

Bishop Mark cut him off. "You are not a minister, are you? Have
you been ordained to lead the Lord's people?"

Ernest pulled himself up straight. "I have been called to lead my
home, and Susanna was my intended promised one. In this I have
a right to speak when someone takes her from me."

"I see," Bishop Mark said. "In this you would be right, so let's
speak further on the matter—now that I know you are not chal-
lenging Bishop Enos's authority."

Ernest nodded and set his face again. "Far be it from me to do
such a thing, Bishop Mark. I am a humble servant and take no
responsibility that does not belong to me. I have served faithfully
ever since my baptism as a member in the district. You can ask
Bishop Enos if you wish. I would not challenge him on anything.
But I love Susanna, and I have a right to ask questions."

Bishop Mark grunted. "Questions and challenges are close cousins if not brothers, but I will give you the point. I can understand
why you would be distraught over this matter. Susanna Miller is a
beautiful woman, but she has the wild *Englisha* blood of her mother
in her, Ernest. Surely you would not wish to take such a woman as
your *frau*?"

"I think Susanna is being judged too harshly." Ernest kept his voice even. "It is discipline that she lacks, and this is what should have been given to her—and to Emma for that matter. The Lord knows I tried."

Bishop Mark eyed Ernest with a sharp look. "So you say Susanna was judged too harshly, meaning she was *goot* on the inside but only needed stronger discipline. That would imply there were no big problems in her life."

"Does not discipline deal with wrongness?" Ernest tried to keep the desperation out of his voice. "And I realize no one is perfect. I was willing to work with Susanna. We didn't have to lose her to the *Englisha* people. What does this say about our ability to keep people in the faith? Beyond that, one of our own young women helps the erring one in the wrong direction. Emma was clearly out of her place. I don't see how no one can understand that."

"Perhaps because Emma's eyes were wider open then yours were. That's your answer, Ernest." Bishop Mark shifted on his rocker. "At least, that's what I was told by Deacon Herman. Would you claim the deacon was wrong?"

Ernest swallowed twice before he answered. "I am not an ordained man, but I am the husband of my family, and my two daughters need a *mamm*. Badly! Surely no one can question that, and Susanna was the woman to fill that empty spot. Don't I get to decide that?"

"My heart is with you, Ernest," Bishop Mark allowed. "Maybe I would feel the same way in your situation, but clearly you have been blinded by Susanna's beauty. You have allowed her allure to create feelings in your heart that are not wise. In this you had best give way to those who can see clearer and from a better viewpoint. Emma was right. Deacon Herman has told me this, and I have no reason to doubt his word. Especially since Bishop Enos agrees with him. You had best back down on this issue and not complain further.

Seeking counsel is one thing, but pushing things too far is unwise.
Do you understand?"

"I understand." Ernest stared at the living room wall.

"We value peace in the community," Bishop Mark continued.
"Troublemakers are not appreciated. You know this. If I were you, I'd
ask Emma to marry me this weekend. Get this whole thing behind
you, Ernest. Your objections to how Susanna's case was handled are
well known in the community. Perhaps better than you think. Many
are watching to see how you take this, and they will remember—as
our people should. Those who cannot accept the discipline of the
Lord are not appreciated. Everyone except you seems to know that
Susanna has always been a risk to the community. She was granted
patience only because of Ralph's full repentance of his sins and
because of his desire to extend the grace of the Lord to his daughter.
A daughter who—I must remind you—was begotten in sin. The
community extended her that same grace, but Susanna clearly did
not benefit from what the community offered. You had best accept
that fact, Ernest. Stop in at Emma's place on the way home and
speak kind words to her. That would go a long way to settling this
whole matter in the minds of our people."

"I—" Ernest began, but stopped. Further words were useless.
This whole thing had turned on him, and now the community
thought he was to blame and needed repentance. Anger stirred in
him, but he couldn't allow the bishop to see. "I will think on this,"
he concluded.

Esther must have heard the end of the conversation because she
stuck her head out of the kitchen and asked, "Would you like a piece
of pie, perhaps? Before you go?"

Ernest tried to smile and said, "No. I must be going. It's late
already."

"Remember what I said," Bishop Mark hollered after him as Ernest went out the door.

Ernest took the porch steps two at a time, but slowed as he approached the buggy again. He should have stayed home tonight, but he hadn't, and now it was too late. All he had done was make things worse for himself. Bishop Mark thought he should take Emma as his *frau*. Katherine had told him the same thing tonight, but he was not about to listen to a woman. How could he take that low-down, sneaky Emma into his home? How could a woman like Emma call his daughters her own? He was not ready to stoop that low.

"And may it never happen," Ernest whispered into the night as he untied Gambit and drove out of the bishop's lane.

Chapter Thirty-Two

Joey arrived home to the sound of piano music wafting out the window. He grinned, parked his car, and climbed out. That would be Susanna again. With a soft step he cautiously approached the house.

His mother stopped him at the front door. "Shh…don't disturb her until she's finished."

"She's good, isn't she?" Joey asked.

Beatrice smiled. "I knew the girl could play, but I hadn't been paying much attention when she was here over the weekends."

"How's she doing otherwise?"

"She's coming along," Beatrice said. "We've been to the dry-goods store twice. They even had a nice used sewing machine for sale—electric powered, thank goodness. I couldn't stand to see the girl pedal through the sewing of a whole dress. Then we bought patterns at Walmart. It took a little doing on Susanna's part, but the dresses look store-bought to me. The girl is frugal and talented. Not bad qualities to have. She won't waste your money, if it comes to that."

"Come on, Mom," Joey protested halfheartedly. "What are you getting at?"

"I'm your mother." Beatrice patted his arm. "I know what's going on in that mind of yours. But I also know Susanna needs to live somewhere else if you want to win her heart. Something about her upbringing doesn't allow for…romance happening if you live under the same roof."

Joey grinned. "I'm a step ahead of you. I stopped in at Osseo's Bed-and-Breakfast today, and Rosalyn is willing to meet Susanna. Rosalyn could use help around the place in exchange for the rent. She likes the fact that Susanna has an Amish background. And I sang Susanna's praises pretty loudly."

Beatrice chuckled. "I imagine you did. And just so you know, your dad and I both approve of Susanna for you. We never dreamed you'd find an Amish girl to marry!"

"We're not married yet," Joey whispered as the music stopped. "I have a long way to go in that department." He moved away from his mother to call to Susanna, "Keep playing. That's beautiful."

Susanna's face was flushed when Joey peeked at her around the corner. "You shouldn't have been listening," she said. "I thought only your mother was here."

"I just got here." He sat down beside her on the piano bench. "I have good news. I think I've found a place for you to stay."

"You have?" Susanna's face lit up. "Where?"

"I'll tell you all about it at supper. How's that?"

Susanna bounced to her feet to exclaim, "Supper! Oh! I almost forgot. I made potatoes and gravy tonight, and canned beans from the Amish stand down the road. They're ready on the stove whenever you want to eat."

Beatrice glanced at Joey and shrugged. "I told her she didn't have to, but old habits die hard, I guess."

"I have to help out somewhere!" Susanna declared. "And I don't know much besides cooking and sewing, so that's what I do." She left the two of them and hurried toward the kitchen.

"She's something," Beatrice said when Susanna was gone.

"Should I go with her into the kitchen and offer to help?" Joey asked. "I'm not sure how to act."

Beatrice shook her head. "Not so much to help. Just be there, but also give her some space. She's like a wounded animal."

"Yeah, and I've never cared for a wounded animal. I'm not sure how to behave."

Beatrice glanced toward the kitchen and the sounds of rattling dishes. "If you can figure out how an Amish man would act, that might be a good start."

Joey shrugged. "Exactly how does an Amish man act? I don't have a beard, and I'm not going to sit in the living room and wait until the woman has supper ready."

Beatrice laughed. "Just be yourself then."

"That's sounds better," Joey said as he turned to head for the kitchen.

"It's almost ready," Susanna told him.

"Can I help?" Joey asked.

"Usually the men don't help in the kitchen. That's in the Amish world. Most of them only know how to wash dishes."

"Then I'll be Amish." Joey sat in one of the kitchen chairs. "I cooked a carrot cake once when I was younger, but that was with a cake mix."

"That's not exactly fair, you know." Susanna lifted a lid on a steaming pot and peered inside. "You should try it from scratch sometime."

"I suppose I should," Joey allowed. "But enough on my faults for one day. That's a nicely made dress you have on. You made it?"

Susanna blushed and looked away. "I tried my best, but I'll get better before long—until I can afford something better."

"Looks good enough to be store-bought to me," Joey said.

Susanna didn't look convinced and raised her eyebrows at him. "No, it's not that good. Homemade is still homemade."

Joey let it go. "So do you want to hear about your possible new home...for now?"

"*Yah*, while you set the table."

Joey grinned. "That I know how to do." He got up and busied himself with knives and forks. "There's a job and a place to stay at a bed-and-breakfast. The owner, Rosalyn Osseo, will give you your own room and a small salary in exchange for cleaning and helping out in the kitchen. I told her we'd drop by after supper if you're interested."

"*Yah*, I'll go. I'm a little nervous and don't know how to handle myself, but I trust your judgment. If you can assure me this Rosalyn isn't taking me in because she feels sorry for me, then it's okay."

"She's not!" Joey said. "Rosalyn's a kindhearted soul, and our family has known her for years. But she doesn't tolerate people who are..." Joey stopped and searched for the right word. He didn't want to offend Susanna, and she didn't fit the description anyway.

Susanna finished for him. "Moochers?"

Joey grinned as he set two plate settings. "Something like that."

Susanna appeared satisfied, but her face clouded when she looked at the two plates. "Aren't your mother and father eating with us tonight?"

"We'll eat later, Susanna," Beatrice called from the living room. "Langford doesn't come home until late, and I'll warm things up for him."

"Okay," Susanna said. "I'm just not used to the family eating in shifts. We always ate together, even if it meant postponing the meal for an hour or two if something came up." She served up dinner and brought it to the table.

As soon as she sat down, Joey asked, "How are you doing, Susanna? I mean, really. Are you okay?"

Susanna forced a laugh. "Don't worry about me. I'll be fine. Sometimes I find myself thinking about home and wonder what everyone is doing. Mealtimes are the worst."

Joey reached for her hand. "Shall I take you there for a visit tonight, instead of to see the Osseos? That can wait."

Susanna shook her head. "I'm not ready for a visit home yet. Maybe soon, but not tonight. I've seen a few of the community people at the shops your *mamm* took me to. They'll let *Daett* or one of my family know I'm doing okay."

"How did that go?" Joey asked. "I mean seeing your old friends."

Susanna shrugged. "It was okay. We talked about where I was staying and what I was buying. They didn't say much about my family, but I know it must be hard. At least I left the community before anyone had to get punished for my departure." Susanna gave a little laugh. "And I wouldn't have wanted the *bann* placed on me, either. With that infliction I couldn't purchase anything at the Amish stores or ever go home with any degree of comfort. That would have happened if I had been baptized."

"I see," Joey allowed. He wasn't sure what all that meant, but he was interested. "How do you feel about going back? Has that crossed your mind this week?"

"*Yah*." Susanna hung her head. "But it can't be, and that's that. Can we pray now before the food gets cold?"

"Pray, yes." Joey pulled himself upright. "I hope you don't expect a long prayer in German, though."

Susanna's laugh was soft, and she pressed her hand in his. "Silence is fine, but we must pray."

Joey closed his eyes. He'd better brush up on his religion if he wanted to live with a serious, dedicated, ex-Amish girl. He certainly didn't want to change her. "Amen," he said, having figured the silence had lingered long enough.

Susanna's eyes sparkled when she looked up. "That 'amen' sounded almost like a preacher's."

Joey laughed along with her. "I hope you're teasing, because I'll never be a minister."

Susanna's face sobered. "I like you just the way you are, Joey—"

Joey silenced her with a shake of his head. "We'd better eat, remember?" He looked down at his plate. "Wow. Does this taste as good as it looks?"

"I hope so," Susanna ventured. "I did my cooking on a woodstove at home, but yours is electric."

Joey took a bite and said, "It's excellent!"

Susanna beamed and began eating too. They took their time and ate in a comfortable silence. The few girls Joey had dated always chattered nonstop while he was with them. He liked this better. Lots better.

When their plates were empty, Joey stood to take Susanna's hand. "Let's go. I want you to meet Rosalyn."

"But the cleanup!" Susanna protested.

"Remember," he said, "that will be my job…when we get back."

The two walked out to Joey's car and got in. As he headed the car toward the bed-and-breakfast in nearby Canton, he said, "You'll like Rosalyn right off the bat, I'm sure. Like I said, she's been a family friend for many years now, and—"

"I wonder if she knew my mother?" Susanna asked, seemingly lost in her own thoughts. "My real mother."

Joey wasn't sure what to say. His mother had spoken correctly about Susanna's state of mind. There were things that needed time to heal in her life, but he was willing to walk with Susanna on the journey.

Joey let his mind wander as he drove through Canton on Highway 11 and turned south on Route 68. He could imagine how Susanna would bloom over the next few months, and even more in a few years. She had always been a carefree girl, but now the seriousness of womanhood—and the sorrow she had suffered—would change that. But Susanna would be a better person for all of this, and certainly better off here than being married to that Ernest fellow in the closed community.

Joey pressed his teeth together at the thought and slowed the car. "This is it." The driveway ran downhill from the road and was lined on either side by small trees. Susanna drew a sharp breath when he pulled in and stopped beside the garage. Behind one of the small cottages, the waters of a small pond glistened in the last light of the evening. "Beautiful and peaceful, isn't it?" Joey asked.

Susanna nodded, but she seemed tongue-tied at the moment. Rosalyn had appeared through the garage door, and Joey climbed out to greet her.

Rosalyn came forward and offered her hand as Susanna climbed out of the car. "Welcome, Susanna. I'm glad to meet you after all the good things Joey has told me about you."

"Oh, he shouldn't have." Susanna colored slightly. "Joey says too much sometimes."

"I'm sure all of it was true." Rosalyn took in Susanna's dress. "Did you make that yourself?"

Susanna's color deepened. "I'm sorry, is it that obvious?"

Rosalyn laughed. "Not at all. It's just that Joey said you were sewing your own clothes. I was just curious. In all honesty I couldn't have seen the difference in this dress from what I buy off the racks. A little more decent perhaps, and well made."

Susanna turned to give Joey a glare. "You do say too much."

Rosalyn laughed again and took Susanna by the arm. "Come, dear. I think we'll be getting along perfectly, you and I. Anyone who can handle Joey Macalister has made it in my book."

"Hey," Joey protested, but neither of them was listening to him. They had already disappeared into the garage. "Now, what have I started?" Joey asked the open sky before he followed the two women inside.

Chapter Thirty-Three

B y early the following week, Susanna had settled into her room and her duties at Rosalyn's bed-and-breakfast.

On Tuesday morning she was changing the bed in the room where a young couple, Rupert and Joanna, had stayed for a long weekend. They had left right after the second breakfast Rosalyn served at nine o'clock. They had arrived on Saturday morning and had strolled around the spacious grounds all weekend, hand in hand and obviously very much in love.

"We're getting away from all the big city fuss," Rupert had explained when Susanna had checked on them Saturday afternoon.

Already Rosalyn had complimented Susanna on her work. Susanna needed the encouragement, but in many ways the duties at the Osseos' place weren't much different from what they had been at home. She kept house, made meals, washed laundry…The only differences were the *Englisha* people all around her and the modern conveniences. Each cottage had Internet service and its own television.

"Everyone asks for Internet service," Rosalyn had told her. "Even the ones who are here to get away for the weekend. I'm sure that's something you didn't have to deal with at home."

Susanna nodded, unable to answer at the moment. The thought of home brought a brief pang. But Rosalyn seemed to understand. She slipped her hand around Susanna's shoulder for a quick hug—a gesture Rosalyn had given her several times already. Rosalyn was, in fact, becoming like a second *mamm* to her.

All weekend there had been no sign of Joey. Rosalyn was either to blame or be thanked—Susanna wasn't quite sure which. She had heard Rosalyn tell Joey as he dropped her off Friday night, "Let her have some peace and quiet this weekend. Leave her to herself as she settles in."

Joey had been right about Rosalyn and this job. The Osseos' place was exactly what she needed, so why should he be banished for the weekend? But Rosalyn was also right. Susanna needed time alone. Already she had bonded deeply with the older woman. Rosalyn was someone she could trust.

Although she had missed Joey, Susanna had been glad for the quiet as she learned to do her job. But surely Joey would return soon, or she could travel to see him at his home.

Susanna exited the cottage with a garbage bag of laundry in one hand. She closed the door carefully behind her with the other. A cardinal flew into the small tree in front of her and burst into song. The bird's bright red colors glowed among the green bristles of the evergreen.

Susanna paused to listen, and as the song continued, she lowered the bag of laundry onto the deck boards. How beautiful was the music the Lord gave birds to sing. They were such unassuming creatures, untouched by the sorrow of the world. No wonder the Lord had given them an angel's song, for this must be how the angels sang—so full of joy and with utter abandonment. She imagined the little fellow knew she was listening, and he sang not out of pride but for her enjoyment. The Lord must have sent him to touch her heart and give her courage for the journey ahead. She sighed and hoisted the laundry bag again, and the bird stopped his song and tilted his head. He stared at her for a moment before he flew away, vanishing into the limbs of the taller trees.

"Thanks for that concert," Susanna called after him. "And thank You, Lord," she prayed toward the heavens as she made her way to the laundry room.

Rosalyn met her there. "I thought I heard you talking to someone."

Susanna grinned sheepishly and said, "It was a bird."

"A bird?" Rosalyn raised her eyebrows.

"He was sent by God to sing for me," Susanna managed as she lowered the laundry bag. She felt a tear form and run down her cheek.

Rosalyn wrapped Susanna in her arms. "You know what you need?"

"What?" Susanna asked with a sniff.

"We have no guests scheduled for tonight. The laundry can wait. I'm going to take you home to visit your parents."

"Today?" Susanna asked, her heart speeding up.

"Yes, today. Now, in fact. No ifs, ands, or buts about it!" Rosalyn declared. She led the way back into the house and motioned for Susanna to wait while she changed.

"I must change too!" Susanna called out to Rosalyn. She didn't wait for an answer but rushed to her room where she quickly pulled on the Amish dress she had worn the day she left. Oh, to see *Daett* again! Was it going to happen so soon? She knew the day would come…but already? How would *Daett* respond? He would still love her in his heart, and he would speak with her—that much was allowed. She finished with the last pin and hurried out again.

"Ready?" Rosalyn asked. "I mean, emotionally ready? I don't want to force you into anything."

Susanna's voice choked. "I guess I'm as ready as I'll ever be."

"Then come." Rosalyn took her hand. "Let's hit the road. Besides, I want to speak to your father."

Susanna stopped short. "But you can't speak harsh words with him. He's not to blame for anything. I was the one who couldn't live the life he wanted me to live."

Rosalyn pressed her lips together and opened the car door. "Get in, dear. Don't worry. I'm not going to chew him out…even though I think he's been most unfair to you. I just have some questions for him."

Susanna climbed in and leaned back in the seat. It was useless to argue with Rosalyn. She had already learned that in the short time she had been here. Rosalyn could be as stubborn as an Amish bishop, and a smile crept across Susanna's face at the imagined comparison.

"Now you're smiling," Rosalyn commented when she checked for traffic on Route 68. "That's better!"

"*Yah*. It's better than crying," Susanna agreed.

Her thoughts turned next to Ernest. He now seemed far away and distant, as if he and she had never sat together on the porch swing. A shudder ran through Susanna, and she gazed out the window in search of better thoughts.

Once they were out of town, Rosalyn reached over to squeeze Susanna's hand. "You need to get past who's to blame. That's the only way to truly move on. You need to heal and accept your past. You had a very decent upbringing, I'm sure. Be thankful for that. Also, you've done nothing to be ashamed of. Don't feel guilty over leaving. You were right to leave instead of letting them force you into marrying a man you don't love."

Susanna tried to smile. "Well, it wasn't quite like that. I did have a choice, but with my past the choices were to marry Ernest or to stay single for the rest of my life. No other man in the community would have married me. And I suppose all the more so now. Leaving just proved to everyone that I have wild *Englisha* blood in me."

Rosalyn's voice broke through Susanna's daze. "Susanna, dear, listen to me. That may be what your community thinks, but that's not what God thinks. We are loved by the Father even in our sinfulness. That the people around you didn't think so doesn't change anything."

Susanna choked back a sob. "*Daett* loved me. And I left him."

"Dear heart." Rosalyn's voice was urgent. "Many people care a whole lot about you. Joey and his parents care very much for you. I do, too, even after the few short days I've known you. I gladly opened my home to you when Joey asked. I've not regretted that decision for a moment. You're a blessing, Susanna, and I know Joey thinks so too." Rosalyn paused. "In fact, I'm quite sure Joey *more* than cares for you."

"We're friends, Joey and I. I have to keep reminding myself of that. I don't want to end up making promises I can't keep. Joey's been so nice to me, and I've taken advantage of his kindness, but I don't know if I can repay his affections—and I won't force myself again. I promised myself that before I left home."

"You let me take care of Joey." Rosalyn gave Susanna a pat on the arm. "You heal up. That's your first task. A woman's heart is a tender thing, and yours has been bruised considerably. I can't even imagine how much. Just hang in there, and don't worry about Joey right now."

"Joey's a nice man," Susanna allowed.

Rosalyn smiled. "Nice is good, but let's leave it there for now. The Lord will guide you when the time comes. Don't you think so?"

Susanna nodded as Rosalyn drove out of Canton, toward Maple Ridge Road and all that was so familiar to her. Ahead of them the Miller home appeared, and Susanna took a deep breath.

Chapter Thirty-Four

Susanna kept her gaze straight ahead as Rosalyn turned into the driveway. She wanted to glance around wildly like a ten-year-old arriving home after a long absence. But everything would still be the way she'd left it a little over a week ago. The only thing that had changed was that this was no longer her home.

Rosalyn brought her car to a stop near the barn. The barn door stood open in front of them, but no one had appeared yet. *Daett's* buggy was there, so he should be home. Susanna hadn't been able to see the back fields when they drove in, so maybe that's where all the men were working.

This was harder than Susanna had imagined. Her heart was throbbing, and her mouth was dry. She wanted to see *Daett, Mamm,* and her brothers, only she knew it would never again be like it was before. It would be impossible to recapture the past. In her *rumspringa* days the thought of her eventual return had comforted her even as she enjoyed her life in the world. Back then she had gazed without fear into Joey's eyes and called him a friend. Her heart hadn't concerned itself with where she was headed. Now there was no anticipated return to soothe her. The world felt like a heavy basket of laundry in her arms.

"Shall we go in?" Rosalyn asked as the front door opened and *Mamm* appeared.

"*Yah*, of course," Susanna replied.

Rosalyn climbed out of the car without further comment, and Susanna followed. She made her feet move as Rosalyn led the way up the walk. She wouldn't have accomplished this if Rosalyn hadn't come along. She would have fled back to the car in spite of her best resolutions. At least she had thought to change into an Amish dress before she set out on this journey.

Mamm's first glance took in that fact. *Mamm* smiled and greeted them with a soft, "*Goot* morning. This is a surprise."

"Hello, Mrs. Miller." Rosalyn held out her hand and *Mamm* gave it a quick shake.

Susanna tried to say something, but her mouth was too dry.

Mamm didn't seem to mind as her attention was on Rosalyn. "Are you a friend of Susanna's?"

"Yes, a *new* friend…and her employer." Rosalyn laughed. "My name is Rosalyn Osseo. I have a bed-and-breakfast in Canton where Susanna is staying."

Mamm hesitated. The look on her face said, *So you're already moving from place to place, unstable as the wind blowing across the summer fields?* Out loud *Mamm* said, "I'm glad somebody's taking care of you, Susanna."

Rosalyn smiled. "The truth is, she's taking care of us. I've felt downright lazy and spoiled all weekend. You've taught your daughter her household duties quite well, Mrs. Miller."

"It's Linda," *Mamm* muttered, though she had brightened at the praise. "Do you want to come inside?" *Mamm* turned to lead the way toward the house.

"Where's *Daett*?" Susanna asked.

Mamm turned with a hurt look on her face. "He'll be in soon from the back fields, I'm sure." She had a weary smile on her face as she held open the front door. "Sorry about the mess, but I was trying to get lunch ready for the men. I'm sort of alone with the house, since—"

"We'll give you a little help," Rosalyn said at once, "although your house looks spotless compared to mine when Susanna's not around."

Mamm considered the offer for a second and finally nodded. "Do you want to fix lunch, Susanna? And I'll clean up the house before the men arrive from the fields? Rosalyn can keep me busy with chatter." She forced a smile. "I don't have much of that anymore—female talk in the house."

"I'll help, of course," Rosalyn said.

Susanna left them and hurried into the kitchen. *Mamm* had begun what was clearly potato soup. A large bowl was set on the table, and half-peeled potatoes were spread across the tabletop. *Mamm* planned to keep things simple apparently, but what choice did *Mamm* have since there was no one to help with the housework? The thoughts raced through Susanna's mind as she finished peeling the potatoes. Was there some way she could come home a few days a week and help?

Could she? Surely *Mamm* wouldn't object. Or was she desperately attempting to live a sort of double life—with one foot in each world? But she no longer had a foot in this world, Susanna reminded herself. Maybe she could come home on slow days at the bed-and-breakfast. *Mamm* needed the help—badly, from the looks of things. Surely something could be worked out.

Of course, she would have to ask *Daett*, but when and how? The dinner table was not the appropriate time. Oh, if only...Susanna glanced out of the kitchen window and gasped. *Daett's* erect figure strode purposefully across the lawn from the open barn door. Susanna sat down and tried to breathe. She didn't dare peel another potato until her emotions were under control. The knife would cut her fingers more readily than it sliced the potatoes.

The outside washroom door opened with a bang, and Susanna stood to her feet. *Daett* burst in the kitchen door and came to a sudden stop.

"*Daett*," Susanna whispered.

"My own daughter in my kitchen," he said. "Where have you come from?" *Daett* looked as though he thought he was dreaming.

Susanna stepped closer. He opened his arms, and she wrapped hers around him. The sobs came quickly, in quiet gasps.

Daett tried to speak. "Are you…but there is a car in the driveway."

Susanna shook her head, unable to speak.

"So you…" *Daett* tried again.

"I'm only here for a few hours," Susanna said.

Daett took in the potatoes with a quick glance. "Then why the kitchen work?"

"*Mamm* needed help," Susanna replied. "And Rosalyn is helping *Mamm* clean the house."

"Who is Rosalyn?" *Daett* asked. But he didn't wait for an answer before his arms closed around Susanna again. "My own daughter has come home," *Daett* muttered. "Let me hold you close and never let go."

Susanna let the hug linger and then gently pulled back. "*Daett*, I've not come back to stay. This is only a visit." Susanna looked away from the pain written on his face. "Please don't make this harder than it is. We have to live with what is true, and being an Amish girl is no longer possible for me."

"But it is," *Daett* objected, sitting down on a kitchen chair close to her.

Susanna didn't answer. *Daett* was only saying what was in his heart, but he also knew the truth. Reality took a while to face. "*Daett*, I have a job and a place to stay at the Osseo's Bed-and-Breakfast," she said, trying to sound upbeat. "Out in Canton. You know the place?"

Daett nodded. "*Yah*, I do, but how did you get a job there?"

"Joey's family is friends with the Osseos."

"That's better than staying with him," *Daett* said.

Susanna blushed and then jumped to her feet to move the bowl of potatoes over to the stove. *Mamm* had begun a fire earlier, and the stove top was glowing hot. *Daett* watched her work with a pensive look on his face.

"We miss you, Susanna," he said.

"I know. I miss you too," she answered. "I know *Mamm* misses my help around the house. And that has given me an idea, *Daett*. What would you think about me coming to help *Mamm* when I can? Like, maybe on Tuesday or Thursday when the bed-and-breakfast is slow. I haven't spoken with Rosalyn yet, but I think we can work it out. *Mamm* needs the help."

Daett didn't say anything, so Susanna let the silence linger. At least he hadn't said no.

"And how would you get here?" *Daett* finally asked.

"In a car." Susanna forced a laugh. "I can't drive a horse and buggy any longer, and it's too far anyway."

"And you'll soon drive your own car?"

"I don't know," Susanna said. "I haven't really thought about it."

"It would be *goot* to have you here," *Daett* said.

Susanna saw that tears had formed in his eyes. She stepped away from the stove to wrap her arms around his shoulders, but when *Mamm*'s face appeared in the kitchen doorway, Susanna let go.

"I didn't hear you come in," *Mamm* said.

"My daughter has come back," *Daett* told her, as if that were all the answer *Mamm* needed. "And she is asking if she can come home and help you out a few days of the week. Surely that would be okay, don't you think?"

Mamm didn't answer, and Rosalyn appeared behind her.

"Welcome to our home," *Daett* said in Rosalyn's direction. He stood to his feet and smiled.

Rosalyn stepped forward to offer her hand. "I'm so happy to meet you, Mr. Miller. I hope we're not intruding."

Daett accepted Rosalyn's handshake. "No, of course not. The boys noticed a car drive in, and when it didn't leave after a while, I thought I'd come up and—"

"I don't know about Susanna coming home to help out," *Mamm* interrupted. "What will Deacon Herman say?"

Daett gave Rosalyn a quick glance. "Susanna hasn't spoken with Rosalyn about this, so we can talk later, but I think we should consider the idea."

"I'm sure something can be worked out," Rosalyn responded. "I'm not sure what Susanna has in mind—but considering the way the girl works, she could probably be in two places at one time and not surprise me at all."

Rosalyn's and *Daett*'s laughter filled the room. Even *Mamm* smiled a little. Susanna returned to busying herself with the food preparations, and warm circles raced around her heart. *Daett* wanted her home, even on her terms. He was also willing to face Deacon Herman's possible disapproval. *Mamm* still loved her too, Susanna reassured herself. Somehow they would all come to terms with what life had given them and allow the Lord to lead the way. Rosalyn had been right. Susanna had needed to come home. She stirred the potatoes and listened to the sounds of the conversation behind her. *Daett* had taken Rosalyn and *Mamm* into the living room, where Rosalyn had charmed even *Mamm* from the sounds of their voices. Truly the Lord was at work in their lives. She would comfort herself with that thought. The Lord was seeing fit to extend mercy toward them, and she would rejoice in every small gift of grace.

Chapter Thirty-Five

The following Tuesday morning found Susanna and Rosalyn lingering at the breakfast table with coffee cups in their hands. Outside the open kitchen window, birds could be heard chirping, and the two women listened to them with soft smiles on their faces. Susanna allowed herself to relax and let the quiet of the morning soothe her spirit. She still wasn't used to the *Englisha* world, but Rosalyn had done her part in making the transition easy. Staying busy helped, and this past weekend had been a rush. All the cottages had been at full capacity, and two of the couples had stayed over into Monday.

Rosalyn knew the value of hard work to heal the soul of its wounds. This morning they had risen early. Susanna had been raised on a farm where you got out of bed before the sun rose each day. From what she had seen of Rosalyn, the woman must have acquired similar habits long ago. In many ways this place was like home, which must be the Lord's grace to help her ease into the *Englisha* world. She would have made it at the Macalister's place, but this was so much better.

Rosalyn interrupted Susanna's quiet thoughts by saying, "Joey's picking you up this morning to drive you over to your parents' house."

Susanna almost spilled her coffee at Rosalyn's words. "What! I thought you were driving me."

Rosalyn smiled slyly. "I think it's time you and Joey see more of each other, don't you think? You've been hiding out here for over a week, and he's getting quite impatient."

"But why?" Susanna sputtered, though she knew exactly why Joey wanted to see her. "I've made him no promises."

"And that's how it should be," Rosalyn agreed. "But you do need to see him, and you have my approval if you choose to spend more time with each other. We'll make it work with the schedule around here." Rosalyn gave a little laugh. "I can exist on my own, you know."

"Of course you can!" Susanna said, wrinkling her face. "You were doing just fine before I came. You didn't even have to take me in, but you did. For that I should be on my knees all day in thanks, and yet I hardly ever tell you how much I appreciate what you've done."

Rosalyn reached across the table to touch her hand. "It's an honor, dear. How else could I have enlivened my boring life? Meeting you was exactly what I needed. And through you I finally got to see the inside of an Amish home! And to meet your parents." Rosalyn gave Susanna a tender look. "Susanna, you do know they love you, even though it may not feel so at times. Even your Amish mother does in her own way. I hope you know that."

Susanna looked away. "I try to remember. They have always done the best they could for me. I'm only sorry it wasn't enough... or what I really needed. I thought I would turn out to be a happy Amish girl, and now—"

"Your father doted on you, didn't he?" Rosalyn interrupted.

"*Daett* spoiled me," Susanna said. "I see that now. He let me get away with things he shouldn't have. *Daett* didn't want to know what I was doing all those weekends on my *rumspringa* time. I was in my own dream world. Now it's all come crashing down."

"Don't look back, dear," Rosalyn chided. "I know the pain is there, but it will heal."

Susanna forced herself to laugh. "Oh, I know it will. Perhaps I'm just too self-absorbed. Everyone has problems, I guess. Why should I be any different?"

"That's true. Many young women your age have far worse problems." Rosalyn glanced at her watch. "You'd better get ready for Joey. He'll be here any minute."

Susanna sat up straight and fixed a smile on her face. "I'm ready now."

"Good. I'm going to do some book work in the office. You and Joey enjoy each other, okay? He's a good young man," Rosalyn said as she stood to leave.

"Joey has been a true friend," Susanna agreed. "I've come to realize that more than ever the last few weeks."

"I think I hear him now," Rosalyn said with a twinkle in her eye.

"Thanks for everything," Susanna said over her shoulder as she dashed toward the door. Then she slowed, realizing a wild dash out to Joey's car would leave the wrong impression. Joey shouldn't know about the delight that stirred inside her at the thought of his smiling face. Susanna stepped slowly outside.

"Good morning," Joey called through his open car window. "You look cheerful this morning. Rosalyn must not have worked you too hard."

"She's a jewel," Susanna said, climbing in the car. "And *goot* morning to you."

"Off to Amish land again." Joey gave her a long look. "You're not thinking of moving back, are you?"

"I'm not going back," Susanna answered. "Don't look so worried." She reached over to give his hand a quick squeeze. "And thank you for taking me this morning—and picking me up again tonight, I assume."

"Yep! I'm yours for the day," Joey chirped.

"Were you worried, thinking I'd consider going back?"

Joey started the car and drove out of the lane before he answered. "Not really, it's just that—"

Susanna stopped him. "You don't have to say it. I understand, and I'm thankful." She paused. How was she to express her feelings to him? So much in her present world was still new, and Joey was her friend—only now she wondered if he might be more than that to her. She had to be honest about that too.

Joey smiled as he settled back into his seat. "So what does the day hold when you get to the homeplace? Will you scrub pots and pans all day and wash laundry and clean the fireplace cinders?"

"Maybe. What's wrong with that?"

"You're a real Cinderella, I suppose," Joey teased.

Susanna thought for a moment before she remembered the *Englisha* tale of the servant girl who worked for her harsh stepsisters and stepmother before she finally married the prince.

Joey chuckled. "You do know the story, don't you?"

"*Yah.*" Susanna hid her face. "But I'm not Cinderella."

"And neither am I the prince," Joey said. "But like the prince, I do care about you, Susanna. More than I can ever say. I hope you know that."

"I suppose I do," Susanna allowed, but she didn't look at him. Could she love this man as her husband? The thought left her weak. She had always known she would never love Ernest Helmuth even if she married him. Yet he had been the only man she had ever considered for a husband. As for Joey, what if her feeling for him was just gratitude? Joey deserved better than that. He deserved a wife who could love him with her whole heart.

"Did I offend you?" Joey asked, and his hand found hers.

Susanna forced herself to look at him and smile. "It's not that, Joey. You brought up the Cinderella story, which I know little about. But I know the Amish Humpty Dumpty story better. We chanted the little rhyme in the school yard all the time." Susanna closed her eyes and said the words from memory. "'Humpty Dumpty sat on a wall; Humpty Dumpty had a great fall. All the king's horses and all the king's men couldn't put Humpty Dumpty together again.' That," Susanna said when she opened her eyes, "is who I am."

"I disagree," he said. "You *are* Cinderella, and the Lord will give you a new heart. That's why I was worried you would try to put the old one together again. You could never be the wife of that…" Joey appeared angry and waved his free hand about the car. "Whatever his name was. I'm glad that egg is broken."

Susanna couldn't keep the smile off her face.

"That's better," Joey said, glancing at her.

"In truth, you probably pushed this poor Humpty Dumpty off the wall."

Joey laughed. "No, it just had to happen. But I'm here to help put Humpty back together again. Maybe all the king's horses and all the king's men just weren't up to the task."

Susanna joined in his laughter as Joey slowed for the Millers' driveway. "I wish I had all the answers for you, Susanna," he said. "That way you'd fall into my arms like Cinderella did with the prince, but I don't. I just know that I love you. I know your past, and I believe your best years are ahead." A mischievous look crossed Joey's face as he parked beside the barn. "With me, of course," he finished.

"Oh, Joey," Susanna said, meeting his gaze. "You know I can't make promises. I wish I could, but I—"

"Go," he said. He placed his hand on hers again. "Have a good day, and don't work too hard. I'll see you at five, and we'll go out to eat. Will you give me that much of a promise?"

Susanna took a deep breath. "That I can do."

"And we'll go shopping," he teased.

"I'm holding you to that," she shot back as she stepped out of the car.

A grin filled Joey's face as he turned the car around and drove out onto the road. Susanna watched until the car disappeared from sight before she moved toward the house.

This was not her home anymore. She was only here for the day. She no longer had to think about Ernest Helmuth or how she could fit herself into his life as his *frau*. That was all behind her. She would go eat with Joey tonight, and she would hold him to his promise to shop. She had no idea what to buy, but she didn't *have* to buy anything. She could use the time to familiarize herself with her new world. Maybe Joey was right. Maybe she could be put back together again. Maybe she could even return Joey's love. The thought took her breath away. *That is more than I can handle,* Susanna told herself as she hurried up the sidewalk.

Mamm greeted Susanna at the front door. "*Goot* morning. I see you've come."

"*Yah*, I said I would," Susanna responded. "Put me to work!"

Mamm led the way back inside. "I started the laundry before breakfast, but the first load is still in the basement. I guess you…" *Mamm* paused. "Susanna, I still feel bad about this. You don't have to—"

"I *want* to." Susanna gave *Mamm* a hug. *Mamm* clung to her and tried to say something when Susanna let go. "It's all right," Susanna said.

Susanna hurried toward the basement door.

"I'm glad you're home," *Mamm* called after her, "even if it's just for the day."

"So am I," Susanna responded before she took the familiar basement steps one at a time.

Chapter Thirty-Six

That evening the clock on the Millers' kitchen wall ticked toward five. Susanna placed the last plate on the table and arranged the utensils in their proper places. She stood back to take in the familiar sight as *Mamm* walked in the room. *Mamm*'s quick glance took in her work. Everything was set as it should have been, but Susanna knew why *Mamm* frowned. They had avoided the subject all day.

"I'm leaving at five with Joey," Susanna said before the question was asked. "But I'll be back tomorrow."

Mamm's frown didn't fade.

"Maybe I can stay for supper tomorrow night," Susanna suggested. "But tonight Joey asked me to eat out with him, and—" Susanna stopped. *Mamm*'s distress would only increase with details of Susanna's evening plans.

"I'm glad you could come today." *Mamm* tried to smile. "And for all the work you did. This was a godsend. But can't you think of what's best for yourself, Susanna? It can't be the way you're headed right now out in the *Englisha* world. Maybe if you came back slowly into the community it would work this time?"

Susanna opened her mouth to speak, but *Mamm* rushed on. "I know I've failed you often over the years, but I'd try hard to make things work this time. Your old room is still upstairs waiting for you." *Mamm* ended on a hopeful note.

Susanna stepped toward *Mamm*. With both hands she reached out to touch *Mamm*'s arm. "*Mamm*, I can't come back. It's not about you trying hard…or me, for that matter. You're certainly not to blame for any of this. I know you loved me like your own child. I'll always be grateful for that. I had a great childhood, *Mamm*." Susanna forced a laugh. "It's not as if you chained me up in a dungeon or something."

Mamm laughed with her and then fell silent.

"Can we slowly build a new relationship?" Susanna searched *Mamm*'s face. "Please?"

Mamm seemed confused. "A new relationship? But…"

"What once was can never be again," Susanna said. "I think you know it can't. And would you have wanted me to live with Ernest Helmuth as his *frau* if I didn't love him?"

"But you would have learned to," *Mamm* protested. "And Ernest will still take you, even now. He looks like a man lost in the woods at the service. You could love the man."

"You know I couldn't," Susanna insisted.

Mamm reached up to tuck a few hairs under Susanna's *kapp*. "At least you're still wearing this."

Susanna took a deep breath. "I'm not making any promises about even that, *Mamm*. I'm *Englisha* now, and I'll act like an *Englisha* woman soon."

Alarm filled *Mamm*'s face. "You'll come home looking like them? You know *Daett* will be getting in enough trouble already."

Susanna shook her head. "Don't worry. I'll look decent here. I'll keep my Amish dresses and my *kapp*, but I can no longer dress like I'm Amish when I'm out there in the *Englisha* world."

The sound of Joey's car pulling into the driveway came through the open kitchen window. Susanna gave *Mamm* a quick hug. "Let's just love each other," Susanna said. "Okay?"

"Okay," *Mamm* whispered, through tears.

Susanna nodded and slipped outside. She had seen Henry and James and *Daett* at lunch, and Noah when he came home from school. Tobias had been busy playing most of the day and was now resting quietly in his room upstairs. Susanna still hoped some of them might come out to see her off, but no one came through the barn door as Susanna climbed in the car.

"No tears?" Joey teased as he turned the car around. "That's progress."

"No tears," Susanna repeated. "But that doesn't mean it was easy."

"I'm sure it wasn't, but you held up well," Joey said tenderly. "So, what restaurant will it be?"

"You choose," Susanna said. "But first I have to go home and change."

Joey raised his eyebrows and gave her a long look. "You appear fine to me even after a long day's labor. That's one of your gifts. Perfection whatever the situation, you know."

"You never used to be this irritating," she teased. "Now take me back to Rosalyn's place, and I'll put something on that I haven't worked in."

"Okay," he said with a grin. "I still say you look fine."

"Does Rosalyn know about our going out to supper?" Susanna asked.

"Does she need to know?" he asked as he slowed for the town limits of Canton.

"It just seems like the right thing to do," Susanna said. "She'll want to know."

"She knows," Joey said. "I called her, and she's ecstatic that we're having an evening out."

Joey took his time to work through the stoplights in Canton. He seemed lost in thought, and finally Susanna glanced at him. "Did you have a difficult day at school?"

"A little, but nothing unusual," he said. "I want to start law school next term, so I've had to take some extra classes to make that happen."

"That's sounds interesting. I've never..." Susanna searched for words. She knew next to nothing about the *Englisha* ways of schooling. "I've always wanted to learn more but never had the chance."

"It's never too late," Joey said. "You could go back to school if you want to."

Susanna sighed. "No, I don't think so. Learning this new way of life is going to be more schooling than I can handle. But I'll always want to learn, I'm sure. Beyond that I'm still a little Amish. Maybe that's something that will stay with me. I want things like a home, a husband, children, and of course..." Susanna stopped. She had best not go on.

"I think that's perfectly beautiful." Joey's voice soothed Susanna's ruffled spirit. "You need not have regrets about that. Education isn't all there is to life."

"But all your family is educated, aren't they?"

"Yes, but that can be both a blessing and a drawback," Joey said. "I grew up in the home of a successful lawyer who was always busy with his work. Dad tried to make time for his children, but there was never enough. I don't want to live like that, even if do become a lawyer. So don't devalue yourself, Susanna. You have graces I greatly admire and need."

Susanna avoided his glance and began to blush. "You shouldn't say such things," she whispered.

"I'll say what I wish," Joey declared, "and that's that."

Susanna managed to laugh as Joey sped up once they neared the other side of Canton. When Joey pulled in the lane to the bed-and-breakfast, Susanna hopped out of the car and called out, "I'll be right back."

Rosalyn met her on her way to her room. "Why are you here? I thought Joey was taking you out to eat."

"He is," Susanna said. "I have to change."

Rosalyn took in her dress and shoes. "I suppose you could, but you look clean to me."

"I want to look like someone from his world," Susanna said. As she went into her room, Rosalyn followed her. Without hesitation Susanna picked out the best *Englisha* dress she had made so far and slipped it on. With a flourish she loosened her hair bun and allowed the curls to flow over her shoulders and all the way to her hips. She would have to cut her hair to shoulder length soon, but this would do for now. A few brush strokes would be *goot* enough with clips for the loose sides. Susanna finished her hair and turned in the mirror to check the results.

"Okay, I guess," she muttered to herself. "Different—that's for sure." She knew her *mamm* would have passed out from shock.

Susanna turned to Rosalyn, who had been waiting. "Is it okay?"

"You look stunning," Rosalyn said. "Now go."

Susanna stepped outside and carefully kept her back to the car. That couldn't last for long. She would have to face Joey. Susanna gathered herself together and moved toward the car. When she climbed in and closed the door, Joey stared.

"Is it that bad?" Susanna asked.

"Oh, sure. It's just awful," he teased.

"It's the most *Englisha* looking I've ventured so far," she said.

Joey started the car and drove down the lane. "It's stunning... stupendous." He looked both ways before he pulled out on Route 68. "I think I have to go home and change to match how good you look."

"You don't have to," she said.

"I was kidding." He reached for her hand. "You don't know what this means to me. After all this time, and to see you like this. My heart overflows with…well…"

"Stop it," she ordered. She pulled her hand away with a shy smile.

Silence filled the car as Joey grinned. As they approached town again, his gaze drifted toward her at regular intervals. Susanna smiled each time, and Joey's face lit up. Susanna finally asked, "Are we going to do this all the way to wherever we're going?"

Joey chuckled and cleared his throat. "We will be adults now and behave," he said. "I will look straight ahead and not at the beautiful woman next to me. When we get to the restaurant I will pretend she's my sister and that I can barely stand the sight of her."

"Joey," Susanna giggled. "Stop it."

"I can't help it," Joey said. His face was sober, and his hand found hers. "I love you, Susanna. I have for a long time."

Susanna wanted to say the words too, but they stuck in her throat. Joey seemed to understand. *You'll have to give me more time*, she almost said, but she was sure Joey already knew that.

When the car came to a stop at a red light, Susanna leaned across the seat and gave him a quick kiss on the cheek.

Chapter Thirty-Seven

The following Saturday morning, Ernest Helmuth drove his buggy east of DeKalb toward Deacon Herman's place. His hands hung loose on the reins, and Gambit took his time.

"Getup, there," Ernest shouted through the buggy windshield, but the effect was nil.

Even Gambit no longer responded to his commands. Ernest's frown deepened. How was he to keep his head up at the Sunday services with things in the condition they were? The younger boys who gathered in the barnyard after the services had begun to snicker unashamedly when he walked past them. He was an embarrassment. Susanna should be the center of the community's outrage and concern, but she wasn't.

Now that the issue had been resolved, everyone seemed to have heaved a collective sigh and moved on. He hadn't. How could he when the humiliation was so great? Even the news of his rejection by Bishop Mark from the neighboring district had somehow leaked out—as it always did in such a close-knit community. He should have known better than to risk the visit to Bishop Mark, but he hadn't been able to help himself. No danger seemed too great when it came to Susanna. He had desperately wanted her as his *frau* and as a *mamm* for Lizzie and Martha. Was there shame in that?

There was no shame, Ernest reminded himself—except the community didn't see things that way. What they saw was a man jilted by a beautiful woman. Furthermore, she had jumped the fence rather than marry him. It would have been better for him to have never made a move for Susanna's affections, than to have her reject him for such a lowly option. He would never regain his former high standing in the community, but somehow he must try. In the meantime, the risk he had taken for Susanna's sake had gotten him into deep water. Could any further risk make things worse? He would speak with Deacon Herman again this morning, regardless of the cost.

Ernest tightened his grip on the reins as Deacon Herman's place came into view. Even Gambit perked up his ears a bit. Maybe there was hope in his morning errand. As low as he felt, even the smallest expression of sympathy for his cause from Deacon Herman would be like a fresh breeze on a hot summer day.

Ernest pulled in Deacon Herman's driveway and parked his buggy beside the barn. He had Gambit tied to the hitching ring when Deacon Herman appeared in the barn doorway.

Deacon Herman greeted him. "I thought I heard someone drive in."

"*Goot* morning," Ernest responded. "How is everything?"

Deacon Herman ignored the question to say, "If you're here to convince me to discipline the Miller family because Susanna's helping her *mamm* during the week, it's not going to work. At least when she's there, she dresses Amish and wears her *kapp* around the family. I'd say we'd best leave things the way they are."

Ernest stood in stunned silence before he sputtered, "But this is so wrong, so out of whack, so, so, so, ungodly. How can you stand there and tell me otherwise?"

"Be careful there," Deacon Herman chided. "You've already over-reached with your visit to Bishop Mark. It's an undeserved blessing for you that Bishop Enos didn't require a church confession for that stunt."

"A stunt!" Ernest exclaimed. "How can you say that? I was only doing my duty."

Deacon Herman grinned. "I think your desire for a beautiful *frau* like Susanna is clouding your eyes, Ernest. The Scriptures warn against such an attitude, and you should take the holy words to heart. All beauty is vain and deceitful when the heart isn't right. Susanna had set her heart on the *Englisha* world where her real *mamm* came from, and there's nothing any of us can do about that. Ralph has repented to the Lord and the church for his past sins, and there's no sense in adding to his sorrow. That's what would have happened if Susanna had married you and jumped the fence afterward. Actions have consequences, and Ralph understands that. Maybe our pride would have been too great if we had succeeded? We might think others can sin willfully like Ralph did and have everything turn out well. You have to be honest, Ernest. Would that not be the lesson our young people learned if Susanna had turned out the way all of us wished she had? So leave the final judgment of Susanna in the Lord's hand, because you need to get on with your life. That's my word for you. We have plenty of unwed sisters in the community who would take your hand in marriage. Even with the embarrassment you've made out of yourself. Visit one of them this morning and you can have that wedding this fall. How about that?" Deacon Herman reached over to slap Ernest on the back. "Isn't it time your daughters had a real *mamm* and you had a *frau* instead of your sister to take care of your house? Katherine has done a great job, I'm sure, but the Lord's gift to a man is a *frau*, not a sister." Deacon Herman's hand came down in another solid whack. "How about it, Ernest? Shall I visit a woman with you, and speak a *goot* word on your behalf?"

Ernest choked and tried to speak, but the words stuck.

Deacon Herman laughed. "I see you're overcome with the weight and depth of my wisdom. At least that's a *goot* sign, I think."

"I…I…this is such a great shame," Ernest managed. "I cannot see—"

"Save your words for later," Deacon Herman interrupted. "You might need them. Shall we talk about whom you should visit this morning?" When Ernest didn't answer, Deacon Herman continued. "So let's see—there are the widows Laura and Hannah. They would both be busy this morning, but I suppose they'd have time for a few moments with you, or—"

"I can make up my own mind," Ernest snapped. He drew himself erect. "I was quite able to woo Naomi, I'll remind you. Has everyone forgotten that I was once married and fathered two children? They are both *goot* and decent little girls."

"They are four and three years old," Deacon Herman said with a straight face. "I'd say you have a ways to go before you can crow about your daughters as decent church members. There's still their *rumspringa* ahead, you know."

"My girls will not jump the fence into the *Englisha* world or even think about it." Ernest glared. "I will see to that."

"I hope you're right," Deacon Herman said. "But we all fail sometimes. You thought you wouldn't fail with Susanna. Why else would you have taken such wild risks? But I heard you never achieved an engagement with Susanna…that she never did agree to marry you. Is this not true?"

Ernest stared off into the distance. This conversation had gone on long enough, and he dared not say anything more that he'd regret.

"Maybe I can help with your next marriage proposal," Deacon Herman offered. "I don't mean that as an insult. I'm here to help whenever a member needs aid."

Ernest turned to go. "Thanks," he muttered. "But I'd best be going."

Without a backward glance, Ernest untied Gambit and climbed back in his buggy. He was off with a shake of the lines.

"The best to you," Deacon Herman shouted after him.

Ernest nodded, but he didn't look in Deacon Herman's direction. His humiliation had been enough for one morning, and Deacon Herman knew it. He wouldn't live this down for an awful long time—unless he took drastic steps. For one thing, he was not about to visit either of the widows. Desperate as either of them might be for a husband, their noses would be high in the air at the moment and not likely to come down anytime soon. Deacon Herman should know that. No, he wouldn't visit either of them, or accept Deacon Herman's offer of help. He could imagine how that conversation would go.

"Ernest is still in *goot* standing with the church," Deacon Herman would inform either of the two women. "You can have confidence that the community will soon forget how he has behaved himself recently. So trust me when I say that Ernest will make a decent husband—if you choose to wed him."

No, he would not take that route. That was one final humiliation he would not subject himself to.

Ernest shook the reins and turned east. He had made up his mind. The situation had become desperate, and he didn't care whom he married. With Susanna gone it didn't matter. He would forget Susanna. He would forget how close he had come to a marriage with her. He wanted this nightmare to end. He wanted no more risk, and only one woman in the community carried no risk.

Emma Yutzy. Ernest groaned. *Yah*, that would be the final humiliation, but at least the woman loved him. That would comfort a man's soul, and he needed his soul comforted. And Emma would care for Lizzie and Martha. Not the way Susanna would have, but *goot* enough. The two girls would have a *mamm*, and he would have a *frau* in the house.

Ernest set his beard straight forward and shook the reins. Gambit increased the pace, and ten minutes later they were at Emma's driveway. Ernest turned in, and the buggy bounced as one wheel hit the ditch, but he didn't notice. His gaze was fixed on the front porch, where the swing moved slowly in the morning breeze. Someone had been there moments before. Likely Emma. Had she anticipated his visit?

That wasn't possible, Ernest told himself. He had only decided to come here moments before, and Deacon Herman had mentioned nothing about Emma this morning. Or did Deacon Herman pull some trick on him when he had neglected to mention Emma? Ernest sighed and pulled up to the barn, where he climbed out to tie Gambit. He had been outfoxed to the last, it appeared. But what did it matter? He had best eat his humble pie and get it over with.

With slow steps he approached the front door and knocked. Thankfully Emma didn't answer. He didn't want to see her at the moment.

Emma's *mamm*, Sarah, greeted him. "*Goot* morning." Her head tilted sideways as if to question his arrival.

"Ah, could I, perhaps if it was convenient this morning, see Emma?" Ernest stammered.

Sarah's face brightened. "Of course. So that's why Emma went up the stairs in such haste. I thought something had frightened her, but she must have been expecting you."

"I…" Ernest began, but gave up. Sarah wouldn't believe him anyway. "*Yah*," he said. "She probably was."

Sarah turned almost giddy. "Do you want to wait in the living room or out on the swing?"

"The swing is fine," Ernest said.

Sarah held the front door open for a few moments longer as if she couldn't believe he was actually there. "I didn't know you had an arrangement with Emma," she called after him.

I didn't, Ernest almost said. He forced a smile instead, and the front door swung slowly on its hinges. Sarah had vanished.

The moments ticked past as Ernest waited. He pushed the swing with one foot, and the chains creaked in protest. He would not take this much longer, he told himself. Emma had better appear soon. Ten minutes later he was still there when Emma appeared in a Sunday dress.

"Shall I?" Emma motioned toward the swing. "Or would you rather walk in the yard?"

"Sit," Ernest muttered. "Did you know I was coming?" He glared at her.

Emma sat down and smoothed her dress. "I'm not sure how to answer that, Ernest. I had prayed earnestly for some time now, about…" She paused. "I prayed about what my heart desired, and I've spoken with others about this matter and sought counsel. I've laid out my heart in the Lord's presence. I've asked that all would turn out as the Lord willed." Emma lowered her head. "Forgive my boldness, but I had hoped this moment would come, but I did not know for sure that it would. How is one to know for sure what the Lord decides?" She raised her head. "But I am overjoyed that you're here."

Ernest shifted on the swing, and the chains groaned above them.

"I can get you something to eat." Emma glanced at him. "It's almost lunchtime."

Ernest took the leap. "Maybe I will stay for lunch."

A hint of a smile crept across Emma's face. "We can talk perhaps afterward?"

Ernest studied her face for a few moments before he reached over to take one of Emma's hands in his. She took a sharp breath, but didn't pull her hand back.

"Emma," he began.

"*Yah*." Her voice was steady.

"There isn't much time," he said, "or I would make this more proper and all, but would you be my *frau*? Would you say the wedding vows with me this fall? See, Lizzie and Martha need a *mamm*, and I need a *frau* in the house. I know that Susanna—"

"I will, Ernest," Emma interrupted. "The answer is *yah*, a thousand times *yah*. You don't know how I've prayed and longed for this day. On my knees I have wept before the Lord with my desire to mother your children, and to…" Emma looked away. "To love you, Ernest. I gladly accept your offer."

"Then we have much to speak about after lunch." Ernest settled back in the swing without letting go of Emma's hand. Slowly they swung in the breeze. "Did you speak with Deacon Herman?" Ernest finally asked.

Emma didn't even blush. "Was his recommendation for me?" A big smile filled her face. "He's a *goot* man, that deacon is."

Chapter Thirty-Eight

The late spring twilight was still hanging heavy on the horizon when Joey arrived at home.

His mother greeted him. "You're home early."

Joey chuckled. "For a Saturday night, I suppose so."

"Were you with Susanna?" his mother asked.

"No." Joey sighed and sat down on the couch. "I'm taking things slow."

"Is she doing okay over at the Osseos'?" Joey's father asked, setting aside his folder of papers. "We haven't seen her around here lately."

Joey grimaced. "Susanna hasn't asked to come, and I haven't pushed the point. Like I said, I'm going slowly."

"But if you like the girl," Langford insisted, "there's no sense in waiting around."

"I don't want to lose her," Joey said. "That's for sure."

"I don't think that's going to happen," Langford declared, picking up his folder again.

"She's a wonderful girl," Beatrice added.

"That she is," Joey said, staring at the ceiling.

"Well, there's plenty of time," Beatrice continued. "You still have law school to finish."

"What if I don't want plenty of time?" Joey replied. "Maybe I want to marry the girl now?"

His parents glanced at each other.

"I thought you were moving slowly," Langford said.

"That's because of her, not me. I don't think she should be rushed. But if it were up to me, we'd be off on our honeymoon by summer."

"Well," Beatrice said, "in that case, ask her. Wives have gone along to law school before. It's difficult but doable."

"You should be telling all this to Susanna, not us," Langford said.

Joey turned to his mother. "So what would you do, Mom? Or more to the point, what would you want done if you were in Susanna's shoes?"

Beatrice thought for a moment. "I think the girl likes you, but she's afraid. What to do in that case? Well, tenderness and gentleness are always in order. Her heart has been bruised by what happened between her and her father, and that strange marriage attempt you told us about. She does come from another world, but underneath all that Susanna is not unlike most other women. I'd say I wouldn't mind a declaration of intentions, but without pressure."

"Like the four years I waited for you," Langford got in edgewise.

Beatrice gave him a smile. "I was worth the wait, wasn't I?"

"Did she really make you wait four years, Dad?" Joey asked.

Langford chuckled and busied himself with his file folder.

"Don't mind your father, Joey," Beatrice said. "I fell into his hand like a ripe fruit."

Joey joined in his parents' laughter. "Sometimes I can't believe I snuck a cell phone into an Amish home."

"You are a very naughty boy," Beatrice chided. "No wonder the girl's in love with you."

"You want to tell us the story?" Langford asked.

"There's not much to it," Joey told him. "Cell phones are a big taboo with the Amish, and I just left one under a tree for Susanna to pick up."

Langford whistled. "Real cloak-and-dagger stuff."

"Let's just say there has been intrigue," Joey said. "And I've even faced down bearded Amish men."

"With all that effort, I'm sure things will work out," Beatrice said.

Langford nodded. "I think you've set your heart on this girl, and there's little that can stop you now."

Joey grinned and headed to his room. All he knew was that he wanted to see Susanna tonight, and he wanted to ask her if she would marry him. He wanted to see her beautiful face light up with hope and love. He wanted to hear her say, *I love you, Joey.*

Joey paced his room until he noticed the full moon. It rose over the horizon outside of his bedroom window, and he stopped and stared. The full globe seemed to inch upward. Joey pulled himself away, deciding he would see Susanna tonight. Her duties would soon be over for the day, even with a full slate of guests. Rosalyn wouldn't mind the intrusion at this hour unless Susanna had already retired. If she had, he would leave again without Susanna's knowledge. More than likely, though, Susanna would still be up, stirred by the same moon he had seen and conflicted with the same emotions.

Joey hurried outside. He tossed an "I'll be back soon" over his shoulder at his parents.

He drove rapidly toward Canton. Most of the lights on Main Street were in his favor, and he ran through the last one just after it turned yellow. With a nervous glance around, he again saw the full glory of the moon. He dimmed his headlights on the empty road and sped on.

Moments later he turned into the Osseos' lane to park in the only available parking space. Vehicles were everywhere, and the low voices of Rosalyn's guests came from the shadowed pond behind the small line of poplar trees. Everyone apparently was still awake, but so much the better. Susanna would be astir, and if the pond was the center of attention, Susanna might agree to a walk by the water's edge. They could meander to the other side on the footpath circling the pond.

Joey walked slowly up to the office area, where Rosalyn looked up in surprise from her desk. "I was just finishing the bookkeeping for the night. We are full to the hilt as usual." She gave him a pensive look. "But why are you here?"

"To see Susanna, of course." Joey glanced around, but she was nowhere to be seen.

Rosalyn studied him for a moment before her gaze drifted toward Susanna's room in the back of the house. "I'll tell her you're here." Rosalyn disappeared down the hallway and came back moments later to say, "She'll be right out."

Joey shifted from foot to foot until Susanna appeared.

"Hi," he greeted her. "Sorry for the interruption at this time of the night, but the moon is full, and it's lovely. Want to go for a walk around the pond?"

"You came over for that?" Susanna asked.

"I came over to see you," Joey said.

Susanna hesitated only a moment. "Sure, let's go." She took Joey's arm, and he led the way outside.

He glanced back to Rosalyn, who gave him an encouraging wink. She must have figured out his intention—*Just like a woman,* he thought. Well, it was good to have one person on his side.

"It's beautiful out here," Susanna said as they came to a stop beyond the first of the poplars lining the pond.

Their view was unobstructed across the pond and toward the horizon beyond. Faint forms of guests were outlined on lawn chairs near the water's edge and on blankets spread out on the ground.

Joey took her hand and slowly led the way around the pond on the east side.

"We've been busy today. All the cottages and rooms are full," Susanna said, as if the information were extremely urgent.

"I'm sure Rosalyn's grateful she has you to help," Joey said. His palms were beginning to sweat.

They were both silent for a while, and then Susanna asked, "How are your parents? I haven't seen them for days."

Joey chuckled. "Oh, my mom is as feisty as always. I had a nice talk with them tonight about my future...and law school."

Susanna's hand tightened in his. "Will you visit home often? I mean, after you leave."

"When I can, I suppose," he allowed. "Law school is pretty intense."

Susanna looked up at him with a sad smile. "You'll come home all smart and be a real-life lawyer. That will make the sacrifice worth it, I suppose. Nothing good comes without pain, they say. I mean, look at what I've had to face in the last months."

"Has it been worth it?" Joey gently pulled on her hand and they came to a stop near the far side of the pond.

Susanna smiled. "*Yah*, every moment of it. Part of it was finding you, Joey. It's been one of the best parts. You've been a *goot* friend."

Her long hair shimmered in the moonlight, and the shadows deepened beneath her eyes. Joey reached up to touch her face, and Susanna didn't flinch.

He stood motionless. Did he dare? Susanna didn't seem to object to his closeness, but perhaps she had never been kissed before. She nestled against him, but said nothing.

Susanna was too tender in his arms, too injured, too trusting—too *something*. He couldn't put his finger on what. He simply held her.

"You are an angel," she finally said.

"I'm not," he objected.

She laughed. "We could go around this point all night."

"Then I'm an angel," he agreed.

They stood there until Joey tugged on her hand and led the way back around the other side of the pond. Susanna followed close beside him, matching her step to his.

He would claim this woman someday as his wife. Joey promised himself. He would accomplish what that Amish man couldn't do. He was just sorry it wouldn't be tonight.

Chapter Thirty-Nine

A month later, Susanna stepped out of the car and waved as Rosalyn drove out of the Millers' driveway. Stillness settled over the barnyard, broken only by the soft bellows of the cows as they made their way from the barn to the pasture.

Susanna straightened her *kapp* and headed for the front door. As she entered, she heard the rise and fall of soft voices from the kitchen as the family ate breakfast. Her arrival must have been noted, but these regular visits of hers had become fully engrained in the Millers' routine and needed no special attention. She was part of the family again—in a limited way.

Daett called from the kitchen. "*Goot* morning, Susanna. Come and eat some of *Mamm's* delicious oatmeal. There's still a little left."

"I've already eaten," Susanna hollered back. She hung her coat on the hook behind the living room stove and entered the kitchen.

"Sit down at least." *Mamm* gave her a big smile. "*Daett* was just ready to read the morning's devotions."

Susanna nodded and greeted her brothers as she pulled out a kitchen chair. They responded with mumbled greetings. *Daett* gave her a kind look, after which he opened the huge family Bible and began to read. "'The Spirit of the Lord is upon me, because he hath anointed me to preach the gospel to the poor; he hath sent me to heal the brokenhearted…'" *Daett's* voice broke for a second. "'To preach deliverance…'"

There were tears on *Daett's* face. Had there been a family quarrel this morning? None of her brothers appeared upset, and *Mamm* wasn't troubled. Why, then, was *Daett* in tears while he read the Scriptures? There seemed no clear answer as *Daett* finished and smiled at her again. "That is a *goot* Scripture," he said to no one in particular. "Let us pray."

Chairs and benches scraped on the hardwood floor, and the Miller family knelt. Susanna missed this tradition and always would. Neither the Macalister family nor the Osseos practiced such an ancient custom. She still knelt to pray at night in her room, and hopefully someday she would kneel with her husband in prayer—whoever he might be.

When *Daett* called out "Amen," Susanna sat up with everyone else and *Mamm* started directing the boys on their chores. The boys responded slowly while Susanna cleared the table.

Minutes later Henry and James told her to have a *goot* day as they went out the washroom door to the barn. Susanna gave them a quick wave and reached over to tickle Tobias's chin.

Noah came down from getting ready, and Susanna asked him, "How are things going at school?"

The boy's eyes shone as he said, "We studied horses yesterday, and today we're going to write about them."

As he headed off for school, Susanna turned to *Daett*, still seated at the table. His tears were gone, but a pensive look still filled his face. Little Tobias took the moment to scurry past his *daett* and head toward the living room. *Daett's* gaze followed the boy, and then his eyes turned back to Susanna. "I have something planned today that we need to do."

The tears glistened again on *Daett's* cheeks. *Mamm* must have noticed because she stepped away from the stove to give *Daett* a quick hug. With a pat on *Daett's* shoulder, *Mamm* went into the living room. Susanna and her *daett* were alone by design. *Daett* had requested this from *Mamm*, but for what reason? A thousand thoughts raced through Susanna's mind as *Daett* studied the kitchen tabletop.

Was *Daett* ready to propose another way she could come back to the community?

Had another Amish man made a proposal of marriage that *Daett* thought might lure her in again?

Did *Daett* know about Joey, how close they had become since she had left? Did *Daett* plan to warn against the obvious?

Or maybe the community had lost its patience with her having such easy access to her family each week. That would be the worse option of them all.

Susanna waited until *Daett* cleared his throat and looked up again. "*Mamm* knows where we're going, and she agrees," *Daett* said, standing to his feet. "Come, daughter. We have some traveling ahead of us today."

Daett grabbed his coat in the washroom, and Susanna retrieved hers from the living room.

"Wait while I get the horse," *Daett* said once they were near the barn.

Moments later *Daett* reappeared with his hands on Charlie's bridle. "I thought we'd drive your old horse today," *Daett* said, his smile thin.

Susanna held the buggy shafts up for him and fastened the tugs on her side. *Daett* had something special in mind. She wanted to ask what, but perhaps it was best to wait and see.

They climbed in the buggy, and *Daett* drove out of the driveway and took a left on Highway 17. From there he took Ritchie Road north until they reached Route 812 toward Heuvelton. Susanna waited while the miles rolled past slowly, and *Daett* finally began to speak. "This is difficult for me today, Susanna. I have a serious confession to make. But before I tell you, I want to say again that my sins lay heavy upon me, and yet you have brought much joy to my life. I can never express fully how much I love you. I didn't know that such sorrow and happiness could live together in a human heart."

"I'm sorry I didn't turn out the way you hoped," Susanna whispered.

"It's not that!" *Daett* shook his head. "I was out of my place to plan your life like I did. I added pride to the sins that already were laid to my account, and yet I feel the Lord had mercy upon me. I am unworthy of such kindness, Susanna. I want to say that I have not been the man I should have been."

"*Daett*, please." Susanna reached over to loop her arm in his.

He fell silent again and didn't speak until they reached the edge of Heuvelton. "I want to take you down by the river's edge, Susanna," *Daett* said. "I once brought you here when you were very small, but I haven't dared come back with you since. I didn't want you to remember the place."

"The river's edge?" Susanna held her breath as *Daett* brought Charlie to a stop. The reins hung limply in his hands. "But I do know this place, *Daett*. I've come here often. There is nothing to be ashamed of, unless…"

Daett looked away. "*Yah*, you already know, I see. Or maybe you can guess." *Daett* groaned. "What a fool I have been to think I could run from the past. The Lord will have none of it, I see. All that was broken must be healed regardless of the pain we suffer. But come." He climbed down from the buggy and came around to offer his hand to Susanna.

She lowered herself down the buggy steps. With her hand still on *Daett*'s arm, she followed him to the swift flowing water's edge.

"I use to bring your *mamm* here," *Daett* said, the pain strong on his face. "I need to tell you this, Susanna, and some other things also."

Susanna waited as the moments passed. *Daett* seemed to have difficulty breathing, and Susanna slid her arm around his waist and pulled him close.

"Your *mamm* could also play the *Englisha* music," *Daett* said. "I'm sorry I haven't told you this before, but I had hoped you—"

"*Daett*, please," Susanna begged again. "You don't have to do this to yourself. I'm okay."

"These things must be said." *Daett* fixed his eyes on the river. "I have erred greatly in not saying them before. I have wished often to hear your *mamm* play again, and now I have a daughter who loves music, but for me this cannot be." *Daett* glanced toward her. "I hope you understand that. I have no plans to jump the fence with you. I cannot listen to such music or allow it in my life, even if you play like your *mamm* did. I only wish to make things right with you, Susanna, and they will not be right if I am not honest." *Daett* paused to catch his breath. "Come," he said. "We have a ways to travel yet."

"Where are we going?" Susanna asked on the walk back to the buggy.

"You will see when we get there," *Daett* said, and would say no more.

He had explained some things, but there must be much more. *Daett* wouldn't have been so disturbed this morning over the revelations he had given her so far.

Only the beat of Charlie's hooves on the pavement filled the buggy as *Daett* drove north on Route 812 toward Ogdensburg. Each mile deepened the somber look on *Daett's* face.

"Can't you tell me where we're going?" Susanna finally asked him.

"I was up here last week," *Daett* said, as if that answered things. "They agreed to see you. I can't say that I would have blamed them if they had refused, but they are more righteous than I am."

Susanna waited, but *Daett* didn't speak again until they had reached the outskirts of Ogdensburg. "I have hidden something from you all these years." *Daett* turned down a side street and lapsed into silence again.

"You had best just say it, *Daett*," Susanna said. "Whatever this is, I will still love you like before. Haven't I already proven that point?"

"*Yah*, you have," *Daett* agreed.

Susanna was ready to probe again, but *Daett* said, "Your *Englisha* grandparents are still alive, Susanna. That's where I'm taking you. I made an arrangement with them all those years back when I took you into my home that they would not try to contact you or interfere with your upbringing in any way. They were reluctant, but Mindy had told them that if she ever passed, they should place you in my care if I wished to have you—which I did. They agreed to my conditions out of respect for their daughter's instructions and for the ways of our people."

Daett choked up and Susanna waited. Her chest burned with fear and delight. A strange joy that was mingled with terror filled her. Her *mamm's* parents were still alive?

"You never told me." Susanna's words rang in the buggy.

Tears trickled down *Daett's* cheeks. "Now you see what my greatest sin has been, daughter. I thought it was when I sinned with your *mamm*, but this has only made things worse. I don't ask that you forgive me, but you need to know. Somehow I must make right what little I can—*if* I can."

Susanna could scarcely believe it. She had *Englisha* grandparents! A woman who was her *mamm's mamm* was still alive!

"This is the house," *Daett* said. He brought Charlie to a stop, and the reins dangled in his hand. "This is the same place I came to all those years ago. This is where your *mamm* would bring me in my *rumspringa* time."

"What are their names?" Susanna asked.

"Hunter and Alice," *Daett* said. "They are *goot* people. They have always been very *goot* people."

"And they want to see me?" She felt cold all over. She suddenly wished Joey was with her, but that wasn't possible.

"*Yah*, daughter," *Daett* said. "They were overjoyed when I came last week. They wanted to drive out and meet you at once, but I begged them to allow me this moment. I wanted to bring you, to atone in a small way for what I have done." *Daett's* eyes had filled with tears again.

Susanna gathered herself together and reached for *Daett's* hand. "I will go see them," she told him. "Take me to my grandparents, my own flesh and blood."

"*Yah*," *Daett* said, and his eyes shone as with a bright light.

Chapter Forty

Susanna didn't move as *Daett* knocked on the front door of the fancy *Englisha* home. The ground under her feet was still moving in circles. It was so hard to fathom. Her *Englisha mamm's* parents were still alive, and *Daett* had known all these years. It made perfect sense from *Daett's* point of view. He had been worried she would be drawn into the *Englisha* world if she had regular contact with *Englisha* relatives. But that had happened anyway, and now *Daett* was seeking to make amends.

Susanna jumped when she heard a man's voice come from the side yard. "I thought I heard a buggy drive up."

"Hunter," *Daett* said. He held his hat in his hand.

The man came around the corner of the house. He stepped forward and nodded to *Daett*, but quickly turned to Susanna. He hesitated in front of her and seemed to search for words. "Is this who I think it is?" he finally asked, extending his hand.

Susanna reached for his hand. The grip was gentle and kind. This, then, was her grandfather.

"Susanna," he said. "Mindy's girl." Tears filled his eyes. "Please give me a moment while I fetch Alice. We were expecting you

today, but we didn't know when." He glanced back the way he had
come. "Alice is still in the garden. She—" He paused. "On second
thought, come! Let me take you to her." He turned to lead the way.
Susanna's knees trembled, but she followed close behind the two
men. When they rounded the corner of the house, an older woman
was kneeling in the dirt. She rose slowly to her feet and turned to
face the three of them. Susanna held back, half-hidden behind the
two men. All of this was so sudden and awkward. How did one see
one's grandmother for the first time as an adult?

"Alice," Hunter said. "They have come."

Alice seemed to waver, and Hunter reached out to take her arm.
"Alice," he repeated. "Susanna is here."

"I know," Alice said. She took a step forward and Susanna forced
herself to move.

Alice searched Susanna's face. "My granddaughter. Is it really
you?" Alice reached out her hand and then drew Susanna into a
hug. Susanna held on as the years seemed to crash over each other
and break on some distant shore. She was a little girl again and seeing Grandma for the first time, only she was all grown-up and tow-
ering above the elderly woman in her arms.

"I'm dreaming. It is Mindy, is it not, Hunter? She looks just like
her."

Hunter just smiled as Alice continued, taking Susanna by the
hand. "Come sit, dear, and tell me all about yourself. There is a garden bench over there. Hunter and I sit here in the summer evenings.
I can't tell you how many times we've wondered aloud about you,
hoping you've been having a happy life."

Susanna was at a loss for words, but it didn't seem to matter to
Alice. "Let me look at you again." Alice studied Susanna's face and
reached up to move a few wisps of hair on Susanna's forehead. "You
really do look like her," Alice whispered, her face aglow. "You *are*

Mindy's daughter." Alice looked skyward and prayed, "Oh, dear Lord, thank You for this day. Thank You that I have lived to see her this side of eternity."

Daett and Hunter left them alone, and stayed at a distance.

"You're all grown-up!" Alice said as she studied Susanna. "You were so tiny when we saw you last, your little fingers curled around mine." Alice's face clouded. "Oh, how we wished to see you again and again…but your father—"

"I know," Susanna interrupted. "*Daett* is very sorry for what he did."

"Sweet girl." Alice pressed Susanna's hand tightly. "You are welcome in our world, but we respected our daughter's and your father's wishes, difficult as that was. I think the years aged me faster because of that decision, but I never felt we could back away from it." Alice's face brightened. "I prayed often that this day would come, and now it has."

"I'm glad this day has arrived too," Susanna said with a slight laugh. "I'm still trying to get my head around the fact that you even exist. *Daett* never told me."

"Now, just think," Alice said. "We have the rest of our lives to make up for all those lost years." Alice gave Susanna a tender look. "You'll be able to come often, won't you? I understand you're no longer Amish."

"No, I'm not." Susanna dropped her gaze to the ground.

"Come." Alice stood to her feet. "There's no sense in being sorrowful on a day like this. Shall I show you the house?"

Alice didn't wait for an answer and led Susanna by the hand in through the back door. As they walked through the kitchen and dining room, the massive living room opened up in front of them with a vast expanse of ceiling. Susanna drew in a quick breath as she took in a beautiful antique piano near a stone fireplace.

Alice's gaze followed Susanna's eyes. "Can you play?" Alice asked.

Susanna approached the piano and pulled up the small bench. She seated herself and ran her fingers slowly over the keys. The sound trembled and hung for long moments in the heights of the ceiling. With greater assurance, Susanna played faster and yet more gently. She didn't stop even when the front door opened and she saw *Daett* and Hunter out of the corner of her eye. *Daett* would have to think what he wished. She was no longer his little Amish girl, and he might as well see who she had become. And had *Daett* not spoken of how her *Englisha mamm* played music, likely on this very piano?

Susanna's fingers stumbled at the thought, but she recovered herself. With renewed zeal she allowed the music to flow out of her. The sorrow of the past months, the pain of what had been left behind, the agony of impossible dreams, and the look in Joey's eyes that night he held her hand in the moonlight at the Osseos' pond. They all seemed to melt into one exquisite symphony.

Susanna felt hope enter her heart and let the emotion sweep through her. If there was sorrow in the world, there was also joy. If there was pain, the Lord had also supplied an escape. Could she not walk the road ahead of her, no matter where it led? Maybe *Daett* had brought her here today for that reason, even if he didn't fully understand why himself. Thankfulness filled her heart as the notes slowly died away. Susanna turned around with trembling hands to see Alice and Hunter both beaming. Even *Daett* had tears streaming down his face.

"You are the Lord's angel," Alice said. "How many years has it been since I heard such music?" Alice wrapped Susanna in a tight embrace and didn't let go for a long time.

Daett finally interrupted them when he loudly cleared his throat. "We have a long way back home, and we'd best be going now," he said.

"So soon?" Alice protested.

"Susanna will come again," *Daett* said. "She will come without me, of course." *Daett* hung his head. "We really have to go."

"You are welcome here anytime, Ralph," Hunter said.

Daett nodded but said nothing.

Alice and Susanna hugged again, and then Susanna turned to Hunter and gave him a hug as well. "I will come again," she said to both of them.

"Thanks for bringing her, Ralph," Alice said. "I can't thank you enough."

"I am shamed greatly," *Daett* muttered from halfway down the sidewalk.

Susanna hurried to catch up. Already *Daett* had begun to change from what he had been this morning. Did he regret his decision to bring her here? If he did, the deed was already done. He had opened up the way for her into a new life in ways even she could not fully understand. For that she would forever be grateful.

"Thank you for this day," Susanna said as they climbed in the buggy.

Daett hung his head and drove down the street without an answer. Susanna kept her silence. If *Daett* wished to mourn further she would respect him, but she was thankful for what he had given her.

"You play even better than she did," *Daett* finally said.

"Why didn't you marry Mindy?" Susanna asked, and wished at once that she hadn't. She already knew the answer, and the pain that flashed across *Daett*'s face cut deep into her heart.

"Following the Lord is a higher calling than human love." *Daett* kept his gaze fixed on the road ahead. "I made my choice, but I should not have tried to make yours."

"I also seek to follow the Lord," Susanna whispered.

Daett's face darkened, but he said nothing. There would always be a gulf between them. She was not to blame that the bridge to cross had not been built. Perhaps such a thing could never be, but at least they were at peace with each other.

Daett looked at her and managed to smile as if in confirmation of Susanna's thoughts. "Do you plan to marry him?" he asked as they neared the outskirts of Heuvelton.

"He hasn't asked…yet," Susanna said.

Daett pulled back on the reins and slowed Charlie for the town's first stoplight. "I might as well make all my apologizes today," *Daett* said. "So, *yah*, I'm also sorry about Ernest and the part I played in that mess."

Susanna glanced at him. "It's in the past now, and I'm thankful you let me keep in touch with the family. It lessens the pain."

Daett didn't say anything for a moment. "You will always be my daughter," he finally said.

Susanna reached over and took his hand.

Chapter Forty-One

As planned, Joey left for law school the next term. As the weeks sped by, Susanna was able to keep herself occupied with work at the bed-and-breakfast, plus she had taken on a few sewing jobs from *Englisha* women who either needed something mended or wanted a dress made from a fancy new pattern.

She also continued sewing for herself and now had several nice, modest dresses from which to choose.

Tonight she chose carefully. Joey was home for a long weekend and wanted to take her out to dinner. Susanna browsed through her closet and picked out an emerald green dress she had made just last week. She slipped it on and paused in front of the full-length mirror. A faint blush spread over her face. Not that long ago she wouldn't have dared more than a brief glance at herself in the mirror, even with a new dress. The glass above the dresser in the old farmhouse might have glared back at her.

Susanna looked away and then back again. She would be careful that pride didn't enter her heart even as she wore nice *Englisha* dresses, but she wished to appear her best tonight. Ever since Joey's call, she had felt butterflies in her stomach. One thing she had requested of Joey—that supper be at Hunter and Alice's home in Ogdensburg.

"Whatever you work out is fine with me," Joey had said.

She had made the arrangement at once to the Whithuses' great delight. She wanted to be with Joey around family rather than at some fancy *Englisha* restaurant, and she couldn't take him home to *Mamm* and *Daett's*.

For such a long time she had repeated over and over to others and to herself that Joey was just a friend, but now she had to admit to herself that he had become more than that.

Susanna blushed into the mirror at the thought. Joey was up to something. There had been a special light in his eyes when he was home for his most recent long weekend. It was the same gleam Joey had that moonlit night when they walked hand in hand around the Osseos' pond. That night she wasn't ready for Joey's words. Tonight she was ready.

A hunger for new horizons had crept over her these past weeks. *Daett's* revelation about her grandparents, the happy hours she had spent at their home in Ogdensburg since then, and the continued days spent helping *Mamm* had only added to the urge.

Henry had driven Charlotte Yoder home from the hymn singing just last month. The two were a charming couple, and *Mamm* had glowed with happiness when she shared the news. Such a life had been planned for Susanna, but it was not to be. She was glad for Henry and Charlotte, as she was for Ernest and Emma. Their wedding had occurred late in the wedding season—a hurried affair, no doubt—but Emma was now Ernest's *frau*. She, of course, hadn't been invited to the wedding, as she wouldn't be to any of the Amish weddings.

Things were the way they were, and she held no bitterness against the community. She was thankful she could freely go home during the week. That might change after she owned her own car, but then again, maybe not. Deacon Herman and Bishop Enos seemed to go as far out of their way as they could to make things easy for her, but her attendance at weddings would definitely be across the line. Maybe she could visit with Henry and Charlotte on the day before their wedding—once the date was set. *Mamm* and *Daett* would try to involve her the best they could.

Susanna eyed the mirror again.

"It's *goot* enough," she told the reflection.

Susanna opened the bedroom door and went out to the patio area, where several guests sat talking around a table.

"Hello everyone," she greeted them. She had checked all of them in earlier. "Everything okay?"

"Splendid!" one of the men exclaimed.

"Off with someone special?" the man's wife teased.

Susanna smiled shyly, nodded, and then hurried on. Joey was always on time and should be in the driveway by now. A quick glance out to the lane confirmed her suspicions.

Rosalyn stepped up beside her. "Off for a big date?" she asked.

"*Yah*, but I'm so sorry about leaving you alone for the evening!" Susanna exclaimed. "I really am. I should stay and—"

Rosalyn stopped her. "No, you've worked hard and you deserve this. Run along and forget all about Osseos' for the evening."

Susanna gave Rosalyn a long hug. "You have done so much for me."

Rosalyn pushed her away gently. "Go, dear. Joey's waiting."

Susanna nodded and headed up the driveway with slower steps. Joey didn't need to think she was overly eager, even when she wanted nothing more than for him to take her in his arms on sight.

"Hi there, beautiful," Joey's voice called out.

"Hi, handsome," she chirped.

Joey had stepped out of his car and came closer, his arms open. She rushed forward and allowed herself to fall into them. She pulled him close and rested her head on his shoulder. His arms closed snugly around her.

Delight flooded Joey's face when he peered down at her. "Now *that* was a welcome!" he pronounced.

"I've missed you so much," she whispered. "You are such a sight for sore eyes."

Joey laughed and held her at arm's length. "That would be true of you," he said, "and not me. You are lovely, dear, with a beauty only the Lord could have given you."

"Hush," Susanna told him, and then climbed in the car before he could open the door for her. He hesitated only a second before he hopped in the other side.

"Your grandparents' home in Ogdensburg, right?"

Susanna nodded. "Is that still okay? I mean…"

"It's fine." Joey's smile didn't fade as he backed up and drove out on Highway 68. "In fact, it's an excellent idea," he added. "As all your ideas are."

"Stop it," Susanna ordered, but Joey only grinned.

"Do we have a few moments before we have to arrive?" he asked.

Susanna glanced at the clock on his dashboard. "I guess so. I didn't give them an exact time."

"See?" Joey glowed. "You always know the perfect answer."

Susanna reached over to squeeze his hand. "So how's school going?"

Joey groaned. "Tough! As law school always is. Things only get worse, they say, but I've managed to keep my grades up. Couldn't disappoint Dad, you know."

"You couldn't disappoint yourself," she said with another squeeze of his hand. "You'll make it, I'm sure."

Joey smiled. "I hope so. Thanks for the confidence."

Silence settled in the car as they approached Canton. "Where are we going?" Susanna asked when Joey turned south instead of continuing north toward Ogdensburg.

"A little detour," he teased. "We won't be long."

Susanna looked out her window. She didn't dare look at Joey. Somehow she knew this was the night. How like Joey to tuck precious times into the spaces available. He had always been like this, from the time she first met him during her *rumspringa*. Joey had the patience and the touch of an angel.

"You've never flown away, though," she said out loud.

Joey gave her a strange look. "Say that again?"

"Just musing," she said, "about how wonderful you are. But I think your head would swell too much if I gave you all the details."

"I want to hear them." He pretended to pout, and Susanna laughed.

"You are an angel," she told him. "Remember? I've told you that before. But you're an angel who's never flown away. You're still with me."

He reached for her hand as the outskirts of Heuvelton appeared. "I'd like to always be with you, Susanna," he whispered. "I love you. You know that."

She nodded and looked away. No words would come at the moment, and Joey seemed to understand perfectly. Joey always did.

He pulled off the road at the right place and parked the car along the familiar riverbank. Joey climbed out and came around to open the door for her. Susanna took his hand, and together they walked to the edge of the bank and gazed across the river. Water splashed softly over the small rocks that were scattered in the shallow parts.

"I think of this as our place," Joey said, "and I wanted to bring you here now. We've been through so much…"

Susanna smiled up at him. "You don't have to say it."

He paused. "I've wanted to ask before...but you weren't ready, and I had law school to think about." He paused for a moment and laced one of her curls around his finger. "You have become such a part of my life, Susanna." He paused again and then drew her into another embrace. "The truth is, I can't wait until I'm through law school to know the answer to the biggest question I've ever asked anyone. Susanna Miller, will you be my wife? I love you with all my heart."

"Joey!" She reached up to touch his face.

"Will you?" he pleaded.

Susanna nodded through moist eyes. "But I don't deserve your love."

"You deserve the love of a prince...just like Cinderella."

"Kiss me, Joey," she said.

He hesitated, and tears glistened in his eyes. Without a word he drew her close, and Susanna closed her eyes. She didn't want to ever open them lest the angel fly away after all. Surely only an angel could fill her with such joy and happiness. Was this what it felt like to love? Why hadn't she dared to love him a long, long time ago?

Susanna opened her eyes. He was still there. The angel in her life was still at her side.

"Are you sure you know what you're getting into?" Susanna asked.

"Yes, I know," he said, placing his fingertips on her chin and lifting her face to his for another kiss.

Susanna dropped her gaze. "Joey, I want to go to law school with you."

"Law school?" Joey said, tilting his head.

Susanna smiled. "Not as a student, silly. As your wife. Can we get married when you come home at the end of this semester? Then I can return with you for the new semester."

"Of course. The sooner the better," Joey said, taking Susanna by the waist and lifting her gently in the air.

When her feet were back on the ground, she said, "Let's tell my grandparents. They'll be so excited."

Joey looked at his watch. "Yes, and I imagine they're wondering what became of us."

Susanna held Joey's hand as they walked back to the car and he helped her in. She took his hand again for the drive to Ogdensburg. Joey parked in the Whithuses' driveway, and Hunter and Alice met them at the front door.

"Welcome! We've been waiting for you," Hunter exclaimed.

"Thank you," Joey replied, following Hunter inside.

Susanna gave Alice a quick hug and whispered in her ear, "We have something to tell you."

"Oh?" Alice's face glowed.

Joey came close again, and slipped his arm around Susanna's shoulder. "Your lovely granddaughter has consented to be my wife. We'll marry at the end of the present school term."

Susanna clung to Joey as Hunter and Alice rushed forward with their congratulations. Afterward the table was laid out in the dining room, with the spread of food Alice had prepared. Baked potatoes, green beans, corn casserole, tossed salad, and layered cake for dessert.

They were seated with Joey by Susanna's side. She knew she could never be this happy again. It simply wasn't possible, and yet when she looked up into Joey's eyes, the years of joy stretched out in front of her and never seemed to stop.

Chapter Forty-Two

A special morning weeks later dawned without a cloud in the sky. A soft breeze blew across the Osseos' pond and stirred only the slightest of ripples on the water. Susanna stood in front of the full-length mirror with Rosalyn and Alice behind her.

"She's so beautiful," Alice whispered. "And the girl made the dress herself."

Susanna wanted to protest both points, but she couldn't bring herself to speak. The moment seemed too sacred for words. Here she was on her wedding day, and the blessing and the joy of the Lord filled her to overflowing. Such had been her happiness that she had dared take the dress pattern home to *Mamm* and ask for advice.

Mamm had raised her eyebrows and had given her the advice she wanted. But none of the elegant dress had been sewn at the Millers' home. There were limits to everything. The work had been done at Alice's house, where there was plenty of peace and quiet and music when Susanna needed to relax her tense nerves. The wedding dress must be perfect. Only her best effort would do.

Susanna stepped back from the mirror and relaxed every muscle in her body. She would soak in the moments of this day and store them away in her memory. If she lived for a hundred years she could never give thanks enough for what the Lord had given her. Joey's love had built up in her heart until it felt as if she would burst with joy.

"Come, we need to go," Rosalyn prodded. "The guests are here."

The guests, of course, didn't include *Mamm* and *Daett*. They could not attend their daughter's *Englisha* wedding. It was simply forbidden by the *ordnung*. Her spirits sank a little at the thought, but only for a moment. She understood her parents' position. At least Joey's parents were here. But *Daett* had given his blessing. For that she could also give thanks. She and Joey would stop in this afternoon at the Millers' place, before flying out the next day on their honeymoon to Paris. Joey had suggested the plan, as if he knew what moved her heart before she said the words. Paris! Only in her dreams as an Amish schoolgirl had she ever thought of Paris.

Rosalyn waved her hand in front of Susanna's face. "Back to earth, dear. Time to wed the handsome prince."

"And a prince he is," Alice agreed. "The Lord has blessed us more than we ever dared dream…"

Alice didn't finish the thought. Both Susanna and Rosalyn knew what Alice meant. At Rosalyn's suggestion, Susanna had asked if Hunter would lead her down the aisle. The question had brought a tear to her grandfather's eye, and he had said, "I would be greatly honored, Susanna."

What the big deal was, Susanna wasn't really sure. The Amish didn't walk anyone down the aisle at weddings, but she wasn't Amish any longer, even if the simple elegance of her wedding dress reflected her upbringing. Such things were not easily left behind, and neither did she want them to be.

"Coming," Susanna said. She followed the two women out of the bedroom and into the kitchen, where Hunter was waiting for them. His face lit up when they walked in.

"Isn't she beautiful?" Alice gushed.

"Absolutely angelic," Hunter said. He stepped closer to hold out his arm.

Susanna took his arm, and muttered softly, "I can't cry. I can't cry."

Rosalyn, who had tears in her own eyes, said, "That's okay, honey. We'll do the crying for you."

Behind them the young photographer had his camera up to his eye, getting shots of the whole scene. She must not pay him any attention, Susanna reminded herself. She was *Englisha* now, and there was no pride in her heart—only joy that she would be Joey's *frau*.

Rosalyn held the door open for them, and Hunter led the way outside into the bright sunlight. The faint sound of music echoed from the pond. That would be Joey's cousin Marisa, who had volunteered to play the piano for the wedding. Joey's parents were seated up front.

"She plays well," Hunter told Susanna, "but nothing like you."

Susanna smiled, and the tempo of the music changed. It was time for them to walk toward Joey, who stood waiting for his bride. The small group of guests stood and turned to watch them approach, with a smile on every face. Several of the couples were regular guests at the cottages who had been warned in advance of the wedding but had still booked the rooms. Rosalyn had invited them to attend the short ceremony, and all of the guests had accepted.

Susanna kept her gaze steady as they made their way toward Joey and the minister. Joey's face glowed with happiness, and Susanna pressed back the tears. To fill this man's life with joy was an honor she couldn't begin to comprehend.

"He sure loves you," Hunter whispered in Susanna's ear.

As they reached the end of their walk, Susanna reached out and took Joey's outstretched hand. The couple then turned to face Pastor Rosen. At home Bishop Enos would be standing in front of her, but she was now a new person in a new world. Her life with Joey would be greatly blessed by the Lord. She no longer doubted that for a moment.

Pastor Rosen cleared his throat and smiled. "I am honored," he said, "to attend this union in marriage today of two wonderful young people. I have known Joey all of his life, but Susanna not so well. Yet the Lord has known both of you since before you were born. It is to Him and before Him that you have come today to commit your lives as husband and wife." Pastor Rosen paused. "With that being said, the young couple has decided to read their own vows to each other. Joey, if you will, please."

Joey fixed his gaze on his bride and began. "I met you a long time ago, Susanna, and yet it seems like only yesterday. I've known almost since our first day together that I loved you, and yet the Lord saw fit to allow it to deepen and grow while we both waited for the right time to declare our love. I have spoken to you often of my love," Joey continued, "and I vow to you today to love you always, to think not of what is best for me, but what is best for us. I will seek to take my place as your husband in a way that fulfills your dreams and hopes, even your highest expectations. I will be there for you, in the good times, in the dark valleys, when things go well, and when they go badly. I will not say 'I said so,' even when I am right, and I will laugh at myself when I am wrong. I will always love you for what you are and for what you will become. I will never regret this day or what the Lord has given us, because He had led us together. For that, I promise, I will always be thankful."

Pastor Rosen turned to Susanna and nodded.

Susanna lifted her head and looked into Joey's eyes. There was no way she could speak right now. She had not known that Joey would say such things. Thankfully no one shifted on their feet or cleared their throat. Pastor Rosen's smile never dimmed as he waited.

After a few moments, she gathered her emotions and began to speak in a shaky voice. "You have been my angel, Joey. You have been there when I needed you, and often when I didn't know I did. You have read my heart well, and your touch has been the touch of the Lord. You have been His friend first, and for that I will always be grateful. You have loved Him before you loved me. I thank you for loving me, Joey, and I will always love you. I will always look up to you as the angel the Lord sent into my life to walk beside me as my husband. I will always reach for your hand when trouble comes. I will always think of you when I am in need of comfort. I will try to be the kind of wife you need, Joey, because you are a truly wonderful man."

Susanna lowered her head. That little speech sounded stupid next to Joey's *wunderbah* words, but it had come out of her heart. Pastor Rosen seemed pleased when she looked up to meet his gaze.

"Thank you, both of you," he said. "That was beautiful, and now for my little part." He grinned. "Do you, Joseph Delaney Macalister, take this woman, Susanna Miller, as your lawful wedded wife?"

"I do," Joey said, his voice firm.

Pastor Rosen turned to Susanna. "And do you, Susanna Miller, take this young man, Joseph Delaney Macalister, as your lawful wedded husband?"

"I do," Susanna said, her voice still shaking.

Pastor Rosen took both of their hands in his. "Then by virtue of the authority vested in me by the state of New York, I now pronounce you husband and wife before the Lord and these witnesses. May the Lord bless you greatly and keep you always in His divine care."

With that said, Pastor Rosen motioned for them to turn around. "It is my pleasure," he announced, "to introduce you to Mr. and Mrs. Joseph Delaney Macalister."

The brief ceremony over, the couple walked back down the aisle. For the next twenty minutes they accepted congratulations and tight hugs from loved ones and the guests who had attended.

When the time seemed right, after many well wishes, Joey took Susanna by the hand and led her to his car. The remaining guests crowded around them and threw rice as Joey quickly turned the car around and drove his bride out of the lane.

Once they were on the highway, Joey turned to Susanna and said, "You made the most beautiful bride I've ever seen."

"And you," she said without hesitation, "said the most wonderful vows. I'll never forget a word of what you said."

"You deserved them and then some," Joey said. He reached over for her hand. "I do love you, Mrs. Macalister."

Susanna closed her eyes. The wonder of the short wedding still filled her heart. She didn't want the moment to fade.

A few minutes later, Joey pulled into the Millers' driveway.

Susanna gasped at the sight before her. Everyone was out on the front porch in their Sunday best.

"Looks like we're in for a warm welcome," Joey said with a grin.

Susanna drew a long breath, and an idea rose in her mind. Could she dare ask this of Joey on their wedding day? Surely *Mamm* and *Daett* wouldn't refuse the request.

Susanna clutched Joey's arm as they came to a stop near the barn. "Will you do your new wife a tremendous favor?" she asked.

"The marriage test already?" he said, grinning from ear to ear. "Of course I will. Anything you want. What dost thou wish?"

"Let's stay here for the night instead of at the hotel in Ogdensburg. They'll let us use my old room, Joey. I know they will. It's still empty."

"I suppose this is what an Amish couple would do," he said. "Okay, just give me a moment to think about it."

"Oh, Joey," she said. "You are an angel."

He laughed. "I doubt that, but come—we have your family to meet, and the whole evening in front of us."

Susanna waited until Joey had opened the car door for her. She held his hand for the walk toward the house, but they didn't get far. *Mamm* arrived first and wrapped Susanna in a hug while *Daett* shook Joey's hand.

"So this is your wife?" *Daett* teased.

"Yep!" Joey joined in the laughter. "Did you ever see a fairer bride?"

"She was my fair daughter first," *Daett* said. "And a mighty fine one."

Susanna let go of *Mamm* to fly into *Daett's* arms, and silent sobs shook both of them.

Daett finally released his embrace and held Susanna at arm's length. "My heart is right full of joy today."

"Oh, *Daett!*" Susanna exclaimed as they embraced again.

Henry cleared his throat loudly. "If all this hugging doesn't stop, I'm leaving."

"No you're not!" Susanna said as she let go of *Daett* to open her arms to him.

Henry grinned but offered a handshake instead. "That's *goot* enough for me," he said.

They all laughed as Susanna shook hands with the rest of her brothers, right down to little Tobias. Joey took her hand when she finished, and Susanna led him toward the house. *Mamm* and *Daett* followed behind while the others ran ahead to change back into their regular clothing.

Susanna turned to *Mamm* and said, "If it's all right, we'd like to stay for supper and for the night—in my old room. Then we'll fly out early tomorrow from Ogdensburg for the honeymoon."

"Of course it's all right," *Mamm* said, a pleased look on her face. "This is a great honor indeed."

"*Yah*, it is," *Daett* added.

"Come." Susanna led Joey through the living room and upstairs. Slowly she opened her old bedroom door and led Joey inside. *Mamm* had cleaned the room and polished the furniture since she had been up here last. In this bedroom she had lived another life, and here she hoped to spend the first night of her new life with Joey.

"So this is it," Joey said as he looked around at the humble furnishings in the room. "I do believe we can stay until the morning."

"Thank you, Joey," she told him, gazing up into this face. "You are my love, my sweet, sweet love."

Discussion Questions

1. What was the source of Susanna's conflicted feelings at the beginning of the story? What would you have done about them?

2. What triggered Susanna's father to share the secret of Susanna's past with her? Would he have done this without this trigger?

3. How would you react to a similar revelation from your father?

4. What is your opinion of the two main male characters, Joey and Ernest?

5. Would you have had any advice for Joey in his confrontations with Susanna's father?

6. Should Susanna have cooperated as her family lay down rules for the end of her *rumspringa*?

7. Do you have sympathies for Susanna's long hesitation in jumping the fence?

8. What is your opinion of Bishop Enos and Deacon Herman? Should either of them have done things differently?

9. Did you hope Ernest would win Susanna's hand in marriage?

10. What are your feelings on Emma's crush for Ernest? Do you think Emma was happy with the outcome of events?

11. What are your feelings toward Susanna's *daett* when he takes Susanna to visit her unknown grandparents?

12. What was your opinion of Susanna's wedding? What about Susanna's decision to follow an Amish tradition and spend her wedding night in her parent's home?

Want more from Jerry Eicher?

The following excerpt is from another engaging, heart-tugging
story in The St. Lawrence County Amish series.

A Heart Once Broken

Chapter One

Lydia Troyer smoothed the wrinkles in her dress with a quick brush of her hand as she watched Ezra Wagler's buggy pull into Deacon Schrock's lane on Kelley Road. Now Ezra would put his horse, Midnight, in the barn and join the other St. Lawrence County Amish young people with the work at hand.

They had all gathered on this Friday evening to help clean the house and yard of the recently arrived deacon and his *frau,* Ruth Ann, who had both just joined the community. After their tiring move from Holmes County, Ohio, the couple appeared happy and had settled easily into the North Country in upstate New York.

Lydia gave her dress another quick brush and glanced at the barn door, hoping to catch Ezra's attention as he joined the young workers. A minute later and still no Ezra, Lydia looked across the yard to where her cousin Sandra Troyer was on her knees in the garden, pulling weeds with several of the other girls. Lydia allowed a smile to creep across her face. Tonight she had the advantage over Sandra. Her brush-cutting assignment wouldn't leave smudges on her dress or dark streaks on her hands. Sandra, too, was looking at the barn door for the same reason she was. As were a few of the other young girls with similar aspirations.

That was one of the things so maddening about Ezra, besides his handsome *goot* looks. He was the young man many of the community girls set their *kapps* for…though everyone knew she and her cousin Sandra had the inside track. The two had vied for Ezra's attentions ever since they finished their *rumspringa* days—about the same time Ezra and his family joined the community.

The rivalry of the two cousins had begun in their school days, long before Ezra had arrived. Even as rivals, they had managed to stay steadfast friends, though lately things had become a little grim. What had begun as a healthy competition—such as who could get the most 100s in school—had turned into something more serious after their *rumspringa* convinced both of them to be baptized and settle into Amish life. The cousins had wasted no time making their interest in the newcomer known. And Ezra, seeming to enjoy the attention, was obviously in no hurry to choose between the two cousins.

"Maddening!" Lydia muttered aloud.

"I know," Rosemary said from a few feet away. "These weeds are stubborn as all get-out." Lydia took another whack with her hoe as she gave Rosemary a smile. Thankfully the younger girl couldn't read her thoughts.

Though Lydia's rivalry with Sandra descended to low depths at times, neither she nor Sandra seemed able to back off. On this point they were equally determined. Whoever won Ezra's hand in marriage would have won the most important competition between the two girls.

For this contest they were evenly matched indeed. Both Sandra and Lydia had decent looks—among the best in the St. Lawrence County Amish community. Lydia had heard whispered more than once by one of the younger girls in frustration, "Those pretty Troyer cousins!"

Lydia stood up straighter as she caught sight of Ezra's smiling face. He walked her way, but then he glanced across the barnyard to where Sandra was working and waved toward her. Sandra waved back, but stayed on her knees. Lydia grinned as Sandra tried in desperation to tuck a few loose strands of hair under her *kapp* with one hand. The attempt, no doubt, left further smudges of dirt on Sandra's face.

Ezra hollered something toward Sandra she couldn't understand. Sandra appeared to smile and hollered something back as Ezra moved closer. Lydia could see the girls near Sandra giggle at this exchange between the two. After a few words, Ezra moved on, walking toward Lydia.

"Looks like you get your chance now," Rosemary said with a wicked smile. "When are Sandra and you going to settle this matter?"

Lydia didn't answer. There wasn't anything to say. Ezra would choose soon. He would have to. She so wanted to win this competition. It had always been difficult to tell who would gain the upper hand, whether Sandra or herself. Back in their school days Sandra would have the best average grade one week, and the next week Lydia would be ahead. But with this contest, someone would be left heartbroken. That would hurt worse than any defeat they'd suffered at school.

Lydia rallied her emotions as Ezra drew near.

"Hi there, Ezra," Rosemary chirped before Lydia could speak. "We've been needing a man on this fencerow for some time."

Lydia gave Ezra a sly smile, but remained quiet now that Rosemary had spoken up first. She used a low-key approach. Sandra, on the other hand, could chatter a hundred miles a minute when she had the opportunity.

"Well, then. It looks like I've come to the right place," Ezra said with a chuckle.

Lydia gave Ezra an admiring look. "You should be able to handle the rest of this fencerow all by yourself then."

"Oh no," Ezra protested. "I wouldn't want to lose the company of two such pretty females. Please stay."

Rosemary gave a sly grin. "Your sugar tongue will get you nowhere with me, you know."

Ezra grinned. "A man's gotta try, doesn't he?"

Lydia joined in their laughter. That was what she loved about Ezra. He could joke and laugh with any of the young people and make everyone feel special and appreciated.

Rosemary handed her hoe to Ezra. "Here, I'll go get another one."

"Thanks," Ezra replied, seemingly pleased with the offer.

Lydia worked on a tall thistle as Rosemary hurried away. This gave her a few moments alone with Ezra. Giving him a quick glance, she said, "You look handsome tonight. Did your *mamm* make that new shirt for you?"

Ezra grinned and said, "*Yah.* Thanks for the compliment. Now I can relax for the rest of the evening knowing everything's fine. There's nothing like arriving at a gathering and finding out your *mamm* forgot to sew a seam."

"You're *mamm* wouldn't do that," she chided. "She's among the best seamstresses in the community."

"*Yah*, I was teasing." Ezra whacked away at the weeds again before he looked up to say, "I heard there was another new family moving into the community. Have you met them?"

"No." Lydia busied herself with a stubborn root.

"The oldest boy is around our age, I was told." Ezra gave Lydia a quick glance. "His name's Clyde Helmuth. He's the boy right over there—the one with the pitchfork."

Lydia looked toward where Ezra had motioned with his chin. There was indeed a new boy near the barn. She had been too wrapped up in Ezra to notice. His straw hat cast shadows on his face, but he looked handsome enough.

"I imagine you girls will have him matched up with someone before long," Ezra teased.

Lydia teased back by saying, "Maybe so. Maybe it'll be me. I seem to be available." She gave the weeds in front of her another wallop.

"Surely you wouldn't fall for a strange man so quickly," Ezra scolded.

"Maybe I would and maybe I wouldn't," Lydia said. "And who knows. My cousin Sandra might fall for him."

"Are you wishing she would?" Ezra's eyes twinkled. He was on to her now.

"*Yah*," Lydia admitted. She knew she might as well say the truth. "That might help you make up your mind."

Ezra grinned from ear to ear. "Maybe it would and maybe it wouldn't," he teased back.

Ezra was still grinning when Rosemary returned with her new hoe. She gave them both a quick look and said, "Is something funny going on that you want to share with me?"

"No," Ezra said, teasing again. "We thought maybe you got hung up talking with the new fellow over by the barn. Young and handsome Clyde Helmuth?"

Rosemary colored a little. "Clyde who?"

Ezra laughed. "I can go tell him you're available."

"No need," Rosemary snapped. "He already knows that. Clyde and I go way back. Our families have been friends for years…before his family moved here."

Ezra's tone softened. "I didn't know that. Did something happen between the two of you?"

The look on Rosemary's face was enough of an answer, but she still said, "I used to date him, but we broke up."

"I'm sorry to hear that." Lydia reached over to give Rosemary a quick squeeze on the arm. "I had no idea."

Rosemary shrugged. "Most people don't know. It was only for a few dates. Clyde felt like the relationship wasn't what he wanted."

"There will be someone for you, I'm sure," Ezra encouraged her.

"I can see why your heart is still attached to the man," Lydia whispered to Rosemary, loud enough for Ezra to hear. "He's quite handsome."

"*Yah.*" Rosemary bit her lip and attacked a thick weed with her hoe.

Ezra gathered up an armful of thornbushes and headed toward the garden where Sandra was working. Lydia tried to keep busy and not pay attention to what Ezra was doing. The burn pile was near the garden's edge, and Lydia was sure Ezra would stop to speak with Sandra.

Lydia turned her attention to Rosemary. "Is it hard for you, then? With Clyde now living right here in the community?"

"No, it's fine." Rosemary put on a brave face. "I have to get over him, that's all. And I will. He and his *daett* just moved here after his *mamm* died. He's carrying a heavy load now."

"Oh, I'm sorry to hear that," Lydia said.

Rosemary paused with her hoe in one hand. "And as for me, you or Ezra don't need to feel bad. It's not as though I want another chance with Clyde. That's clearly in the past."

Lydia didn't respond, and the girls turned their attention to their work. Their tools rose and fell in unison as they attacked the thornbushes. The simple peace and camaraderie of their shared disappointments was comfort enough for the moment. But before long, both of them glanced toward the garden where Sandra and Ezra were engaged in a lively conversation.

"See what I mean?" Lydia muttered. "It's maddening."

Rosemary choked back a laugh. "*Yah*, I see what you mean. So that's what you were muttering about earlier. I thought it was the weeds."

"Maybe it *is* a weed," Lydia said, but she knew it was the bitterness in her heart speaking. The truth was, she loved Ezra.

Chapter Two

The following Saturday evening, Lydia ran to the front window of the Troyers' living room and peeked through the drapes. A buggy had rolled into the drive a few moments earlier, and Lydia watched as the lengthy form of Deacon Schrock climbed out. The deacon tied his horse to the hitching post, but he made no move to go any farther. Rather, the deacon stood beside his horse with clasped hands. Lydia pulled back from the window. Did Bishop Henry already have the deacon busy on church work—even though he'd only recently arrived in the community? That was possible, but what anyone in the family could have done to provoke a visit from the deacon was beyond her. All of her older brothers and sisters were married. The deacon would visit their homes if there was a problem, and she certainly hadn't disobeyed the *ordnung*. Her younger sisters, Emma and Rhoda, were still in their *rumspringa* time. They would be gone for the evening in thirty minutes or so, but they weren't subject to the deacon's jurisdiction. Unless her sisters had brought embarrassment to the community. She should check with her sisters more often, Lydia told herself. Maybe the two were up to something that had aroused the community's concern. Everyone kept close tabs on the young people in the North Country.

Rumspringa in St. Lawrence County wasn't quite the loose affair it was in other Amish communities. All of the families had made sacrifices to move this far upstate in New York, and they didn't want the problems from the old community to follow them. Lydia hesitated but looked past the drapes again. *Daett* had just come out of the barn. She watched as he walked up to the buggy and shook hands with Deacon Schrock. The two were soon deep in conversation. Did Deacon Schrock want something with *Daett* after all?

Lydia ducked behind the drapes again. Come to think of it, *Daett* had seemed distracted lately and so had *Mamm*. But what could *Daett* have done wrong? Lydia peeked out and saw *Daett* and Deacon Schrock still talking beside the buggy. The deacon's visit must have involved some other member of the family. She dropped the drape's edge from her fingertips and walked toward the kitchen, where Emma and Rhoda were busy at work with supper preparations. Neither of them looked up—which wasn't necessarily a sign of innocence. Her sisters always rushed through the supper preparations on a Saturday night so they could leave sooner for their weekend's taste of the world's freedom.

"What have you two been up to?" Lydia demanded. "The deacon's here."

The girls acted as if they hadn't heard. Emma hummed a worldly tune she must have learned from her *Englisha* friends. If *Mamm* had been in the kitchen, Emma would have quit this nonsense at once. But Lydia was too soon out of her own *rumspringa* to complain about an *Englisha* tune being hummed. At least she'd had the decency not to bring anything from the world into the house.

Lydia sighed and glanced toward the living room window again. Maybe one of her sisters had hidden a radio upstairs and had let the fact slip at the Sunday evening hymn singing. That could provoke a visit from the deacon. There would be no discipline for her sisters, but *Mamm* and *Daett's* reputation would suffer if they failed to keep control of their children's *rumspringa* time. The parents were expected to draw the lines clearly between the world and their home. Nothing but trouble would come from such a situation, and trouble was something Lydia didn't need right now. Everything needed to be in order at the Troyer's house so Ezra Wagler would have no excuse to choose Cousin Sandra over her. After all, Ezra came from a well-thought-of family, and his parents would see to it that Ezra chose a *frau* who would uphold the family's tradition as faithful Amish church members.

Lydia tried again in a louder voice. "Why else would the deacon be here if you're not up to no good?"

Emma ceased her humming long enough to say, "I don't know and I don't care."

"That's not a decent attitude," Lydia scolded. "Sounds like the deacon should speak with you while he's here anyway."

Rhoda added her two cents. "That's why I'm in no hurry for church membership. And you wouldn't have been either if you didn't have Ezra Wagler on the brain."

Emma and Rhoda giggled and high-fived each other. That was another thing they wouldn't have dared to do with *Mamm* around.

Lydia exploded. "I didn't join the church for Ezra's sake, and don't do that silly gesture in the house."

"You used to act just like this yourself," Emma shot back. "So don't go all high-and-mighty on us."

"At least I had enough sense to leave that *Englisha* stuff out there," Lydia snapped. "If you two get too silly, you'll never make your way back into the faith."

"Maybe we don't want to," Emma said with a glare. "Look how we work ourselves to the bone when a little electricity in the house would save so much labor. Benny Coon's sister, Avery, had us in her house for a party last weekend, and you should have seen all the fancy things she has. Even the clothes dryer is inside the house and runs on electricity."

"You should be ashamed of yourselves with such talk!" Lydia said, trying to keep the tension out of her voice. "You're supposed to taste the things of the world and get them out of your system, not get used to them or bring them home with you."

"Speak for yourself." Rhoda gave Lydia a rebellious look. "Be thankful we made supper so you can work on that new dress to impress Ezra Wagler with tomorrow."

Lydia winced but kept the confidence in her voice. "*Yah*, and maybe I'll be sewing his shirts soon—if the two of you don't destroy the family's reputation first."

The two girls were silent, and Lydia refrained from any further protest. Where was *Mamm*? Without *Mamm* around, Lydia always seemed to stoop to silly arguments with her younger sisters. If her two older sisters, Lucy and Betty, were still at home instead of married, they'd know how to handle Emma and Rhoda. Lucy was wise beyond her years and a true asset to the family's standing in the community. And Betty had married Bishop Henry's son, Lonnie. Lydia could never match the reputations of her older sisters, but that didn't mean she had to descend to Emma and Rhoda's level.

"I'm going to find *Mamm*," Lydia mumbled. The two girls giggled as Lydia walked off. Clearly Emma and Rhoda thought they held the high ground. *More like the low ground,* Lydia told herself. But she had other concerns at the moment. Why was Deacon Schrock there? That question still wasn't answered. Her sisters acted too confident. They obviously hadn't done anything wrong—at least that they knew of.

Lydia peeked out of the living room window again as she passed. *Daett* had his head bowed, and Deacon Schrock appeared to be in the middle of a lecture. Could *Daett* have done something wrong after all? Fear stabbed at Lydia. But what could that be? *Daett* didn't bend the *ordnung* in any way, and both of her parents gave the community their full support. Betty couldn't have married Bishop Henry's son under any other circumstances.

Lydia opened the stair door and glanced up the steps. Only silence greeted her, so *Mamm* must have finished the Saturday cleaning and was no longer upstairs. Had *Mamm* gone outside? Maybe she was in the garden? But that was unlike her on a Saturday evening. Lydia closed the door but paused to listen. She had heard something—a faint sob coming from the first-floor bedroom. Lydia held her breath as she tiptoed in that direction. Did *Mamm* know why Deacon Schrock was there?

The bedroom door was ajar, and Lydia entered to find *Mamm* seated on the edge of the bed, her face in her hands.

"*Mamm*, what's wrong?" Lydia sat down beside her.

"We're ruined," *Mamm* whispered.

"Ruined?" Lydia tried to breathe. "Why are we ruined?"

"We just are. That's why Deacon Schrock is here." *Mamm* stifled a sob.

Lydia gripped *Mamm*'s arm. "How can we be ruined?"

Mamm stared blankly across the room. "*Daett* made some bad business investments and all our savings are gone. He still owes much more than we can ever pay back." *Mamm* placed her head back in her hands, but the sobs had ceased.

"But *Mamm*." Lydia slipped her arm around *Mamm*'s shoulder. "Deacon Schrock is here to help in our time of trouble. You mustn't let this shame overcome you. Others in the community have had financial problems. It's not like this is—"

Mamm stopped Lydia with a shake of her head. "Deacon Schrock isn't here to help, not after *Daett* tells him everything."

"There's shame, *yah*," Lydia allowed. "But you shouldn't take this so hard. Money isn't everything. You know this."

Mamm lifted her face and sat up straight on the bed. "The shame is too great. *Daett* is telling the deacon because he must. I didn't want him to, but I know that's not possible. Not if we're to get support from the church, which we must. We can't go bankrupt. That would bring an even greater shame on the community."

"I still don't understand," Lydia said. "But then what do I know about money?"

"Thank the Lord you don't," *Mamm* whispered. "I have learned so many things the past few weeks that I think my hair must have all turned white."

Lydia glanced over at *Mamm*'s hair. "Your hair is not white," she said as she reached over to hug *Mamm*. "It will turn out okay, I'm sure."

Mamm didn't look convinced as she got up from the bed, wiped her eyes, and headed toward the kitchen with Lydia following her. Thankfully Emma had begun to hum the Sunday morning praise song by the time they walked in, and *Mamm* joined in the supper preparations as if nothing was wrong.

Lydia returned to working on the new dress she had started that morning. She focused on the pieces of cloth as the foot-pedaled sewing machine hummed under her. Emma and Rhoda had been correct about her interest in Ezra. Her failure to keep Ezra's attention at the youth gathering this week troubled her more than her family's financial problems. Ezra couldn't go on forever in his undecided state. If she wore a new dress this Sunday at the services, it might push him in her direction. Of course, Sandra likely had the same idea. They thought alike in most areas—maddeningly so.

The sewing machine hummed again. This competition was so silly and beneath both of them, Lydia told herself. Maybe the seriousness of Deacon Schrock's visit would stop some of this foolishness. Sandra would certainly find out about her family's problems—eventually, at least. Maybe she should have a talk with Sandra on Sunday to settle the matter of Ezra between them. But how would they do such a thing? They had never been able to settle even the simplest matter before. Now their competition involved love. You couldn't divide a man's heart, or your own, for that matter. They both couldn't marry Ezra, so one of them would have to back down. But who? She wasn't ready to give in, and she was sure the same was true of Sandra. They both wanted Ezra's hand in marriage. A King Solomon was needed to decide between them, but King Solomon had long ago passed from the earth.

Behind Lydia, Emma and Rhoda burst out of the kitchen and raced upstairs. Moments later they came back with carry-on bags in their hands.

"Have fun tonight working on that dress," Emma chirped. "'Cause we're sure going to have fun!"

"Behave yourselves," Lydia chided, but both of them were already out the door. Her sisters had some nerve to set out in their open buggy right in front of Deacon Schrock. She would have waited until Deacon Schrock had left before dashing outside, broadcasting her intentions for the evening. Not that Deacon Schrock disapproved of a *rumspringa* time, but a little discretion was called for. That was a lesson her younger sisters had obviously failed to learn. Lydia laid down the dress with a sigh. She would finish after supper when things had calmed down. Whatever the extent of the problem *Daett* was discussing with Deacon Schrock, his mood wouldn't be improved by his two youngest daughters spiritedly bursting out of the house to set out for a night on the town.

Lydia peeked out of the drapes again. Sure enough, *Daett* still stood with his head bowed as Deacon Schrock glared in the direction of her sisters. *Daett* made no effort to help Emma and Rhoda as they giggled and hitched Archer, the oldest driving horse, to the open buggy. Emma and Rhoda soon climbed in and drove off, without a backward glance.

About the Author

Jerry Eicher's Amish fiction has sold more than 700,000 books. After a traditional Amish childhood, Jerry taught for two terms in Amish and Mennonite schools in Ohio and Illinois. Since then he's been involved in church renewal, preaching, and teaching Bible studies. Jerry lives with his wife, Tina, in Virginia.

To learn more about Harvest House books and
to read sample chapters, visit our website:

www.harvesthousepublishers.com

HARVEST HOUSE PUBLISHERS
EUGENE, OREGON